ALL SHALL MOURN

ALL SHALL MOURN

ELLIE MARNEY

Black 🖐 Hand

For all the patient ones

Beware; for I am fearless, and therefore powerful.

Mary Shelley, *Frankenstein*

Peace, my heart, let the time for the parting be sweet.
Let it not be a death, but completeness.
Let love melt into memory, and pain into songs.

Rabindranath Tagore, *The Gardener*

CHAPTER ONE

Tangier, 25 October 1982

They rise late, around noon, pushing off cotton sheets and draperies to go drink thick coffee on the balcony. The sun is at its apex, and the scent of Old Medina – cumin and thuja wood, and smoke from the snail-sellers, and vehicle exhaust – rises from the streets below the apartment like steam. They open the windows, but keep the curtains half-closed and the big ceiling fans turning.

The housekeeper has left a mound of sweet briouat pastries on a metal platter. In silk pyjamas, still waking and languid from the heat, Kristin moistens the pad of her thumb to press on the sticky pastry crumbs, then licks her fingers clean.

Piping hot coffee, rich with cinnamon, is delivered by the seller at the bottom of the stone stairwell. Simon sips from the distinctive tall glass tucked in its metal holder, sets it down on the balcony table beside the platter with the pastries. In a smaller enamel bowl, ripe figs: Simon likes to smoke his first cigarette of the day with the coffee, then slice a fig in half and scoop out the innards with a spoon. He has removed his black djellaba for sleeping and changed into camel-colored trousers and a loose white linen shirt, soft slippers on his feet. His hair is the color of snow on the Atlas mountains.

Peering out at the city through round, wire-framed sunglasses, he surveys the landscape for anything that seems out of place: White faces in the crowd, or local people glancing too frequently at their second-floor eyrie, or an overheard snippet of an American accent. But there is no cause for concern at present, so Simon returns his attention to the foreign newspapers piled on top of his stack of medical texts.

He selects a copy of *The New York Times* and examines the headlines. "And what is on the menu for us today, dearest?"

"The gemstone man again, sadly, as our coffers are getting low." Bothered by the sun, Kristin rakes her long hair back from her face. She fans herself with one pale hand. "Then I can pay all our accounts, and perhaps buy more paints. And I should visit Dimity for a while this afternoon."

"Give her my very best regards," Simon says absently, turning a page.

"I was rather hoping you'd come along." Kristin gestures for his cigarette. When he hands it to her, she draws deeply, blows out smoke in a thin stream. "It'll be martini hour, and you know she'd be delighted to see you. And it's lovely and cool in the riad."

Simon recovers his cigarette and smiles. Impossible to see his eyes behind the black lenses of the sunglasses. "I'm afraid I have some business in town."

"By *business*, you mean *chess*." Kristin rolls her eyes indulgently.

"Mr. Bennani has invited me for coffee and chess," Simon acknowledges, still reading.

"I don't know what you see in Mr. Bennani."

"Much the same as what you see in the gemstone man, I think." Simon raises his eyebrows.

"Hmm. Oh goodness, it's far too hot out here." Kristin rises from her cushioned chair. She is unaccustomed to these temperatures in

October. "I'm going to take a bath before I dress. Do you want anything from the souk while I'm there?"

"I don't think so, dearest." Simon finally detaches his attention from his newspaper, removes his sunglasses. Beneath them, his eyes are the same startling blue as the khamsa hanging by the balcony doors.

"Simon…" Kristin bites her full bottom lip over a smile. "Would you fix my hair before I bathe? I don't like to be a bother, but you do it so well."

"Of course." His gaze softens, and he stands. Simon is very tall, even in his slippers.

They stand away from the sun, in the cool, green-tiled shadow of the apartment kitchen. Kristin turns, and Simon sinks his fingers into her hair, rubbing her skull gently before separating the thick strands of ice white and beginning to weave.

Kristin closes her eyes, shoulders relaxing. "Thank you, Simon."

"I like that you ask me," Simon whispers, his lips behind her ear. From the hook on the kitchen wall, he collects a length of ribbon, ties off the braid.

Kristin turns in his arms, hugs him around the neck, her eyes damp. She presses her length against him, as if she might ease her body into his. Even now, she seems intoxicated by this closeness with him, closeness so long denied. It's only been five weeks since they set themselves free.

She kisses him on the cheek, wipes her eyes on her hand. "Enough – I simply must bathe."

"Go bathe," he grins, tweaks her braid.

Kristin laughs, disappears inside.

Simon Gutmunsson – doting twin of Kristin Gutmunsson,

3

American fugitive, former resident of jails and hospitals for the criminally insane, sociopathic murderer of fifteen – settles back into his chair on the balcony and picks up his coffee, lights another cigarette.

CHAPTER TWO

Mexico, 27 October 1982

She does the journey in slow stages, the way she does everything.

First, taking a few days to check over the Rabbit's tires and engine with her dad, then driving from Apple Creek to Columbus, then to Cincinnati and Nashville, then onward, farther south. She sees a lot of beautiful country that way. Red skies above the mountains outside Louisville. Snow glistening in the Ozarks. A full moon over San Antonio, where she stays a night.

Emma Lewis enjoys all of it, drinks it in. She doesn't want to miss anything anymore.

In Encinal, she stops to tank up at a little mom-and-pop Chevron station, and when the kid comes out for the money, she tries her halting Spanish. She sticks to English at the border, where they check her passport and inside the trunk of her car. Maybe she looks suspect, she thinks after driving on, because her hair is still so short: Five weeks of growth has only given her the equivalent of a pixie cut, and she looks pale in the rear-view mirror.

But her eyes are clear and she's alert. She's recovered. Recovering. She doesn't think she'll really feel better until she gets to Guanajuato, and that was the argument she used to convince her mother to let her go.

The drive is long, but she's always liked to drive. Her sister gave her a bunch of cassette tapes to listen to on the road; she's mostly been playing an old album by Edgar Froese. She checks the route maps she bought, concentrates while navigating the toll lanes. On the country roads, she rolls her window down and watches the horizon undulate around her as the desert gives way to mesquite and pasture. The landscape is unlike anything she's used to.

Ten hours past the border: Water and snacks are in the car, but she takes rest stops to use the bathroom and stretch. Lots of grime on the Rabbit. She was hoping to avoid San Miguel de Allende, because the city is busy with Día de Muertos preparations, but she has to stop for directions. The address she has is twenty minutes out of the city, to the north.

Finally, well after sundown, she reaches a dry dirt road and a farm gate. Night is a blanket, and dust swirls in her headlights. The approach to the house is wide, with wooden horse-yard fencing at the right and a few old sheds. At the end of the driveway, a stand of saguaro near the lights of a broad, low house behind more fence and some big trees. Another gate closer to the house; Emma parks before it in a sandy patch on the left, gets out. Cool gloom, and the smell of limes.

Squinting, Emma sees a flashlight: A slim woman in pants, with a beige apron, walks toward her, surrounded by a crowd of excited dogs. In her wake, backlit by the illumination from the house, another figure, taller. Emma keeps her eyes on the tall figure as he gets closer. She pulls on her jacket and takes her backpack out of the car, shuts the door, walks to the gate.

Even in the dark, Travis looks different. Emma tries to remember if she's ever seen him in anything but an FBI suit, or law enforcement sweats. There were the nightclub clothes for the Paradise sting, and his hospital gown, but those don't count. Now he's in his home clothes: a chambray shirt over jeans, with a familiar-looking brown Harrington jacket.

His shirt hem is loose and he's smiling, although he looks tired. "You made it."

"Javi, let the girl in the yard," the woman in the apron tuts.

She is old; as she waves the flashlight, her wrinkles become visible. She moves with the fluttering rapidity of a bird, dogs yapping as she opens the gate. "Come in, come in. Do you have many bags?"

"No, just this," Emma says. "Gracias, señora –"

"Mariana – I am Mariana. Come through, come through."

Mariana pushes doggy faces away with her knee, ushers Emma forward and shuts the gate. Emma holds still as the dogs start snuffling around her. One is a black Labrador, one is a pitbull, and three are of indeterminate heritage. The woman makes shooing noises, takes off one chancla and waves it around.

"They like visitors," Travis says, wading toward Emma through the dogs.

"They are ridiculous," Mariana declares. "Javi, you should be laying down."

"I've been laying down for five weeks, abuelita." His dark hair is longer, messy. He's looking right at Emma. "I'm glad you came."

"Me, too." Emma smiles. They're standing within inches of each other as the dogs weave through their legs. If they hug right now, she's not sure what will happen – she's been thinking about it a lot. Better to wait. She glances down, and the spell is broken. "This is quite a welcome."

"It is nice to meet you, Emma." Mariana puts her chancla back on her foot and snaps her fingers for canine attention. "I'm taking these silly dogs to the stables."

"Good idea," Travis says. He looks back at Emma. "Long drive, huh?"

"About thirty-three hours." She hitches her bag higher.

He nods. "Come on up to the house."

A dirt path leads up past the saguaro, eventually turns to gravel. Mariana has gone off to the right with her pack. Travis doesn't offer to take Emma's bag and she doesn't ask him to, unsure what he's capable of physically since his injury – she's not the only one recovering. He walks slow, and she wonders if that's because he's unable to walk fast or if he's allowing her to get her bearings in the dark.

Under the moon, it's possible to see some details even at night; the long, one-story house is stone and wood, surrounded by lavender bushes. Terracotta barrel roof tiles. Small lanterns are set at intervals along a wide front patio and strings of marigolds are everywhere, for the coming celebration. A century plant stabs toward the dark sky.

"Thirty-three hours – phew," Travis says, leading past a mesquite tree to the right. "You must be sick of sitting down."

"It was okay," Emma says. "I like driving."

His lips quirk on one side. "Guess *I'm* the one sick of sitting down."

"You've been doing it longer." Emma grins. She gets a split-second flash of memory: Travis in front of her, blood spilling from his mouth and a gory length of rebar protruding from his torso while she screams. She blinks and the image is gone, but her expression gets more sober. "I feel like I should've stayed with you."

"Hey, no," he says. "Don't worry about that. I told you on the phone not to worry about that. You stayed with me ten days. It was a long time for your folks to wait."

Emma watches the gravel at her feet. "It felt weird, walking away with my parents while you were still in the hospital."

"Yeah, but I checked out four days later." Before them now, two wide shallow steps onto the patio of the ranch house. Travis's face – his olive complexion, strong cheekbones, the warm brown of his eyes – is lit by a wall lantern. "My mom and my sisters looked after me. It was good. I needed to go home."

Emma looks up at the stars. "This isn't Texas, though."

Travis shrugs, faintly abashed. "Yeah, well. I tried to stay until Christmas, but after three weeks with my mom, I needed a break."

Emma understands that. She looks again at the house. Bougainvillea climbs the stone arch above them; ahead, a set of wicker patio furniture. "Your uncle's place seems nice."

Travis expression is soft and happy. He lifts his chin forward. "Let me show you inside."

Up the steps onto the patio, past the wicker furniture, a series of arched windows and bracing posts. The smell of lavender and peppers. Further along, a wide wooden door with iron rivets – there is a decorated ofrenda beside the door. The warm inside of the house: dark walnut vigas, thick adobe walls, whitewash, flagstones, globe light fixtures. A big kitchen and open-plan dining area in classic Spanish colonial style. Travis leads her through a living room with a couple of big couches, one with a plastic cover, then along a hallway.

"Where is everyone?" Emma asks.

"My aunt and uncle are in San Miguel, at a wedding. They'll be back later. Mariana – my aunt's mom – has probably gone to check the horses."

"Uh, I don't mean to impose –"

"Emma, you're not imposing. I invited you." He stops at the open door of a room. "Will this be okay?"

Lamps with soft shades beside the bed, a cowhide rug on the floor. Her own bathroom – blue and green painted adobe. A wooden study desk and chair nested inside a small alcove with curtained windows.

Emma turns back, her mouth open. "Are all the rooms in this house amazing?"

Travis grins, gestures to a door near the end of the hallway on the right. "I'm just down there. The rest of the family lives on the other side of the house."

"Why does your aunt's mom call you Javi?"

"It's my middle name – Javier." He waves a hand. "Go on in. Set your stuff down and take a minute, wash up. I'll be out on the patio when you're ready."

She drifts into the room, marvelling. Takes a minute to use the bathroom, wash her face, unpack a few things to find a change of shirt. For a moment she wishes she had something more fancy than just long-sleeved T-shirts and jeans. But that's not how she and Travis Bell are with each other: They don't do fancy. They're just themselves, and that's how she likes it. She pulls on her warm white thermal and her jacket and leaves the room.

Out on the patio, Travis is occupying the wicker patio couch. A low coffee table in front holds an earthenware plate with peanuts, cucumber slices. There's one bottle of Estrella on the table and one already in Travis's hand. He's reclined against the arm of the couch with his legs stretched across the well-used cushions – the first real concession she's seen for his injury since she arrived.

Seeing her approach, he sits up a little and slides his boots off the couch. "Sorry, I just had to lay down a second –"

"Don't apologize. And don't move your feet." Emma collects her beer from the table and plonks herself in the vacant spot. Hauls his boots back up into her lap. "I can sit this way."

Travis blinks at her. "Okay."

"How's the healing going?"

"Slow." He relaxes, sips his beer. "I hate going so slow, but I'm getting there. The scar doesn't hurt so much anymore, and I can drive and stuff. I went for my first horse ride today, which is cheating, so I'm a little sore. Self-inflicted. How's your leg?"

"Good." The beer is refreshing. Emma takes another swig. Travis's boots are heavy in her lap, but she's comfortable. "There's still tenderness when I run, but it's improving. It'll leave a mark, but that doesn't bother me."

Travis examines her, his eyes soft. "Your hair's grown out."

Emma ducks her chin, her free hand lifting to the nape of her neck where the hair is smooth and dark. "Yeah. I just…got tired of clipping it."

The lantern on the stone wall behind them glows enough for comfort, without disturbing the view of the stars beyond the patio roof. Where the flagstones end, a hedge of lavender makes a low border. The night is cool. She sips from her bottle, leans for some peanuts.

"You hungry?" Travis asks. "You want dinner or something?"

"Nah, this is good," Emma says. "I had a burrito in Matehuala."

"All right." Travis slips his left boot to the flagstones and moves his right boot off her lap and onto the couch, so he can sit up more. He leans forward with an open hand. "Then gimme some of those peanuts and tell me how your folks are doing."

Emma obliges. "My folks are doing fine. Columbus Day was… interesting."

"How's that?" He shells peanuts onto the couch cushion. His jacket is open and his shirt falls away from his collarbones.

"Remember I told you my sister's roommate came for Columbus Day and October break?"

"Yeah.' He nods as he works on the peanuts. They've been calling each other with more and more frequency over the last five weeks. "Julie... Julia. Something like that."

"Julia, yeah." Emma tries a cucumber slice, washes it down with the beer. "So she came over for the break, and Robbie's invited her for Thanksgiving as well."

"There's a reveal here I'm missing, right?" Travis alternates peanuts with beer.

Emma passes him her empty shells. "I was missing it, too, until I went to the barn to get my dad's socket wrench set and saw them kissing."

"Your sister and her roommate." His eyebrows go high. "Okay."

"I knew Robbie was dating someone, but she wouldn't tell me who. Now I don't know what to think."

Travis pauses. Shrugs.

"What?" She stares. "That's it? You just shrug?"

"I mean, what else is there? They're dating." He sips his beer. "Is your sister happy?"

Emma thinks about it. "Yeah, she's happy."

He shrugs again. "Then that's it."

Emma snorts in the beat. "Okay... Yeah, okay."

"Hey, it's nineteen eighty-two, we're making social progress." He makes a wry grin around the lip of his beer bottle as he takes another sip. "And it could be worse. Your sister could be dating a known juvenile delinquent from San Angelo."

Emma sucks in a breath. "Oh no. Lena or Connie?"

"Lena."

"Jesus."

"He has a motorbike."

"Oh my god." Emma rolls her eyes. "How's your mom taking it?"

Travis grimaces. "She's not thrilled. But she's…philosophical. Says she dated this roughneck blond white boy and it turned out okay."

"Your dad, right?"

He nods, smiling. Emma laughs, finishes her peanuts, brushes her hands off on her jeans. "So tell me again what the deal is with you staying here?"

"The house belongs to my uncle Luiz, my mom's brother." Travis washes the remains of his peanuts down. "It's just him and my aunt Sofia, and her mom, my abuelita."

"And they don't mind me coming to visit?"

"Hell, no."

Emma takes that in. "So…how long are you planning to stay?"

He shrugs. "Long as I need to. How about you?"

Emma bites her lip. "Long as you'll let me."

"Okay, then." Travis puts the shells on the table, wipes his hands on the sides of his jacket, like that answer settles things. "I mean, it's just the horses, ranch stuff. Orange picking now and next month. Swimming in the river, when it's warm. It might get boring."

"I could handle a little boring," Emma says, dry.

"Fair." Travis finishes the dregs of his beer, looks out beyond the lavender hedge. "But it's pretty quiet here. Not many people. My cousins are all grown up, they mostly live around San Miguel. They come by sometimes."

"That doesn't sound so bad." She studies Travis's profile. Studies the label of her half-finished beer. She killed a man five weeks ago. Does that disqualify her from living? She doesn't know. Her therapist, Audrey, says no.

Emma makes her decision. Leans and puts the beer on the table.

"There's a rancho guy, Mateo," Travis continues. "He's sixty, he lives here with his grandson, Elias, who's thirteen. They're in one of the outbuildings off thataway, I'll introduce you in the morning. And a bunch of charro guys help out with the horses, but none of them live on the property."

"Okay." Emma reaches over and plucks the empty Estrella bottle from his hand. "You done with this?"

"Uh – yeah." Travis watches her set it on the table. "You want another one?"

"Nope," Emma says, and she shifts to kneel on the cushion between his legs. She puts one hand on the wicker couch and another hand on the top of his chest, near his collarbone, easing him back.

Travis is suddenly very still, except for his heart, which drums through the chambray under her palm.

"Okay," he whispers, swallows hard. Their faces are a lot closer now. He's searching her eyes with his own. "Emma, I didn't invite you because –"

"Shh. I know you didn't. But I want to." She wets her lips. "I'm just not very..." Her breaths are shaky. "I'm not sure how all this works."

His expression goes impossibly soft. He reaches up between them and traces the backs of his fingers over her cheek.

"I think," he says, voice husky, "it mostly works like this."

He strokes down the side of her neck. Her breath catches at the sensations and at the look in his eyes – all wonder. He hooks a finger into the collar of her thermal shirt and gently pulls, until they're inhaling together. Their lips greet one another, make friends.

Emma feels warmth spread through her, rich and dark and slow as molasses. *This is kissing,* part of her thinks, *this is kissing,* then she switches the thinking part off.

CHAPTER THREE

Tangier, 27 October 1982

Simon has a standing invitation at Dar Laurent in the evenings, where they drink coffee and play chess at the rattan table with the cushioned chairs and overhanging potted palm fronds.

Laurent is about eight years Simon's senior, an aesthete, French Canadian, with brown hair and a great deal of inherited money. He favors hashish while he plays, but Simon declines the shisha and smokes his preferred French tobacco, flavorsome and dark. He is expecting Kristin at any moment, and little of his attention is on the game.

Laurent puffs, sets his pipe down. Shifts his piece after examining Simon's previous move. "I hear you've been playing that local gendarme, Bennani."

"I have," Simon acknowledges. The chess set they are playing on is lovely – turned malachite and mahogany. It is at least one hundred years old. Simon's expression doesn't alter when he detects the sound of light footsteps in the hall.

"Bennani may share all the Tangier gossip," Laurent informs him, "but you should know he is a terrible cheat."

"Which is perfectly acceptable," Simon admits, "as I also cheat."

Laurent laughs, catches himself as he realizes Simon is not joking. He makes a small frown. "I do not see the point of cheating at chess."

"The point is that Bennani and I aren't really playing chess." Simon shifts a piece and grins. The grin is primarily for his sister, who has come through the sitting room and crossed the checkerboard floor to reach them

"Mr. Bennani cheats to win," Kristin declares, throwing an arm around her twin's neck and kissing him on the cheek, "and Simon cheats to lose. Bonsoir, Laurent, are you having an enjoyable game?"

"Bien sur, cher." Laurent accepts his own kiss on each cheek, before sitting back to regard his guests. "But your brother's approach is unusual, non?" Although Laurent is likely already aware that these American twins are an unusual pair.

"Judicious losses are an essential part of a larger strategy," Simon reminds him before turning to Kristin. "How was the market, dearest?"

"Oh, it was very pleasant." She slips free of his hand to settle her string bag and parcels on the lounging couch nearby, pulling back her headscarf as the plaintive lilt of the adhan filters through the window. She brushes her fingers through the leaves of a nearby fern and selects a date from the tray on the rattan table. "I love to walk about as everything is cooling and all the evening sweetmeat sellers emerge. I should like to paint the market, from the top of the hill just on sundown. The colors would be glorious."

"Indeed." Simon returns his attention to the game, and Laurent's last move. "Ah, you have me in checkmate."

"Assurement." Laurent blinks at the board, perturbed. "But now I'm wondering if you have made a judicious loss."

Simon simply smiles.

They dine with Laurent in his solarium – it's very enjoyable to occupy the couches, with the handsome tapestried cushions, and admire the tadelakt plaster of the walls that blends so well against the décor of terracotta and wood colors, with ruby accents. Laurent and Simon resume their conversation about the Tangier expatriate demi monde while eating flatbreads and lamb tagine from large ceramic bowls. Expatriates love gossip and novelty – the twins were absorbed into the community within a fortnight of their arrival, and have made many friends.

"Oh, I've been meaning to ask, have you seen Jeremy lately?" Kristin dabs her flatbread piece delicately in the rich sauce. "He was due to join Dimity and I for an evening picnic yesterday, but he never arrived."

"Mm." Laurent finishes sucking the marrow from a bone, sets it aside and rinses his fingers in a clay water bowl. "I have not seen him. His gardener says he is out of town. I thought you were vexed with him – did he not try to, eh, make une avance...?"

"Oh yes," Kristin says, waving Jeremy's indiscretion away with a hand. "But I am less offended by *that* than by him failing to tell me he'd be unable to attend our picnic."

"Both things are certainly rather rude," Simon agrees, eyes downcast as he examines his nails. He directs the conversation away from further discussion of Jeremy's whereabouts.

After dinner is complete – or rather, an early lunch, for Simon and Kristin – they depart. On the way toward the door, Simon sees an American newspaper atop a large stack on the occasional table in the hall.

"May I borrow this paper, Laurent?"

"Bien entendu. I collect the newspapers from the embassy, or friends pass them on, but I have no time, at present, to read. Have it, with my compliments."

The twins take their leave.

They walk the long way home along the Tangier wall, listening to the cars on Borj Dar Baroud near the water below. Kristin has covered her hair once more. She crooks her arm through Simon's elbow as they pass La Marino café, greets the cats that inhabit every nook and cranny of the Old City as they prowl by. The muted sound of radios and the smell of garbage and oranges and shisha smoke lilts around the cobbled streets.

Simon seems relaxed, but his eyes are in constant motion, observing people in alleyways, where the lantern-light falls, how far shadows extend and what they conceal. It is a hunting practice he cannot shake, would not want to. He has roamed the kasbah at night many times, its turns and secrets as familiar to him now as the darkness he sees in sleep.

Through a tunnel, past a tourist kiosk, Kristin stops to admire a birdcage-maker's stall, switches to French to make inquiries with the stallholder. Nearby, through a window, an old woman in a dark kaftan and headscarf labors at a treadle sewing machine. She sees Simon, looks away quickly, her right hand raised. Palm out toward him, she mutters something inaudible.

"Come," Kristin says, reverting back to English as she pulls him farther. "You shouldn't look. It makes them nervous."

"Do they still call us 'shabah' in the market?"

"Of course," Kristin says. "How can they not? With our coloring, we look like ghosts to them."

They are back at their two-tier apartment by ten in the evening. Simon retreats to the sitting room as Kristin goes downstairs for her dance lesson with a local girl. After Kristin returns, she takes to her easel while Simon studies his medical texts. They have a late supper after eleven, retrieving the bowls and food prepared by the housekeeper from the cooler.

At midnight, Kristin has one of her baths. The whole apartment is scented with pomegranate and amber and rose petals, which Simon finds distracting; he moves from the sitting room to the large bedroom with the wooden table, and begins clipping the newspapers. After a time, his sister emerges wearing her soft, deep blue robe, smoothing her damp hair.

"What are you clipping now?" She stops by the table, rests a hand on his neck and peers over his shoulder. "Simon, what is that?"

He passes her the clipping, so she may see properly.

Now her expression is less serene. "This is about an FBI case."

"I know," he says softly.

"You're not saying this interests you?" Kristin returns the clipping, eyes wide. She continues to stare at him as she steps back to sit on the bed. Through the low vee of her robe, her skin shines white. "Simon, aren't you happy here? We have everything we've ever wanted. We're free, we're together…How could you possibly want more?"

He turns in his seat to face her. "Darling, don't upset yourself."

"I *do* upset myself," she exclaims. "I *do*."

When she throws herself back on the bed, Simon stands and comes closer.

"Kristin…" She will not be cajoled. He settles his length beside her on the sheets and blankets. "Do you trust me?"

"Of course. You know I trust you." But even though they lie on their sides facing one another, she will not look at him.

Simon tucks a cool lock of her hair behind her ear. "Then you must trust that I do what I do for the benefit of us both."

"Oh, Simon!" Kristin looks away again, tears brimming in her eyes.

"Calm yourself, dearest. You know I will always make intelligent choices."

Kristin wipes her eyes against the cuff of her robe. "Simon, you say you use only intellect, that you don't allow your biases to sway your logic. But I *know* that feelings still have an impact."

"I don't know if I experience what you describe as feelings." He tries to explain gently. "It's more like what you experience when you dream of painting the market – it's the pull of a strong current." He touches his finger to the tip of her nose. "*You* allow yourself to be carried along by it. But I like to use my movements to allow the current to take me where I wish to go."

"And you wish to return…home?" Kristin blinks at him, confused.

"I don't know yet. The current is unclear."

Kristin is still upset. Simon holds her chin in his fingers like he would hold a delicate egg. "Sister. Kristin. Look at me." He bites his lip. "Do you love me?"

Kristin raises her eyes to his. Takes his hand and draws it slowly down to the soft, exposed skin between her breasts, in the vee of her robe. Presses his palm to her heart. "Can you not feel how much?"

"Then let me take care of you," Simon whispers.

He drifts his hand from Kristin's breast, up her neck to her temple, into her hair. Brings their faces together. When their pillowed lips meet, the fit is so exact it's like clouds settling over land.

In the night, Simon rises, draws on his robe, goes barefoot to the desk. The desk lamp is still burning, an orange wash. A pack of Gitanes lies atop the arrangement of clipped newspapers; Simon extracts a cigarette, lights it. Examines the top clipping, holds it up to smell the newsprint. Air circulates beneath the ceiling fan, cooling the sweat on his neck.

A muffled sound of padding steps, then a soft hand slides into the damp hair at his nape.

"You're intrigued by this case," Kristin says quietly. She presses herself warm against him.

Simon ashes the cigarette, brings the clipping closer. "I would like more information about it, I think."

Kristin extends a finger to touch the clipping carefully, as if it might bite. "Laurent keeps up with news from American sources. You could ask him to find out more – discreetly, of course."

"This is an option." Simon inclines his head. "Although I don't wish to arouse his suspicions. He lied about not reading, you understand. He reads everything."

Laurent also takes liberties, entertaining Kristin with amusing stories that allow him to gesticulate, showing off his bare chest beneath his flowing banyan robe. Perhaps Simon should return to visit Laurent tomorrow night, find out what further information he has – an extra lump of hashish may be the key to unlocking Laurent's insight. And then Laurent, like Jeremy, could go out of town unexpectedly...

His attention is drawn back at the sound of Kristin's soft gasp. "What is it, dearest?"

She has brushed clippings aside to see the most recent newspaper headlines. Now she points a trembling finger at the article, her face blanched in the low light.

Simon scans quickly, and his eyes land on a typed name. It's a name he has turned over in his mind many times, painted in shades of red.

"Oh my." He stubs out his cigarette with a snorting laugh. "Do the bureau think they're being subtle with this kind of thing, I wonder?"

"Simon…" Kristin stiffens beside him. "Are you saying this is a trap?"

"Assurement, mon cher." His voice is very jaunty.

"Then surely that is all you need to know." She brings a hand up to his face and draws him around to look at her. "Listen to me. You don't have to take the FBI's bait."

"Do you think me such a minnow, dearest?" Simon leans forward, whispers in her ear. "But I am a shark of the deep…"

He kisses her white-blond crown, and lures her back to bed.

CHAPTER FOUR

Guanajuato, 29 October 1982

Sun is bright through Travis's room as he stands by the window, pulling on a shirt. His most recent scar is an untidy keloid Z just below his breastbone – the entry wound scar on his back is much smaller – but it's only a little red now, and Travis doesn't pay it any mind.

The view through the window is a good one. Emma is out in the yard. Her jeans are dusty, and the sleeves of her T-shirt are rolled up her arms to her shoulders. She's walking along with Mariana, both of them lugging baskets – maybe something for the horses or the dogs, maybe peppers from the garden. These last two days, Emma has fit in comfortably with the chores and routines of a working ranch, and Travis keeps reminding himself that she grew up on a farm.

She looks so much healthier now than she did in September: more wiry than skinny, solid in her boots, dark hair coming in soft and spiky. Her smile is still guarded, but she's smiling. Like now: Out in the yard, Mariana leans and says something, and Emma grins. Her arms and cheeks are burnished by the sun. Travis buttons his shirt, can't take his eyes off her.

Once he's dressed, he drags himself away from the window and out, down the hall and through the living room. His aunt Sofia is setting the table for lunch, when all the men down tools and come in from the yard – there's a platter of tortillas on the kitchen pass-through bench, and Travis can smell frijoles charros and the tang of roasted chiles.

"Travis, hand me that platter?" Sofia speaks only Spanish when it's just family. She gestures with her elbow as she sets a plastic jug of water on the table. "Are you and Emma still okay to do the deliveries for me in San Miguel?"

He diverts to find the platter and pass it over. "Yeah, no problem."

"Can you drop off one more thing?"

"What do you need?" Travis helps himself to a gordita, cups a hand under his chin to catch the drips.

"Emilio called, said Gabriela hurt her foot. Wanna drive out to La Angostura?"

"We were gonna come home early…." He trails off and sighs at the sight of her raised eyebrows. "But sure. We can go out to Emilio's."

"You're a good boy, Travis." She smiles now she's got her way, nods with her chin toward the front door. "I packed all the food deliveries in the tote, plus some extras for you and Emma. The parcel for Luisa has the address on the paper. There's another box of empanadas there for Gabriela."

Travis wipes his fingers on a dishcloth, heads for the door. On the wooden hall table beside the jamb, two pie-sized boxes wrapped in brown paper and string, one with a marked address, as well as a woven plastic tote stuffed with brown paper bags, grease-spotted and still warm from the kitchen.

"Got it. Thanks for the extra food, auntie."

Sofia lays out paper napkins. "Thanks for doing this! You've really saved me today."

Travis heads out into the yard. Dogs are chasing each other around in the driveway, and Mateo is bringing a wheelbarrow up from the direction of the chicken coop. Travis passes left of the old century plant, and a stone horse-mounting block that he used as a child, and Emma is suddenly there with her basket.

"Hey." Her face is dewy with sweat. "Is it time for us to go? Let me just take this basket inside and wash my hands."

They take his uncle's Chevy truck, and Emma drives. The woven tote is on the floor in the passenger footwell, but Travis holds the boxes on his lap to protect them from Chico – one of the corriente dogs, coming along for the ride. They navigate through San Miguel to drop off small parcels of celebration food to various friends of Sofia's, then the parcel for her sister, Luisa. They eat some of the extra gorditas and drink from bottles of Sidral Mundet on the hour-long drive to Emilio's place near La Angostura.

Emilio, wearing a pale yellow guayabera, comes out to greet them. He accepts the empanadas for his wife, Gabriela, before introducing Travis and Emma to his twelve-year-old granddaughter, Flora. Chico runs around, sniffing everything. Emma smiles and begins halting chat with Flora; with time, her Spanish-language skills will keep improving. Emilio thanks them for the food parcel and the visit, wants to show off two new horses, waves them over to the yard.

The horses are a bay and a grey, a pair of Aztecas – the grey has some paint markings. Travis admires them, blows in their noses, lets them smell him. The horses hang their heads over the fence as he and Emilio discuss family news, farm news, the weather. It's been warm for Día de Muertos. There's some high cloud developing today, but Emilio doesn't think the rain will come before late evening.

Travis watches Emma stroke the bay horse's nose as it gets to know her, sunlight glancing off her face. She runs her hands over the animal's neck and chest, and Travis feels a tightening low in his belly.

He keeps talking with Emilio about celebration plans, but a steady awareness of Emma builds up and down his nerves. He watches her feed the horse a sandita; she smiles when the animal lips her palm. Tiny silver hoops glint at her ears. Travis thinks about touching her neck.

When they say their goodbyes and get back in the truck, Emma lets Chico clamber over her lap to sit by the window and Travis takes the wheel. Beside him, Emma's clean, bright scent. About two miles down the road, he recognizes that he is too distracted. He pulls over, unclips his seatbelt.

Emma looks confused. "What? What is it?"

"Come 'ere," he whispers, and reaches for her hand, tugging gently.

He kisses her first on the forehead, reassuring. All this stuff, she's still figuring it out. What she wants, and when, and how much, and how to do it. It was only after the first time she kissed him that he realized it was the first time she'd kissed *anybody*. Both shocking and humbling, that knowledge.

The engine rumbles beneath them. They touch noses, smiling, breathing together. Travis feels his hunger well up, warm and fine. Emma's eyes gradually darken and her breaths begin to hitch. She lays the flat of her palm against his cheek. Desire suffuses his body like a syrupy haze. But he is not a child. He can exercise control in service to doing this right – she's been hurt too badly to get it wrong. He lets her lead.

She draws his face closer and their lips meet, tentative at first, then soft and pliant. Tension falls away. Every time they kiss, it's like coming home. She sinks her mouth against his, draws back to nibble on his bottom lip. Then in again, deeper. Withdraw, advance. The rhythm of it is inflaming, and it is her rhythm. Her fingers are cool on his neck. This goes on for some minutes. He's panting.

The moment she starts to shiver, he curls his hands around her shoulders, pulls gently away.

"Okay." He is goddamn superhuman, keeping his voice this level. "All right. We should keep driving."

"What?" She's glaze-eyed. "No."

It's a good sign. "We want to get back to the ranch by four, right?"

"Yeah, but…" She looks at him, breaths slowing. Her gaze is clearing. She huffs out a laugh. "Oh my god – you're winding me up."

"Am I?" He grins, puts the truck in gear. "Clip your seatbelt back on."

She laughs again, but she clips her seatbelt. They keep driving. Some song by Silvio Rodriguez wafts from the radio, and the afternoon rolls on. Warm air blows in the cab of the truck. Emma looks out the window.

"This is nice," she says finally. She glances over. Her cheeks are pink and she looks happy. "I mean it. This is really nice."

Travis feels it, too. He's trying to remember the last time he was this content. "Yeah, it is. I'm really glad you're here."

"Me, too." Emma's hand slips across the bench seat and squeezes his non-driving hand. "Hey, you were up again last night," she says softly. "I heard you from my room."

"Yeah, I was up. But it's not every night now."

"Wanna talk about it?"

"Not yet." He just wants this golden afternoon to go on and on.

Sun dapples them through the windshield. Chico falls asleep on the seat.

It's just after four when they make it back to the ranch, and the first thing Travis notices is the black car parked in the driveway. The warm contented feeling he's been enjoying drains so fast it's like someone pulled the plug out of him: The plug hole seems to be located near his impalement scar.

Beside him, Emma sucks in a breath. Travis turns the truck into a sandy spot near the gate, leaves the engine idling as they both stare at the car.

The spit has dried up in his mouth. He clears his throat. "That's a very official-looking rental."

"I've only been here two days." Emma's hugging Chico. "Is that all we get? Two days?"

Travis doesn't trust himself to speak.

"I don't know if I'm ready for this," Emma whispers.

There's a pause, as the engine rumbles.

"Do you want me to turn the truck around?" He says it in a rush. "We could go back to San Miguel. Stay with my cousin in town –"

"No." Emma takes a beat, exhales long and low. "No. Let's just get it over with."

Travis turns the key to off.

When they get up to the patio steps, Travis sees a man in a dark suit sitting on one of the wicker chairs. He's about thirty-five, his blond hair cut in a high and tight. He has an oddly broad face, with eyes of such a pale grey they look almost silver. A glass of agua de fresca, half empty, sweats on the low table in front of him.

Seeing the car and this man has forced a mental gear shift; now Travis recalls everything he knows about Special Agent Jack Kirby. They have not worked together much, so the connection is not solid. But Kirby has a reputation in the bureau: He is adaptive, intelligent, prepared to negotiate. And he's a true believer. The ideals of the FBI – fidelity, bravery, integrity – are Kirby's ideals.

Travis once felt the same. He's not sure now if he is still soldered to those principles. Or maybe he is, but not in the same way.

Emma leads onto the patio and straight into confrontation. "Mariana made you wait out here? Pretty sure that means she doesn't like you."

Kirby stands from his chair. "Emma Lewis? Miss Lewis, we were never properly introduced at Quantico –"

"No, we weren't." Emma's face is a flat mask. "But that's fine. I don't like you either."

"I'm sorry to hear that." Kirby gives her an assessing look, before turning to Travis with his hand extended. "Mr. Bell."

"Just Travis." But after a beat, Travis shakes. Direct confrontation is not his way. "How's Virginia?"

"Chilly." Kirby's eyes flick to Emma, move onward to the view from the patio. "This is nicer."

"But you didn't come to enjoy the weather." Emma's standing firm, both feet planted. "What do you want, Mr. Kirby?"

"I've mainly come to speak with you, Miss Lewis." He looks between them both. "Can we sit and talk?"

Emma expression doesn't change one iota. "You can't tell us standing up?"

"Not this I can't." Kirby's suit is soft at the edges, from the afternoon heat. "If you could give me just a few minutes of your time –"

"We've already given a few pints of blood to the bureau," Emma says. "Travis almost gave his *life*. Now you want a few minutes of our time?"

"Emma..." Travis touches her forearm gently.

"It's important," Kirby says.

Travis looks back at him with a humorless snort. "When is it ever *not* important?"

"Please." Kirby somehow maintains his dignity while making his appeal. "I've come a long way."

This is undoubtedly true. Kirby would have flown from DC to Guanajuato, probably with a stop in Atlanta or Houston. Then the hire car, and at least five hours to his destination. He wouldn't have been able to flash his tin, the Mexican government doesn't recognise FBI jurisdiction – he has no police powers down here. Kirby has come with no visible symbols of authority, apart from his suit, and he's come alone.

Travis recognizes this, checks Emma for her response. She hesitates, bites her lip. Finally nods.

Travis gestures toward the wicker patio chairs. "Have a seat, I guess."

They all sit. Kirby returns to his chair, Travis takes the corner of the couch and Emma claims the chair nearby.

Travis can smell horses and truck diesel on himself, on his clothes. His loose shirt and jeans and boots are a long way from FBI standard. He reminds himself that this is his territory – Kirby is the one who's out of place here.

But Kirby is the one who speaks first. "I've come to talk to you about Simon and Kristin Gutmunsson."

Every muscle in Travis's body braces. He breathes through it. Emma immediately crosses her arms.

"I know it's a difficult subject for you." Kirby's expression is appropriately solemn. "And it's taken us a while. We lost them after Pittsburgh

– they went to ground in Europe, and things got busy for the bureau at the end of September."

"The Tylenol case, right?" Travis has to unclench his jaw to ask.

"Yes." Kirby nods, reaches to take a sip of his drink. "You heard about that here?"

"I was still in the hospital, but I keep up with the news. Not as much these days." Travis glances at Emma, back. "So you got the guy?"

"Yeah, we think so. We're still pulling all the evidence together." Kirby returns his glass to the table. "Anyway, by the time matters in Chicago were resolved, the Gutmunssons' trail had gone pretty cold. We had a few spot sightings forwarded from Interpol – for a while we thought they were in Switzerland, or Portugal."

"They were both educated in Europe." Emma's voice is stiff.

"Yes," Kirby confirms. "But early this month, we had a concrete hit. We're pretty sure they're in Morocco."

"Kristin, too?" Emma is holding herself so tightly it's a wonder her tendons don't crack in protest. The question of Kristin's involvement in Simon's bloody escape from Allegheny Jail in Pennsylvania, and whether she's being held against her will, clearly still preys on Emma's mind. It preys on Travis's mind as well.

Kirby sits back in his chair for the first time. "It seems fairly evident now that where her brother goes, Kristin Gutmunsson follows."

"You can't extradite from Morocco," Travis points out.

"No. Which is why we've been trying another strategy." Kirby waits a beat for emphasis. "We've accepted advice about Simon Gutmunsson's personality profile and behaviors from Dr. Stanley Becher, a professor of psychology at Columbia. He's given us information that's allowed us to develop a plan to lure Gutmunsson back to the States."

"You want to *lure* Simon?" Emma is momentarily surprised into a dumbfounded expression.

"Becher has done a full psychoanalytic report on Gutmunsson – studied his upbringing, his relationships with his parents and victims and his sister, the written work he submitted for Georgetown University, the crimes he committed. Becher thinks Gutmunsson is deeply attached to his identity and, uh, 'legacy' as the Artist. So we've been challenging that legacy."

Travis gets a bad feeling. "How?"

"We faked a homicide case." For something so radical, Kirby makes it sound very bland. "More than one, in fact."

"Fake murders." Travis can't believe an institution as buttoned-up as the bureau would try something so ballsy.

"Yes," Kirby says. "The cases have been designed to seem linked, and they all feature elements similar to Simon Gutmunsson's crimes."

"And you've seeded those stories in the media." Emma extrapolates, in that way she does. Her eyebrows are still raised.

Kirby nods. "That's correct, yes. We've supplied information to a number of syndicated newspapers, including three majors we know have international reach. The *New York Herald Tribune*, the *Washington Post*, and the *Wall Street Journal* have all run stories on the 'investigation into the new Artist'. We even got a few column inches in *Newsweek*."

Kirby seems pleased with himself. Travis meets Emma's eyes. Her expression is disbelieving.

He looks back at Kirby. "You think he'll see this stuff in Morocco?"

"We know he keeps up with the news. We believe the stories will get his attention, yes. We're hoping he'll be intrigued and annoyed at the idea of someone else committing murder and using his nom de plume to take credit. If it's enough of an insult to his ego, we think he'll come home."

"Great." Emma opens her hands. "So you've laid a trap, and now you just have to reel him in. You don't need me."

Kirby wets his lips, finally getting to the point. "Miss Lewis, we'd like to ask you to come aboard on this operation. We want Gutmunsson to think you're involved in the hunt for this 'new Artist'."

"No." Travis speaks on automatic. Relents for more information. "Why?"

"Because Simon is…" Emma slowly exhales. "He thinks he has some kind of connection with me. He's talked to me before, and he's left me alive twice now."

"Dr. Becher suspects he has a form of psychological attachment to you, yes," Kirby says softly.

Travis has a sudden, almost overwhelming urge to punch something. He has to dig his nails into the wicker arm of the couch to control it. More than anything, he wants to turn back the clock to the moments in the truck with Emma only a few hours ago, when they were ignorant of all this, when the afternoon stretched out before them in a mellow glow.

"Fuck." Emma whispers it, but the word still comes out harsh. She rubs a hand across the back of her neck, eyes closed.

"I know…" Kirby stops, rephrases. "Miss Lewis, I understand that this is a tough decision. You have difficult history with Gutmunsson. But if you elect to come aboard, we would take good care of you. We –"

"Hold up," Travis interrupts. He can feel himself being subtly cut out from this conversation and he wants to remedy that. "First of all, Emma and I are partners. We work together."

He's not looking at Emma, but he senses her startle, feels her alarm like a fine tremor on his skin. "Travis –"

"Hey." He gives her his full gaze. "I would never let you walk into something like this alone. Not a chance. You should know that before you make a call on it."

"You're not recovered yet." She's got that *Are you crazy?* expression on her face which always makes him grin.

"I don't care." There's no way he's gonna sit at home wondering if she's okay. "And I have skin in this game, too."

Kirby clears his throat. "Uh, Mr. Bell, considering that you're not in full health, the bureau would prefer if only Miss Lewis –"

"The bureau can prefer whatever it likes," Travis says calmly, turning back. "We're a team. A package deal. You want Emma, you've gotta bring me in as well. You need her, right?"

Kirby makes a tight-lipped nod, looking between them.

"Then I guess if you want me, you get both of us," Emma says.

Travis can see her fingers twitching on the arm of her chair, like she wants to reach over and hold his hand. It gives him a good feeling.

"Okay." Kirby sighs, conceding defeat. "If it's a deal-breaker, I can authorize that."

"I still don't know *why* you want me," Emma says.

"We want to use your name and your picture." Kirby warms to his subject again. "Your involvement would give this operation the authenticity it needs to draw Gutmunsson into the open."

"So I'm the bait." Emma's voice is dry. "Again."

"Not at all." Kirby backtracks. "We're not planning to dangle you in front of Gutmunsson – we don't want to put you in harm's way. But we'd like to be able to leak to the media that you're being consulted. Later, we'd like you to give an interview to syndicated news about the 'investigation' –"

"Why would she do any of that?" Travis interrupts. "I understand it's good for the case, but how is it good for Emma?"

Now he feels Emma's soft hand on his forearm. When he glances over, he sees her eyes narrow as she stares at Kirby, watchful as a bird.

"Travis, I don't think that's the question. I think the question is, why wouldn't the FBI have leaked my name *already*?" She cocks her head. "That's it, isn't it, Mr. Kirby? That's why you seem so eager. Because you've already done it. You've already leaked my name."

The man is caught with his mouth open, but he recovers his business-like expression quickly. "Miss Lewis –"

"Jesus Christ." Part of Travis is thinking how the FBI always underestimates Emma's intelligence, but the other part of him is just plain outraged.

"There it is." Emma shakes her head at Kirby in wonder. "The good ole FBI."

Kirby scrambles to regain ground. "Look, we were under some time pressure –"

"So you decided, what, *We may as well go for it?*" Travis says. "For one, leaking Emma's name to the media in relation to an active investigation can't be legal."

"That's how desperate we are." Kirby volleys his attention between them, his pale eyes intense. "Miss Lewis, I know you want to get Simon Gutmunsson back behind bars as much as we do. Mr. Bell, I imagine you feel the same way."

Emma has already stood up. "Goodbye, Mr. Kirby."

Kirby stands to match her. "Miss Lewis, please. We all want the same thing –"

But Emma has already walked away, off the porch and down the steps. Travis pulls himself to his feet.

"Mr. Bell –" Kirby starts.

"You could have *asked*." Travis feels a heaviness in his limbs, which is the weight of disappointment. "You could have just asked first."

Kirby bites his lip. "You're one of us, Travis. You understand how this works."

Travis shakes his head slowly. *Fidelity, Bravery, Integrity*. During his time with the bureau, it was the integrity part that was always the most important, and the most difficult for people to sustain. He turns away from Kirby, follows Emma's trail off the porch.

Cool air drifts across the yard.

Emma has gone for a walk. After Kirby leaves, Travis returns to the truck for Sofia's woven tote. On the way back to the house, he discovers Kirby's card sitting in the small pool of condensation from the man's glass, there on the patio table. Travis stares at the card for a long moment, then reluctantly picks it up.

He fields his uncle and aunt's questions about the official visitor – there's not a lot he can say – before going back outside and walking down to the gate. The sun has lowered toward the horizon and the sky is turning salmon pink. Travis watches as it darkens.

The most difficult thing is knowing that Kirby has got them backed into a corner. He cheated, but he still won. Travis wonders if that's the way the FBI works now. Maybe that's the way the FBI has always worked, and he's only just realizing.

It's not fair, but there's a lot of things in life that aren't fair.

Emma approaches with a series of scuffs from behind. She leans on the gate beside him, regarding the same horizon. "It's nearly time, isn't it."

"Yeah." Travis is filled with a complex sadness, consisting mostly of grief.

Emma makes a humorless huff of laughter. "I know I said, when you were in the hospital, that we have to do something about Simon Gutmunsson. But now I kinda wish someone else would do it instead."

Travis nods. "I kinda wish that, too."

"I don't want to leave here," she says softly.

"Me either."

"Do we have a choice?"

Travis has been thinking about this for the last hour. No, he realizes – he's been thinking about it for the last five weeks. But didn't he know the conclusion all along? Ultimately, it's all very simple.

"Kirby's doing this completely wrong," he says. "But Simon Gutmunsson murdered my dad. I don't think he deserves to be walking around, pleasing himself."

"Simon will hurt other people," Emma agrees. "I'd be surprised if he hasn't done that already." She leans against Travis's shoulder, looking at the dirt. "Kirby's an asshole. But I keep thinking about Simon out in the world. And I keep thinking about how I killed a man five weeks ago. I had every reason to shoot Peter Kirke, and I did it, but it was not a good feeling and I'd like to get rid of it."

"Emma –"

"Simon called me a murderer like him." When she lifts her head, her eyes are shiny. "He said that we're drawn together. That we understand each other. I guess if I can harness just a little of that understanding to catch him, I need to do it."

Travis presses his arm against hers, keeps his voice gentle. "You're not a murderer."

"Then I'm having a shitty run of luck with people dying lately." She kicks a clump of dry grass with the toe of her boot. Looks up again at the fading light, her face becoming radiant. "I love it here."

"I know," Travis says.

Emma smiles sadly. "If we leave, how will your aunt bring the oranges in?"

"We can stay." Travis has to keep reminding himself they have options.

She turns her face into his shoulder. "If you get hurt again, I don't think I could handle it."

"We can stay," he whispers.

But he knows they won't stay. Emma presses her wet cheek against the sleeve of his shirt, and they stand together, consoling each other. He slips an arm around her and she rests, warm against him, as they watch the horizon together. The final edge of the sun creates a corona of fire in the dusk as it disappears.

"God," Emma says. "The sky is so bright here."

Travis squeezes her, unable to speak.

CHAPTER FIVE

Virginia, 30 October 1982

Quantico FBI training base is quiet at 8:00PM, when the bureau car brings them to the entry of Jefferson residential. But of course, Quantico is never really quiet: The base is a military facility, and in other buildings here lectures are being attended, residents are studying or eating meals, firearms are being broken down and quickly reassembled.

A young MP named Coleman – skinny, cap pulled down to the bridge of his nose, hair clipped close in a way Emma's familiar with – met them for the hour-long drive from Washington International. The trip from Guanajuato to DC, via Houston, has taken an entire day and involved a mental and environmental adjustment: Mexico was warm, but it is fall in Virginia. Everything is hard and cold, and there is frost on the sidewalk outside Jefferson. Now they've arrived, Emma would like a moment to sit in the car and gather herself, but moments like that never seem to come, and anyway, this is not her car. She left the Rabbit at the ranch.

They enter the building and Emma sheds her heavy jacket in the atrium, where the temperature is set at a consistent sixty-eight degrees. "Now where to?"

"Elevator." Travis's boots are dripping on the hardwood floor. "But we should dump our bags at the desk first."

They were already ID-checked at the base gate; now they're issued interim passes and allowed to set down their luggage. Emma has only her backpack, Travis has his duffel. His suit-bag is conspicuous by its absence. He's still in jeans and boots and his dad's old jacket, and Emma realized a while ago that he plans to stay this way. She likes it pretty good. She guesses this is what the FBI is going to get now – the real Travis Bell. She hopes they're ready for it.

They stand together waiting for the elevator and Emma wants to get one thing straight. "I'm still not totally sure why you're doing this. You're not fully recovered. You don't have full mobility, and you get sore and tired."

Travis just shrugs and smiles. "I'm here now. You can't get rid of me."

Emma rolls her eyes. "You know what I mean."

"Package deal, remember?" When the elevator doors open, Travis walks in after her and pushes the button for basement level. Inside the car, there's a suspended quiet. "Do you remember the first day we met, in the foyer of Behavioral Science?"

That was only five months ago, Emma's shocked to realize. She's not sure where he's going with this, but she remembers. "You were looking at the Most Wanted posters. I thought you looked kinda uptight."

"Really?" He grins. "You thought I looked uptight?"

"I think it was your chinos. Or maybe your posture." Emma considers the moment again. "But you had a good handshake."

"A good handshake, huh?"

She feels her cheeks warm. "It made me trust you."

He turns to her then, sticks out his hand. "Bell, Travis J." When she gives him a disbelieving look, he finds her hand with his own anyway. "Do you still trust me?"

She takes a lot of comfort in the contact between them, but her lips press together all the same. "I worry."

"Speak plain, Emma."

"I can't lose you," she says softly.

His eyes narrow. "Then stick close. Something tells me we're gonna need each other."

The elevator doors open.

They walk the confusing gerbil-run corridors to Behavioral Science. The bureau has re-painted, so there's a three-foot gray dado marking the white cinderblock walls – it doesn't actually help much with finding your way around. The ducted ceiling is the same as always, and as they approach the glass doors, Emma sees that the Behavioral Science foyer is also the same: no chairs, buffed concrete floor, Most Wanted posters on the right-hand side. She wonders if the criminals in the pictures have changed at all in the last five months.

Special Agent Kirby is leaning against the unoccupied reception desk, leafing through a file. Even at this time of night, his gray suit is immaculate. As they enter, his eyes light and he tucks the file under his arm, extends his other hand to shake.

"Miss Lewis, Mr. Bell." His smile is easy; he lifts his chin at the ceiling to indicate the facility above them. "Folks from upstairs called, said you were on your way. I really appreciate you coming aboard. How was your trip?"

"Long," Emma says.

Kirby nods. "And I'm sure you're tired, so this briefing will be just to get you oriented. This way, please."

He ushers with the file, and they walk through the door. Emma looks around, curious. Although she's slept in this building, been many times to this floor, this basement, it's the first time she's actually entered the offices of FBI Behavioral Science.

She's surprised at how dingy it is. The low ceilings are coffered, the colors are muted, the carpet is an industrial beige. Wall signs point toward evidence storage and inform visitors that they are at Lower Level, which the concrete buttresses already made obvious. Emma's regular anxiety at being underground manifests as goosebumps on her arms, but she thinks her reactions to basement areas have improved a great deal since June.

Kirby leads them through a series of cubicle hallways, past cork boards covered in staff notices, various wood veneer doors. As they weave closer to the heart of this maze, the décor becomes more commensurate with the section's purpose: tacked-up scene-of-crime photos, suspects with staring eyes, victims with open mouths. The criminal and the dead clamor for equal attention here.

Kirby finally steers them through a door on the left. It's a tiny conference room; walking three steps inside brings Emma's legs up against a large blond-wood table. The wall by the corridor is all glass, and the room smells faintly of Pledge. More immediate and jarring is the way the entire wall straight ahead is taken up with photos and information about the Gutmunsson twins.

There are printouts, profiles, a world map with marked locations, and a large chalkboard with keywords – Emma blinks at terms like 'ego' and 'repressed memories?' and 'sadist'. But it's the photographs that dominate: mug shots, stills from prison CCTV cameras, candid family photos. In each of them, Simon's white hair and full lips, and Kristin's curiously detached expressions, create unnerving textures. The twins' blue eyes stare out, blank and appraising.

Travis balks at the sight. "Jesus."

"We're using this as home base for the duration," Kirby says over his shoulder, as he skirts around the table to introduce another person in the room. "I understand you already know Special Agent Martino?"

"Yeah." Travis conjures a smile and moves closer for a handshake. "But he probably hasn't seen me in civvies before. How're you doing, Mike?"

"Good, yeah, really good." Mike Martino is affable and consistent: His dark hair and moustache and unsubtle cologne are all unchanged, although his tan suit is now a three-piece, which suggests to Emma that his star is rising in the bureau. He looks genuinely happy to see Travis, claps him on the arm. "I just stayed back to say hi, I've got a meeting in a few minutes. But man, I'm glad to see you walking around, you had us all worried back in September. You look healthy enough now."

"I'm healthy enough for this," Travis says.

"Where's your work suit?"

Emma stiffens but Travis just shrugs it off. "I figured I'd hold off on the suits until I can stop getting blood all over them. I'm strictly advisory here this time. You remember Emma?"

"Of course, of course – good to see you again, Miss Lewis." Martino nods at her, waves at the strategy wall. "What do you think of this, huh? It's the whole Gutmunsson file in one place."

"It's...certainly something," Emma agrees. She thinks it's unlikely Martino will catch her tone.

Kirby may have caught her tone, but he seems to be electing to ignore it. He looks over Emma's shoulder at another person standing behind her. "Travis Bell, Emma Lewis, I'd also like you to meet our psychoanalysis expert, Doctor Stanley Becher."

Emma turns and immediately wants to take a step back. Becher is an imposing figure. Heavy-boned, white, well over six feet tall, the man wears a pale buttoned shirt, brown trousers, and a blue tweed sport coat that seems too warm for inside. He has sleek dark hair and a downward-sloping moustache, thick glasses. Everything about him seems contained and oddly prim.

"Miss Lewis." Becher's jowls are shaven smooth, and his quiet voice seems to fall into a register somewhere below the basement's hum. "Delighted to meet you."

"Doctor." Emma nods to avoid shaking hands. She thinks Becher is standing closer than he really needs to be.

"I'm very pleased you could join us." Through his glasses, Becher's dark eyes radiate an intimidating calm. "I think the combination of your experience and my expertise will be very helpful for dealing with the bureau's little problem, don't you?"

"Yes." Emma controls her knee-jerk reaction, which is to run around the other side of the table and out of the room. "The little problem."

"And Mr. Bell." Becher switches his attention.

"Doctor," Travis says, shaking hands. "It'll be good to work with you."

"Yes, I understand you'll both be assisting Special Agent Kirby with this operation." Becher has a slow way of talking, with weird hesitations between words, and his attention lingers on their faces just a beat too long. "I'm sure you've had a strenuous journey, but I'm looking forward to discussing matters with you once you've recovered."

For a man with such a large physical presence, Becher has an awkward sluggish energy. Emma finds him unnerving. She nods again in reply, angles away from Becher and toward Kirby for a diversion. "So where do you believe Simon and Kristin currently are?"

"Sorry to interrupt, but I'm gonna leave you to it." Martino gestures to Kirby, points at the door. "Jack, I've got that budgetary meeting with Cubbins –"

"No problem, Mike, see you tomorrow." Kirby nods at the exiting Martino, moves to the wall, where the maps and papers and photos whirlpool together in a bloodthirsty collage. "Okay, the Gutmunssons' location. Our sources have indicated that they're living here, in Tangier, Morocco. They have an apartment in Old Medina where they're living off their mother's jewelry."

"That's where they *were*," Travis says, getting to the point. "What are the chances they're back in the States already?"

Kirby shakes his head. "We only released the, uh, relevant newspaper articles a few days ago." He doesn't even blush when he says this, which Emma definitely notices. "But news often takes time to circulate in the expatriate community. So we're not expecting –"

"When were the articles released?" Emma asks. "Which dates?"

"October twenty-third and twenty-fourth," Kirby says. "Two outlets, *New York Herald Tribune* and WaPo."

Emma finds Travis is speaking only to her. "What do you think?"

"I think it's enough time for them to come home." She glances across the assembled mess of paperwork. "Other than that, it's hard to say. Simon probably already knows what this whole sting entails. The question is whether he considers it a warning or a challenge."

"You think Gutmunsson knows this is a ruse?" Kirby's brow furrows.

She's gonna have to break it to him gently. Well, not that gently. "Mr. Kirby, you're dealing with someone whose IQ tests are totally off the charts. So it's really just a matter of whether Simon's pride outweighs

46

his common sense, and whether Kristin has managed to persuade him to hold fast in Morocco."

Travis nods. "Believe it or not, Kristin's actually the sensible one in this situation."

Becher is in curious agreement. "That's likely true. It will depend, of course, on how much influence Simon's sister has over him."

"Interesting." Kirby looks disturbed by these ideas, even as he wrests back control of the conversation. "Although I'm not sure I agree with your assessment that Simon's already ahead of us…But let's have a quick look at the news articles, and then I'll let you go."

He motions to the big table in the room; Emma turns to see a manila folder of newspaper clippings on the blond wood table-top. She flips the cover of the folder with her finger, stirs the clippings around. Some tacky headlines, some gory photos in black and white – and a recent picture of her face, cropped from what looks like OSU student enrolment files. Her name is appended underneath in tiny letters: *Emma Lewis, serial killer survivor now consulting with the FBI.*

She looks up at Kirby, her mouth tight. "I'm still pissed about this, you know."

"It was my fault really, Miss Lewis." Becher, in his slow way, with a finger on his glasses. He drops his chin in a gesture of humility. "I was the one who suggested Agent Kirby needed to mention you in the news articles."

Travis has the man pinned in his sights. "Were you the one who suggested they do it without prior consent?"

Becher lifts his gaze to Travis's, unflappable. "It was a group decision."

"We want to do a feature for the next article." Kirby is re-directing. "Miss Lewis, we'd like you to give an interview in which we cover some aspects of your history and how you came to work with the bureau, and also some details about these fake homicide cases."

He's tenacious, she'll give him that. His pale eyes show no embarrassment at all, only confidence – which is understandable, given that she and Travis are already here.

"She's gonna be talking about everything with a reporter?" Travis asks.

"Yes," Kirby confirms. "A WaPo contact known to Doctor Linda Brown, from FBI Scientific Analysis. We originally appealed to Dr. Brown to write the articles needed, and she was very helpful. But she's had a series of court engagements which meant she couldn't construct the interview, and in any case, we think a personal dialogue with a professional journalist will come across as more authentic."

"How much detail of my own history am I expected to reveal?" Emma wipes the newsprint off her fingers onto her jeans. "I don't want to rehash everything about the Huxton case in the newspapers – it's painful for my family, and for me."

Kirby makes a considering frown. "We think Gutmunsson's fascination is really centered on you, so honestly, I'll take as much detail as I can get. But let's talk about it further tomorrow."

Travis steps forward. "And how are you going to protect her?"

"You'll both be sequestered here, at Quantico, so there's absolutely no need for you to be in the field. We'll keep an eye out for Gutmunsson, you don't have to worry."

"And our families?" Emma asks.

"Protection detail coverage in Ohio and Texas has already been set in place."

"Lena's gonna love that," Travis murmurs, glancing at Emma.

Emma bites her lip, looks at Kirby. "I still think Simon's way ahead of you on this. He's been ahead of you all along."

Kirby seems resolute. "If he's already back in the country, then that's good for us. We just need to tweak the schedule for his recapture."

Emma squints up at a nearby photo of Simon smoking a cigarette while seated on edge of the bed in his old cell in Byberry State Hospital. "Have you tried contacting him directly?"

"What do you mean?"

Emma shrugs, motions toward one of the paper notes affixed to the wall. "Well, his lawyer's number is right there."

It's a spur-of-the-moment idea; she steps back and grabs the phone conference unit in the centre of the table. Presses a button for an outside line and gets through the first three numbers...until a large, thick index finger descends onto the switch hook, and her ear registers the dial tone.

"We don't believe," Dr. Becher says, "that a direct approach will be productive."

Emma holds Becher's gaze for a long moment, until she decides she's had enough. Fuck it: It's late, and she's been travelling all day. She doesn't need this.

She breaks eye contact with Becher to glance back at Kirby. "Right. So you construct this elaborate hoax that you think is gonna fool a guy who's too smart for Mensa, but you don't want to deal with him directly...Okay. Are we done?"

"We are," Kirby says. "I want to thank you again for agreeing to participate –"

"Yes, absolutely. Can we go now?"

"Of course. Make sure to set your alarm for tomorrow – we'll have an 8:00AM meeting and then the journalist interview before lunch."

"Fine." Emma turns away, wants to hold Travis's hand but figures that can wait until they're in the elevator.

Travis looks at the other two men, and his gaze isn't entirely friendly. "Agent Kirby, Dr. Becher. We'll see you both tomorrow."

They find their way out through the maze of cubicles in Behavioral Science, and once they emerge, Emma thinks it's funny: For the first time, she's relieved to be out in the regular basement corridors. She breathes like she's had a weight removed off her lungs. The air conditioning is cool on her face.

Travis shoves his hands into the pockets of his jacket, gazes back at the office doors. Emma finds her eyes straying to him constantly: Her old, faded image of him in his FBI suit refuses to align with the current image. In this environment, with his hair uncombed and his boots dusty, he looks a lot less domesticated – about as far from *uptight* as she could imagine.

Right now, he's squinting like something's bothering him. "That was weird, right? It wasn't just me?"

Emma shakes her head. "Not just you. It was weird."

Travis lowers his voice as they start walking away. "I shook Becher's hand and it was like, I don't know. This…meat sock."

"Becher." Emma blows out air as she walks. "Holy hell."

"He must be six-five," Travis says. "He towers over me."

"I guessed six-three, but you've got the height advantage." Travis has taken a corner she wasn't anticipating. "Where are we going now? Shouldn't we head back to the elevators? We need to get our room assignments."

"Not yet." Travis frowns as he walks them through the hallways. "I wanna go to the Cool Room first."

"The Cool Room?" Last time Emma arrived at Quantico, their old office was her first port of call. It occurs to her now that her primary reason for visiting the office then was to see Travis – she just hadn't wanted to admit it to herself. "Okay, Cool Room it is."

Travis nods. "I've got a hunch about something and I want to check it out. Plus, I'd kind of like to have a place to go that's not some tiny room plastered in pictures of the Gutmunssons."

"I hear that," Emma says fervently.

They turn the final corner and front up to the door. Travis reaches for the knob, rattles it. There's no give.

"They locked it?" Emma finds the idea that Kirby has cut them off from their usual refuge disturbing.

"Yeah, I thought they might." Travis has been fishing in his jeans pocket; now he pulls out a green plastic keyring. "Which is why I kept this."

Emma coughs a laugh, glances behind them to ensure they're not being observed. "Travis, are you breaking and entering on FBI property?"

"Hey, it's not breaking and entering if you've got a copy of the key." He winks and unlocks the door, and they walk inside.

CHAPTER SIX

Virginia, 30 October 1982

Travis looks around at how the interior of the Cool Room has been stripped.

Every small convenience from their last case is gone: There's no extra desk, no coffee maker, no pencil holder, no carpet tiles. All that remains is a single wooden desk with a lamp, a heavy metal filing cabinet, one folding metal chair with a cushioned seat, and the hard old couch, which was obviously too awkward to remove. Travis finds the reduced conditions oddly poignant.

Emma scans the dour gray basement space, wincing. "I mean, this place was never homey, but now…"

"Old FBI maxim – everything not nailed down is free to be cannibalized for further use." Travis moves to the desk, switches on the lamp, then goes to the filing cabinet. He opens the top drawer, which only holds empty suspension files, all letter size.

"What are you looking for?"

He pushes back the files, checks underneath: nothing. Tries the next drawer. "I tucked it in here last time, and if our luck holds, they might have forgotten to…Oh yeah. Got it."

The beige business phone unit is wrapped in its own cord. Travis works it free from under the suspension files, shuts the drawer, turns around with a victorious smile.

"Uh-*huh*." Emma's admiring expression is an added bonus. "Smart."

"Yep. One second."

Travis kneels to plug the phone line in at the jack, feels a sharp twinge as he stands back up. Reminds himself he's been going hard for the last thirty-six hours, and he'll need to take some pain relief and lay down soon. But for the moment, that can wait. He dumps the phone on the desk, consults his mental Rolodex, lifts the receiver and starts punching numbers.

Emma walks closer to the desk, opening out the one remaining folding chair. "Here – sit down before you fall down. Who are you calling?"

"We need allies." Travis settles onto the seat with gratitude, leans on his elbows as the ringtone chirps. "I'm calling the folks at Scientific Analysis."

"It's after nine. Will anyone even be there?"

"The lab never sleeps, remember?" Travis raises his eyebrows at her, but now the phone is being picked up.

The voice is a warm, female contralto. "Good evening, Gerry Westfall's office."

"Dr. Brown?" Travis exchanges a fast glance with Emma. "Dr. Brown, this is Travis Bell. I'm calling from Quantico, and you're actually the person I'm trying to reach. Is it okay if I put this call on conference?"

"Hi, Travis. Of course." And now Dr. Linda Brown's voice is echoing in the dim gloom of the Cool Room. "Nice to hear from you. I'm glad to hear you recovered all right, and I'm really glad you got in touch. I've been hoping to talk with you about –"

"About the news articles that Special Agent Kirby wanted prepared?" Emma, perched on the desk, angles toward the phone. "Hi, Dr. Brown, this is Emma Lewis here. Sorry to butt in."

"You're not butting in, this concerns you, too." A pause from Brown. "I'm honestly relieved to talk with you. Special Agent Kirby made a request in relation to you a few weeks ago that I wasn't entirely comfortable with."

It all tracks: Dr. Linda Brown is an expert in forensic documents. Her skills were a huge advantage in both of the FBI cases that Travis has been involved with. It makes sense that Kirby would consult her in the creation of the fake news articles, to get the tone and language exact.

"You mean the articles Kirby is using for the sting on Simon Gutmunsson?" Travis catches Emma's eye. "Yeah, we just got out of a briefing about it with Kirby and his psych consultant."

"Then you know I prepared the initial articles as requested," Brown confirms. Her golden voice resonates in the quiet space, taking on a disapproving tone. "Except in the final article, Agent Kirby wanted me to include Emma's name. When I asked him about it, he wouldn't give me a straight answer about Emma's involvement. That's when I contacted Howard to find out more."

Travis leans in. "You've been in touch with Howard Carter?"

"Yes," Brown confirms. "He's been on leave, but I've spoken with him."

"Tell me they didn't bench him after the Kirke case." Travis eases back, queasy over the fate of his former mentor. While things didn't go to plan during the College Killer case, Special Agent Howard Carter's a good agent and taught him a lot.

"It had nothing to do with your injury during the Kirke case, or with the Gutmunssons' escape," Brown reassures quickly. "Howard's been on compassionate leave – his wife, Angela, passed in late September."

"Oh god, that's awful," Emma says softly. Travis knows she had a dimmer view of Carter's behavior during the Kirke case in Pittsburgh, but she's never been devoid of empathy.

"Yes, I believe it was quite sudden and unexpected." Brown's voice regains a more professional tone. "But I've been liaising with Howard about the articles, and he told me that Kirby didn't have your consent prior to their publication. Which is why I elected to share the name of a WaPo contact for the proposed interview, but not to contribute further documents to Agent Kirby's case."

Emma catches Travis's eye, and he believes they're both remembering the same thing: The moment Kirby said, *She's had a series of court engagements which meant she couldn't construct the interview*…It's likely that Brown's court engagements were a fiction.

"Okay, we really appreciate you giving us that information, Dr. Brown." Travis hunts in his pocket for a pen, finds that Emma is passing him one. "And can I ask one last thing? Is it possible for us to get in contact with Agent Carter at home? I know it's out of order, but Kirby has brought me and Emma into Behavioral Science, and we're…kind of out of our depth."

Emma angles closer to contribute. "Linda? We're basically swimming with the sharks here."

"I understand." Brown hesitates. "Look, I don't think it would be a good idea if I pass on Howard's personal number – that could get us all in a little trouble. But I can get in touch with him directly myself, and let him know what's happening. Would that work?"

"That'd be an excellent start," Travis says. "Only problem is, I don't know if I can give you a direct line of contact if he wants to call us."

"It's fine," Brown insists. "I'll get him to contact Betty, the receptionist in Behavioral Science. She's discreet, and she can find you."

"Okay, sounds like a plan. Dr. Brown, thank you."

"Yeah," Emma agrees. "Thanks, Linda. We really appreciate this."

"No problem." Brown sounds lightly amused. "Travis, you can call me Linda, too, you know. I was only awarded my doctorate a month ago, and we've known each other longer than that. All right, I'd better get back to work – we'll talk again soon."

As soon as the call ends, Travis sits back in his chair. He taps the pen on the desktop, thinking about what a mess this is turning out to be. "It's still blowing my mind that Kirby signed off on all this. The fake homicides? The way he tried to squeeze Linda about the articles? It all sounds really sketchy."

"I know." Emma scoots herself farther onto the desktop and into a cross-legged position. "You think he's being pressured from above?"

"Maybe. Still no excuse for using you like chum in the water." The whole idea gives Travis a sour taste. He sees Emma turn the phone unit around, lift the receiver. "Who're you calling?"

"More allies – there's some information we need." The number rings five times, and as soon as it's answered, she hits the conference button. "Audrey? Hi, it's Emma. I'm sorry to call so late."

"Emma, hello again. And don't worry, I'm just finishing my final notes for the day, it's no problem." The speaker on the line this time has the faint quaver of an elderly person, and Travis recognizes the voice of Doctor Audrey Klein, Emma's therapist. She's a highly respected trauma psychologist in Ohio, and just listening to her makes Travis feel calm.

"You said you wanted me to check in," Emma says. "Audrey, I've put this call on conference – Travis is here, too."

"Hello, Travis." Audrey sounds like she's smiling. "That's fine, and I did ask you to call once you arrived at Quantico."

"Hey, Dr. Klein," Travis says. "Sorry about the time. The FBI runs kinda weird hours."

"Then we can be flexible," Audrey says placidly. "So, Emma, how are you and Travis finding things on base?"

Emma gives Travis a look, tilts her head. "Yeah, there's a strange energy here."

He can almost hear Audrey's interest pique. "Can you tell me a little more about it?"

"The FBI seem...kind of desperate?" Emma makes a grimace. "I don't know. It's a brittle feeling. I don't think it's just coming from me. There's always tension because of the nature of the work, but this feels a little different."

"Are you managing it okay?"

Emma nods, although Audrey can't see. "So far. I'll call you if I'm struggling." She pauses. "Audrey, I want to ask you about someone here who's been hired as a consultant with the FBI. Someone in your line of work. I don't know if this will cross some kind of professional boundary, or..."

"Ask your question," Audrey says, "and let me decide the ethics of it. I can always say that I can't answer."

"Okay, fair. So, Special Agent Kirby has a consultant here, a psychoanalyst. His name is Dr. Stanley Becher —"

"Out of Columbia?"

From the way Emma's eyes immediately seek his out, Travis can tell it's unusual for Audrey to interrupt like this. "Yeah," Emma says. "That's him. He seems...I don't know. He makes me uncomfortable."

A hesitation from Klein. "Emma, can I give you some information and trust you'll hold it in confidence? And Travis, you too?"

"Of course," Emma says.

Now Travis is the one nodding. "Absolutely. Go ahead, Dr. Klein."

"I think it might be useful for you both to know," Audrey says, "as you're dealing with this together. Yes, I'm familiar with Dr. Becher. He is not a clinician, which means that he no longer sees patients. But he has a solid reputation as a research academic. He's published a lot – studies and extracts, mainly. Although, in my personal opinion, the conclusions he draws from his research tend to be very…open to interpretation."

"He's subjective?" Emma asks, translating Audrey's terms.

"Let's just say, I think his facts tend to fit his theories and not the other way around."

"Hi, Dr. Klein," Travis says. "Can I ask about Dr. Becher's specialty area?"

"Maladaptive behaviors, including conduct disorders and violent mental illness," Audrey says. "Basically, he studies psychopathy – what you may know as sociopathy, or antisocial personality. So I can understand why Agent Kirby has brought him in."

Emma sits up straighter in her cross-legged pose. "I don't like him."

"I've met him once before," Audrey admits, "and I can understand your reaction. Dr. Becher has a very flat affect in conversation, and that can be off-putting. But he spends a lot of time examining the most hostile and damaged minds. That can have an impact on a person, and how they interact."

"Well, *you* spend time with some pretty damaged minds," Emma notes, "and you don't creep me out like Becher."

Audrey makes a soft noise, which might be a gentle laugh. Then her tone becomes more serious. "This is just a hypothesis, all right? But

I imagine Becher would have a lot of professional curiosity about you, Emma. It might…spill out in conversation. That may be why you feel an aversion."

Travis doesn't like the sound of that.

Emma's posture stiffens – clearly, she doesn't like the sound of it, either. "You mean, he wants to study me? Why would he want to do that?"

"Think about it, Emma. Men like Becher tend to feel that their research and position makes them experts. But you've encountered four serial offenders now, without any kind of buffer, and survived. That experiential knowledge makes *you* the authority. These are the kinds of people Becher's spent his life studying, but in a situation like this, you're the expert."

Emma releases a slow breath. "So you don't think I'm overreacting?"

"You're naturally perceptive, Emma," Audrey says. "And there's something else I have to mention. Are you comfortable if I talk about it with Travis present?"

"Yes." Emma meets his eyes, and her look warms him, even in the grimness of the Cool Room.

"Okay," Audrey goes on. "Right now, at Quantico, in this situation, it's likely you're also experiencing some anxiety and hypervigilance. I don't think it would be strange if you were having a strong reaction."

"You think it's just my trauma responses kicking in." Emma seems to deflate a little.

"Possibly, yes." Then Audrey continues. "But I also think you have good instincts, Emma. So I'm going to encourage you to trust your feelings here."

Emma bites her lip, meets Travis's eyes again. "You think I should be careful around Becher."

"Yes, I do." Audrey's certainty is a warning. "And call me again if you feel he's digging at you. That would be a serious discourtesy on his part, as you're already under the care of another therapist."

"Okay." Emma exhales again, and it's more like relief this time. "Thanks, Audrey."

Travis gives his thanks along with Emma, and they conclude the call. The vents hum and tap in the resulting quiet. Travis leans back in his chair, wonders what the hell they've gotten themselves into.

"I mean, it's all good information to have." Emma squeezes the nape of her neck as she looks at a shadowed corner of the room, not really seeing it.

He feels less equanimous. "Yeah, but this is layers upon layers. Should we really be involved with this?"

Her eyes cut sideways at him and she drops her hand. "It's funny you think we have a choice at this point."

"There's always a choice. Even if the options are less than ideal."

"No. Come on, we discussed this, and we decided."

"We can change our minds."

"Simon isn't going to." Her expression is very flat. A blunt reminder. "The ball is rolling now – Kirby kicked it off down the hill. All we can do is try to make sure it doesn't smash into something."

"Or someone."

"It's like you said, we'll be okay if we stick together." But Emma sounds more hopeful than certain. She picks up the phone receiver again. "All right, one more call."

"Who are you calling this time?" Travis frowns.

"The same person I wanted to call back at Behavioral Science." Emma's eyes are very bright as she stabs the numbers. "Otto Jasper – the Gutmunssons' lawyer. If they're back in the country, he'll know."

It's too late for the lawyer's offices, but Emma leaves a message with her name, and the contact number for Behavioral Science. Now the evening is well advanced, and Travis has a deep, throbbing ache in his diaphragm that he knows will only be relieved by drugs and genuine rest. Once Emma tucks the clandestine phone away in the filing cabinet again, he locks the Cool Room door behind them and they return to the elevators, the atrium desk, their room assignments and luggage.

Emma looks at his face and flatly refuses to let him carry his bag, hefts her pack onto her back and shoulders his duffel. Travis wishes he were whole for her. He wishes he could at least pretend to be fine so she'd feel more comforted, more protected. But he's in too much pain to fake it, and Emma's too smart for that kind of bullshit anyway. They're on the same floor, so at least she's not carrying his bag far.

At his dorm room, she walks inside and drops his duffel on the bed, hitches her own pack and turns around. Cups his face with both hands. "Go to bed. Get some rest."

"I will," he promises. "I've got some Percocet, so I should sleep okay."

He doesn't, though. The same dream wakes him again, and he rolls over in tangled sheets, gasping at the smell of blood. Once his vision clears, he changes his damp T-shirt and flips the pillow, spreads a towel on the bed so he can lay back down.

But it's too late. By the time his heart rate has settled, it's nearly six in the morning, and time to get coffee.

CHAPTER SEVEN

Virginia, 31 October 1982

A t the morning briefing, in the cramped 'home base' office, Kirby explains that the interview with the WaPo reporter will be conducted upstairs, in the library of Jefferson.

Travis can tell, from a subtle curtness in Kirby's speech, how much he wanted to conduct the interview off-base to make it look as though Emma was staying somewhere temptingly accessible. As though Emma is a piece of cheese, and all it will take for the FBI to catch their target is to position her in the middle of a trap that Kirby can snap shut.

But arranging the interview photos to make it look as if Emma is staying outside Quantico would have obliged the team to keep an alternative location under surveillance once the story runs; Kirby didn't have the budget for that. Like most bureaucracies, the FBI are penny-pinchers, and surveillance manpower is at a premium. Hence, the library.

And first, this briefing. The tiny conference room still has a chemical, lemony smell. Emma and Kirby sit under fluorescent strip lights, kitty-corner at the overlarge table, and go through the case file with the invented murder details and the 'new Artist' information, so she'll sound like she knows what she's talking about with the reporter.

Travis sits a little apart, drinks his coffee, listens and watches. Runs through his own mental storehouse for more information about Special Agent Jack Kirby. The man's reputation is solid: trained hostage negotiator, bureau leading light, one of the most zealous hunters in Ed Cooper's elite Behavioral Science squad. Cooper always took on good people – he'd trusted Kirby, who clearly feels he's honoring his old boss's legacy by recapturing Gutmunsson, who Cooper once helped put away.

But watching Kirby try to manage Emma now, Travis searches for the facets of the man's professional personality that inspired Cooper's trust and comes up short. When he'd approached them in Guanajuato, Kirby had seemed genuine. Perhaps here, back at Quantico, he's under too much pressure to be sincere, preferring to dictate rather than persuade. Kirby also seems too young to be so senior. There had to have been some jostling for position after Cooper's death; Travis wonders if Kirby got caught up in that.

Overall, the data points blend together to create an unappetizing picture, and the man's self-assured manner isn't helping, for all that he makes some good arguments.

"We need Dr. Becher at this interview," Kirby insists. "Think of the logic. We want to give the impression that we're pulling in as much expertise as we can muster."

Emma makes a face, unconvinced. "It won't matter to Simon. He despises psych professionals. And he's the audience we're aiming at, right?"

"It's just a smokescreen, Miss Lewis. A little theatre."

Travis leans forward, forced to agree despite his own misgivings. "Emma, if it's just you in the interview, the purpose of the article seems too obvious."

She shakes her head, sliding the gray case file away from her across the table-top. "I don't think it matters. Simon pulled back the curtain on this in the first act. But fine, whatever."

As Kirby continues brokering Emma's approach for the interview, Travis gets up from the table. He takes his to-go coffee over to the wall where all the pictures of the Gutmunsson twins are displayed. In the nearest photo, at eye level, Simon Gutmunsson is smirking.

Travis stares at the photo and holds his warm polystyrene cup and wonders why things feel different. If he were wearing his suit and tie right now, he'd be angry. But standing in his boots and plaid and jeans, he feels steady. He sips his coffee and examines Gutmunsson's malevolent eyes.

I know you. You're just like any other spoiled rich boy — smart but unwise. Too accustomed to getting your own way.

For the first time, Travis gets a sense of possibility: Simon Gutmunsson is just a boy. And he can be defeated.

When the clock on the beige wall ticks over to 9:00AM, Kirby ushers them out toward the main doors of Behavioral Science. As they reach the reception desk in the foyer, Travis sees a figure he recognizes: A woman in her sixties, impeccably dressed in a green boucle skirt suit, her white hair in a classic French twist.

The woman angles in her seat to address Kirby, peering over her bifocals. "Excuse me, sir, I have Miss Lewis and Mr. Bell's lanyards."

"Betty!" Emma can't stop the informality slipping out.

Travis feels his own expression lighten. "Ma'am, it's good to see you."

Betty, the redoubtable unit receptionist, keeps her smile professional but her eyes reveal more warmth as she holds out their ID. "It's good to see you, too. Both of you. Welcome back to Behavioral Science."

"Thank you." Travis slips his lanyard over his head.

"Much appreciated." Emma accepts her ID and examines the laminated photo. "My hair's grown out since this was taken."

"And it looks very nice on you," Betty notes.

"Thanks, Betty," Kirby says, cutting off further conversation and gesturing for the corridor. "All right, this way, folks."

They take the elevator up to the third floor. Quantico library is a quiet, open space with lots of pale brick and long windows, dotted with students in red polo shirts and khaki trousers. The WaPo reporter – Burt LaFriche, a stocky guy in a tan suit with a shock of auburn hair – is waiting by his equipment at a maple-wood table, with an MP stationed nearby. The FBI is always leery of journalists, and they don't like civilians coming onto the training base, so someone higher up has signed a special dispensation for this interview to take place here. LaFriche seems appropriately awestruck, gazing around at the environment of the building, the official FBI plaques on the walls.

Kirby has dismissed the MP and they've just finished exchanging handshakes and introductions when Dr. Becher emerges from the elevator. The man is wearing the same blue sport jacket as yesterday, with a different shirt, exuding the same heavy energy. Travis thinks he's the kind of person Mariana would cross herself against if she passed him on the street. But he feels a guilty relief about the psychologist's presence, too: If Becher wasn't joining Emma for the interview, it's possible that Kirby would've asked Travis himself to participate, and he's not sure he'd be able to talk about Simon Gutmunsson with any kind of equanimity.

Emma bristles as Becher comes closer. She takes some measured breaths, and Travis is reminded that it's not just Becher; she's nervous about how probing this interview is going to be.

"It's all good." Travis puts a hand on her forearm and leans in to keep his voice quiet. "You can back off anytime you want."

Emma sets her shoulders, steadies. "I'm okay."

"Right," LaFriche says. "Miss Lewis, Dr. Becher, are we ready to go?"

He sets up the tape recorder on a library table for the interview. Becher seats himself on one of the study chairs beside Emma, dwarfing her with his bulk. She moves her chair over unobtrusively.

Kirby directs Travis to the library stacks, to give the reporter space to work. He glances back at Emma as proceedings begin. "She gonna be able to hold it for this? She seems tense."

Travis thinks of all the ways he could reply. Lets it go with a brief, "She'll be fine."

And in the end, Emma manages the interview with LaFriche extremely well. She sits upright at the glossy table, looks attentive when Becher explains his theories around the new Artist, and how the murders seem to be a kind of deliberate homage. She seems calm, projecting the appropriate seriousness. She talks about Becher's assessment, neither agreeing nor disagreeing, and about what she knows of the original Artist, Simon Gutmunsson.

She handles some personal questions from LaFriche, talking in short sentences about her history. Travis sees the quiver in her facial expression, sees her control it. She continues smoothly once the personal stuff is out of the way, explains the importance of the FBI's work, makes a dry, off-record joke. It's a solid performance.

The only time she balks is when LaFriche sets up for the photos, grouping both subjects in a collegial pose at a decorative mantlepiece under a large FBI seal. Travis sees the moment Becher puts his hand on Emma's shoulder, knows straight away she won't like it. As soon as the shutter clicks, Emma twists out from under the man's heavy palm and walks back to the table, where LaFriche arranges another shot of her solo, poring through the 'murder' file. Her T-shirt and jeans make her look very normal, very relatable. Natural light from the big window glances off her face, her pixie hair.

Kirby nods, sucking his front teeth. "That's the shot they'll use."

"Probably," Travis acknowledges.

"She's doing good." Kirby cocks his head. "I thought she'd be too fragile in the interview, but she's keeping it together really well."

Travis doesn't respond to that. They're standing together at a remove, amongst the library stacks. Travis crosses his arms in front of his chest; he's watching Emma carefully, but also the way Becher behaves and how he moves.

"And how're you holding up?" Kirby asks.

Travis has been waiting for this conversation. Bracing for it. "Fine. A little sore, still."

"So, when are you coming back?"

Travis wants to say, *I'm already here*, refrains. He considers how to reply when he himself isn't sure of the answer, and thinks of the dark hours this morning, when he woke up in sweaty, tangled sheets. "I won't be cleared by medical for another five weeks."

"Sure, but come on. You've been involved in two major investigations already, and you're not even qualified. I know the admin folks have your paperwork prepped and ready to go." Kirby's hands are on his hips, his white shirt crisp and his suit jacket open. His gaze has an assured gleam. "There's always going to be a place here for you, Bell, you know that."

"Thank you, sir."

Kirby wants more than this. "You have a promising career ahead of you with the bureau. I'd hate to see you waste that. And let's face it – you can't follow Miss Lewis around, playing bodyguard forever."

Again, Travis is forced to consider and discard a number of responses. "I'll keep that in mind."

After the interview and the photo shoot are done, LaFriche begins packing up his equipment and Becher makes his farewells – he has to return to the university to give afternoon lectures. Travis feels relieved when the man leaves. He and Emma excuse themselves to let Kirby finish up with the reporter.

In the elevator on the way back to home base, Emma turns to Travis and says, "I'm glad that's over. Thanks for being there."

"Anytime."

"Do you think this 'lure' thing is going to work?"

Travis examines the numbers above the elevator door and thinks about memories he'd prefer to avoid. How Simon Gutmunsson looked at Emma amongst the stones of Allegheny County Jail. How he looked at her in the moonlit dark of the College Killer's warehouse barn. Those memories taste sour in the back of Travis's throat.

He can feel how his shoulders have tightened. "I think Kirby is hanging you out there, with your face and name splashed all over the newspapers. And I think Gutmunsson is arrogant enough, and enough of an asshole, to take the bait."

Emma chews on a thumbnail, eyes forward. "So we have to assume Simon and Kristin are in the country."

Travis nods. "If not already, then soon."

"What's the first thing he's going to want to do, once he's back on American soil?"

Don't you know? Travis wants to say it, can't. No one likes to be reminded that a killer has you in his crosshairs.

Instead, he says, "We need to think about Gutmunsson's long

game. About the personal connections he has here. People, places, experiences."

"I'm one of those people." Emma is still worrying at her thumb.

"You're just the most visible," Travis reassures. He wants to draw her hand away from her mouth, squeeze it gently, give her a hug. But now the elevator dings as the door opens.

Betty has left the reception desk unattended as she goes to deliver some paperwork. Travis wonders how she copes, working so far underground all day in the cold basement offices, never seeing the sun. As they weave back through the cubicle hallways, he thinks of Mexico, of the salmon light of dusk and the smell of limes.

In the home base room, a man is standing with his back to them, examining the display wall and comparing it with the notes in the gray case file he's holding. He's dressed like a professor in brown wool trousers and a white shirt, and a cardigan in a grandpa style, with a Fair Isle pattern in faded red and camel colors. Even before he closes the file and turns around, Travis knows who he is.

"I wasn't sure how long Kirby would keep you busy," Special Agent Howard Carter says. "Come on in."

Carter is a Black man in his late fifties, of average height, with cropped hair and peppered streaks in his moustache and clipped beard. His bearing is upright, and his glasses are on a chain at his chest.

Familiar faces are always a relief at Quantico, and this one is especially welcome. Travis moves around the desk immediately, extends a hand. "Sir, it's really good to see you."

Carter returns the handshake. "Mr. Bell, you look way better than last time we met. I'm glad you recovered okay."

"No one's more glad than me, sir."

"I believe it." Carter's expression is wry as he turns to Emma. "It's good to see you too, Miss Lewis. How are you?"

"I'm…fine." Emma seems mostly confused, which is probably diluting an angrier response. "Linda gave you our message already?"

"She did," Carter says. "She mentioned something about swimming with sharks?"

"Yes." Emma visibly relaxes. "That was it."

"Well, hopefully this old salt can help." Carter's face livens with self-deprecating amusement.

But Travis notices that Carter also seems to have aged. His calm, serious visage is more lined and the skin under his eyes is puffy. Plus, the clothes signify: Travis knows what Carter's civilian cardigan means. His old supervisor is apparently much diminished, which is concerning.

"We're both really sorry for your loss, Sir," Travis says. "It was a shock when Linda told me you were on leave."

"Thank you. I appreciate that." Carter's cheeks tighten and he glances down at the folder in his hands, like he can't quite remember how it got there. After a beat, he recovers. "Suffice to say, I was out of the loop when this new strategy to catch the Gutmunsson twins was being hashed out with Becher. Let's just say I don't entirely approve of Jack Kirby's approach here. Using your name in the articles before he'd secured your permission, Miss Lewis…That was an unethical move on Kirby's part. Dr. Brown and I both had concerns about that. But I'm also worried about outcomes here."

Travis shoves his hands in his jeans pockets. "Outcomes?"

Carter's face takes on a stern aspect. "Think of it this way – while I'm sure Kirby's strategy will get Simon Gutmunsson's attention, I'm not convinced that his attention is something the unit is currently prepared for."

Emma seems to agree with this assessment. "Simon isn't like other perpetrators the FBI has attempted to catch."

Carter nods. "You tried to warn me in Pittsburgh, but I didn't listen. I've done some research since then. The only way we caught him in nineteen eighty was because his sister incapacitated him long enough for us to get an arrest. The manner of his escape in Pittsburgh suggests he has a greater ferocity and capacity for long-term planning than we ever anticipated. Setting a flimsy trap for him now seems…"

"Stupid?" Emma's expression is very dry under the harsh fluorescents. "Juvenile?"

Carter meets her gaze. "*Juvenile* is actually a good word. Kirby still thinks of Simon Gutmunsson as a juvenile, because of his youth. But it's a gross underestimation, in my opinion. I'd certainly like to know more about Kirby's intentions for capture, or if he's even thought that far."

Travis can hear voices approaching. "Sounds like Agent Kirby's on his way back, so maybe you can ask him."

Carter straightens. "If you don't mind, let me do some talking here."

Emma comes alert. "You want to argue with Kirby about it?"

"Not argue. I want to provide operational support." Carter raises his eyebrows at her as he sets the file down. "You want backup, right?"

"Backup." The idea seems foreign to her.

"Yes." Carter gives her a fast, serious look. "Listen – you know serial killers, but I know the bureau. That's why you reached out to me, yes? You don't want to be stuck here with no allies, and no exit strategy. Let me help, Miss Lewis."

Travis gets that goose-bumping sense of possibility again, just as Jack Kirby enters the room with Mike Martino, both of them in apparent good humor.

Kirby's sunny expression holds when he sees Carter in the room; he walks forward with his hand out. "Howard! Man, it's good to see you, I was just saying to Mike it's been quite a while."

"Too long," Carter says. "You're looking fit, Jack – you still playing squash with Allan Ford from Hostage Rescue on Sundays? Allan's got a mean slice…"

The three men exchange handshakes and cordialities. Travis stands back with Emma, watches the way Carter strums the unseen chords of the bureau old-boy network, playing all the greatest hits before he lets Kirby get to the point.

"So what brings you back to the office, Howard?" Kirby puts his folder on the table with a studied casualness. "Your leave period isn't up for another few weeks, am I right?"

Carter spreads his hands. "You know me, Jack – I always had trouble staying away. I got the new report on the Gutmunssons from Phil Drexler, and of course I have an interest. Then I heard Mr. Bell and Miss Lewis here were back in play. I figured I'd come see what was going on."

Mike Martino, who's always had a more finely-tuned awareness of political brine than operational detail, backs out of this fight. "Uh, Jack, that phone call with Bryant from NCIC –"

"Sure, Mike, go on." Kirby watches Martino leave the room before turning back to Carter, his tone only half joking. "Trying to cut in on my action, Howard?"

"Not at all. But I'm curious, Jack – you're running the whole operation? And organizing the young people, on top of everything else?"

Kirby can obviously see where this is going. "Martino's helping me out."

"It's a lot, even for a two-man team. Mike probably has his hands full with unit support and dealing with state and district police." Carter plays his hand. "Drexler suggested I come aboard as liaison for Mr. Bell and Miss Lewis – not as oversight, just to help with coordination."

Travis puts his hand gently on Emma's lower back. She's looking at the photos of the Gutmunssons on the wall, apparently ignoring the ongoing conversation, but she's gone very still.

Kirby's pleasant expression flattens slightly at the corners. "You're on leave, Howard."

"And I'm not trying to run it." Carter nods toward Travis. "I'm like Mr. Bell here – I've come off the injury bench to help out, in an advisory capacity."

"Howard –"

"I spoke to Cubbins, who spoke to Rasche." Carter lays down his winning card. "They've given preliminary approval. Of course, it all depends on you – and the young people. They have to sign off as well."

Kirby vainly tries to take it to the net. "Well, they're not minors, Howard. They can handle themselves."

"But they're not agents. And you can't treat them like agents." Carter glances at Travis, who recognizes the callback to words he used himself one time, in Pittsburgh: It warms him that his former boss uses them now. Carter continues, digging in. "The inclusion of Miss Lewis's name in those articles, for instance…"

Kirby's cheeks color but he holds his ground. "That was a timing issue, and I'm sure you know –"

"Excuse me." A knock, and a new voice. Betty stands in the open doorway of the office, washed out under the lights. She's holding a rectangular, sage-green box about the size of a toaster oven, with postal markings. "Excuse me, gentlemen, I'm sorry to interrupt."

Kirby looks frustrated. "Betty, we're kind of in the middle of –"

"Miss Lewis has received a parcel, and there's also a phone call." The receptionist walks over to the business phone unit on the far side of the table, sets the box down nearby, and presses some buttons on the phone – a light begins blinking. "I've directed it here. The caller introduced himself as Mr. Otto Jasper."

Travis feels Emma twitch. She moves toward the phone.

"The Gutmunssons' lawyer?" Kirby frowns. "Why's the lawyer calling?"

"Let's answer and find out," Travis suggests. "We left him a message last night."

Kirby seems appalled. "You *called* him?"

"Yes." Emma is unapologetic. "Mr. Kirby, we need information, and Jasper might have some."

"I expressly told you not to –"

"Miss Lewis," Betty interrupts, her expression stern. "The man on the phone said he's Otto Jasper, but you should know – that is *not* Mr. Jasper's office number."

Emma looks over, immediately alert. "Travis."

The sudden awareness rolls in his stomach, a seasick feeling. He nods. "Has to be."

"What do you mean?" Kirby asks, nonplussed. "You think the call's from…"

"Betty?" Carter speaks directly to the receptionist, his eyes hawklike. "Have you got systems in place for this?"

"Yes." Betty has worked at Quantico for longer than either of the two senior agents in the room. "I've told the caller that I had to page Miss Lewis, to give us some time, and I've notified Laura Steadman in the communications room to prep for recording, and to open a line to the Bell switching centre. With the new electronic switching, we might get a trace."

"Excellent work." Carter collects a legal pad and a pen, talking as he moves. "But could this call be from Jasper's home number?"

"I don't have Mr. Jasper's personal contact information," she admits. "It's possible."

Emma is shaking her head. "It's got to be Simon."

Travis exhales, steadies. "Well he won't stay on the line forever."

"Answer it," Carter says. It's as if Kirby isn't even in the room. To Betty, Carter says, "Open speaker. And start the trace and recording."

"Yes, sir." Betty presses buttons, lifts the receiver. "Laura? It's me. Begin recording and instruct ESS to start the trace, BSU9, on line two. Put them through to BSU7. Thank you." She puts a hand over the receiver. "Mr. Carter? Bell ESS is on line one, at Mr. Kirby's desk." Then she takes a breath, counts to ten, presses another button. "Thank you for holding, sir. Miss Lewis is coming out of her meeting. Transferring you to Behavioral Science offices now." She depresses her finger hard on a button, hands the receiver to Emma. "Are you ready?"

The two women exchange a look. In this sharp, frozen moment, Carter and Kirby have both shut up. The atmosphere in the office has gone still, like the moment before an electrical storm.

Emma swallows, nods. "As I'm gonna be. Okay, hit it." Betty releases the button, and Emma's entire focus centers on the phone. "This is Emma Lewis."

"*Hello, Emma.*" Simon Gutmunsson's voice echoes from the phone speaker. "How lovely to hear your dulcet tones once more. How are things at Quantico?"

For a blinding second, Travis is shocked through with a white-hot bolt of rage. It's like a camera flash, so sudden and clean and pure that he's caught off balance, has to sink down onto the office chair nearby. The rage in his chest flares, radiating, then the light dims as Gutmunsson's slippery voice comes out of the speaker once again.

"The receptionist for Behavioral Science is *so* professional," Gutmunssons says. "I imagine she knew straight away that I wasn't Otto. Isn't it curious how FBI support staff are more intelligent than the field agents?"

"Hello, Simon," Emma says. She glances at Betty, who has paled to hear herself mentioned in this conversation, by this particular caller. Emma gestures for her to leave, keeps talking as she watches the receptionist's departure. "But I'm sure you didn't just call me to unnerve the women on the FBI switchboard. What do you want, Simon?"

"To renew our acquaintance, of course." Gutmunsson sounds amused. "And to find out more about the latest excitement at Quantico. A new murderer in town! How thrilling!"

In reaction to this drollness, Kirby looks deflated. Carter raises his eyebrows. Travis clenches his hands hard on the edge of the table, keeps his eyes on Emma where she stands across from him.

"Emma, please tell me they're paying you well to advise them on the case," Gutmunsson goes on. "Or is the payment as fictional as the investigation details?"

Kirby's voice is a hiss. "*How can he –*"

Emma waves at Kirby to shut him up. "Staying ahead of the game, Simon?"

"Well, it's not as if it's difficult." Gutmunsson's voice is acrid, and Travis can almost hear him rolling his eyes.

"So you just rang to gloat," Emma observes.

Carter moves briskly out of the room, probably to check on the call-tracking progress. Kirby leans on the table, watching Emma and the business phone unit with equal frustration. The lapels of his jacket hang open, and his pale gray eyes glint like mica.

"You can console your FBI handlers that the newspaper campaign wasn't a complete loss," Gutmunsson says. "After all – here I am again, on American soil. That's what the bureau wanted, correct?"

Carter steps back into the doorway, gestures at Emma to keep Simon talking.

She nods in response, grips the plastic receiver. "Is Kristin with you?"

"My sister is perfectly safe." The sibilance in Gutmunsson's voice is unsettling, feels greasy on the air. "She sends her best regards. We've had a very pleasant time overseas, as I'm sure you're aware, and I thought it was prudent to make a short pilgrimage back home…"

Travis hears these words and remembers the poem that Gutmunsson sent to Emma in the mail: An excerpt from Byron's *Childe Harold's Pilgrimage*.

Now Gutmunsson sounds as if he's grinning. "If we're catching up with old acquaintances, how is Mr. Bell? What a hardy fellow. I trust he's made a swift recovery after that unfortunate business in Peter Kirke's warehouse."

Nausea roils in Travis's gut. He tries to ignore it, keeps his eyes open. If he closes them, the sensations and memories will come back: the explosion of gunshots, blood and fire, a feeling like his chest is splintering…

A scratch on the table-top draws his attention; when he looks over, Emma is tapping a nail on the wood.

"Bell's fine," Emma says, her eyes on him.

"That's all you're going to say about it?" Gutmunsson makes a huffing laugh. "How very close-mouthed of you, Emma. Does that mean he's back in the field already? Goodness – so soon after Pittsburgh! But he's a man of action, after all. One might say he seems *compelled* to act. Out of ego, perhaps. Does he have to stay busy to avoid thinking about his daddy? Or is being FBI such a crucial aspect of his persona that he can't let go even long enough to make a full recovery?"

For the first time in nearly six weeks, Travis is angry enough to go for his hip, reaching for a gun that isn't there. Emma is still watching him. Holding the phone to her ear, she slowly shakes her head – *No. Don't you believe him.* But Travis feels hot in the face. Gutmunsson's words always have a papercut sting that's hard to salve.

Carter makes a soft rap on the jamb: He's back in the open doorway, holding up a scrawled sign – *PHONE BOOTH, DC.* Emma nods.

"Mm." She lifts her chin. "Simon, if you can't be polite, I think I'll hang up."

Kirby yelps softly. "*No –*"

"Oh, *Emma*," Gutmunsson drawls. "Don't be like that. We're past all that now. And you must allow me my petty amusements."

"Really?" Emma continues to pick at the wood of the table, frowning. "Why?"

"I told you – we're connected." Gutmunsson's voice is a slithering worm. "You're a murderer now, like me."

"I'm nothing like you, but fine. Get to the point, Simon." Now Emma sounds bored. Travis finds it mind-boggling, how she handles this shit.

"I'd like to see you," Gutmunsson says.

Travis's gaze snaps up.

"Why would I agree to that?" Emma asks.

Travis can hear Gutmunsson grinning again. "Wouldn't you like to have this conversation in person? At the Kennedy Center, perhaps, over a glass of wine? I even sent you something to suit the occasion…"

All eyes in the room suddenly turn to the sage-green parcel sitting innocuously on the table, ignored since the phone call began. Emma looks at the postal marks, pokes one corner with a finger and then wipes her fingertip on her jeans, like the box is poison. Carter strides out of the room again.

Emma swallows. "Okay. When?"

"I'm sure you can figure that out. Let's make sure it's soon, though – it's been an age, and I'm *longing* to see if my memory of you matches the current reality."

Emma is aware she needs to draw out the conversation as long as she can. "Simon, I don't think –"

"You can give my best to Mr. Bell. He doesn't need to attend. Adieu, Emma, until we next meet."

"Simon –"

The dial tone sounds as Gutmunsson hangs up. Emma returns the receiver to the cradle and exhales tension. Carter walks back into the room with a piece of yellow memo paper, and a copy of the newspaper under his arm.

"The phone booth is at the corner of F Street and Eighth," Carter says, reading from his memo. "Near the National Portrait Gallery."

Travis straightens. "That's right by Scientific Analysis at FBI head-quarters."

Kirby looks as if he'd like to strangle someone. "That son of a *bitch*."

"The district police unit is stuck in traffic about a block over, on E Street. When they arrive, they'll set up a cordon and do a forensic sweep, but I think it's safe to assume that apart from fingerprints, Gutmunsson will be long gone. You want this?"

Carter offers the newspaper to Travis, at his 'give it' gesture. Travis lays the broadsheet down on the table and wets a finger to catch the paper edges, starts paging through, searching for what he knows he'll find. From the corner of his eye, he sees Carter take a pair of nitrile evidence gloves out of his back pocket, hand them to Emma.

"He *called the office* from goddamn *headquarters!*" Kirby is having trouble containing his fury. "If you hadn't contacted the lawyer and tipped him off –"

"Mr. Kirby, nobody tipped Simon off." Emma snaps on one glove. "My phone call to Jasper's office gave him confirmation I was at Quantico – but he knew that already, because *you* put my name in the newspaper articles. I explained all this from the start, but you still don't get it. And calling from headquarters…Simon probably thought that was hilarious."

Carter nods. "Jack, you need to adjust your ideas about how to deal with this guy."

"Mr. Kirby, please listen, okay?" Emma centers Kirby in her gaze. "*Simon Gutmunsson is smarter than you.* He's smarter than all of us. He knew the end game of this before he and Kristin even left Morocco."

"You think his sister is with him?" Kirby asks, controlling himself with an effort.

"I hope so." Emma blows into the other glove before putting it on. "If she's back in the States, there's a chance we can get her away from her brother."

"If she wants to get away," Carter reminds her.

Finally, Kirby seems as if he's paying attention. "What did he mean about having a conversation in person? Is that a threat?"

"An invitation." Travis has found the item in the Entertainment section, where he knew it would be. He folds the section of the newspaper over to reveal the advertisement, lays it flat on the table. "He said the Kennedy Center, right?"

Emma nods. "It's something he mentioned way back at St Elizabeths. The night he killed Anthony Hoyt."

"Here." Travis points at the ad in question. "The Liceu Company from Barcelona is visiting for a series of performances at the Kennedy Center."

"I need scissors or something," Emma says. Carter passes her a letter opener, and she slits the paper on the box in front of her, glancing up at Travis. "When are they performing *Turandot*?"

Travis sighs. "The first performance is tonight."

But Emma has opened the parcel now: Nestled in tissue paper, the contents are exposed. Travis can see the black fabric of a dress, the edge of a shoe. On the top of this display is a note: heavy purple card stock, and a looping cursive hand that Travis instantly recognizes is Kristin Gutmunsson's handwriting.

The message is short, only one line. It reads: *None Shall Sleep.*

Emma looks Travis right in the eye. "This is circling back to where it all started."

CHAPTER EIGHT

Washington DC, 31 October 1982

They came up on the 395, took a route past the Pentagon and over Arlington Memorial Bridge that was clearly familiar to the driver, then turned onto Rock Creek and Potomac Parkway exactly five minutes ago. Now they're making the turn onto F Street NW, on the approach to the John F. Kennedy Center for the Performing Arts.

The car is a black Lincoln Continental Executive limousine, an older stretch model. Emma figures it's an ex-Secret Service vehicle, and there's no way she'd be riding in it except that showing up to the opera in a Dodge Ram van would look too sketchy. The limo, by contrast, has shag carpet in the footwells. Cooper is sitting to her left, and Kirby is perched opposite her on one of the rear-facing jump seats, near the mini TV. Emma thinks her father would be delighted by this car, and even the most fleeting thought of her dad gives her a jolt of courage she needs right now.

She's very alert to the hum of operational strategy around her – it's been like that all afternoon, but she's feeling it most sharply in this moment, before events begin. Kirby and Carter arranged the set up, and while it was a scramble, everything appears to have fallen into place in time for tonight's performance. During the car trip from Quantico, they've gone over deployment of agents, exit points, support teams, surveillance. Nobody talked about weapons, which Emma thinks is probably deliberate – she's bad with guns. The first time she was given a gun, she missed; the last time, she shot a man in the face. Right now, Emma is wishing she still had the extendable baton that Agent Reyes once gave her in Pittsburgh.

She forces herself to focus back on Kirby, who is finishing his final review of what will happen next and why.

"You'll be met at the front entrance by Mr. Bell." Kirby's dressed exactly to regulation, in his dark suit and tie, and his expression has a fixed, battleground intensity. "There's an agent with him, Steven Denis, who'll be shadowing you both all night."

"Steve Denis is solid." Dressed now in a dark brown suit and waistcoat and a maroon tie, Cooper seems more serene, but his manner is always very contained. He's holding a clipboard and a pen. "I've worked with him, he's good at his job. You should feel secure."

Emma nods automatically. "And his job is…"

"Close personal protection," Cooper supplies.

"Right." Emma presses down hard on a writhing tendril of panic. She's meeting Simon in a crowded place. There'll be people around. She has close personal protection. Travis will be there, which means he'll be in danger, but she's trying not to worry about that aspect and just stay fixed on the operational details. "I'm still confused about why I don't have a wire."

"We don't want Gutmunsson to talk to you," Kirby reminds. "We don't want him anywhere near you. We see him, we take him down. This is the trap closing."

"Okay," she says, and mentally, *If you think so.* She stretches her fingers inside her black net gloves. "And you feel confident he'll arrive.

You don't think he's just running you around to get a sense of who's involved in this operation and how they work."

"That's a risk," Kirby admits. "But talking with Dr. Becher on the phone this afternoon, he's pretty convinced that Gutmunsson will show up to see you."

She's actually pretty convinced of it herself. Mentioning it feels unnecessary. She swallows, for about the hundredth time, to clear her throat of tension.

"Are you gonna be okay with this, Miss Lewis?" Cooper has been watching her. His expression suggests he places some value on how she chooses to reply.

"I'm okay to do this," Emma says. No hesitation. She's worried about Travis's safety, but she's not prepared to say that in front of Kirby.

Kirby seems to have pre-empted this awareness. "We've got you and Mr. Bell as covered as we can."

Which is to say, they're covered adequately, but not as thoroughly as Emma or anyone else would like. The Kennedy Center, it turns out, is a terrible place for a stakeout. The Center administration absolutely refused a SWAT presence on-site: They threatened to shut down the performance – their primary responsibility being the safety of patrons – and only some fast talking from Kirby and the Section Chief, Adam Rasche, had allowed this evening's activities to happen at all. Emma knows she should feel grateful for this strategic opportunity, but she wishes the night were already over.

"We drive up," Kirby explains, "drop you at the front. Lots of people, lots of eyes. You and Bell go with Denis to the balcony box on the second tier of the auditorium, you stay there."

"Stay in the box, got it," Emma repeats. She can smell the faint powdery scent of the makeup she's wearing.

"You stay in the box, which has limited exit points and where surveillance is completely covered. Four agents to a tier, three tiers. When we see Gutmunsson on approach, we throw the net – the agents on each side close in, Denis locks the door of the box, agents from the other tiers provide additional support, and the target is hemmed in."

"Okay." Her tone is flat. She's too aware that these things never go to plan. And this is Simon.

The driver glides them toward the main entrance. Lights are illuminating the immense *War or Peace* sculpture in the forecourt. Frost glistens near a fountain. There are Halloween decorations – sparkling black skulls and autumn-leaf bunting – strung around the main doors, and it gives Emma a shock; she'd been involved in Día de Muertos preparations at the ranch, but she completely forgot about Halloween.

People move to get out of the cold and go inside; Emma blinks at the glitter of their clothes. She seeks out the figure of Travis by the big doors, finds him at last – he's a stationary figure in black tuxedo pants, a black jacket, white shirt. His posture reads as 'static, prepped for action' and she sees his attention swing between her approaching limousine and the security-threat-rich environment. With relief, she notes another man, clearly an agent, standing beside him.

Carter is also watching the scene out the car window. "This forecourt area is where you're most exposed. Go straight to Bell, get inside, let the CPP agents take it from there."

"All good, Miss Lewis?" Kirby, always asking the most obvious questions.

Emma nods her head when she'd like to shake it. "All good. Get to Travis, get inside – no problem."

"Good luck."

She should wish Kirby good luck in return. Instead, she chooses to warn him. "I know you think this is too good a chance to pass up, but I don't think you're going to catch Simon tonight."

"We'll just see," Kirby says, and she wants to slap the man. He's not the one squaring up to meet with a monster.

She sighs to herself, nods at Carter. "Good hunting."

Carter nods, opens the door on his side. Emma slides forward and out of the car.

It's a shock to be outside, in the open air. Also, it's freezing. She pulls her black velvet shawl tighter with one hand, finding herself slightly encumbered by skirts. The dress she received is black tulle, the bodice form-fitting, with layers of black organza ruffles cascading down from the hips to her knees. Her arms, shoulders, and decolletage are tightly covered by fine black net, like the accompanying gloves. Despite the cold, her hands are sweating in the gloves, slipping on the velvet.

The fountain leaps to her left. Lights stretch out the walkway on either side, and people – other opera-goers – stride briskly nearby, call out to each other, laugh. They're about to see a performance; but Emma feels like she's the one performing on a stage right now. Through her black ballet flats, the chill from the paving tiles of the forecourt prickles into the soles of her feet as she walks directly toward Travis.

Golden illumination from the Center entrance spills over him, giving his strong shoulders emphasis. This is the most formally he's dressed since they arrived back in the States, but he's expressed some subtle rebellions: He has no tie, his shirt open at the throat, his dark hair raked back.

Emma takes in the sight of him and feels a hot, familiar rush of longing. She thinks of their last night on the ranch outside San Miguel, when she'd walked into his room, saying, *Are we really going back? We must be insane.* They'd hugged, and her hands had slipped under the soft chambray of his shirt. She'd touched the warm, smooth skin of his back, and the contact had helped her feel solid. She wishes they'd let themselves go that night. She wishes they were back in his room right now, taking their time, her fingers loosening his buttons. He'd laugh softly, in that way he does, making desire feel comfortable, homely…

It's a bad time to be thinking about such things. *Focus.* She walks toward his welcoming hand.

"Hey." They clasp forearms. Travis's eyes scan all of her, then he meets her gaze, his expression unhappy. "You look beautiful, and I fucking hate that he put you in that dress."

Emma feels the same, and it grinds on her like a toothache. "On the upside, I didn't have to go shopping for something to wear to the opera."

Travis shakes his head; his suit was borrowed from another male agent. "Come on, let's get inside. Emma, this is Special Agent Denis."

He indicates the man at his shoulder, as they move as a group for the doors. Denis is clean-shaven, with an FBI haircut, moderately handsome. There's a covert communications device spooling out between his collar and his right ear. He seems about thirty, young for this detail, but every agent Emma's ever been assigned to for close protection has had a competent, reassuring calmness, and Denis is no different.

"Miss Lewis, nice to meet you, we're going this way," he says, and ushers them into the Hall of States.

The warmth inside the doors immediately makes the blood rush to her cheeks. The Center itself is massive, a concrete aircraft hangar with no visible ornamentation in its structure, made dignified inside by the addition of long red carpets and the judicious placement of artworks.

Crowds of people swirl everywhere. Emma glances up as they pass beneath the massed laundry line of national flags. They come out of the entry hall and turn left under a row of extraordinary chandeliers in a modern style.

Denis guides them around clumps of patrons and toward a sculpture – an enormous bust of John F. Kennedy that looks as if it's been slapped together with handfuls of mud – as he continues giving instructions in a normal-sounding voice.

"Your tickets are here." He distributes them. "We have a private box position on the top tier, which is highly controllable. And of course, you'll get a good view of the performance."

"Did you work with Special Agent Carter for long?" Emma asks him. As they make their way up the grand foyer, she spots additional agents subtly flanking them at a distance.

Denis directs her toward a set of stairs at right. "I worked a few times with Agent Carter, more times with Agent Kirby."

Travis glances up at the chandeliers, around at the people, hyper-alert. "Has Mike Martino finished coordinating on-site?"

"Yes. His team has already verified ticketing and waitstaff, and they just cleared the kitchen staff about thirty minutes ago. It's been kind of a rush job. Watch your step here, Miss Lewis."

The ruffles on the dress obscure her feet; she pushes fabric aside as they take the stairs. The dress is lovely, but not something she ever would have chosen for herself. Emma has a strong sense that Kristin had a hand in selecting it: Apart from the ruffles, it's a considerate dress, knee-length and fitted for movement. The ballet flats are the clincher: They allow a freedom which high heels would've made impossible, and that feels like a detail only another girl would think about. Wearing the outfit is still galling.

At the top of the stairs – which are decorated with orange and black pumpkins on the side of each riser – a wooden lectern with a staff member in black. Their tickets are checked, and they're issued programs.

"Now this way," Denis says.

He directs them to the right, up a flight of stairs, then another flight of stairs. Other theater-goers are moving in this direction. Denis nods at the two agents in position at the first tier foyer, who nod in reply and speak into their wrists to notify Control.

Another turn; they pass an older woman in a mink coat, guided by her escort. Then two more flights of stairs. Emma loses track of all the decorative pumpkins.

"So many stairs," Emma says.

Travis grimaces. "Carter suggested the elevator, but Kirby vetoed. He said if Gutmunsson is here, he should get a good look at us arriving."

"Wonderful."

Denis says, "It's close now, Miss Lewis," just as they arrive at the second tier foyer. He greets the two suited agents situated either side of the entrance to a right-hand corridor. The corridor is carpeted in red, and the walls are also papered in red felt, which dampens sound, with elegant autumn-leaf bunting. Emma feels her feet sink into the carpet.

They pass three doors, arrive at the fourth door, where an agent stands in wait.

"Thanks, Fletch," Denis says to him. "All good?"

"You're good to go," Fletch says, with no more expression than a robot.

"I'll send the signal." Denis turns. "Mr. Bell, Miss Lewis, this is our spot."

Fletch stands aside and Denis opens the door of the box onto a dark red velvet curtain, which creates a momentary anteroom so patrons and staff can use the door without creating disruptive noise. Once the curtain is pushed aside, Emma finds the opera box is a kind of fenced balcony, with a vertigo-inducing view of the auditorium. It's an intimate space, enough for three armchairs, with a curtained concrete partition at left. Two of the armchairs are grouped together near the partition, separated from the third by a spindly wooden side table with a Halloween centerpiece: a tiny black skull with a candle inside.

Denis stands off to the right of the box and speaks into his wrist. "Control, we're at the location and our principal is in position."

Emma knows that in Close Protection parlance, the principal is the person being safeguarded, and she wishes she wasn't the focus of all this intensity once again.

She squashes her frustration down, settles into her seat at centre as Travis takes the chair closest to the partition. As she slides off her velvet shawl, she realizes that she never thought to ask to use the bathroom before they got here – and now they're locked in, it'll be hard to leave. Luckily, she's too anxious for this to be a problem.

She takes in the scenery: An immense chandelier glows like a giant phosphorescent jellyfish against the red ceiling of the auditorium, and she can see the President's box, currently unoccupied, one tier down along the long crimson curve suspended to their left. Candles in the other boxes flicker prettily; Emma tries not to read all the skull ornaments as ominous. The chairs are comfortable, and the view of the proscenium stage is amazing. These primo seats must have cost a small fortune; it's a shame she can't let herself enjoy it.

Beneath them, in the auditorium, the ranked seating is filling up. At this angle, Emma can see men's bald spots, and the tags on women's dresses.

"How long until the performance starts?" she asks, picking at her gloves.

On her left, Travis checks his watch. "Nine minutes."

"Okay. So now we wait."

"You think he'll show, don't you?"

"Yes. Don't you?"

Travis exhales. "Yep. Gutmunsson set it all up. I don't think he's just bluffing to make the FBI jump around."

Denis is still standing, exchanging quiet communication with folks in other positions. Travis shifts in his chair, examines the program. He smells good, like amber and orange and bergamot – it's his usual aftershave, a scent Emma always associates with him, and she finds it both sensual and soothing. She forces herself to stop glancing at his collar, the way it reveals the open line of his throat as he leans on the balcony and squints at the arrangement down in the auditorium.

"Working out how hard it might be to climb down from here?" She's trying to keep things light.

"Or how far to fall." He leans back again, gestures with his program. "You ever been to the opera before?"

"I remember…a school excursion to see a musical theatre group in Wooster, when I was a kid. But it was nothing like this. How about you?"

"Nope. Seems kind of like going to see a play, except all the words for the show are in the program."

"That's the English translation. The opera's in Italian."

His eyebrows lift. "We're gonna be listening to people singing in Italian for the next three hours?"

Emma grins. "Uh-huh."

"Damn." He scratches his jaw. "Okay."

His arm is warm beside hers. She's still horribly jittery: The patrons in the area below provide some distraction. One woman is wearing a low-cut purple cocktail dress, her neck encrusted with flashing sparkles. Another woman, much older, has a blond beehive hair-do.

A moment later, the musicians enter the orchestra pit, and there's the prologue sounds of bassoon and flutes and strings gently tuning. The house lights flicker three times, then go down; attendees blow out their candles. The audience is still murmuring. Even after the jellyfish chandelier dims, Emma feels a suspended tension hanging above her.

"This could be over tonight." She says it like a prayer, quiet enough only Travis can hear. "They could catch him."

Travis reaches across her to lift their candle, blow it out. "It's a nice idea, but I kind of doubt it."

"Me, too." She puts a hand on his forearm before he can draw it back. "Listen, what Simon said about you on the phone this morning… He's wrong."

Only Travis's shadowed profile shows in this darkness, but his jaw seems tight. "You think he lied about that?"

She shakes her head, finds his hand with her own. "Simon doesn't lie much. But he can be wrong. He's wrong about that. About you."

Travis's eyes flash white in the gloom. "Again, it's a nice idea. But I've wondered the same shit. I've thrown myself back in – I could've given myself more time." He breathes out his nose. "We both could have."

"Kirby didn't give us a chance," she points out.

"*Gutmunsson* didn't give us a chance." He looks away. "But I don't know where I stand with the FBI, with my job. So, maybe he's right – maybe I *am* staying busy to avoid thinking about stuff."

She squeezes his hand. "Don't let Simon get in your head. He's messing with you for a reason. He digs at you, insults you, because you challenge him. Something about you, he can't handle, so he reacts like this – pulling you down, messing you up. Reducing the threat."

Travis makes a snort. "I'm not a *threat* to Simon Gutmunsson –"

"You are." Emma laces his fingers with her own. "Believe me, in a million ways, you are."

And that's the essential truth of it. Travis is something Simon will never be: a good person. Real, wholehearted, genuine. As a creature of pure selfishness, Simon finds that anathema. He's trying to wipe it out, shut it down, but Emma believes – has always believed – that Travis's will is strong.

Agent Denis takes his seat to her right, and she and Travis untangle. Applause starts below, as a man in a tuxedo enters the pit. The entire orchestra stands as he turns to the audience and bows. When the conductor turns back, the orchestra takes their seats, and the audience settles as violinists lift their bows.

Emma leans against Travis's shoulder. "It's starting."

He nestles up closer. "Do you know anything about *Turandot*?"

After St Elizabeths, Emma had made a point of doing some research. "I know it's written by Puccini, and set in China –"

"It's set in China, but they're singing in Italian?"

"Yes. Shh, it's a thing." Emma smiles. "It's about a guy who falls in love with a princess. But the princess has sworn never to marry, and commands all her suitors to answer three riddles – if they give wrong answers, they're beheaded."

"Gruesome, but okay."

"The guy decides to woo the princess and try the riddles anyway."

"Oh boy."

The first three dramatic notes sound, and the stage curtains lift on the people of Peking. Travis puts an arm around her in the dark.

Emma finds her gaze can't stay fixed on the stage, is constantly circling the auditorium. And through the good-quality fabric of his suit, she can feel the tension in Travis's body: When the Prince of Persia is beheaded, he flinches.

It would be nice if they were both just here enjoying their first experience of the opera. Instead, they're stuck in this box, and she's wearing a scratchy dress, and feeling like her ribs are tight around her lungs because for some reason, a homicidal boy simply can't leave her alone.

But nothing sets off her alarms, and they reach the end of Act I – the audience applauding thunderously and the curtains dropping for the fifteen-minute interval – before Emma glances down into the orchestra pit and sees the girl who was turning pages for the harpist rise from her seat and sweep back her hair.

Travis is checking the program. Emma leans forward.

"Travis." Without looking, she reaches for his nearest hand. "*Travis.*"

With the lights up, he can see the direction of her gaze. "What is it?"

"Left-hand side, in the pit. I know the hair is different, but that looks like –"

"*Kristin,*" Travis says, and there really is no question about it.

Kristin Gutmunsson is down in the orchestra pit, wearing a wig of smooth black hair that spills down her back in a rippling fall, plus dramatic eyeshadow in peacock blue. The change of hair color, and her black lashes, somehow gives her an exotic beauty, a more gauntly structured face. She turns, and Emma notices that she's skinnier than she was in Pittsburgh: Her emerald green slip dress shows her spine. Maybe she hasn't been eating enough while she and her brother have been overseas.

Emma clutches Travis's hand. "She's heading for the orchestra door –"

"You've sighted Kristin Gutmunsson?" Agent Denis lifts his wrist to report. "Where? Keep an eye on her!"

"I can't believe Simon brought her," Emma says, genuinely shocked.

"She can be insistent." Travis leans over the balcony.

Denis is leaning, too, scanning everywhere. "Is it possible she's here alone, to pass on a message?"

"Anything's possible with the Gutmunssons," Travis says.

Emma plucks at Travis's jacket sleeve. "What about her brother?"

Denis shakes his head. "No sightings."

"How the *fuck* is she in the orchestra pit?"

"*There.*" Travis points. "Now she's in the auditorium, on the edge of the front row of seats –"

"I see her. Is she looking for us?"

"Seems like it," Denis says.

Travis glances at him. "Recon?"

"Maybe." Denis frowns, his communication earpiece squawking. "We've got agents moving to intercept."

"I should go down there," Travis says.

Emma startles, aghast. "No way!"

"Safer in the box," Denis says.

"If she's playing messenger," Travis points out, "she's not going to talk with the FBI."

"What if Simon's down there?" Emma asks.

Travis snaps a glance. "Denis?"

"No sightings." Denis makes a grimace, frustrated.

Travis turns and grips both of Emma's hands. "Emma –"

"*No.*" Emma feels like she's going to be sick.

"Listen, okay? Kristin won't spook with me." His expression becomes imploring. "Let's get this over with. Get the message and get the hell out."

"She could be bait! You don't know!"

"I know I'm tired of waiting for Gutmunsson to make his next move." Travis stands abruptly and turns to Davis. "Five minutes. We could end this right now."

Denis's pursed mouth works. Finally, he nods.

"Okay, five minutes –"

"Don't do this," Emma gasps.

" – and take Fletcher with you, he'll coordinate support."

"*Travis –*"

"Trust me." Travis swoops close, kisses her firmly on the mouth, backs away. "Five minutes."

When he exits the box, ushered out by Denis and flanked by the agent called Fletcher, Emma throws her balled-up program at the door.

"God*dammit!*" She spins in place, her entire body prickling with fear and fury.

"Miss Lewis, he'll be fine." Denis returns, holding up his hands, trying to reassure. "He's not my principal here, and he's trained. He'll get the message and go, he's got plenty of support –"

"Simon uses Travis to get to *me.*" She wants to rip her hair out. "That's why I didn't want him here. You don't *get it!*"

"Miss Lewis –"

"To hell with this," she snarls, and starts for the door.

Denis grabs her by the shoulders. "Absolutely not."

"*Fuck*!" She pushes away, leans over her knees.

But Agent Denis will not be moved. Emma marches back to her chair and the view from the balcony, searches the auditorium. She tries to keep a bead on Kristin, who's glancing everywhere like she isn't sure what happens next.

There's nothing to see for a moment. But Emma knows what she's looking for: a flash of white hair, the angle of a shoulder in a jacket, someone standing with a predatory stillness while everyone else is moving. *Damn you, Simon, where are you?* She scans so hard, her eyes start hurting.

"Miss Lewis, sit down please," Denis requests. "You're making an easy target."

Emma wants to ignore him but she can't. She flumps into her chair, sitting close to the edge as possible. It can't be long before the lights go down for the end of the interval; she prays they don't dim too soon.

Denis is clearly feeling regrets, because he starts offering concessions. "Let me get you something. A bottle of water, or –"

"No thanks." Emma keeps her attention on the scene below.

Now Travis arrives into the swarm of patrons milling before the start of Act II. Emma can see the top of his head, with his rough dark hair, and the masculine black lines of his suit. Agent Fletcher is sticking close, about an arm's-length away.

Another squawk from Denis's earpiece. He turns for the curtain, the door. Still looking down, Emma feels a souf of cool air on her cheek.

Travis moves through the crowd against the flow of traffic, twisting to find passage. He reaches Kristin, and Emma sees Kristin see him: The girl turns to face him, with her smoky blue eyes. Travis puts his hand on Kristin's arm, and Emma catches her breath.

A glass of champagne is placed on the small, skull-decorated table beside her on the right, between her seat and Denis's.

Emma glances at it. "I said I didn't want –"

She realizes too late why the hair on the back of her neck has lifted. Everything inside her goes very quiet and still. She's afraid to turn her head.

She clears her throat, so her words don't come out hoarse. "I said I didn't want anything."

"Compliments of the house."

Emma would know that voice anywhere. If she were on the moon, she would know it. She closes her eyes, opens them. "Where's Agent Denis?"

Simon Gutmunsson slides into Denis's armchair. He's wearing a dark suit, like Denis, but the fabric is clearly of a much better quality; Emma thinks the lapels might be silk. The shirt he's wearing is white, with a point collar and double French cuffs. His cufflinks are silver, heavy, and the silver rings he is wearing on each middle finger are also heavy. One has a black cabochon stone deeply inset, and one is engraved with markings like a coin; Emma suspects they are Moroccan.

Simon's eyes are sapphire blue, flashing more vivid than the silver rings. His typical blaze of white hair has been dyed a polished brown and tamed into a Princeton clip with a sharp side part. In every other respect, he is just as Emma remembers: Tall, urbane, insane.

"I'm afraid your agent has stepped out for a moment." Simon picks up her rejected champagne and takes a sip. There is dark red blood on the stem of the glass, and on the fingers of his left hand. A large, suspended drop breaks and falls onto the fabric of his trousers. "He may not be back for some time."

Emma absorbs this. She thinks of Denis's politeness, when he told her to watch her feet on the stairs, and feels a jagged catch in her breathing. "Simon –"

"Hush now, the conductor is returning."

The lights flicker three times and begin to dim all over the auditorium. Emma has lost sight of Travis down below, in his standoff with Kristin. She cannot help but focus on Simon as he takes a snowy-white handkerchief from his breast pocket and wipes his hands. In the gloom, the handkerchief moves – smoothing, scrubbing. When he discards the stained fabric onto the floor, Emma forces herself to look away. Her heartbeat is fluttering, her skin is cold, and her head is rigid on her neck. She is familiar with the feeling of freezing into stillness, when your entire body is stiff with fear.

"I do love attending the opera," Simon admits, smiling. "Although I don't think much of this mezzo in the role of Liu – unidiomatic singing, no attack on the high notes, and such *rote* pronunciation of the Italian… That dress is lovely on you, Emma. Kristin was right. And look at your hair!"

Despite her terror, there's a deep well of anger inside her that Emma finds impossible to control. "*Stop it.* Just *stop it*, all right? Just say what you want to say and go."

"'*Principessa, have mercy.*'" Simon grins, takes another swallow of champagne, his cold blue eyes softening. "I dreamt of you in Tangier, you know."

She trains her focus on the stage as her gloved hands curl into fists. "Well, I didn't dream about you."

"Oh, Emma." He relaxes back in his armchair, disappointed. "Tsk tsk. You've always been so honest until now. But you've changed since we last met, haven't you? Perhaps that's the worthy Mr. Bell's influence –"

"Leave Travis out of this," Emma growls.

"Or maybe it's the effect of your new handlers at the FBI." Simon waves a languid hand. "They'll discard you when they're through using you, of course, like they discard all their tools. I suppose they gave you no choice but to participate."

Emma glances at him, shakes her head. "You know what you are, Simon. You know they can't leave you walking around." She exhales heavily, watching the Lord Chancellor of the Imperial palace sing of his longing for his homeland. "Neither could I."

"Do you hate me so much?"

Emma looks him full in the face for the first time, surprised at his tone. "Wasn't it always going to come to this?"

"I suppose it was." Simon leans forward, a smile playing about his full lips and his ultramarine eyes ready to swallow her whole. He smells of rosemary and oakmoss, and the salty tang of blood. "You and I – two killers facing each other at last."

"No." She's as motionless as if she were seated next to a live cobra. "I'm not like you."

"Aren't you?" Simon's shadowed gaze is insistent. "You were shaped in your first incarnation by Daniel Huxton. I like to think I've had a hand in shaping the new you." He gestures with his fingers. "Just a little more, and you can transcend all this…artifice. The FBI…Mr. Bell…normalcy."

His tone drips with condescension, and Emma snorts.

"Don't try to tell me this is about transcendence, Simon. Your sister might fall for that – not me." Compelled by a sudden fury, and perhaps a trace of insanity all her own, she leans in and grips his wrist as she spits the words of the libretto into his face. "'*Hurry, hasten back to your country. Here, the graveyards are full.*'"

It is the first time she's touched him voluntarily. Simon snatches his wrist away, his expression flaring. "You've always been a stubborn girl."

But Emma feels like she has the upper hand now. "*I'm* stubborn? *You're* the one who left Morocco to come home. Why walk into the trap?"

His full lips open to reply – but there is movement down below in the shadowed auditorium. Murmurs come from disturbed patrons. Emma strains to see; she suspects agents are pursuing Kristin in the darkness.

Simon twists out of his seat; whatever his goals were with this interview, having his twin under threat is something he cannot tolerate. "Well, it's been a pleasure as always, Emma."

"Simon –" Emma starts.

"*Arrivederci, cruel one.*" He salutes her with a flourish. As trumpets sound in the orchestra pit, he slips behind the curtain.

Emma makes a wrenching gasp as his departure registers, and her blood pressure drops in a dizzying rush. Still regaining her breath, spots in her vision dancing, she pushes herself up and fights her way through the curtain. The door to the box is half-open. Emma shoves through it, trips over the bulky object at floor level, her hands landing on lax flesh.

With a screaming sense of shock, she realizes she's fallen onto Denis's body.

The man lies facedown, limbs splayed. Emma scrambles quickly to kneel beside him, turn him over. *There's still a chance, there's a chance he's not dead –*

A great gout of residual blood spills onto her from Denis's severed throat, and Emma cries out in shock. Denis's skin is cooling, and his eyes have no more life than the glass orbs of a mannequin.

When Travis and three other agents arrive, breathless from running, Emma is still on her knees. She stares at them wordlessly and holds up her bloody hands.

CHAPTER NINE

Washington DC, 31 October 1982

The limo, currently doing fifty miles per hour with lights and sirens blazing, is full to capacity with Kirby, Carter, Emma, and Travis, who braces when they take a corner off Memorial Bridge onto Washington Boulevard. He wishes this night were over – but more immediately, he wishes they would slow down, and that everyone would stop talking over the top of each other. He is so angry he can hardly see.

Carter calls instructions to the driver, turns and asks, "Do you need medical attention?" for the second time, his question directed at Emma, as Kirby gives terse, loud directions into a handheld transceiver, occasionally breaking off to curse.

"It's not mine. It's not mine." Emma, bundled into the back seat, her face blank and shock-y, seems to be talking about the blood all over her hands and the front of her dress.

Travis, one arm around her, rubs her shoulder and glares at Carter. "He slit Denis's throat in the doorway –"

"No, I *can't*, you're breaking up –" Kirby looks up from the transceiver to give an update. "Martino set up the crime scene. He's contacting Scientific Analysis to come right now."

"Miss Lewis," Carter says, over the screaming of the siren, "are you all right?"

"Of course she's not all right!" Travis exclaims loud enough to be heard over the siren. But this knee-jerk fury makes him seem overwrought, so he tries to control it as he makes his point to Kirby. "She wouldn't be put in harm's way – that's what you *said*."

"We did all we could," Kirby replies stolidly. "There was no way to predict –"

"I want to get this dress off," Emma whispers.

Travis turns to her immediately, knowing exactly how she feels: The smell of blood is grotesque in the car, is almost as loud as the siren.

"Show me your hands." Travis takes her wrist gently, looks toward Carter and Kirby. "Is there a towel? A handkerchief?"

"I've got a handkerchief." Carter seems to have just remembered; he digs it out of his jacket pocket, hands it to Travis.

Kirby proffers a plastic bottle of water. "What did Gutmunsson say to you Miss Lewis?"

"*Back off*," Travis snaps. "Give her a minute to get the blood off before you start interrogating her."

But Emma seems to be recovering herself. She looks up at him as he swipes her net-gloved hands with the damp handkerchief.

"It's okay. It's okay, Travis." She meets Kirby's eyes. "I'll write it down for you – I have a good memory. But it was mostly personal…"

She blushes in the gloom of the car, and Travis wants to punch the car door.

"Simon thinks this is some kind of final showdown between him and me," Emma continues, then her voice drops. "Maybe he's right."

The drive back to Quantico is rapid with the siren. Travis just keeps holding Emma close; she's shivering, and he puts his jacket around her, cursing that there's no blanket in the car.

By the time they pass Newington, they've turned the siren off, and Emma's recouped enough to sit forward with a pen and a pad of sticky notes, the best approximation of writing materials Kirby could dig up. She scrawls note after note, stripping away each top one and handing it to Carter, continuing on the blank pad underneath.

Travis watches her and wishes his mind could be that simple – tearing off the damaged and dirty top sheet, starting fresh with a smooth, clean page each morning. He wants the memory of Denis's waxy, blood-smeared face erased, never to be thought of again.

When she's done, as they're coming toward the turn-off for Woodbridge, Emma presses the pad and pen into his hands.

"You, too." She looks improved, still not great. "You should write it down while you've got it."

"What?" Travis blinks.

"You met with Kristin," Emma reminds him. "You spoke with her."

Carter regards him solemnly. "Miss Lewis is correct."

"We need everything," Emma insists. "What she said, how she looked – everything you noticed."

"Yeah. Yeah, of course." Some part of Travis still balks. He turns to Kirby. "But don't you need an official –"

"Just write it." Kirby's eyes are red and tired. His blond hair glints gray as he reaches for the Motorola phone pack once more to make another call. "Write it down, we'll type it up with Miss Lewis's report."

Still disoriented, Travis takes the writing materials, begins the process of recalling and setting down the whole sad business of the night.

They reach Quantico by about twenty-two thirty, bumping into the motor pool garage. Travis is standing in the concrete bay by the limo's rear door, handing Emma out and retrieving his jacket, when a brown bureau Plymouth jounces down the ramp at above regulation speed. As soon as it's parked, Mike Martino exits the car and strides their way.

Kirby looks like he needs a win. "Mike, give me some good news."

"Afraid not." Martino's mouth is tight and he looks sweaty with worry. "Paul McKnight is in George Washington hospital ICU – Gutmunsson stuck him in the neck. McKnight and Gene Tyrell chased the twin sister into the opera house backstage area, got separated, and the whole thing went to hell."

Carter is frowning. "McKnight's in the ICU? How bad?"

"The knife went in the back of his neck, close to the spine."

"Jesus," Emma says faintly. Travis gets a firmer grip on her as she sinks against him.

Kirby's barely holding onto his outrage now. "And the twins *both* got away?"

Martino nods. "Faster than spit. I swear to god, Gutmunsson just racks up bodies everywhere he goes. The embassy in Morocco got in touch about a missing expat, Jeremy Welch, twenty-three years, seen in the targets' vicinity while they were overseas –"

"Not our priority now." Kirby cuts him off with the chop of a hand, then starts leading toward the exit, assuming everyone will follow. "Mike, I want a call with the Washington group in Buzzard Point, I want every assigned agent to call in for instructions, and everyone involved in this operation in the briefing room in forty-five minutes –"

"No." Emma stops dead. She looks frazzled, and there's a brown blood streak at the side of her chin which Travis never noticed in the car. She plucks black tulle away from herself. "I'm not…I can't do this. I need to get out of this dress."

Kirby halts his progress and turns on her, eyebrows mashed together. "Miss Lewis, I've got one man dead, and another in the hospital –"

"That's not her fault!" Travis is incensed at the unfairness of it.

Carter steps in, appealing to Kirby. "Jack, she's given her report. We can correct anything else in the morning, when she's had some rest. Let her and Mr. Bell go."

Kirby is tight-lipped. "Howard –"

"Jack, the hospital called to say McKnight goes into surgery in twenty minutes," Martino interrupts. His concerns are larger than whether Emma and Travis attend the debrief. "So we need to contact his family asap, plus Steve Denis's family, then the district boys are going to want some answers, and the chairman of the Kennedy Center committee will be in my ear any second –"

"Dammit!" Kirby whirls, drops his fist to his side. "Okay, fine – Miss Lewis, Mr. Bell, you're dismissed. Get cleaned up. Then get some rest, because I'm going to want you at oh six hundred tomorrow, no later."

"Jack –" Carter starts.

"I'm going to be up all night with this, Carter," Kirby snarls, "so they can damn well help set things straight from early!"

But Travis only heard 'dismissed' – he's already urging Emma toward the corridor, the elevator. Inside the elevator car, Emma's greenish, although she makes an effort to stand unassisted. When they get to their floor on Jefferson and get into her room, she goes straight to the bathroom and lifts the lid of the toilet, hangs over it, hands on the wall.

"You gonna hurl?" Travis asks.

"Maybe." Emma closes her eyes, head down. Then she's suddenly allergic to what she's wearing, wrenching off the clammy, bloodstained gloves and tossing them away. "*Fuck.* Undo this zip for me?"

Travis undoes the black button at her nape and her zip at the back, retreats as she kicks off her shoes.

"They might want to examine the clothes," he warns.

The dress parts behind her, revealing an upside-down triangle of bare, pale skin. Travis sees the line of her backbone, the black band of her strapless bra – and a number of silver-white scars. He knows she has others, but these ones are new to him.

She reaches for the faucet of the shower, spins it hard. "I'll put everything in a pile."

"You need me?"

"Not for this." She glances over her shoulder. "Give me a minute."

Travis backs out of the bathroom, closes the door. He shoves a hand through his hair, unsure whether he should stay, in case she collapses in the shower. He listens at the door. But nothing untoward seems to be happening and he feels like a creep lurking outside. Backtracking from Emma's room, he returns to his own.

His Quantico room is more spacious for this stay: There's a king single bed with a cream coverlet, a study desk, an ensuite bathroom. Everything smells like carpet shampoo, but it's not top of his mind right now.

He's sweaty in his formal clothes, and more than that, he feels grimy from the events of the night. He tosses his tuxedo jacket on a chair, unbuttons his cuffs and pulls off his shirt, goes to the bathroom and runs the water. Stands there in front of the mirror in his undershirt and dress trousers, holding the basin for a minute, searching for calm. Then he splashes his face and dries off with a towel.

His chest is aching, and he rubs it. Percocet would make him feel better, but he's not sure if the pain is physical or just a result of the stress of the last ninety minutes.

The moment he'd looked up to the opera box and seen agents scrambling for Emma's position had felt like a heart attack.

His hands are still trembling a little; he tries to settle them. Out of the bathroom, there's a hooded sweatshirt poking out of his duffel so he pulls it on, takes off his shoes, changes his trousers for sweatpants. Should he go back to Emma's room? Probably. He sits on the edge of the bed to think.

Kristin Gutmunsson had seemed worried. Thin and anxious, drawn in the face. *Travis? Oh my god, it's you…Oh, please don't be angry with me…It's not about you at all…*

All the way toward her, as auditorium lights started to dim, he'd been furious. But confronted by this distressed, vulnerable, too-thin girl, his first reaction had been to feel sorry for her.

She'd grabbed him by the arm, eyes huge. *I didn't want to come back, you have to know that…It's just that Simon takes over, and everything I tell him is completely swept away…* Then she'd trapped him with her hands on his shoulders, and leaned in to whisper in his ear: *My brother loves me too well, you see…*

The implications of that had made Travis cold in his very bones.

He'd barely registered the sounds of tenors singing in the background when Kristin pulled back to stare into his face and say, *Up there*, her eyes finding the box he and Emma had shared. He'd jerked, looked back, and Agent Fletcher had reached him, seen the direction he was staring in, immediately started talking into his wrist, bolted away.

Travis hadn't sensed Kristin let go. He'd been too busy with the heart attack feeling, and with watching agents on the tier levels moving, and being jostled by other agents who'd pushed past him to give chase to the slip of emerald silk disappearing toward the backstage areas. After that, he'd moved faster than he had in over a month, faster than was probably wise.

Which is why his chest is aching. He should take the Percocet.

He's washing the tablets down in the bathroom when there's a knock on the door. Travis answers it.

"I just…I left everything on the floor in the bathroom." Emma, in a loose white T-shirt, and sweatpants like his own, only gray. Hair spiky with damp, her hands wave toward her room vaguely, and she doesn't look as if she's quite present. "I don't know what they want to do with the dress, but I figured –"

"Come inside," Travis says, and he draws her into the room, closes the door. "It's okay. It doesn't matter about the clothes."

Emma's arms wrap around his waist immediately, and her breath hitches against his sweatshirt. "I hate this. I hate it. Denis is dead because of me –"

"No way." Travis holds her firmly, and the contact is soothing. "That's not on you. Denis was doing his job. It was a dangerous job, and he knew that."

"I still feel it." She shakes her head, shivering. "All the casualties. I *feel* them, Travis."

"I know."

"Every one of them."

"Me, too." What he feels is relief, that it was Denis and not Emma. That maybe makes him a selfish person, but he can't help it. "It's okay. It's okay."

"Keep holding me."

"I'm not gonna stop."

They hug for a long time. Emma rubs her face against his chest, over the place where the scarred skin is tender. Then she curls her arms up around his neck, pushes him back to the bed, pushes him to sit down. He finds he's completely unable to resist her, although she's about six-ty-five pounds lighter and built of nothing but whippy runner's tendon and slow-twitch muscle.

She climbs onto his lap, knees on the mattress either side of his hips. Puts her hands each side of his face and kisses him, intense and deep. Travis feels her fingers slide up and clutch his hair as his head lolls back. He closes his eyes and sees fireworks bloom, gold and silver. Warmth unfurls inside.

Emma tugs off his sweatshirt, smooths her hands over his bare shoulders, presses herself against him. When she kisses him again, her lips are feverish, urgent; Travis feels like he's burning. There's more heat in the room than he knows what to do with. Emma makes a low moan in her throat. But after a few blazing minutes, he realizes she's shaking.

"Slow down, slow down," he whispers.

"I don't want to." Her eyes are screwed up tight.

He cups her cheek. "Emma –"

She bats his hand away. "I want this. This is what I want."

"Easy," he says. "There's no hurry. We have time."

"Do we?" Her eyes snap open. The words have rung inside her like a gong, and she clambers off him, steadies herself on wobbly legs. "This might be it. This might be all the time we get."

"What?" Already, being apart from her makes him feel chilled. "Emma –"

"Especially if you keep doing shit like you did tonight." She swipes a hand across her face. Her lips are trembling. "*You left me*, Travis. You *left* me. You were with me in that box, and you walked away."

Now he's beginning to get where this is all coming from. "Emma, I'm sorry. It was a mistake –"

"You're *damn right* it was a mistake." She takes a step back, forward again. "Why? Why did you do that? What were you *thinking*?"

He stands up, but the flash of resentment inside quickly fades. He can see how affected she is. She's pacing back and forth. And she's not just berating him – she's genuinely asking, trying to understand. She deserves a genuine response, and he's not sure he's got one.

"*I don't know*," he blurts. It's the first time he's acknowledged it to himself, which gives him pause. He looks within for answers. "I don't know. I was…angry. I got frustrated. I wanted us both *out* of there."

Her hands drop to her sides, but her energy is still heightened.

"I know this…" She waves around. "All this *shit* – Simon's mind games, the FBI, the bullshit…It works on you. Like it works on me, only in different ways. But if you let it pull us apart, we'll both end up dead."

She's right. It strikes a bolt of fear through his heart so fast, he's forced to rub at his ribs.

Emma steps closer, entreating. "You want me to trust you. You said we have to stick together, so let's *stick together*."

"Okay," he whispers.

Now she moves right in, holds his waist in both hands, looking up at him. Her expression is so raw, so utterly vulnerable, it steals his breath.

"I'm nowhere near as terrified of Simon Gutmunsson as I am of losing you." Her chin is quivering. "You hear me, Travis Bell? You scared me *so much* tonight."

"I'm sorry," he says, and wraps her up tight in his arms. "I'm sorry."

She holds on for dear life, face mashed into his chest. "Kristin wasn't a message, she was a distraction."

"You're right." He presses his lips to her crown and closes his eyes. But it's coming back to him again: Kristin's pale, troubled presence, her disjointed words. "She was a message, too, though."

"What do you mean?" Emma eases back gently.

"She said some stuff that I..." Travis grimaces. He remembers everything he wrote on those damn sticky notes. He backs against the bed, sits himself down, trying to think. "She's worried, Emma. Her brother doesn't show emotion, but she does. And tonight, she was real worried. I don't think she wanted to come back to the States."

Emma settles on the mattress beside him, still keeping contact. "Can we use that somehow? Can we get her away from Simon?"

"I don't know. It'll be tough." He runs a hand across his mouth, but he has to tell her. "I think she's sleeping with him."

"What?" Emma looks horrified. "With Simon? With her *brother*?"

"Yeah. I just...It was something she said – *My brother loves me too well.*" Even repeating it gives him a bad taste. "And the look on her face..."

"Oh *god*. Oh god, that's messed up."

"They're messed up," he agrees. He only has to turn his head to look into Emma's eyes. "And it's like you said – they're trying to mess *us* up."

Emma glances down at where their hands are joined, fingers laced together. She meets his gaze, matches the intensity. "Travis, don't walk away from me again."

"Okay," he says simply, and for all that the words are plain, he knows it's a pact they've made. They've been honest with each other, and cleared the air, and now this moment of important stillness – something about it makes him feel calm. "Lay down with me awhile?"

"Yeah," Emma says.

They lie together on the bed, facing each other, knees bumping, kissing some but hugging more. Travis turns off the lamp. Soon the post-adrenaline blowback works on them both, until their hands slow and their eyes close and they spoon up under the blankets, and sleep. It's the first full night's sleep Travis has had since he woke up in the hospital in September.

He's grateful for it come morning when the phone rings a wake-up call. He eases away from Emma's back and reaches for the receiver.

"This's Bell." His voice has a new-wakened rasp.

"Mr. Bell, this is Betty from Behavioral Science – it's oh five thirty. Mr. Kirby requested that I check you were up."

"Got it."

"I've tried Miss Lewis, but she's not answering –"

"I'll get her," he says, his gaze straying over Emma's deeply breathing form beside him. "Thanks, Betty. We'll be down in a half hour."

He hangs up. When he turns on the lamp and slides his arms around Emma again, she startles. He holds her firmly until she's properly awake, his lips tucked into the side of her neck. Waking up together is new; the emotions of it are like a tiny sun radiating in his chest.

"Hey." She stretches, cheeks pink. "S'morning?"

"Uh-huh."

She sounds different first thing after waking, drowsy and soft. "Have we got to go?"

"Uh-huh." But she's warm and silky against him, and he doesn't want to move away. He rubs his lips at the place where her neck meets her shoulder.

She turns in his arms. "How long have we got?"

"Thirty minutes." He nuzzles her throat, contemplates working his way down.

"Not long enough," she says, pushing him off, but she's smiling. "Come on, let me up, I've gotta go wash my face."

He groans, releases her.

She doesn't even have shoes to put on, so she heads for the door. "Elevator in five?"

"And coffee in ten," he agrees. He's up now, moving for the bathroom.

They meet near the elevator, and Emma is still tugging a black pea coat over her jeans and green flannel shirt, the laces of her running shoes flopping loose. Travis loops his lanyard over his head and hits the elevator button, glances down the hall. Quantico runs on a twenty-four-hour clock, and other residents are stirring into action.

Emma kneels to tie one shoe. "So are you going to tell Kirby about Simon and Kristin?"

"Well, he's got my report." Travis buttons his black Henley; his dad's jacket is caught in the crook of his arm. "It feels weird to share it, like it's their personal business. But it's probably important – it's certainly relevant."

"Becher will go apeshit over it." The doors open, and Emma leads into the car, pulling her lanyard out of her coat pocket.

"Becher." Travis makes a face. "I mean, it's all supposition."

"Yeah, but you always had a better read on Kristin than I did." Emma dons her lanyard and ties her other shoe. "If you think that's the inference from what she said, I believe it."

In the atrium, they line up for to-go coffee; the cafeteria is bustling, even this early. They don't have to queue long. Travis buys two sandwiches, inhales one and pushes Emma to have the other one – she's bad at remembering to eat.

It's unfortunate timing that they arrive at the elevator at the same time as Dr. Becher. Today the man's sport jacket is brown houndstooth, his polyester work shirt is white with double-breasted pockets, and his trousers are a dark, drab olive. Travis can't get over how big this guy is; the normal-sized brown briefcase he's carrying seems like a child's toy.

Becher approaches with his hand raised, his glasses flashing as the doors prepare to close. "Hold the elevator, please."

There's no earthly reason Travis can think of to deny this request without being rude, so he presses the button to let the man in. Immediately, the car feels crowded. Emma shifts back to give herself more personal space.

"Thank you." Becher seems to recognize that his presence in the car is less than welcome.

Travis feels compelled to deliver an icebreaker. "Good morning, Doctor."

"Not a very good morning for Agent Kirby, I'm afraid." Becher's ponderous voice, his serious expression, seem to hammer the point home almost to the point of satire. "Or the men who were killed or injured last night."

"I guess not," Emma says. Her tone is slightly dry.

Becher's eyes, magnified by his glasses, zero in on her as he turns. "You saw Simon Gutmunsson. He spoke with you."

"Yes."

"I haven't examined your report, as yet."

"It doesn't make particularly thrilling reading." Now her voice is definitely dry. "Simon was just there to goad me, and hurt people."

"I suspected he would be there." Becher nods sagely.

Emma narrows her gaze. "Did you suspect he'd murder another law enforcement officer?"

The man looks her right in the face. "I can imagine him thinking it would make an appropriate sacrifice, for the opportunity to meet with you again."

Travis feels his hackles spring. "Emma wasn't responsible for Denis's death."

Becher straightens. "I would never intimate such a thing. I only extrapolate from what I know of Simon Gutmunsson's psychology and recorded behavior."

Emma's lips are tight; Travis isn't inclined to let Becher's comment go. "I think you're drawing a long bow, sir."

The man blinks, owlish, finally realizing that he has over-stepped. "Mr. Bell, if I have offended you or Miss Lewis in any way –" The door of the car opens at basement level; he breaks off to gesture politely. "After you."

Travis leads out, Emma follows. Becher is right behind them. Emma's steps have quickened in the corridor and Travis can tell she's pissed, wants to make some distance; her to-go cup is sloshing in her hand.

"Drink some coffee," Travis suggests. It's a good distraction. He sips his own as they walk and finds it grounding.

Betty nods as they enter the foyer and flash their ID, walk through the doors into the beige caverns of Behavioral Science. Behind them, Becher has to dig for his own identification. They reach the home base office first, to find Jack Kirby in his shirtsleeves, adding new photos to the Wall of Gutmunsson: a glancing picture of Kristin in her emerald dress, a blurry on-site camera still of a tall figure in a dark suit and white cuffs.

"Hey." Kirby finishes pressing in a thumbtack before turning. "You both look better."

Travis thought he'd find Kirby all crisp action, but the agent seems worn down today. He's in the same pants and shirt from the night before, his tie loosened. His eyes have a washed-out, silvery paleness.

"You look worse," Emma notes, softening the lack of diplomacy with a considerate tone. "Did you even go to bed?"

"It's been a long night." Kirby shears a hand through his hair, straightens a little as Becher walks through the door. "Ah, Dr. Becher, thank you for coming in at such an early hour."

"I would have come last night," Becher says, setting his briefcase on the table-top, "but I imagine things were purely operational by the time you called."

"Pretty much, yes." Kirby's focus swivels as Carter comes through the door. "Dr. Becher, you haven't met Special Agent Howard Carter…"

Travis finds seats for Emma and himself as introductions are made. Carter and Becher shake, Becher settles into his own chair across the table as Carter and Kirby remain standing, sorting through manila folders on the table-top.

"Miss Lewis, have you recovered somewhat from last night's events?" Carter's also in shirtsleeves, cuffs rolled, but his tie and waistcoat are both neat.

"It was good to change out of bloody clothes and get some sleep." Emma's words have a stiffness, but it dissolves with her next acknowledgement. "You guys have been up for too long, though – you probably want to get started."

Kirby nods, pushes a folder in her direction. "We have some paperwork to deal with. If you and Mr. Bell could read through the transcriptions of your reports, note any changes, then sign off on them, that would be helpful."

Becher raises a finger, moustache twitching. "May I read through them also?"

"Of course."

But Travis's attention has switched to a dry-erase board mounted on the wall, covered in a kind of architectural schematic, a floor plan with dots and red arrows suggesting dynamic action. "You mapped out everyone's movements at the location?"

"Yeah." Kirby's face is tired as he gestures. "We needed to work out what went wrong. I owe Steve Denis's family that much."

Carter shifts closer to the wall. "With a bit more digging, we discovered how the Gutmunssons managed to get in and out, all under the radar."

He moves aside to reveal a photo of a tall, angular-looking man in his thirties. The man is fair-skinned, and very blond. He has one hand in the pocket of his dark trousers, the other hand lifted as he smokes a cigarette; it's unclear if he's squinting into the sun or scowling at the camera. Shadows from the tall hedge nearby mottle his white short-sleeved work shirt, much like the type that Dr. Becher is wearing now. The hedge almost completely shades out a figure beside him: a slim, ethereal-looking white woman in a vintage dress. The photo looks old – it has the foxed yellow tint of sixties Kodachrome. But the family resemblance is unmistakeable.

Carter taps the photo. "The parents, Ivar and Alice Gutmunsson – you're aware the family is very wealthy? They were donors to the Kennedy Center committee for many years, and have connections to the National Symphony Orchestra, including sponsorship of the orchestra, scholarships for musicians, and so on."

Emma sighs her understanding. "I get it now."

Becher raises a hand, confused. "I myself do not 'get it' – how do donations and sponsorships impact last night's situation?"

"The National Symphony is the Kennedy Center's home company," Carter explains. "As sponsors back in the day, the Gutmunssons, both senior and junior, attended symphony recitals and green-room preview events. The twins also play instruments – Simon, the piano, Kristin, the cello – and the family toured the backstage areas of the Kennedy Center many times."

Travis examines the old Kodak. "That's how Kristin ended up in the orchestra pit?"

Carter nods. "A number of the musicians know her by name. They'd met her socially. When the harpist's page-turner, Harriet Sinclair, didn't show for the performance, Kristin took her place. We're still looking for Miss Sinclair, by the way."

Kirby takes up the reins. "But that history is how Kristin and Simon knew the backstage areas so well. Simon Gutmunsson accessed backstage hallways here and here…" Kirby uncaps a dry-erase pen and makes notations on the map, "…to reach you on the second tier, Miss Lewis. This door, these steps, then this hall…" He draws a slashing curve on the board, glances back. "The hall leads directly to the wing areas of the performance stage."

"Kristin lost Agent Tyrell here, near the women's dressing rooms." Carter finds his own pen, makes his own marks. "Simon caught up with them here, stabbed Agent McKnight. Then he and Kristin probably cut through the bus parking garage to get out of the building."

"So the Kennedy Center wasn't just a convenient meeting point, or a callback to Simon's conversation with me at St Elizabeths," Emma says. "It was actually a place they both knew well enough to strategize a getaway."

"It was very familiar ground for them, yes."

Kirby is biting his lip. "We should have done more homework."

"Not your fault." Travis feels the urge to throw the guy a bone. "The timeline was crazy short."

"We had, what, six or seven hours?" Kirby grimaces. "We should've checked. It's on me."

Emma looks at him. "Did McKnight make it?"

Kirby shakes his head slowly before facing her, his gray eyes more direct and his face drawn. "Miss Lewis, I owe you an apology. You were right. Gutmunsson has been planning ten steps ahead of us from the start."

"So what do you intend to do now?" Becher asks, sitting primly in his chair.

Kirby glances at him, at the dry-erase board. "I think we put a lid on the 'new Artist' sting. It seems pretty clear that Gutmunsson has anticipated our every move with that."

Becher blinks. "But the interview with Mr. LaFriche –"

"We contacted WaPo early this morning," Carter says, "with a request to hold the story until we can clarify some details. It won't be hard to pull it."

Travis sees Carter and Kirby exchange glances, Kirby nodding. It's obvious the two agents have come to a better working relationship, or maybe Kirby just needed all the support he could get.

But Travis is stuck on the usefulness of the newspaper interview. If they can't utilize it one way, maybe it could be repurposed? "What if… What if you asked LaFriche to tweak it, then let it run?"

"What do you –" Emma starts, then he sees her follow his thread. "Oh, right."

"What do you mean?" Kirby asks.

Travis leans forward, elbows on the table. "Call LaFriche, tell him we've had a breakthrough in the case. That we've realized there was no 'new Artist'. That the original Artist is back. Dr. Becher's analysis won't be applicable – sorry, doctor –"

"Not at all," Becher says, his mouth a straight line.

Travis needs to address that. "Alternatively, Doctor, you could contact LaFriche for a follow up. Give him additional background on the twins." He turns to Carter and Kirby. "Then WaPo runs the story, and the news is basically reporting the truth – that Emma is here, assisting the FBI to recapture the Gutmunssons."

Kirby's eyes narrow as he looks at Carter for guidance. "Will it cause public panic, for people to know the real Artist is back?"

Carter seems to have already been considering that. "We'd have to manage it carefully. Make some calls, especially to families of Gutmunsson's previous victims. And we'd have to clear it with Rasche."

"What does all this achieve?" Becher asks.

"It creates a big red arrow pointing at Simon and Kristin, which will make it harder for them to walk around unnoticed." Emma sits back in her chair, shrugs. "Even with their hair dyed."

"Ah, I see…" Becher now seems to be slowly coming on-side. "Then Mr. Bell might be correct. Removing Simon Gutmunsson's anonymity while he's back in the States could be an advantage."

"Okay." Kirby's expression has lightened by a few degrees. "Okay, I can see it. Then what?"

"Then we get out in front of him." Emma leans forward again. "Dr. Becher, you said you studied Simon's background, his relationships, his papers for Georgetown – all of it."

"Yes." The man steeples his fingers together. "They gave me some understanding of his character, particularly his connection with his sister."

"What about Simon's letters? His correspondence? Something more recent. We want to understand his *current* state of mind."

"In the last year?" Travis thinks he can see where she's going with this.

Emma nods. "It's like you said, we need to start looking into his personal connections. People, places, experiences – anything he's left behind or written down, anything that gives us some insight into his mental state."

"So we can start imagining what he might do next."

There's a web here." Emma gestures toward the wall of pictures. "Simon's at the center of it, but if we can figure out where each strand leads…And there's another thing. When he was in Allegheny, he told me that he made videotapes of his crimes. Those might be really important."

"I would like to see any videotapes," Becher agrees.

"If Simon Gutmunsson ever created videotapes, they were never recovered. I'm sure of that." Carter is frowning. "As for letters, I'm not sure what correspondence of Gutmunsson's we've got from the last year."

"He sent letters to Special Agent Cooper." Travis remembers this very well. "Gerry Westfall and the team at Scientific Analysis will have them."

"Is that all we've got?" Kirby asks. "He left nothing at Byberry, according to reports."

Emma's face has a sharp, single-minded cast. It's the energy of the hunt. "What about his papers and books from St Elizabeths?"

CHAPTER TEN

Washington DC, 1 November 1982

They're in a bureau Plymouth by 08:00AM, with Carter driving. Emma is in the back, with a notebook in her lap and headphones over her ears, clicking buttons on an Olympus SR11 microcassette player. She's listening to a copy of a voice recording of McKnight's encounter with Kristin and Simon. She's not sure how the recording was documented, but Kirby had it, and she asked to hear it, to see if there were more words, phrases, anything at all that might help them piece this puzzle together.

She stops and rewinds again and again to catch the sounds of Kristin's voice, and the dark purr of Simon's. She needs to brace every time, hearing McKnight's scream. The recording is useful evidence, but it's the soundtrack of a man's death, and along with the disorienting low hiss and flutter of the tape, it's uncomfortable listening.

When she clicks the button to stop, conversation drifts in. It sounds like Travis and Carter have already been talking for a while.

"...not an easy life," Carter is saying. "You miss out on a lot of family dinners, a lot of elementary school concerts and little league games. You miss out on your kids' childhoods entirely, if you're unlucky. And it's hard on your spouse, not just the long hours, but the worry – even if your spouse is unsure of what to worry about."

Emma knows what they're talking about now.

"Yeah, I get that," Travis says, and of course he gets it. His own father lived that life.

Carter continues. "So I understand, if that's what's driving your uncertainty. Is that what you're concerned about?"

"Not so much." Travis is looking forward, and all Emma can see is the dark curl of his hair at the back, the collar of his shirt. "The lifestyle worked okay in my family. My folks found a way to balance it."

"Good for them." Carter's hands move smoothly on the steering wheel. "So that's not your biggest problem. What else? Is it the racial stuff? Is that hard to deal with? I mean, if you want to talk that over with someone else, there's always Dr. Brown, or Carlos Dixon, or Special Agent Leeds at the DC field office…"

Travis rubs his nape. "I mean, the racial stuff is everywhere, right?"

"Yes," Carter says. "Yes, it is."

She's not sure if she should be listening; they obviously think she's preoccupied in the rear seat. But this is the first time she's heard Travis talk about his deliberations over his future with another law enforcement officer, and his answers feel important. Emma thinks she knows what's driving him toward the FBI; she's not certain what's driving him away.

"It's not really that so much, either," Travis says. "There's just… other stuff." He hesitates. "I keep thinking about Peter Kirke. What happened in the warehouse in September. Kirke was psychologically screwed-up, he was a killer, he inflicted pain on other people…But that pain, it's everywhere."

"That's right – and it's our job to find the men who continually inflict pain on others and stop them." Carter sounds firm, beyond all doubt. "That's what Behavioral Science is supposed to be about."

124

"I just don't know how effective it is to combat it like that, one screwed-up guy at a time." Travis looks out the front passenger window, where the trees in Fort Greble Park are dressed in orange and brown leaves. "It feels like chipping at a glacier with an icepick."

"I mean, it can definitely feel like that some days," Carter admits. He darts a glance over. "That's not all, though, is it?"

Travis is still looking elsewhere. "I've had this…missing piece inside. Since my dad died. I thought that by taking on his role, becoming like him, I could maybe absorb something of him into myself. A piece of him, to replace the piece I lost."

That's not how it works, Emma thinks.

"It doesn't really work that way, though," Carter echoes gently.

"Not really." Travis looks back. "I guess I'm wondering, if doing this isn't about getting closer to my dad anymore…"

"Then why are you doing it?" Carter nods. Clouds are scudding high above the car. "That's an important question. A question worth asking. You need to find out the answer before you re-commit to your training." Carter sets the turn signal, rolls the wheel, nice and steady. "There's another issue you need to consider, though, before you make a decision about becoming a LEO."

"What's that?"

"The fact that you're good at it."

But does Travis want to be? Emma knows that sometimes in this life, you get insight, you develop a skill. Doesn't necessarily mean that your future path is pre-determined along those lines. She knows herself what it's like to be expert in something you find uncomfortable, something you have no desire to pursue. Something that sickens you, even.

According to Audrey, Emma's knowledge of serial killers gives her expertise, authority in the field. But if someone informed her that it was now her duty and destiny to chase killers forever, she'd get out of this car and walk off into the woods, never to be found again.

Travis's upbringing and circumstances are different, though. Maybe he feels an allegiance to law enforcement she can't understand. The idea gives her a pang.

Emma fusses with the tape unit so they know she's no longer quiet in the back, before she leans forward to ask a question. "Mr. Carter? I think you mentioned back in Pittsburgh that Dr. Scott was no longer at St Elizabeths, and I want to ask you about that."

"That's right, Miss Lewis." Carter takes another turn onto Malcolm X Avenue SE. They're on territory that Emma remembers now. "Dr. Scott resigned from her position at St Elizabeths after Gutmunsson's transfer to Byberry State Hospital. It wasn't just Anthony Hoyt's death, the night of the FBI operation – I think the knowledge that the Berryville Butcher had been working on her staff gave her an additional sense of culpability."

"Who's running St Elizabeths now?"

"An administrative director by the name of Francis Perry. He does things a little differently, and I understand some areas of the facility have been closed down."

"Budget cuts?"

"With all the fallout, I imagine so." Carter brings them to a pause at a stop sign, checks left and right. "Director Perry let some staff go, consolidated in other areas. I don't know if he's preserved any of Simon Gutmunsson's papers, or even realized what they were. But it doesn't hurt to check."

They've reached the rise of the hospital's curved driveway, and here are the buildings of St Elizabeths once again – Emma can't prevent a shiver. The gothic, red-brick towers lurch upward as the wind whips through the gravel car park. All the windows are barred. She can hardly believe she's back here.

Carter parks the Plymouth in shadow, and Emma gets out of the car, looks up. She reminds herself that this is not the place where she faced down her fears: It was in West Virginia, with McMurtry, that she sat across a table from the first serial killer she'd encountered since Daniel Huxton and held her ground. That should be her marker, the place where she realized the smallness of these men; St Elizabeths should be of no significance, except as the site where one of them once resided, and where another died.

But it's where she first met Simon, and survived Hoyt. And it's where Travis got shot.

She hunches inside her pea coat, glances at him. "Well, here we are again."

"Yeah." He pulls up the collar on his jacket, squinting from the chill sunlight spiking off an upper-story window. "This place still gives me the creeps."

She feels it, too, can't shake it. "I'm pretty sure it was designed that way."

In a long, regulation-dark overcoat, Carter walks around the Plymouth's hood and toward the large open doorway. "I was told on the phone that Director Perry would meet us when we check in at reception. You folks coming?"

"We know the way," Emma says, then more quietly to Travis, "You don't have to come inside, you know."

He grimaces, wind pushing at his hair. "Yeah, I do."

Even without looking at it directly, Emma can sense the building like a presence. "This place makes me anxious. It makes me feel…grimy. It's where I set Simon free."

Travis makes eye contact. "If you hadn't done that, Hoyt would have killed you. Then he would have walked up that big hallway and killed me and Kristin."

"I want to start letting all this stuff go," Emma blurts.

"So let's let it go. Come on."

When they get inside, the reception area foyer is unchanged, although it has a booth now, instead of a desk – during Raymond's botched operation, the FBI 'receptionist' was brutally murdered while sitting at the foyer desk, so perhaps the new administrator saw the deficiencies in such an arrangement. The new booth is sturdy, bolted into the parquet floor. Behind a plexiglass window, a matronly woman wearing a green kirta blouse and an embroidered indigo scarf sits at the counter on a high stool. Her dark hair is centre-parted and tightened into a low bun, and her eyes are rimmed with kohl. She checks Emma's signature in the visitors ledger and gives her an appraising nod.

Director Perry has arrived and is already exchanging handshakes and pleasantries with Carter. Perry is a small man with a thin moustache and combed-back hair. The fabric of his dark brown suit has a faint shine, and he wears a knitted burgundy tie. Carter makes the introductions; Emma thinks Perry has the soft hands of middle management.

"Thank you for calling ahead." He makes a polite, tight smile. "That section of the hospital is sealed off now. I'm the only one with the key to open it for you."

"We appreciate you making the time to show us around," Carter says.

"Well, you're the FBI." Perry's manner is obsequious in the way of someone who will fawn to your face, then be vitriolic behind your back. "I don't know if there's anything there that will still be of use to you –"

"We don't either," Travis interrupts. Being here seems to be wearing at his patience. "That's why it's good to have a chance to look at it."

Perry's rat-like eyes dart between Travis and Emma, their civilian clothes, their youth. Finally, it comes to him. "You…You were the young people who were here that night."

"We were," Travis acknowledges.

"Still are," Emma says, trying not to sound too acerbic. "Is it okay if we go straight through to the chapel room?"

"Of course, of course." Flustered, Perry ushers them toward the undercarriage of the grand reception area staircase. "It's this way – I mean, I'm sure you remember."

He unlocks the door under the staircase with the same ornate black key that Emma knows so well. Her palm itches: She can still feel that iron key in her hand, from the night Anthony Hoyt made her cooperate with him in exchange for Travis and Kristin's lives. Through the door, the huge hallway – pillared and high-ceilinged – is gloomy. The old steel-barred sliding doors are all open wide, which seems wrong somehow.

"We've left everything much as it was," Perry says, waving at the bars, the cobwebs, as they walk. "This area was being sealed off in any case, so there didn't seem much point in rearranging things…"

Emma smells dust, and the coldness of wood and metal as Perry continues talking to Carter. Travis is looking around as they walk; maybe he's recalling the way they fled up this hall that night, while he was still injured. Everyone's footsteps echo, and it reminds her of the sound of Dr. Evelyn Scott's heels on the wooden floor. Unlike Perry, Scott would have made this seem more like a clinical visit and less like a tour.

When they reach the oak door which once barred entry to Simon's room, Perry uses another key. Tumblers turn inside the lock.

He pushes the heavy door open and makes a flourish. "Here it is!"

Emma hesitates, then steps inside. Her breathing is tight with memory. But after a moment, she realizes that the chapel room has a different feeling now, probably because its notorious occupant is gone. High buttresses still soar at the ceiling, decommissioned pews are still arranged against the walls, tattered velvet curtains remain drawn aside near the chancel. But the frisson of imminent danger is absent, and that's the feeling she most associates with this place.

She walks past the thick desk of the guard station, toward Simon's free-standing cell, and makes a second realization: The chapel room is identical to how they left it five months ago. The pincer tool, once used to ferry Simon's cigarettes, lies dumped in one corner; Emma blinks, gets a flash of Kristin attacking Hoyt with it. Ahead, a twist of bed-linen and rope hangs down from the roof of Simon's old cell. The charcoal shadow of fingerprint powder coats various surfaces. Dark stains are smeared on the cell floor, and on the wooden floor of the chapel. Barricade sawhorses stand nearby; one is knocked over. Most disturbing are the two hypodermic syringes, murky with brown residue, that lie discarded by the cell bars.

Travis turns to Perry with an expression of confusion, and a touch of horror. "It's exactly the same. You haven't cleaned it up at all?"

"As I said, this is an area of the hospital which is no longer open for patients or staff." Perry clasps his hands together, prim. "In light of the police investigation of the crime that occurred here, we decided it would be easier to simply quarantine this room off."

"Sure," Emma says, "but this is like…some kind of museum."

Carter has walked forward, taken a knee beside the syringes. He uses a pen from his jacket pocket to nudge at them. "Has the bureau cleared the crime scene, Mr. Perry?"

"I've never received any documents about that," Perry says.

Travis is beside Emma now. "This is so weird."

She nods, her lip curling involuntarily. "It's like a shrine."

"Or...a theater set." Travis's eyes narrow. "Did you notice something? The floor in here isn't dusty."

"We have our cleaners sweep the whole facility," Perry says promptly. "For safety reasons, we're obliged –"

"That's not it." Travis turns to Perry. "You keep the floor clean for visitors, don't you? Are you running tours of this crime scene, Mr. Perry?"

"Of *course* not." But Perry's cheeks and nose have gone an uncomfortable pink, and Emma thinks he's lying. He doubles down all the same. "That would be disgusting, and in terrible taste, not to mention illegal without official notification from the FBI that the room has been cleared."

"Also a violation of your remit, as director of a mental health facility," Carter notes dryly. "Although I do understand if it's taking time to obtain a letter of release – the wheels of law enforcement turn slow."

"I resent the implication that such a thing may have happened in a facility that I manage," Perry sputters.

Carter opens out his hands. "We're not trying to cause trouble or get your license revoked, Director. But we *are* trying to locate any papers, books, or documents that may have been left behind by Simon Gutmunsson when he was confined here as a patient. Would you happen to know where those items might be?"

"I do not." Perry's posture and manner are stiff.

"Why?" Emma's curious, because it's the one thing he *doesn't* seem to be lying about. "You've got everything else – the syringes, the bloodstains, the bedding. Even Simon's moldy old fruit bowl is there on the desk."

"There were no papers here when I arrived." Perry gestures around at the tableau. "Only this…mess. I didn't even know that any books or papers existed until the FBI asked me for an audit of all the documents at the scene. I assume that when Evelyn Scott packed up and left, she took it all with her."

"Why would Scott take it?" Travis asks.

"I have no idea."

Carter frowns. "As far as I know, she's in Seattle."

"That's right," Perry acknowledges. "I have a forwarding address if you'd like to contact her…"

The two men begin negotiating on this subject. Emma groans internally; if they have to find Scott, this will take time they don't have.

She walks closer to Travis, whose face is stiff with repressed revulsion as he stares at the self-contained cell. The steel bars don't have the same power without Simon behind them, but there's still a touch of the old resonance, like a dying star's echoing ring. Emma looks at the open door of the cell; she should probably go in and check for books or scraps of paper under Simon's bed. But the idea makes her recoil. She doesn't ever want to be inside that cage. She never wants to be inside a cage again.

Everything in this room makes her stomach tense with nausea. There's the abandoned scalpel that Hoyt stuck in her arm, that Simon used on Hoyt in turn; there's the rubber tourniquet, half perished, which Hoyt forced her to use to draw Travis and Kristin's blood 'donations'; there's the dark streak on the floorboards where Hoyt made her drag an injured Travis to the desk.

"We're done here." Travis's expression is disgusted. He shakes his head and kicks at the traces of his own blood, sunk into the wood. "Let's get the fuck out."

"Yeah." Her throat is thick. Now she's seen his bloodstains, her eyes want to search out her own, an impulse she resists. "I've had enough."

They walk out of the chapel room and together up the hall, with Perry and Carter trailing – Carter is still fishing for whatever final details he can get out of the hospital director. Travis slowly becomes less taut as they move toward the exit.

"Long trip for no result." His shoulders have released by the time they sign out at reception. "Nothing but a whole lot of bad memories."

"We had to check." Emma exchanges nods again with the female attendant. "And I guess now we have to chase up Scott."

"Then we'll have to wait for the paperwork, whenever it arrives Federal Express."

"If she still has it," Emma notes. "Do we just sit on our hands until then?"

"No way." Travis takes a lot of comfort in routine and thoroughness, and he leans into that now. "We go back through the other reports. We look for commonalities, differences, red flags."

"Busywork."

"Sometimes busywork is the only work."

Emma is in the doorway when she pauses, looks over her shoulder at the foyer area of St Elizabeths. She takes in the grand, gothic staircase, the parquet, the dust sparking in sizzling shafts of light. "I don't want to come back here again."

"I'm with you on that." Travis is looking in the same direction, reaching for her hand. "I want to leave this place behind."

They exit to the cold wind of the car park, and it's like she can finally take a clear breath again.

But here's something new: On the gravel outside, another car is set immediately beside Carter's bureau Plymouth. Emma has never seen anything like this car before – it's a dark bottle green, with chrome trim. The rounded edges and white-wall tires suggest the car is at least twenty years old, but it's been beautifully maintained. It has a European flavor, and reminds Emma of a vehicle she once saw in a James Bond movie.

Standing by the driver's side door is a big man, barrel-chested and heavily bearded, wearing a mushroom-colored shirt, argyle sweater, and neat brown trousers beneath his brown woollen coat. His turban is the same dark blue as his tie, and his posture is almost military-straight.

Emma knows this man. "Pradeep?"

His friendly expression of greeting is somewhat obscured by his beard and moustache. "Good morning, miss. I have been waiting for you."

Her last memory of Simon Gutmunsson's former jail attendant is from the same night she and Travis were just forced to relive in the old chapel room. She has never seen Pradeep without his starched, all-white uniform. "You've…been waiting for me?"

"Yes, miss." The man inclines his head in a polite bow, his deep voice resonating. "You will excuse me if I say you are looking well."

Emma makes a soft huff of surprise. "You, too, I guess."

Travis has made the connection. "You're the guy who let us back into the asylum that night."

"Pradeep Singh Sidhu." The man extends his giant hand. "And you are the young trainee officer with his father's gun."

"Travis Bell." Travis nods as they shake. "The FBI returned the gun. I never got to thank you for taking care of it."

"It was a fine weapon. I was honored to safeguard it. I have something else for you now – please." The iron bracelet on Pradeep's right wrist jingles as he takes out his car keys, gestures with them toward the beautiful car's trunk. "My sister, Rupar, has a post in the hospital now. She notified me when you arrived, so I came at once."

"The lady at the reception booth," Travis says immediately.

"Yes. It is good she reached me before you returned to Virginia."

Emma feels a sensation like a mild electric current. "What do you have for us, Mr. Singh?"

"Dr. Scott's departure was quite sudden, and she gave no orders regarding the disposition of Mr. Gutmunsson's effects after he left this facility." Pradeep's eyes are dark and deep. "My hope is that you will take these things, and I may relinquish my responsibility. It is the last task I can perform for Mr. Gutmunsson, and the final burden I carry."

They are all standing before the car's trunk now. Pradeep unlocks the trunk and lifts the lid.

Emma gasps.

CHAPTER ELEVEN

Washington DC, 1 November 1982

They don't have a phone pack, so Carter calls Kirby from the administrative office of St Elizabeths, then he makes another call to Scientific Analysis. It's nearly ten-thirty by the time they get to Pennsylvania Avenue, where Carlos Dixon has arranged their sign-in at FBI headquarters and rolled a pallet trolley to meet them in the underground car park.

There are three cardboard boxes of books, and two smaller boxes of papers. They get the boxes on the trolley, into the elevator and upstairs, where Linda Brown – called back to the office from her rostered day off – is shedding her brown leather trench coat.

"Good to see you, Howard, although I can't say I love the timing." She slides off an orange scarf, glances backward to the lab entrance as she dictates play. "Let's get the books in the lab and the papers in my office – Glenn will do the triage assessment of the books while we look at the papers. Glenn? Are you ready?"

Glenn Neilsen wheels briefly into the doorway of the lab and makes a little wave. "All set up, bring 'em in."

"Man, what a treasure trove." Dixon – wearing blue evidence gloves – hefts the two smaller boxes and heads for Brown's office, calling out over his shoulder. "Linda, I'm putting the papers on your desk!"

"That's fine!" she calls back, pushing the pallet trolley stacked with books into the lab.

Gerry Westfall, looking like a backwoods moonshiner in Carhartt wide-panel pants, a gray flannel shirt, and red braces, watches the flurry of action with less enthusiasm as he smokes a cigarette. "The timeline on this is short as hell. Jack Kirby can't give us a few more days?"

"We're on the back foot here, Gerry," Carter says, slipping out of his overcoat. "The Gutmunssons are on the move and we're trying to nail them down."

"Preferably before Simon kills anyone else." Emma steps out of Dixon's way as he returns, hunting for the clipboard with the trolley paperwork.

"I get that," Westfall says. "Just so long as Jack knows we're gonna lose some detail in the rush. If I had my druthers, I'd get Print and Trace on everything in these boxes, every single scrap. But we'll be working 'round the clock to manage that in such a narrow window."

Travis snorts. "The window's always narrow, right?"

"You got it." Dixon flips the chain-of-evidence papers on the clipboard and signs off, passes it to Carter.

"If it's any consolation," Carter says as he signs, "you'll probably only find Simon Gutmunsson's prints on the books. Maybe the former attendant, or something from the former supervisor? But that should be all."

"Unless they were touched by anyone on the SWAT team, on the night of Hoyt's murder," Emma points out.

Westfall waves a hand, and cigarette ash sprinkles to the floor. "That should be okay, SWAT will all be on file on the computer."

Dr. Brown's hair swings as she pokes her head out the door of the lab. "Can we get a hand with these boxes?"

Travis moves to help, before being snagged by Westfall.

"Gloves, gloves," Westfall says, digging out a pair of nitrile evidence gloves from his pants pocket and passing them over before turning once more to Carter. "What's Jack doing with this anyway? What's he after?"

"We're trying to get a line on Simon Gutmunsson's state of mind," Carter says, passing back the clipboard.

"Plus any personal connections," Emma says. "Dates, names of people, significant events."

Carter nods. "Especially any references to locations. States, towns, places of interest."

"Anything that can position the Gutmunssons at those sites, any signs that they may have a connection or attachment there." Emma looks around as Brown strides out of the lab and into her office. "Uh, can you use us at all? Me and Travis have done document research at Quantico. We could go through the books with Mr. Neilsen –"

"I can use you." Linda Brown snaps on evidence gloves in the doorway to her office. "I've already told Mr. Bell to stay in the lab and help Glenn and Carlos with unpacking, but I could use another set of eyes on these papers."

"Whatever you need," Emma says.

Leaving Carter and Westfall to negotiate over when the report from all this material will go to Jack Kirby, Emma heads for Brown's office. Attached to the open door is a framed quote from the Bible in lovely, distinctive calligraphy. Inside the office, Brown is adjusting a set of lamps. She's arranged some extra space – a card table covered with white paper – and the small cardboard boxes are side by side on her mahogany desk.

Brown hands Emma a pair of blue gloves as soon as she enters. "You've worked with documents before?

"In the Pittsburgh case," Emma confirms. "Mainly photos and reports – mostly copies, but some originals. I've never handled questioned documents before, though."

"And I would normally never do this," Brown admits. "If the timeframe weren't so tight, and if we weren't reasonably certain that all the prints and trace will be from Simon Gutmunsson himself…Well, anyway, here we are." She nods at the box on the left. "You take that one, I'll take this one. I want you to preserve the box itself as much as possible."

Emma shakes off her coat onto a chair and pulls on the gloves. They are powder-free inside, to prevent cross-contamination. "The boxes came from Pradeep Singh Sidhu, Simon's former attendant at St Elizabeths. I think he's had them in the trunk of his car all this time."

"That's fine, Glenn and Carlos will get all the trace from that." Brown's face is alight. "It's quite an opportunity, getting so much material from a long-term offender. Let's go."

They use a scalpel blade on the tape across the boxes, then take sheets out one by one, reading them through and noting their contents on a spreadsheet, no matter how random – *Box 2, Sheet 3; A piece torn from the obituary section of the Washington Post with pencil notation in top R-hand corner that reads: 92, 106, 12, 67, 3011* – before placing them upside-down in an evidence tub. Some of the fragments bear scraps of poetry, or words in foreign languages, or even personal musings, all in Simon's characteristic hand. Emma gets a jolt when she sees lines of Byron; it's like she can hear Simon reciting them.

"I can confirm, at least, that the vast majority of this stuff was written by Simon Gutmunsson," Brown says, laying down another sheet.

"You recognize the writing?" Emma asks.

"Yes – his capitals are very idiosyncratic, and you know I've examined his hand writing before. So there's no question of authenticity, although I'd really love to see if there's any alterations or erasures in these fragments. God, I wish we had more time."

"And I wish we could give it to you." Emma wipes her cheek against her forearm, careful of her gloved hands. "The reality is, we don't know how Simon's going to jump, and we need to find him before he does more damage, or takes off again. He and Kristin could escape back to Europe tomorrow, and then he'll just be…out there. Hurting people somewhere in the world."

The thought is more unnerving after seeing him at the opera last night. In Mexico, the issue of Simon Gutmunsson had started to feel removed, almost academic. Now it feels personal. Now he feels dangerously close.

"You said you're trying to figure out his location." Brown tilts her head.

"He's too smart for us to second guess him, though. We're just trying to figure out the people and places he feels connected to. Maybe we can anticipate his unconscious behaviors." Emma lifts her chin at the papers they're examining, so tedious but so necessary. "It might be a long shot, but every puzzle piece adds something. Everything is useful."

A lot of the fragments don't seem to have any meaning whatsoever. But about thirty minutes later, and halfway through her box, Brown gets a hit. "Box 1, Sheet 34. This is a newspaper article about Sudbury, Massachusetts."

Soon after that, Emma also finds a reference to Sudbury. Then, farther down the pile, there's a reference to a place in Georgia.

"How many properties did the Gutmunsson family own?" Brown asks. "They had generational wealth, is that right?"

"Yep." Emma sets down the letter she's just checked. "Let me find Mr. Carter and ask."

Carter hunts up the details: The Gutmunssons had property in three locations between DC and New England, and two in the south. Some of those properties were sold or re-mortgaged in 1980, for Simon's defense fund.

"Like a lot of wealthy families, they were primarily asset-rich," Carter says, consulting a small spiral notebook. He's taken off his jacket and hung it with his overcoat somewhere, and is once more down to his waistcoat and rolled sleeves. "They had to cash in some chips for the legal team. Then when things got bad, the senior Gutmunssons liquidated property assets to leave for Europe."

Brown considers. "So…which places are still registered for property tax?"

Carter grimaces. "Not sure. But I can find out."

As Carter leaves to use the telephone in Westfall's office, Travis takes his place in the doorway, his expression energized. "Dr. Brown, we found something you really need to see."

Emma and Brown look at each other. They leave their gloves on and hold their hands up like trauma surgeons as they hot-foot it to the lab, with Travis leading.

Workbenches covered in white high-pressure laminate are arrayed around the sides of the big room and in the center. Two of the center benches are identical, except one is standard height and one is lowered to accommodate Glenn Neilsen's wheelchair, so Dixon and Neilsen can work side by side. Beside the preserved cardboard boxes, a number of short stacks of books occupy the surface of each bench; Emma can see the spine of one volume, marked *A Philosophical Enquiry into the Origin of our Ideas of the Sublime and Beautiful* by Edmund Burke.

Dixon looks over from his place at the standard-height bench as they arrive. He's grinning. "Linda, you're gonna love this."

Neilsen turns his chair one-handed, gives her a book: It's leather bound, bulging with swollen pages, and held together with a big rubber band. Brown braces the book carefully in her gloved hand and removes the band, opens the cover. The first page shows a remarkably realistic drawing of a picture frame; sellotaped inside the frame is a lock of white-blond hair.

"Is this a scrapbook?" She examines the paper carefully. "This is watercolor paper."

"Looks like 300gsm," Neilsen confirms.

"It's something Simon Gutmunsson had stashed with his poetry books," Dixon says.

Brown turns another page. Emma makes space for Travis as they both move closer to see. Some written notes are scrawled around the edges of a blurred Polaroid of two young people with white hair, in white clothes, holding croquet mallets against a field of summer green. There is another sellotaped artifact, a four-leaf clover, plus more notes in curling lines of looping script, a hand Emma recognizes.

"Simon Gutmunsson didn't write this," Brown says.

"No." Emma touches the edge of a page with a blue-gloved finger. "That's Kristin's writing. I've seen it before."

Dixon nods at the book. "Look at the dedication on the inside front cover. It's something Kristin Gutmunsson made for her brother while he was in jail."

"I thought they weren't supposed to have contact with each other," Emma says.

"They weren't allowed to meet," Travis confirms. "There was a court order."

Neilsen raises his eyebrows. "Looks like they still found a way to communicate."

Brown brings the journal over to the lower bench so everyone can see. Each successive page holds something different – glued-in leaves, a sequence of photo booth snaps, pressed flowers and strands of dried grass, more Polaroids, cuttings from newspapers and magazines. There are a number of photos and sketches of an old, two-story house amongst trees.

All of these artifacts are interspersed with Kristin's journalled notes and comments, and some of them are very revealing: *...do wish I could still visit with Pippi, I miss her so! Oh Simon, you remember the day when we...find myself becoming very cross with you, but it's horrible, you can't imagine...how much I long for us to be together, watching the leaves change, if only we could...* These are memories or diary notes, personal confidences from Kristin, descriptions of scenes from the Gutmunsson twins' lives and childhoods. Emma's almost embarrassed on their behalf to see their private moments laid out for examination like this.

"Well, this is astonishing," Brown says.

Carter pokes his head through the open doorway of the lab, checking occupancy before walking in. "I looked for you in your office, Dr. Brown. You wanted the information about which properties the Gutmunssons still own?"

"Yes, please." Brown looks away from the scrapbook, pushes her hair back with the inside of her wrist.

Carter moves to the other side of the benchtop as he unrolls a large east coast road map. He lays it down and points. "There are three – this one nearby, in Georgetown, this one in Columbus, Georgia, and this one in Sudbury, Massachusetts."

"It's Massachusetts," Travis says immediately, his eyes strangely intent.

"Kirby said that each of these locations was searched once we knew the Gutmunssons had arrived back on home soil," Carter says.

Emma squints. "But if they knew the location, knew the area, it wouldn't have been hard to avoid a search, right?"

Carter makes a face. "The Georgia property is industrial, and it seems too remote for them to use as a base – we can still search it again to check. The Georgetown one has been searched a number of times, so I don't think he'd still be there, although Simon Gutmunsson has been making all his contact with us from the DC area."

"So, not Georgia, and the Georgetown location is too exposed," Emma says. "But Dr. Brown and I have found two references to Sudbury already. I think Travis is right – they could be in Massachusetts."

"And look at these scrapbook pictures." Brown turns to specific pages in the book: sketches of the house and trees, dried examples of flora. "This looks like New England to me. Glenn, these grasses here, and the flowers…Can we get an exact location match from these, to confirm?"

"Maybe," Neilsen says. "Carlos would know."

"We can get best-closest," Dixon confirms.

Travis uses a gloved fingertip to turn a page, frowning. "If Kristin wrote this, it was before her brother killed Hoyt and was moved to Byberry. So this gives us a window into her state of mind."

"*Her* state of mind," Emma reminds him. "Not Simon's."

"But that's the thing," Travis insists. "Kristin is his emotional touchstone. She's his heart. She directs him in ways we don't really understand."

Carter seems to agree. "Kirby is working on a theory from Becher that Kristin Gutmunsson has an almost symbiotic connection with her brother. She may have greater sway over him than we suspected."

"Think of the kind of relationship they have." Travis makes meaningful eye-contact with Emma, taps the uppermost Polaroid: A picture of Kristin, her white tresses floating around her face as she stands in the doorway of an old stone house. "And this scrapbook shows what's directing her – what's calling to her. This book is a lot of work. This isn't a new thing with her. She *likes* this place."

"Maybe…they grew up there?" Emma suggests.

Carter takes all this in, his expression serious. "Okay, we should contact Jack Kirby again and talk to Dr. Becher. I think we should be going to Sudbury."

CHAPTER TWELVE

Massachusetts, 1 November 1982

Their Delta flight leaves Washington International at 12:49PM, and they've been in the air just over ninety minutes when the seatbelt light comes on, and patrons in the rear are asked to extinguish their cigarettes. Emma reaches for her seatbelt. Travis has been talking with Carter, who is seated on the aisle a half dozen rows ahead, but after a word from the stewardess he returns, keeping his balance by holding onto the tops of seats as the plane judders.

He flumps down next to her at last. "Stewardess said to strap in. We're gonna get some turbulence on approach to Boston."

"Great."

"Not much they can do about bad weather. I'd just prefer it didn't happen when we're riding inside a tin can at altitude. Hold on one sec."

He rises again to collect his jacket out of the overhead bin. His face seems grim, his expressions contained, and Emma is keeping an eye on him – he's been weirdly quiet since Kirby routed everyone to Massachusetts, and she's not sure why. It's not unusual for Travis to be quiet, but this is a different kind of quiet, and it bothers her that she doesn't know where it's coming from.

As he's taking his seat once more, the plane pitches abruptly: little cut-off screams sound in the cabin. Travis is jolted onto Emma. His left hand grips her waist for balance, and his chest is warm at her shoulder.

"Whoa," he says. Their faces are close. "Okay, hi there."

"Hi." She examines his eyes, the strain in them. She's always been a fan of ripping the Band-Aid straight off. "How're you doing? Are you tired?"

Travis pulls away awkwardly and straightens, buckles his seatbelt. "A little. Same as you, I guess. I'll make it to tonight."

That reminds her. "When we get to Massachusetts, I need to check in with my folks and Audrey."

He nods. "I should call home, too. Even just to let Lena blow off steam and bawl me out a while."

Emma sees how he rubs at his breastbone unconsciously. Maybe it's really that simple. "Are you sore?"

"I'm fine." He sees her expression. "Okay, I'm kinda sore since the Kennedy Center. But I've taken some painkillers, so it'll be all right."

He's been taking the painkillers more frequently since they returned to Quantico, which bothers her. It's crazy that he's trying to keep up this pace when he only checked out of the hospital five and a half weeks ago.

"We should slow down a little," she suggests. "We've been going non-stop for the past three days, we should be scheduling in more rest time."

He shakes his head, lays his jacket across his knee. "I'd rather keep busy, get this done."

"Travis —"

"I just want to catch Gutmunsson and go home, you know?"

She does know, but she's not convinced that Travis driving himself into the ground is going to make it happen any faster. And something about his tone is plucking at her.

Out the window on the other side of the cabin, the sky is increasingly gray, like brushed concrete. The cabin rocks; Emma clutches her seat rests. Maybe now, here in public in the middle of flight turbulence, isn't the best time to talk about this.

Better to divert. "What do you think Kirby will do once we all get to Sudbury?"

"Carter said Kirby's already ordered a SWAT team from the Boston field office to high-tail it out there and check the Sudbury house isn't occupied." Travis shrugs. "In an ideal world, the Gutmunssons will be there, and SWAT plus Boston FBI will catch them, with minimal casualties."

Emma doesn't want to dream about guaranteed positive outcomes yet. "What about non-ideal world?"

Travis looks at his hands as he kneads his left palm with his right thumb. "Non-ideal world – the Boston team gets hurt, or the twins just aren't there. In that case, we examine any physical evidence at the house to figure out where they've gone. Heck, maybe we're shooting in the dark and they were never there to begin with."

"I don't believe that." Emma has a gut feeling about it. "I think you're right – there'll be something. Sudbury feels like a significant place. From Kristin's scrapbook, it seems like the place she's most emotionally connected to."

"It should be. Like you said, it's most likely where they grew up. And it's the place her brother was arrested."

"That's where they caught him in nineteen eighty?"

Travis nods, eyes still averted. "He'd been state-hopping – a murder in New Hampshire, a murder in Vermont. That's how the FBI got involved, when the cases crossed state lines. Finally, he killed another victim in Massachusetts, and someone put him at the location, and he became a person of interest."

Emma remembers what Cooper once said about it, long ago last June: That he wasn't at the arrest personally, that he'd been examining a crime scene. Another agent, Joe Gilet, had decided to bring Simon in for routine questioning, with US Marshal assistance.

Nobody realized how much danger they were in...

The knowledge hits her fast as the strobe of lightning outside the window of the plane.

"Oh shit." She stares at Travis. "Oh my god – that's where your dad died. In Sudbury."

"Yeah." Travis is looking determinedly away.

"Oh, Jesus." Now she understands his quiet. Now she gets it. Her hand is at her mouth. "Travis, I'm so sorry, I didn't make the connection –"

"It's okay."

"It's *not*." She drops her hand. "And this is...Wait a second – Travis, this is *nuts*. What are you doing, coming with us on this?"

"What, like I was gonna let you leave me behind?" He glances at her, focuses on the seat in front as his fingers clench in the fabric of his jacket, release. "It's fine."

"Like *hell* it's –" Her voice has climbed. She controls it, leans in, worried for him. "Like hell it's fine, it's the scene of your dad's *murder*. How are you gonna deal with that?"

"Badly, I guess." He meets her gaze at last, and his tone is matter of fact. "Emma, it's no different to what you had to deal with. We investigated Peter Kirke, we talked to serial offenders who assaulted women, murdered women. Every time we handled stuff like that, you had to cope. I'll...I'll cope with this."

She stares at him a moment. He's giving a very good impression of pragmatic resolve, but she can see the lines at the corners of his eyes, can feel the distress leaking out of him, and she's torn: It's very clear that no matter what she says, he's going to do this anyway.

She can share her misgivings, at least. "I think this is a bad idea. For the record."

"Okay." He keeps his eyes firmly elsewhere.

"Look, what you said is true – I coped with all the situations that reminded me of what happened with Huxton. But it wasn't healthy, and it took a toll, and every time I threw myself out there, you called me on it. I'm just saying, this is gonna hurt."

"I know," he says. "I'll deal with it."

Sure you will. But it's his choice. And all those times she confronted her past experiences, Travis was always around to prop her up and glue the pieces back together. Every time, he's been there. He's been her anchor when she needed one. She has to give him the same support, afford him the same dignity.

She still feels terrible about it.

"All right." She bites her lip. "But…keep talking with me. If it's too much, we'll figure out a way to make it easier."

His gaze sneaks her way. "Okay."

"And if you need to tap out, tell me. I'll give you a buffer."

He nods, exhales quietly through his nose. "Thanks."

"Jesus, Travis." The overhead lights flicker in the cabin as she puts her hand on his fist, squeezes. "You don't have to thank me. It's nothing you haven't done for me a hundred times."

His eyes say a lot. The cabin lights dim fully, and in the air-conditioned dark, his fingers open so he can hold her hand.

They reach Logan International in Boston by about twenty past four. Rain lashes the tarmac out the window, and in the Arrivals lounge, the speakers are playing a muzak version of the Captain and Tennille.

Near the lounge seating, they meet up with Kirby, Becher, and a young agent called Sullivan – slim, late twenties, ill-fitting gray suit and a trench coat, prominent ears – from the Boston field office. He's carrying a phone pack, and mixed news: The Boston team found the house empty, but it's not a dead end.

"The Gutmunssons have definitely been there, and recently," he says. "We found positive traces – food packaging, clothes, other items."

"So we're not far behind them." Kirby is pulling a navy woollen topcoat over his suit, adjusting his grip on a leather attaché case as they walk briskly through the terminal. "Has Boston set up a crime scene for examination?"

"The team's still on site, sir."

"Okay, then let's go."

Sullivan has the thankless task of organising cars at the Avis desk. Bad weather has stripped the carpool; Emma and Travis and Carter end up with a blue Chevy Sprint, a distinct step down from the Buick Century sedan claimed by Kirby. Emma still thinks it's a fair trade: Kirby's the one who has to cram in Becher, six-and-a-half-feet tall and bilious after the plane ride.

In the Sprint, Emma drives, because the little hatchback car feels comfortably like the Rabbit. Carter navigates in the front passenger seat, but by the time they get past Fenway Park and through the interchange at Auburndale, the weather's so bad she's wishing she'd given him the keys. Sleet is spattering the windshield, and the wipers are going a mile a minute. Other cars are drifting, throwing spray. Carter reaches to turn up the radio, but music can't compete with the wind; he switches over to a newscast.

"*...strong low-pressure system from the north east, with two to four inches of rain and gusts up to forty-five miles per hour.*" The announcer's

151

voice is inappropriately jaunty. *"If you're on the road, watch out for low visibility and slick asphalt –"*

Carter presses the button off. "Okay, so I guess we take it slow. Miss Lewis, past Weston, we should get off Route 20 and onto 27 at Wayland."

"You say those town names like they mean something to me." Emma's squinting through the windshield, chasing the red flare of Kirby's brake lights in the gray day's gloom.

"You want a candy bar?" Travis grabbed some snacks at the airport; there was lunch service on the plane, but Emma didn't eat much.

"Yes," she admits. "But it's so damn slippery, I don't think I should take my hands off the wheel."

"At least the car heating works," Carter says, droll.

Emma snaps a glance at Travis in the rear view. "You're reading through that precis of the Gutmunsson's history at the Sudbury house, right?"

"Yeah." His head lowers as he returns to studying the file. "It's been in the family since it was built in eighteen fifty-four. It's a two-story, Tudor-style stone villa on twenty-nine acres of land – originally two hundred fifty, but they subdivided and sold off a bunch of plots in the sixties. The house is nine bedrooms, six bathrooms, conservatory, dog kennels, stables and carriage house, yada yada."

Carter makes a low whistle. "Nice work, if you can get it."

"No kidding." Over the pummelling rain and the car's heater fan, the sound of Travis riffling pages in the back. "The land abuts conservation trails near the Sudbury River. Extensive gardens – stone fountains, walls, bridges. Hedge maze. Croquet court. Says here the entrance to the property is guarded by two stone lions imported from Europe? Wild. The whole shebang is currently valued at about four million."

"Out of all their properties," Emma asks, "this is the one the Gutmunssons spent the most time at as a family?"

"If you can call it that." Travis is still reading from the notes. "Ivar Gutmunsson spent months of the year away, overseeing his manufacturing businesses. Their mother, Alice, had social commitments that kept her busy...and she never seems to have been that interested in the whole parenting thing."

"So the twins were just left on their own."

"There were nannies and tutors, but basically, yeah. Remember what Kristin said at Quantico, back in June? Their parents had certain expectations, but there was never much follow-through."

Carter is looking out the windshield, nodding. "So – wealth, parental neglect, upbringing in an isolated fiefdom with disposable staff where you make your own rules but form no real relationships. Mix that with Simon Gutmunsson's psychopathology and you've got quite a combination."

They've reached Wayland, which is a collection of smeared blobs and tossing trees outside. Ten more minutes to Sudbury. As they get closer, the storm eases, and by the time Emma pulls the car right onto Water Row then left onto Plympton Road, the rain has reduced to drizzle.

"Kirby's turning up on the left," Carter says.

"I see it." Emma slows behind Kirby's car. Near the two stone lions, Agent Sullivan gets out of the Buick and pushes the black ironwork gate open on both sides, as his trench coat hems toss against his legs. He gets back in the Buick and Kirby eases the car through, Emma following in the Sprint.

The gravel drive is shaded past the gate. Emma inches the car forward, leaning closer to peer through the windshield as they travel deep into the woods of the estate. It's been over two years since anyone lived here, and everything is overgrown. Trees encroach on the driveway, and wind pushes them closer still, making the road a shadowed tunnel. Both the storm and general neglect has produced a lot of debris; the Sprint's tires crunch on leaf litter and twigs. Ahead, Kirby's switched on his headlights, so Emma does the same. Both cars have to steer around a fallen branch. Rainwater patters on the car, shaken from the trees by the wind gusts. Emma finds the woods give the location a sense of seclusion and gloomy menace, as though visitors are unwelcome.

"Were any of Simon's victims found on this property?" *Apart from Travis's dad.* She doesn't say that aloud.

"Not that I'm aware of," Carter says.

The drive widens out suddenly, the trees receding and shrubs pulling back from the road. The view is opened, and gray-washed light returns. Up ahead, an operations van and another dark sedan are parked near a stone fountain strangled with weeds in the middle of the turning circle. And now the house is exposed: tall and dark and stately, pewter-colored stone tinted green with moss and a riot of ivy, flanked by yew trees.

The house is not as immense or in the same style as St Elizabeths, but Emma notices a strange symmetry in the gothic angles, the black-framed windows. A marble Jacobean arch, at least ten feet high, frames a huge dark door.

"Go right," Carter suggests. "Park near the fountain."

Kirby's car disgorges its passengers, and now officers emerge from the house and the van, some in suits and overcoats, some in SWAT black. Emma shivers just watching the way the freezing wind tosses their clothes. It's going to be hard to leave the warm interior of the car.

Carter drags his own overcoat from the rear seat. "Give me a minute to figure out what's happening."

He exits the car; damp cold blows in hard through the gap as he quickly opens and closes the front passenger door. Travis leans forward, over the center console, watching the parties converge, and watching the house like it's crouched ready for ambush. Maybe, for him, it is.

"Have you been here before?" Emma asks.

"Not in person." His muscles are tense; she can hear how shallow his breathing has become. "In my mind, a lot of times."

The FBI group heads back toward the house. Carter turns as he walks, waves for them to come.

"Are you gonna be able to do this?" Emma asks quietly.

Travis takes a large inhale, grabs the door handle. "Let's find out."

CHAPTER THIRTEEN

Sudbury, 1 November 1982

The house where his father died is not like Travis imagined.

Even though he saw the photos from Simon Gutmunsson's old arrest report, they didn't show a lot of detail of the surrounding landscape. He'd always pictured some sort of Italianate mansion – big windows, fussy décor – nothing like this heavy stone edifice: half mausoleum, half rampart. The house has a presence. Maybe it's his father's spirit, but he guesses there are many old ghosts here.

"Where did it happen?" Emma asks, hunched in her black pea coat as they crunch across the gravel toward the big door.

"In the front hallway." Travis feels slapped in the cheeks by the wind. He's ignoring his slight shortness of breath, the way he's sweating under his jacket. "Gutmunsson was trying to get to a car out here in the drive. He'd seen the officers out front, rushed back to his sister. Grabbed her as a hostage."

"At her suggestion."

"Yeah."

His father had taken point in the hallway, and the other agent – Gilet – had been at the front door. After Simon Gutmunsson had dragged his twin out of the piano room and into the hall, an exchange had taken place: Barton Bell, an ordinary guy, trading himself for Kristin Gutmunsson, a victim of privilege. Travis thinks about this scene a lot, wonders sometimes if some of the numbness he feels around his dad's death is suppressed anger. His father had worried about everyone's safety but his own, when he'd actually been the lynchpin that had held their family together...

There's no time or space for this. He and Emma have slung on their FBI lanyards and taken the two front steps, crossed the marble dais to the massive door, wedged half open to allow entry. Immediately inside, out of the wind, they find Kirby, Martino, Carter, and Becher receiving a briefing on the operation from another man in SWAT fatigues and a police ballcap. Travis can see movement farther ahead: men taking the stairs, men talking, men searching, and documenting the results of those searches.

"...found all the evidence for documentation?" Kirby is digging for notes from his attaché case, to check his data against the SWAT guy's information.

"Yessir," the SWAT guy says. He tugs at his flak vest. "We think we got it all. My recommendation is that we pull back after we've finalized the sweep. Once we've done a last check of the grounds, we can call it."

"I agree." Kirby consults his watch. "I've got someone from the DC Scientific Analysis group coming soon, they're about an hour and a half behind us."

Travis angles sideways and moves past the group and into the entry hallway, dim with brown-stained dado. The hallway spills out into a big flagstone foyer with a grand staircase – dark Tudor balustrade, dark stairs, dark walls. Everything in this house is dark.

Black iron chandeliers hang suspended from the twenty-foot ceiling. There's a green velvet runner on the stairs; the rug under his boots is blood red, probably Persian, heavily napped and smelling of damp. It's very cold; the last time Travis felt this cold was in Peter Kirke's warehouse.

He looks to the right of the balustrade. Some furniture there, draped in white, along with a big grandfather clock. Past that, according to the arrest report, is the old piano room. With all these people moving around, he can't pinpoint the place on the foyer floor where his father bled out. He stands there, feeling anaesthetized. There's a tightness in his chest.

"It's freezing in here." Emma is suddenly nearby, rubbing her arms through her coat. She's squinting at officers coming and going through another marble arch to the left of the stairs, which is better lit. "Come on."

She tugs on his sleeve, and Travis follows because what else can he do? They pass under the arch, and the passage curls around to the right. Light in the passage comes through dozens of panelled-glass windows – while the illumination is palled with gray, it's still an improvement on the darkness of the foyer. Racks of pots below the windows hold dead and dying plants.

Farther along, the space widens into a grotto with a wooden table and chairs, and there's action here: yellow evidence markers, cordon tape. On the table, Travis sees a sketch book, an embroidered pouch with colored pencils spilling out, a teacup and saucer, a hairbrush. It's undeniable proof of life.

"Kristin," Emma breathes.

Travis can almost imagine Kristin Gutmunsson sitting at this table, brushing her long white hair, sipping from her teacup and sketching. He looks around; if he'd come to hide out for a few days, he'd sit in this greenhouse-conservatory, too. The table might be surrounded by dead plants, but it's the only place in the house where the air feels breathable.

There's more than one chair drawn up to the table, though.

"They were both here." Travis signals to one of the team members currently arranging more tape to secure the scene for Gerry Westfall's arrival. "Is there more?"

The man pauses, blinks. "Who are you with?"

Travis taps his lanyard ID, reins his impatience. "We're with Special Agent Kirby. Are there more evidence sites?"

"Plenty." The guy gestures with his chin back the way they've come. "Upstairs, in one of the bedrooms. Some stuff in the bathroom there, and down here in the kitchen, too. If we'd been maybe an hour earlier, the gas ring would've still been warm."

Travis leads Emma back out to the foyer, up the stairs with the green velvet runner. He can see dust on a lot of surfaces. His chest still feels peculiarly squeezed. On the landing, he stops to catch his breath.

When he straightens, Emma touches his waist. "Okay?"

He nods. "Okay."

Second floor. The bedroom is second on the left side of the balcony, and it confirms a lot of what Travis has already suspected.

"There's the suit jacket Simon wore to the Kennedy Center," Emma says, pointing at the dark fabric hanging off the back of a wooden chair.

White dustcloths have been pulled off the furniture in here. There's an overnight bag with a glimpse of emerald silk peeking out between the zipper, opalescent fire. On an otherwise empty dressing table, some cosmetics, a wineglass. There's charcoal in the fireplace, still faintly smoking. A pile of what look like old blankets lies massed on the four-poster; as Travis comes closer, he realizes they're fur coats, four or five of them heaped on the bare mattress.

Emma looks around, stunned. "It's like they just got up and went for a walk."

Travis nods at the fur coats, catches Emma's eye. "One bed."

Emma rubs at her nape. "What do we do now?"

"We go on to town," Carter says. He's appeared behind them, standing in the doorway. "Everyone's waiting for Gerry Westfall to come and examine the evidence – no one's allowed to move anything until he arrives. It's nearly quarter to six. I suggest we go into Sudbury proper, find a place to stay, come back later tonight or early tomorrow morning when we have some results. Sound all right to you?"

Emma looks to Travis for an answer. He sucks his teeth. A longing part of him wants to stay here, dig deeper, turn up every single scrap he can find that will unearth the Gutmunssons.

"The state guys are also worried about the weather." Carter takes a step inside, squints out the second-story lead glass window at the tossing trees. "Either way, there's no electricity to the house – Jack's organizing to rig some lights so we can keep working."

"Sounds like we'll be waiting around awhile," Emma says. "A hotel might be a better option."

"Uh-huh." Carter exhales, and Travis remembers the man was up all night, helping sort out the Kennedy Center mess. "Let's get ourselves set up in town, doorknock at local stores to see if the twins bought supplies or gas for a vehicle there. Maybe an early dinner, then we come back here."

Travis works to uncurl his fists. "It feels like we just missed them."

"They're close, that's for sure." Carter starts walking out the door. "Come on, I'll drive us in to Sudbury."

Travis lets himself be dragged away.

At the Shaw's Grocery in Sudbury, they discover that the Gutmunsson siblings bought cigarettes, coffee, candy, bread, vitamin C, and cheese. Also a bottle of wine, from a guy who said Simon looked over twenty-one.

"Vitamins?" Travis examines the copy of the receipt they were given. "They've got a vitamin deficiency?"

"No." Emma's cheeks are pink from the cold. "I have a hunch it's for Simon's hair – he dyed it for the Kennedy Center. Vitamin C helps strip out hair dye. Sounds like he's trying to get back to white-blond."

"And not a single person recognized them."

Carter takes the receipt and adds it to his file folder. "When they were still owner-occupiers, it's likely the family ordered household supplies to be delivered. Shopping in-person for local groceries might have been a new experience for the Gutmunssons."

They continue door-knocking and making inquiries at stores. It's hard to get a good sense of the shape of the town in the late afternoon half-dark, but Travis thinks it's mostly old cemetery. As they stop at the Sundries & SG Gasoline on Boston Post Road, the Goodwill on Hudson, the clouds build and darken again, and the wind picks up in the streets. Travis feels antsy, and he doesn't think it's the weather: It's the scent of quarry close by. He feels weirdly alert but exhausted. Sometimes, when he looks down, his hands are shaking.

The rain starts back up. It's close to seven when they stop at a historic local hotel and book rooms, including additional reservations for Kirby, Martino, and Becher.

Travis's room is thick-walled with a sway-back armchair and a big window, warm with lamplight and rugs, and the radiator's soft sigh. When he pulls aside the curtain, there's a rumbling crack of lightning outside. He grabbed a toothbrush at the same general store where the

Gutmunsson twins bought snacks, and it's the only thing he has to leave in the hotel room when he emerges to go downstairs.

Emma is closing her own door behind herself, three rooms along.

"Room okay?" he asks.

"Yeah, it's fine." She scratches a hand through her short hair, straightens her flannel shirt. "I called my dad and Audrey, told them we'd be here at least one night. But I'm running out of steam. I really need to sleep."

"I hear that."

"Are you doing all right?"

He tries to make an honest appraisal. "I'm tired. The house was weird, and I feel…on edge." She has experience with this stuff, he recalls. "Is it like this for you?"

"Sometimes." She touches his cheek. "You need a break."

"I need a hug," he says gruffly. "Come 'ere."

She hugs him, and he tries to relax into it. The warmness of her is some respite, as she slips her arms inside his jacket lapels to get closer. Eventually they break apart to go downstairs and eat, before it's time to head back to the estate.

But in the couch area before the dining room, an unexpected surprise: Gerry Westfall and Carlos Dixon are talking to Carter by the big fireplace. Westfall is smoking in an armchair, Dixon is still taking off his overcoat.

"Bad news," Carter says, as he sees Emma and Travis approaching.

"It's crazy out there," Dixon says, lifting his chin to the lashing black out the window, shaking off his flat cap. "We couldn't get through to the Gutmunsson house. A big tree came down across the driveway – a white oak or something."

"A *tree* fell across the driveway?" Travis squints at the two of them.

"I know, right? This is what happens when I leave Washington, I should just never travel." Westfall ashes his smoke in the general direction of the fire. "Road crew can't get there for at least two hours. The guy at the desk here said there's another house in town with a collapsed roof that they have to deal with first. But when they *do* finally get to Plympton Road, it'll take at least an hour to clear."

"What about Kirby and Becher and the others?" Emma asks.

Westfall flicks again with his cigarette. "Carlos got out of the car when we first arrived and talked to this Boston guy, Sullivan, through the tree branches. The wind was tossing everything around, and it was raining...I thought they were both gonna get blown away, or washed away, maybe."

Dixon takes over the story. "Sullivan said SWAT managed to get out before the house was cut off. I dropped Gerry here and drove back with some supplies for Kirby and the others. They're gonna hole up tonight, they've got blankets inside, and wood for the fire."

Emma is frowning. "So they're stuck there? In the Gutmunsson's house?"

The idea makes Travis feel faintly sick.

"They'll be fine for one night," Westfall reassures. "They can babysit my evidence for me and we'll try again in the morning – all our gear is in the rental car outside."

"Doesn't sound like anyone should be driving around tonight," Carter says. "So it might be more correct to say we're *all* stuck in place." He turns to Westfall and Dixon. "I guess you gentlemen can take two of the rooms we reserved for the others, and I'll cancel the third."

Westfall clambers out of his armchair. "You handle the room bookings, I'm going to order dinner."

"If you're gonna smoke in the dining room, get a table away from me," Dixon says, following behind.

Carter heads for the front desk, and the two Scientific Analysis experts continue into the dining area, their gentle squabble ongoing. Emma turns Travis's way with a sigh.

"I mean, I'm glad we're not spending the night stuck at that house?"

His jaw tightens as he stares out the window. "We just missed the Gutmunssons. It's crazy that we just missed them."

"Tomorrow." Emma nudges him. "We'll find evidence and catch up with them."

He looks at her. "You want this over as much as I do."

"So much."

The howling thump of the wind outside echoes in his heart. His chest, which has been bugging him all day, is constricted, and now his middle back is starting to complain.

"Hey," he says, deciding suddenly, "I don't think I can do dinner. You're right about needing a break, I might just go upstairs and lie down."

Emma frowns. "Are you in pain?"

Is he in pain? He isn't sure, but sitting up at dinner is sure to make it worse. "I could do with a few hours of laying flat."

"You want me to bring something up?"

The idea of a tray of covered dishes makes him oddly nauseous. "Nah. Tell Carter and the others I'm sorry."

"They'll probably just sit around talking work," Emma predicts. "I may not be far behind you, actually, I'm pretty beat."

"Okay."

He squeezes her shoulder, walks away from the warm couch area to the stairwell. Taking the stairs is likely his last exertion for the day.

On the second floor, the carpet is spongy in the hall. Lights in their wall sconces dim briefly, recover their glow; Travis thinks of how the lights in the Kennedy Center auditorium dimmed before the second act of *Turandot*, and the terrible outcomes of that.

He lets himself into his room; the rugs in here are nicer, and with the radiator on, the air has lost its chill. He swallows two Percocet with water from the bathroom, brushes his teeth, shucks his shoes and jacket and belt. It's the first time all day that he's had a moment of quiet for himself.

For all that he told Emma he needed to rest, he stands at the window for a while, holding the curtain and peering out beyond the glass as the trees in the street whip their branches in the night. The storm is really going now. Sleet spatters the window, and the way the clouds are moving creates shifting shadows outside.

Travis squints: It looks like someone is standing just beyond the dim circle of light from the streetlamp on the opposite curb. The streetlamp flickers, and for a moment, the figure is his father, blood on his arms and neck. Then it's Kristin Gutmunsson in her shimmering green gown, white hair streaming. Then it's nobody: a USPS mailbox.

He's losing it. He rubs his face with cold hands. What is he doing here? Emma was right: What purpose is served by him being in Massachusetts? He doesn't know anymore.

The lights in the hotel room stutter. All the bulbs – the lamp on his nightstand, the bathroom light – flare briefly, then with a humming pop, all go out. Travis flinches. In the sudden blackness, there's a little exclamation somewhere down the hall, nervous muffled sounds from other rooms.

He calms himself, looks around in the dark, out through the window: The outside streetlamp has blown as well. Town-wide power outage, maybe a line down. The Gutmunsson estate isn't the only place trees are falling tonight.

Hands outstretched, he finds his way to the nightstand, tries the lamp – on-off, on-off. Nothing. He's considering crawling into bed in his clothes when there's a knock at the door, and he startles.

"It's me."

When he fumbles over and opens the door, Emma's standing there with two candles in old-fashioned hurricane glass holders.

"Hey." She moves past him, sets one candle down on the coffee table. "Hotel management is giving these out – I said I'd bring you one. The whole building is blacked out."

"I figured." He closes the door behind her.

She sets the other candle on the nightstand. "Dinner was kind of a bust, I think everyone is just giving up and going to bed." The view out the window catches her eye, and she moves closer to the sill. "Oh my god, look at it out there."

Travis walks over beside her. "Even the weather is fighting us."

"Hey." Emma squeezes his forearm. "We'll find them. Simon and Kristin can't have gone far."

"Every time we get close, they disappear like smoke." Travis leans at the window, his other arm up on the frame. "I feel as if I'm chasing a ghost."

Emma angles to face him. "No – they're real. The ghost is here." She puts her palm on his chest, over his heart. "Travis, do you really think your dad would want you to be here? Seeing the place where he died? Hurting yourself over and over like this?"

The candles behind them are reflecting in the glass. Outside, the storm thrashes in the street and throws rain into the night. Travis feels old, way older than his years.

"I don't know," he says softly.

"You did the best you could for your mom and your sisters." Emma's voice is gentle. "I think he would tell you to let go now. To live."

Travis blinks against the dark. "You're putting words in his mouth, and you never met him."

"I feel like I know him. He raised *you*, didn't he?"

And those words crack him open, or just widen the crack already there, deep under his ribs. He is his father's son. The things that anger him, that frustrate him, about what his father did – the self-sacrifice, the altruism, the honor…Travis knows those are also his own qualities, or qualities he aspires to. *He* would walk into the path of danger to save a life. He would give of himself until there was nothing left. His father led by example, and the idea that Emma can see a reflection of Barton Bell in him – like the golden reflection of the candles – gives Travis an almost overwhelming swell of gratitude and grief.

"I thought I saw my dad outside, near the streetlamp," he whispers in confession.

Emma leans against his shoulder. "Tell me about him."

"He was a big guy. Strong. But patient, you know?"

"Yeah."

"He met my mom when they were still in high school. Her parents didn't like him. He was white, he came from dirt. But he fought his way out of it, became a Marshal. He won my grandparents over in the end." Travis smiles to remember it. "All those times he was teaching me – how to ride a bike, how to catch a fish…How to throw a punch. Shoot a gun. He was giving me a part of himself, for the times when I'd need it."

"He sounds like a good dad."

"I still can't believe it, most days. That he's not around."

"Do you get angry?"

"A lot of times, yeah. I get angry at him almost as often as I get angry at Gutmunsson. I know that's not fair."

Emma shakes her head. "There's no wrong way to feel, with this stuff."

The drugs have loosened his tongue. "I think I've had this hole in my heart since he passed. And maybe part of me has always secretly believed that his destiny was my destiny. That it's what men in this job do – they fight the world's battles, and they die fighting. My dad wasn't the only one. Agent Cooper died the same way. All my role models have died fighting."

Emma goes still beside him. "Is that what you really want?"

Travis turns and looks at Emma – the sharp planes of her face, the spiky darkness of her hair, her wide, questioning eyes. He sees light streaming off her, tracers in his vision. This girl...this girl is like a star. A glimmering north star, a beacon, and he needs that so much right now.

"All I know is that I want you," he blurts, and he reaches out, brings her face to his.

She gasps into his mouth. He catches her breath, draws it down into his own lungs like medicine. Her lips are so soft, and the softness helps assuage the ache in his chest, and her arms slide up around his neck in slow motion as the kiss goes on and on.

When they pull apart, she's breathless, cheeks rosy. "Wait, you're tired..."

He doesn't reply, can't, too busy kissing down her neck. Every place her skin is exposed – ear, nape, wrist – he touches with his lips, with his rough cheek, with the tender pads of his fingers. Emma makes small noises, little mewling gasps, and he wishes he could be less clumsy with this, but he's too desperate. Then she's pushing him back, and he thinks maybe she'll berate him or walk out, but she doesn't do either of those things.

"If you're not tired," she says, voice faintly shaking, "I'm taking off your shirt."

This is not what he was expecting at all. But soon enough, they are on his bed, and Emma is straddling him in that way she likes. The Percocet is flooding his system, and everything is painted in the swirling, glinting colors of the deep ocean, or the night sky, so when she says, "I want to touch you here," his head sinks on the pillow, and he says, "Touch me anywhere you want."

The top of his skull is blowing back a little with the feel of her mouth on his neck, with the way they're panting in unison. The music in the room is the soft sound of clothing being removed or pushed aside, the lash of the storm beyond the window, the noises they make as they please or surprise each other.

"Put your hands on me," Emma whispers, and he obeys, squeezes, is rewarded.

Candlelight flickers as he runs his palms over the scars on her midriff. He always thought he'd be managing this, making everything right for her, exerting control. But it's not like that. She takes over. He can let go. He loses his wits with her. Turns out that's okay.

Afterward, when they're both replete, her naked back tucks long against his bare front. Their arms and legs curl up together, and Travis finds sleep. In his dreams, he's wrapped in a warm, weighted blanket and he feels peaceful.

When he wakes early, there's sun coming through the window. The candles have guttered out, but the bathroom bulb is glowing – the power is back on. Emma's neck is under his lips, and her breast is soft in his hand. It's a good way to wake up.

She turns in his arms, wincing against the daylight. "What time s'it?"

"Just on seven." He plants small kisses from her ear to her collar-bone, like a row of daisies. Her skin is edible. "One of these days, we're gonna get to sleep in."

"But not today," she sighs, strokes his chest. "Are you okay?"

"Better," he says, and he smiles because it's true. Today he feels like he can walk back into the world.

After showers, and doing what they can with the same clothes they had on yesterday, they meet up with Carter and Westfall and Dixon downstairs. Westfall is grumpy until Dixon plies him with cinnamon rolls from the breakfast buffet. Carter orders to-go coffee for Kirby and the others, returns from an outside trip to the Sprint, shaking his head.

"The streets are still slippery as hell, we'll have to take it easy driving back to Plympton Road. Are we caffeinated? Can we go?"

"Take some of these for Jack," Westfall says, waving a roll. "Put him in a good humor."

When they return to the Gutmunsson estate, the road crew is just finishing with their chainsaws in the driveway. In the early light of the morning, steam is rising off the gravel, off the men working. Travis watches Carter speak with them. Chunks of sawed oak-wood are piled to one side. Emma yawns, rests her head on the seat back to get some sun on her face. Westfall gets out of his rental Ford and smokes a cigarette, talks to Dixon through the open passenger window.

Fifteen minutes later, the road crew departs and Carter puts the Sprint in gear, and they drive farther to the turning circle, where Kirby's Plymouth is parked alone.

Travis is surprised neither Kirby nor any of the other men come out to meet them when they arrive, even for the promise of hot coffee and cinnamon rolls. But when they get inside, he realizes why.

It's because everyone is dead.

CHAPTER FOURTEEN

Sudbury, 2 November 1982

On the far west side of the Gutmunsson house, under the front eaves, there's a paper wasp nest. Emma sits on the step of the marble dais in front of the Gutmunsson's front door, tries to stop shaking, watches the nest to see if any wasps emerge. She's always hated wasps, and right now, the idea of encountering one feels like the absolute last straw.

But no wasps appear. The forest around the house is still. After the initial commotion thirty minutes ago, when she and the others arrived, everything is now ominously quiet.

She'll be directing the FBI cars whenever they get here, quarantining the scene, and alerting Carter to their arrival. The Boston field office is sending multiple cars, a paramedic, and a medical examiner's van. It's lucky Simon Gutmunsson left Sullivan's Motorola pack undamaged, or they would've had to drive back to Sudbury proper to use the phone; with the pack, they were able to call for backup straight away.

The drive from Boston only takes a half hour if the support crew is coming in a hurry, which Emma thinks is likely. She's expecting them any minute, but that's not the only reason she's sitting out here on the dais. She's out here because she can't stand to be inside the mansion right now. Because the smell of blood, the abattoir scenes in each room and the imprint of violence in the house, is overwhelming.

For a moment, standing in the hall when they first arrived, she'd been thrown back into a sense-memory of Huxton's basement: the high-pitched sounds of screaming and the iron tang of rent flesh. She'd tried to steady, tried to breathe through it. But when she'd overheard Carter explaining on the phone to Boston that they needed extra body bags, as some of the dead men had been reduced to parts, it had all crowded in on her, and she'd stumbled outside and been violently sick. After that, Carter recommended she stay out front. It makes her feel weak, but she has no task to perform in the house and it's probably for the best.

So now she's just stuck here with her thoughts. It's been very hard to disconnect her memories of Jack Kirby – his bluff, commanding presence and pale, alert eyes, his neat fastidious suits a reflection of his old mentor, Ed Cooper – from the sight of his mutilated body in the mansion's living room. Or her mental image of Mike Martino, who's been present with them through all this from the beginning, from the gory display upstairs. She thinks of the way Martino shook Travis's hand when they first arrived back at Quantico, genuinely collegial; that man is unrecognizable now.

Emma wants very much to uncouple these before-and-after recollections, because not doing so feels wrong; when her time comes, when she dies, she hopes she'll be remembered as a person, not as a cooling chunk of meat. She should afford these men the same decency, but her brain keeps cycling with the juxtaposition: Kirby in life…Kirby in his current form…Martino in life…Martino in pieces…

And she can't stop thinking about what she and Travis did last night, how it changed her, and the way she woke up with Travis's warm hands on her this morning. She feels the sensations even now, in her body. But she doesn't want her memories of last night mixed with today's horrors. It's not fair, and it makes her feel soiled and guilty, as if she got distracted last night and this was the result.

It also gives her the awful sense that Simon Gutmunsson knows them too well, that he's saving all his most horrifying surprises for the moments when they're most vulnerable, most exposed.

We need to catch him. I need to get my shit together.

On the marble step, Emma draws her knees up under her chin. The opposite side of the dais is where she lost her breakfast on the gravel; Westfall has marked that place with a small yellow evidence tag. Above her, maybe twelve feet farther along, the wasp nest hangs suspended like a malevolent gray beach ball. The wasps are in there, dormant. Lurking. It's one of the things she hates most about them: The insects inside are hidden, waiting for the time when they can explode out and inflict pain and wreak havoc, like the Gutmunsson twins have done in this house –

"Miss Lewis?"

"*Jesus!*" Emma startles.

"Oh, hey." Carlos Dixon stands near the door with his palms up. His close-set brown eyes are soft above his moustache and goatee. "Hey, I didn't mean to do that. I'm sorry."

"It's okay." Emma releases her fist from its death-clutch over her heart. "It's fine, I just…I'm a little jumpy. Boston's not here yet."

"I saw. I'm not here for that." Dixon steps nearer, shoulders slumped, digging in his coat pocket and pulling out a single cigarette and a Bic lighter. "I came out for a smoke."

"But you don't smoke," Emma blurts. "You don't even like the smell of Dr. Westfall's cigarettes –"

"Wrong," Dixon says, sticking the filter between his teeth. "I like it too much. That's the problem. I gave up nine years ago. I could easily walk into the nearest store and buy a pack and start right back up, that's how much I still miss it." He lights up and sighs smoke. "Today, especially. I hope I never have to work a crime scene like this again."

Emma moves over so he can sit nearby. Dixon settles on the step, with his forearms resting on his knees, looking spent.

She gives him a minute to inhale and exhale before she asks her question. "Are you able to, um…"

"We can't unhook the bodies from the fishing line he used." Dixon breathes out a gust, rubs his forehead with the edge of the same hand holding the cigarette. "We can't even take Sullivan down, so it's respectful. Gerry still needs to take a bunch of photos, and there's way more evidence and measurements to collect, and a whole heap of other stuff…"

"Will you have more help once Boston arrives?"

"I guess. Although they'll probably tramp over everything like a herd of elephants." Dixon drops his hand, looks off into the wild gardens beside the driveway turning circle. For a moment, his eyes show stark despair. "This is always so much harder when it's colleagues."

"I know," Emma says. "I know, and I'm sorry."

"Jack Kirby could be an asshole," Dixon says, with surprising candor, "but he didn't deserve to die like that. *Nobody* deserves to die like that."

Emma hardly knows what to say.

"This is so…" Dixon struggles to articulate it. "I want to say *brazen*, but it's not the right word. A crime like this isn't just audacious – it shows a kind of defiance. Excuse my language, but Simon Gutmunsson doesn't give a shit about what the FBI does. He's giving everyone a big *Fuck you*."

Dixon is right. Simon has cut a swathe of damage since before his arrest – numerous FBI agents and other law enforcement staff have been killed in action during investigations he's been connected with – but the murders of Kirby and Martino and Sullivan and Becher have dropped like a hammer blow. Simon has struck deep into the command center of *this* investigation, the one designed to catch him. He wants them all to know he's a law unto himself.

But it's the other implication which Emma finds most terrifying. These murders are sending another message, and that message is *Nobody is safe*. If Simon can kill three trained agents and a specialist consultant in such a horrific way, he can kill anybody.

Anybody at all.

The early sun has dulled. Feeling cold in her bones, Emma tucks her coat more firmly under herself. "Um, Boston should be here any minute. But I can go back in, if you really need help with –"

"No." Dixon shakes his head, takes another drag. "Don't do it to yourself. You and Bell have seen enough to give you nightmares already."

"Travis is still in there," she reminds him. "And I saw Berryville."

"This is different. Berryville was an imperative, like a compulsion. And it was utilitarian. It served Anthony Hoyt's purpose. This isn't about purpose, this is just..." Dixon's lip curls. "Gutmunsson was just playing with them. He did this for *fun*."

"Did Dr. Westfall figure out when it happened?" Emma asks quietly.

"Best estimate, between four and five in the morning." Dixon grinds out his smoke against the sole of his shoe, pockets the butt. "None of the bodies are in full rigor. They've been dead two or three hours, tops."

"How did Simon kill all four men on his own?"

"Bell and Carter are trying to step that out right now." Dixon meets her eyes. "I've never seen Howard so mad. He's not saying much, but that man is out for vengeance."

Emma understands. "Tell him as soon as Boston arrives, I'll call for him."

Dixon nods and stands, looks out over the gardens, drinking in the sight and smell of outside before visibly bracing, turning around, and going back into the charnel house that the Gutmunsson residence has become.

Emma rubs her hands to warm them, pressing down hard on the swirl of images in her head, the anxiety deep in her soul. Five minutes later, she hears sirens, and soon after that, three black Diplomats heave out of the forest and into the turning circle. Behind them, an ambulance, and a white Ford F-150 pickup with the county medical examiner's logo.

At last, something useful to do.

Emma stands, holds up her FBI identification on its lanyard as men spill out of the vehicles and approach. "Gentlemen, excuse me, gentlemen. Special Agent Carter requests that you wait here for him to meet with you before entering –"

"Stand aside, miss." The man in front is dough-faced, at least mid-forties, with broad Southie vowels. He's trying to move past her. "Royce Sullivan is one of my men, and I ain't gonna be bossed around by no teenage skirt –"

"Sullivan's dead," Emma says flatly. She counters the man's accent with some Apple Creek twang of her own, raises her voice so they can all hear it: There are eight men in the response group currently crowding in on her, and they're all older and taller and more qualified than she is. Her arms are held out, lanyard dangling, an official block. "I'm real sorry, but he's dead. And there are three other men in this house. Two of them are agents I've worked with. Sir –" She checks the ID facing forward through his coat lapels. "Agent Obersby, I understand how you feel, but you can't go inside yet. I was told to quarantine this crime scene until Agent Carter arrives to escort you, and I'm gonna do just that."

"Whaddya mean *quarantine*?" Obersby's face reddens as he glowers. He stays put, but he's trying to see over her shoulder. "Who gave that order? I wanna speak to –"

"I gave that order." It's Howard Carter's baritone, the man appearing behind her as he steps out and closes the big wooden door. Carter's wearing a blue paper crime scene suit over his clothes. His shoulders are set, and his typically calm, stoic face is stiff and cold. "I'm trying to preserve a crime scene here. If you want to speak to someone, speak to me."

Obersby purses his lips, but he and his men back off. "Special Agent Carter, I'm guessing? Look, I don't wanna butt heads, but I'm the one who's gonna be calling Sullivan's wife. If you can tell me what the hell's going on –"

"Agent Obersby..." Carter softens by one degree. "I'm sorry to hold you up, and I'm sorry your man is dead. I'll give you and your people access, but I already have Scientific Analysis here from DC, so my priority is making sure they get a clear shot at the evidence before folks start walking on it."

"DC squints are here already? So do you know who did this?"

"We know," Carter says gravely, before turning to Emma. "Miss Lewis, you let me sort this out. If you wouldn't mind escorting that man there, who looks like the paramedic –"

"Sanchez." The man in an EMT uniform at the back is pushing his way forward, using his orange medical gear box as a wedge, waving his ID.

Carter nods at him, back to Emma. "Lewis, if you could take Mr. Sanchez through to the kitchen first."

"Got it," Emma says promptly, although the thought of returning to the inside of the house makes her swallow. She ushers with one hand. "This way, sir."

She guides the paramedic through the door as Carter begins his litany: "Agent Obersby, I'm going to need help with moving and transporting the bodies to the Boston ME's office, as well as…"

His voice fades as the door closes. Emma moves to the occasional table that Carlos Dixon set up in the entry way. "Sir? Mr. Sanchez? We've got to put on Tyvek booties before going in."

"Yes, yes." Sanchez is a small, fit-looking older man with gray at his temples, who knows the routine. But his gaze is drawn away from Emma and down the hallway to the dark balustrade of the house's main staircase, where the body of Royce Sullivan hangs suspended.

Emma works to keep to her task, slipping the blue paper booties over her shoes. She pushes down on the feeling of dread that has bubbled up now she's back inside the mansion. Once she and Sanchez are appropriately outfitted, she leads down the hall, veering left.

But they have to pass the balustrade, and she sees Sanchez take in the way Sullivan is displayed: arms out like a crucifixion, his shirt sliced open in front and parted delicately to reveal that his torso has been opened in the same way. Sullivan's innards spill out like a tangle of bloody laundry, and some of his intestines are arranged like bunting around his body, framing his red heart, which has been pulled free from behind his exposed ribs and pinned to his breastbone with a long sharp hatpin. The hatpin has an ostentatious green jewel decorating the pinhead, and it catches the dim light.

Sullivan's head hangs forward, his large ears prominent. His mouth and eyes are open wide, as if he's looking down in surprise to see his heart so badly misplaced, and so strangely embellished.

"Madre de Dios," Sanchez whispers, as they pass. "Are they all like this?"

"Yes. Some are worse." Emma is sorry to inflict this on other people. She keeps her vision trained determinedly down and breathes through her mouth. "This way, please."

They go through the curving hall she thinks of as the greenhouse, although all the plants are dead. She's glad that Carter asked her to escort Sanchez to the kitchen, and not to where Jack Kirby is sawn in half in the living room, or upstairs, where pieces of Mike Martino have been dropped like breadcrumbs leading the way to the bulk of him in the second bedroom...

She feels a kind of blankness in her spirit, exhales slow and even.

She wants to be close to Travis right now. But he's with Carter and Westfall in the living room, 'stepping out' the crime scene, a borrowed FBI jacket over his clothes and his game face on like law enforcement is all he's ever been. She knows he's shaken, and wildly angry, and assuming his old professional persona is helping him cope with the situation. But it's almost physically painful, watching him perform this version of himself. Last night he told her that all his role models had died in this job, and Emma is buffeted by both fear and rage at how he's been pulled back in.

She squeezes her hands into fists. *Wait until we're out of here, and the stink of death has washed off. Then he'll come back.* That's what she hopes.

She and Sanchez have reached the kitchen now. It's a large flag-stone-floored room with big, panelled windows along the right, dark buttresses at the ceiling. A tall black farmhouse door is at the far side, and Carter thinks that's where Simon entered the house. A round iron cande-labra, medieval-looking, hangs above a solid oak kitchen table.

Dr. Stanley Becher lies stretched on that table. Of all the men, his body is the most preserved, although his shirt has been cut off and a broad line of ugly black stitches crawls up from the waistband of his trousers, over his swollen abdomen, splitting into two tracks that reach all the way to each collarbone, like an autopsy Y-incision sewn up by a mad doctor.

Becher's skin is a waxy gray, and above his moustache, his closed eyes look vulnerable without his thick glasses. His wrists and ankles are bound to the table legs. Dried blood has made his skin adhere to the oak table-top in places, and created a dark pool underneath.

Emma has no idea how Simon managed to get Becher – who must weigh at least two hundred and fifty pounds – onto that table.

"We need…" She clears her throat. "I mean, Agent Carter has requested that you verify each man's death, and document injuries at each scene."

"Uh-huh." Sanchez is slowly putting down his orange gear box, his expression shocked, his eyes fixed on Becher's desecrated body.

"Sir?" She knows Sanchez is a professional, but she needs him to focus. "Sir, this whole house is a crime scene, and there are forensic analysts on site, but there's a lot of work to do. Any help you can give us… Well, that would be much appreciated."

"Of course, of course," Sanchez says, snapping back. He takes a knee to open the orange box, grabs examination gloves, a penlight, and drapes a stethoscope around his neck. "Miss…"

"Lewis. You can call me Lewis."

"Miss Lewis, is there any estimate of this man's time of death?"

"The, um, forensic folks think everyone was killed about four or five this morning. And we got here thirty minutes ago, so it's been two or three and a half hours since they all…passed."

"Okay, that's useful, thank you. I might need your assistance for a moment, okay? Take these." He proffers an extra pair of gloves.

Emma dons the gloves. "You need me to…"

"If you go to the left side, I'll go to the right." Sanchez moves toward Becher, pulling on latex.

Unsure what she's supposed to be doing in this situation, Emma sidles closer to the left side. She'd prefer not to be here. In life, Becher unnerved her; in death, he still gives her a powerful revulsion. The smell of blood is rising up into her nostrils, and she's not sure how long she'll be able to stand being inside this house before she loses her cool again.

But Sanchez is issuing instructions. "I'm going to verify death, okay? Check for absence of central pulses on palpation, check for absence of heart sounds, check for absence of respiratory effort."

"Okay."

"Have there been any bystander interventions?"

"Uh…no? I don't know. What do you mean?"

"Has there been any attempt to resuscitate?"

"Uh, no. I don't think so. Most of the victims are in pieces. Becher is the only one who's…" *Whole*, she wants to say, "…like this."

"Okay, I understand." Sanchez is very calm and patient. "But because we're not dealing with decapitation here, or something that looks like immediate death, I need to verify. I'll start with a carotid pulse palpation check. Lift his chin for me, I'll do an inspection first."

Sanchez fishes out a pair of spectacles from his breast pocket, puts them on, adjusts the stethoscope to his ears. Emma swallows. Grimacing, she reaches her right hand toward Becher's face, where his chin is doubled slack against the bottom of his neck.

She doesn't want to touch Becher's jowls, even with gloves on, so she puts two fingers on the very point of his chin and draws it upward.

His head moves back reluctantly; she has to exert a bit of force. Becher's throat extends, his airway is freed.

Suddenly the gray-faced man Emma thought was dead makes a massive, rattling gasp, and his eyes fly open.

When he sees her, he screams, lunatic-loud. Emma also screams. She and Becher stare into each others' faces, screaming on and on.

Sanchez runs for the doorway. "*Hey, we've got a live one here!*"

CHAPTER FIFTEEN

Boston, 2 November 1982

❝Becher will be out of surgery in about thirty minutes," Howard Carter says, returning from the nurses' station along the corridor.

They're in one of the Waiting Room for Families areas of Massachusetts General. It's an oddly-shaped room, narrow and stuck in a corner: Emma reflects that while these spaces are specially designated for stressed-out relatives, they always feel like an afterthought, like the offcuts left over from the building of the hospital.

Out the aluminium frame window, the Boston skyline is drizzly and chilled sallow; by contrast, the hospital's internal heating is up too high. *Avalon* by Roxy Music is playing at a low volume through the waiting room speakers. Emma always associates this band's music with Ed Cooper's death, and it gives her a dragging sense of repetition. She's glad to be out of the Gutmunsson mansion, but this isn't a huge improvement.

There's a small coffee table in the waiting area, and chairs with wooden armrests and padded seats made of some beige fabric. Emma's sitting on one of them, trying to control her shakes. It's nearly midday, she's had hours to calm down, but her heartrate keeps jagging and racing. Her Valium prescription is back at Quantico; she's considered calling Audrey and asking her to speak to staff here about issuing another prescription, but that seems like a lot of trouble, and taking medication now might be unwise.

She clenches her hands, returns her attention to Carter. "Thirty minutes. Okay."

"Any news?" Travis arrives from the vending machine, holding two cardboard cups. He hands one to Carter and sits beside Emma to pass her one. "It's hot chocolate. No caffeine."

"Thanks." The cup is warm, and she's grateful. "Nurses said thirty minutes."

"So far as they know," Carter amends.

Carter's out of Tyvek now, more himself again in his brown suit and FBI vest, but his manner is still far from stoic. His overcoat is puddled on a chair. He travelled in the back of the paramedic van with Sanchez, who was stabilizing Becher as one of Obersby's men drove. Travis and Emma followed the screaming ambulance in the Sprint. Westfall and Dixon have remained in Sudbury, collaborating with the ME and bossing Obersby's staff around while they wait on news.

Carter's slipped out at times – he had to report at the Boston field office and give them a rundown on what's happening, then to talk to a guy called Fish from state police, then to talk to the leader of SWAT. Wheels have been put in rapid motion for a law enforcement response. Carter has a creased, angry expression, he keeps rubbing at his beard and moustache, and tiredness pulls at the corners of his mouth.

Emma sips her hot chocolate, rests the cup on her knee. Her mind keeps vomiting up the image of Becher's huge watery eyes – like blue-yolked eggs – and the black, blood-stained hole of his mouth as he screamed…

She shivers. She wants Travis's arm around her, but he's leaning forward in his chair, the lapels of his FBI jacket loose as he pores over the scrawls in his notebook. He looks wiped but also feverishly alert, and

Emma's worried about him.

She exhales hard. "Okay, so Boston state police are conducting the search?"

"Yes, a full sweep." Carter blows on his coffee. "They're looking for signs of the Gutmunssons in the area surrounding the mansion. Hopefully they'll be able to give us an idea of where and how the twins escaped the scene."

Emma's confused about something else. "You said that the murders at the mansion were a crime of opportunity. But the way the bodies were displayed, that must have taken hours to set up."

Carter's lips twist. "The scene at the house was...elaborate. But all the ligatures, all the tools Simon Gutmunsson used to kill Kirby and the others were all there. Gutmunsson didn't go out and pick up supplies from the hardware store, that stuff was all present in the house."

"The twins must have still been in the house, or nearby, to see that tree go down and take their chance." Travis flicks back a few pages to check his notes, forearms on his knees. "Obersby said Boston SWAT was supposed to have cleared the area around the house, the outbuildings... How did they miss them?"

"They sure as hell missed something." Carter sips, sets his coffee down. "Or maybe it's as simple as the Gutmunssons knowing the area, knowing where to take cover and hide."

Emma thinks of a question she had earlier. "How did Simon get Becher up on that table?"

"I don't know," Carter says, "but –"

He cuts himself off when a woman walks into the waiting area. "Special Agent Carter?"

The woman is in her mid-forties, with dark brown hair in a

tidy professional cut. Her manner is formal, authoritative, in the way of doctors, lawyers, law enforcement, teachers, the world over. A green fabric medical drape is spread over the front of her blue medical scrubs, and she's holding her hands out, latex-ed up. Emma thinks of the way she and Linda Brown held up their hands on their way to the Scientific Analysis lab to see Kristin Gutmunsson's weird scrapbook.

This woman's also got paper surgical booties and a mark on her forehead from a recently removed a surgical cap, like she's just walked out of the operating theater. She's changed her gloves and covered her gown so they won't see bloodstains, Emma realizes, which is a peculiar, doctorly politeness. Travis stands to hear the doctor's news; Emma follows his lead, setting her cup on the table.

"Agent Carter, excuse me if I don't shake, I'm Doctor Julia Rezuto." The doctor gives Carter a nod. "I've just been in surgery with the patient you brought in, Mr. Becher."

"Of course, thank you, Doctor," Carter says. "What can you tell us?"

"Mr. Becher is as stable as we can make him right now." Rezuto's lips pinch as she says this, which Emma takes to mean that Becher's ongoing stability may be tenuous. "His injuries are extensive, but he also suffered respiratory depression before he was properly examined, which has led to cerebral hypoxia. We're concerned about potential brain injury, and we're going to need to contact his family…"

Brain injury. Emma feels nauseous.

"Yes, of course," Carter says, "I've supplied contact details of Becher's next-of-kin to the staff at the admissions desk."

"Then I guess we wait for them to get back to us before we pursue a further course of treatment. Agent Carter, there's one more thing…"

Rezuto notices Emma and Travis for the first time, seems unsure about continuing her explanation. "Are these young people close contacts of the patient?"

"Miss Lewis and Mr. Bell are Dr. Becher's colleagues," Carter reassures. "They're in his unit, they've been working this investigation together."

"Right." Rezuto still looks uncomfortable. Whatever she needs to say, Emma thinks it's probably bad. "Well, something you should know is that Mr. Becher had foreign objects in his abdomen."

Travis looks unnerved. "What?"

Rezuto nods. "When we cut his stitches and went in, we found… this."

She's holding a small object in her gloved fingers. At first, Emma thinks it's an old leaf, or a piece of dark ribbon: thin, curling, black. But then Rezuto lifts it up, and Emma's vision realigns, and she can see it's –

"It's film," Rezuto says. "Magnetic videotape, I mean. Like in a video cassette. Not the actual hard-plastic cassette cases, of course, or his abdomen would've been much more distorted…" Rezuto glances up and realizes no one needs to hear those gory details. "Uh, anyway, this is just a small piece. We've actually found a lot of it."

"How much is a lot?" Emma asks warily.

"About three thousand feet." Rezuto says this calmly, as if it's not a shocking thing, a man with over half a mile of videotape shoved in his belly. "But it's very thin and twisted up, and it's not as stiff as old film negatives or thirty-five millimeter film, so we've managed to get it all out without causing additional damage. I thought you'd want to know, if this is linked to an FBI investigation."

"It is," Carter confirms. "Doctor, the tape will need to go into evidence – I'll have to speak with you and any other staff who had contact with it, so I can complete a chain-of-evidence report. And I'd like to have the tape shipped for further examination."

"What do you need?" Rezuto asks.

"However-much tape you've been able to recover needs to be packed into a dry, sterile container for transport." Carter takes out a card from his vest pocket, scrawls on it. "Send it to this address in Washington DC, care of Dr. Linda Brown. That would be most helpful, Doctor."

"I'll get it taken care of." Rezuto holds the card and the tape scrap together. "In the meantime, the health of the patient is my main priority right now. I'll keep you informed – I assume you're staying in Boston, if we need to contact you?"

"For tonight, yes," Carter says. "You can get in touch through the Boston FBI field office. The number is on the other side of that card, just ask for me."

The doctor departs, and Carter walks over to collect his overcoat. *Videotape* – there's something important about videotape, but right this minute, Emma can hardly think. Her eyes are sore and dry, and she has a strong desire to lie down.

Carter shrugs on his coat. "Okay, I need to be somewhere with a secure phone line. Mr. Bell, I'm going to ask you and Miss Lewis to stay here. Obersby's guy should be back shortly, ask him to call the field office and arrange accommodation near the federal building for the three of us for tonight."

"Yessir." Travis fishes a pen out of the top pocket of his blue jacket and adds another line to his notebook. "Want me to call Betty at Quantico and let her know our movements?"

Carter shakes his head. "I've got to call her myself anyway to get the numbers for Kirby and Martino's families." The concept makes him wince. "But see if you can make contact with Gerry Westfall and Carlos Dixon, get them to phone in a report to Boston. Tell them we'll make transcript copies for Quantico and Washington."

"Yessir."

"I'll talk to Boston's unit chief, then make some calls to sort out chain of command on this mess...Rasche won't be happy, because I'm supposed to be purely advisory on this, but I think that's out the window now. I think lots of things are out the window."

Travis pauses, pen raised. "Will Rasche make it your problem, sir?"

"Hard to say." Carter glances over at Emma. "Miss Lewis, I'm not sure when Obersby's man is returning. Are you going to be comfortable staying here another few hours?"

Another few hours. Emma wants to sprint from the confines of the hospital, but at the same time, she feels exhausted. "Sure. It's not like I'm gonna go out and take in a show."

"All right, then we'll meet again at whatever hotel the local field office puts us in, I guess. Let's say, the hotel restaurant at eighteen hundred for a debrief."

Emma's tempted to say *ten-four* in sarcastic acknowledgement, holds back. "Okay."

Carter looks at her squarely, like he can sense her energy. "Miss Lewis, I know today has been a lot, and you're probably still in shock. But tell me now – have you got the stones to keep going with this?"

It's such a strange, macho-type phrase from Carter, out of character. Emma figures he's resigned to being made lead agent and wants to start stamping out his territorial authority. She tries put aside her resentment about the way Carter is using Travis, about the FBI in general: Carter is mad, and this investigation has gone so terribly wrong, and now, in the middle of his mourning period, it looks like he's being put in charge of salvaging it. She can at least try to meet him where he is.

"I can keep going," she concedes.

"Good. Because I need all the help I can get." Carter's gaze swings between them both. "Listen, we're hunting Simon Gutmunsson, and he retaliated – he took his pound of flesh from the FBI. It's a reminder of the kind of monster we're dealing with. Jack Kirby was a good man, but I told you once before that he didn't seem ready to deal with Gutmunsson when we caught up to him. I hate to be proved right, but here we are. What's important now is that we bring Gutmunsson in."

"Yessir," Travis says.

"Mr. Bell, you can reach me at the Boston office if you need me – I may call you in, if there's a lot of range to cover. Otherwise, I'll see you both at the hotel restaurant at six."

Carter walks briskly out to the hallway, buttoning his coat. Emma turns to see Travis zipping his jacket. The blue nylon catches in the zipper teeth and he has to try again. Travis's jaw is rigid and his fingers are fumbling, and Emma's not sure whether his current stamina is natural or chemical. The fact she's wondering about it at all gives her pause.

He straightens his collar. "I'd better go to the phone bank downstairs and figure out how to reach Westfall and Dixon in Sudbury."

"Call Sullivan's Motorola pack." Emma leans for her hot chocolate – not so hot now – and takes a weary sip. "The Boston field office should have the number."

Travis gives her credit for the idea with a nod. "Are you gonna be okay here? We're still waiting for Obersby's guy, whatever his name is –"

"Fidler. His name is Shaun Fidler." Emma sets her cup back down.

She doesn't really want to bring this up, but looking at Travis right now, she feels obligated to say something. "Carter's just kind of pulled you back in straight away, hasn't he?"

"Emma…" Travis shoves a hand through his hair, frowning. "Carter's in a tough spot, and he needs all the operational support he can get right now. I'm just trying to make things easier for him. And come on – aren't you *angry* about this?"

Beneath Travis's pall of tiredness, Emma can see the fire animating him. He's almost as furious as Carter: Kirby and Martino were men he knew, men he'd worked with before. The connections Travis had with them were stronger than her own, and it's clear that he sees his father's death reflected in theirs.

All she can do to balance that is to tell him how she's feeling. "I'm angry, yeah. But I'm also scared, now we've seen what Simon's willing to do. And I'm worried this is hurting you."

"I get that. But what choice do I have right now?"

She can't reply *You always have a choice* while he's so heightened, and under so much emotional pressure. She tries another way. "Travis, I want to catch Simon and Kristin, too – we all do. But we said we'd stick together. Those were the rules of engagement, that we'd do this on our terms."

His mouth and eyebrows are tight. "Emma, *come on*. You saw that crime scene. The rules of engagement have *changed*, and if Carter needs me as a temporary –"

"It's *never* temporary, don't you get that?" She can feel her frustration spilling over, is powerless to hold it in. "They just keep taking until they use you up. But it doesn't have to be like that – you don't have to jump when the FBI says so, or take orders from Carter."

Travis's hands go wide. "How *else* are we gonna catch Gutmunsson?

It's not like we can do it on our own!"

"I'm not saying that, and honestly, *I don't know.* But listen, you don't have to accept whatever role the FBI wants to shove you into."

"That's not what's happening here!"

"That's *exactly* what's happening here! Goddammit, Travis!" Emma presses her palms to her cheeks, forces a stop. This has escalated way faster than she wanted it to, and they're drawing attention from the nurses' station.

Travis's hands are on his hips, his whole body tense, his lips thin as a knife blade. Her own face feels hot. She doesn't want to cry here, in this hospital waiting room. She needs to exert some control, circuit-break this whole situation.

She steps forward, into his space. Touches his forearm, his muscles tight under the layer of nylon. "Travis, please. I don't want to fight, I swear. Just…think about whether this is what you want. The FBI are focused on Simon. *I'm* focused on getting us both out of this alive."

"I know." He nods tightly, unwillingly, before sighing and pulling away. "I gotta go call."

Emma releases him. "Go. I'll wait for Fidler."

Travis heads for the same hallway exit that Carter took. Emma scrubs at her eyes. She doesn't know what to do, what words to say that will pull him out of this spiral. She can't blame him for it. Maybe it was always going to be like this, since they're pursuing his dad's murderer. But this isn't how it was supposed to go. Last night, they were just themselves. Today, it's like those people never existed. And the closer they get to Simon, the more critical it's all starting to feel.

Unease rises in her, choking, and this pervading sense that they're barrelling headlong into disaster won't dissipate. There's nothing she can do to combat it except sit here in one of the uncomfortable hospital chairs and wait.

Out the window, three stories below, a group of medical students are having their coats blown around as they scurry for shelter on one of the hospital pathways. Emma watches them, thinks of the FBI's response to the murders in the mansion. Simon's terror tactics have been very effective at shocking everyone into a kind of furious, scurrying panic. But they can't afford to panic now – Simon sure as hell won't. He'll be thinking, and planning, and she needs to think and plan, too.

But what is it they're *missing*?

A few minutes later, Agent Fidler – a rangy man in his late thirties who seems quietly scandalized that a nineteen-year-old girl is involved with the FBI in any capacity – returns to the waiting room with Travis's Harrington jacket from the Sprint. Fidler explains that their hotel accommodation in Boston has been arranged. He's not accompanying them, because he has to leave again to drive the car back to the hire desk at Logan airport, but another SWAT guy is escorting them.

The bureau is too cheap to put them up at any of the swanky hotels closer to the federal building: They're staying at the Harborside Inn, in the State Street Block in the financial district. Once Travis finally comes back from his calls, they go downstairs and meet their new SWAT escort, Lesley Garron, a short Irish cop with a bushy moustache. He takes them to a new bureau car, and out of the vast grounds of Massachusetts General, along Merrimac and Congress Streets, then through a series of confusing waterfront back-lanes to the hotel.

With a façade made of granite chunks and numerous segmental arch windows, the Harborside looks like a former prison, or – more likely – an old customs house. There's an envelope already waiting for Travis at the reception desk; he reads it in the elevator on the way up to the floor of their respective rooms.

"Hey, will you be okay here for a little while?" His expression is stiff, although he's trying to keep things harmonious. "Carter wants me at the Boston field office for a few hours."

"Of course he does." Emma sighs, waves a hand. What else can she do? "I'll be fine. You should go – there was a cab out front of the hotel when we arrived."

Travis doesn't even get out of the elevator. He goes straight back down, and Emma is left on her own.

She lets herself into her room. The hotel is okay inside, although Emma gets itchy seeing yet another bed with an apricot-colored comforter, yet another room with bland, anonymous furniture. She takes off her pea coat and sinks onto the end of the bed. There's a pervasive smell of Faultless laundry starch from the sheets.

She should try to nap, but she's too lonely and restless, and she's too wired to watch TV. She puts on her coat again, stuffs her FBI lanyard into the external pocket, then digs in the internal pockets, finds thirty dollars, her OSU library card, her driver's license, and a scrunched-up Kleenex. They really left Quantico yesterday morning with nothing at all, thinking they'd just be visiting St Elizabeths to grab Simon's papers; now here she is in Boston, largely empty-handed, except for some loose cash and the clothes on her back.

She takes the elevator back down, asks the concierge for some directions. He gives her a little letter-sized map of the city. Garron, her security cover, folds up his newspaper to accompany her. Emma's a little tired of being escorted around everywhere, but she grits her teeth and wears it.

Outside, there's a breeze coming up the street, straight off the waterfront; Emma can smell fried fish and car exhaust. The traffic isn't too crazy. She checks the map, goes left, Garron trailing. Turning near an Irish bar and walking up Commercial Street brings her to some kind of market area. The sight of the people drifting around the food and street stalls, the fall colors of the neighborhood trees...it all gives her a nostalgic sense of normalcy. But if she turns her head a little, she can still see Garron behind her.

She bypasses a tobacconist, a Clarks shoe store, and a place selling pizza by the slice to go into a grand columned building called Quincy Market, but it's all butchers and green grocers and ice cream stalls; this isn't what she needs. Back out on the street, she finally gives up and asks Garron; he directs her to an Ames, where she buys a two shirts, underwear for herself, a yellow notepad. Then she finds an Osco Drug and buys a couple toothbrushes. Then she and Garron walk back to the hotel. So that's the sum total of her sight-seeing adventures in Boston. It's still only two-thirty in the afternoon.

The bed in the hotel room looks warm and tempting, and who knows when this downtime will come again, but there's something she needs to do first. After a shower and a room-service burger, Emma wraps herself in one of the too-large hotel bathrobes and sits cross-legged on the bed, settling her notepad and hotel pen and the phone in front of her on the comforter. Dialling the number, she listens as the phone call makes its usual five chirps before being picked up.

The line crackles, and Emma tries to avoid nudging the long curly cord. "Hello, Audrey?"

"Emma, oh my." Dr. Audrey Klein's voice is firm and reassuring. "Nice to hear your voice, but this line is very bad, where are you?"

Emma feels tension release from the back of her neck. "Audrey, I'm in Boston. We're still working on this case, but there've been some...

setbacks. There've been some deaths."

"Oh, that's awful. I'm so sorry. Were they people you knew?"

"Yes." She wonders whether to tell Audrey about what's happened with her colleague, Becher, then decides against it. "Audrey, I'm really tired so I can't talk for long."

"What do you want to talk about, then?" Audrey offers.

"I have a psychology question. You know we're tracking Simon Gutmunsson and his twin sister – I'm trying to work out their state of mind."

"You don't have someone from Quantico who you can talk to about this?"

Emma hedges. "No one I trust. And I'd really like your opinion on it."

"Okay, then, fire away."

"Great, thank you." Emma clicks her pen and thinks of how to frame this. "What kind of impact would it have on their psychology if Simon and his sister were...intimate?"

Audrey is very matter-of-fact about this, as she is with everything. "You think Simon and Kristin are in an incestuous relationship."

"Yes. I mean, it's not confirmed, but yeah."

"Well, sibling incest is very complex." Audrey's mature voice is thoughtful, even through the connection's crackle. "Our society's moral code says that incest is wrong, although with adult siblings, the ethical boundaries are less clear-cut. A consensual relationship between adult siblings, for instance, is still legal in many countries."

"Really?"

"Really. But how does one determine if the relationship is truly consensual? And it's hard to argue that incest is okay, or that it involves a healthy relationship dynamic. Quite often, it involves a power imbalance that started very early. You said Simon and Kristin's sexual relationship isn't confirmed, but if such a relationship exists, the groundwork for it may have begun in childhood."

Emma makes her notes and thinks about Kristin's scrapbook, now sitting in a pile of examined evidence back in Washington DC – the handwritten litany of childhood memories, the curls of hair, the leaves and grass from Kristin's landscape of half-remembered scenes...

Emma taps her pen on the notepad. "I know that some of Simon's victims were boys who Kristin was romantically connected with."

"Well, that's a red flag, wouldn't you say?" Audrey pauses. "Broadly, it all suggests that Simon and Kristin have a level of mutual co-dependence that has tipped over the line. That they trust only each other, and would now find it difficult to exist independently."

"That doesn't sound great."

"It's very different to the kind of relationship you and Travis are working on, which is based on communication, and cooperation, and individual agency."

Emma doesn't know what to say to that, but she knows she must respond. And maybe this was the reason she called Audrey in the first place. "Travis is...He gets drawn back into the FBI. What they want for him."

"You sound worried about him."

"I am." Emma presses her pen nib down hard. "Especially because he's still not completely recovered. And it's complicated...Look, I didn't mean to talk about this, but it's just so complicated, and I don't really know what to do."

Audrey sounds placid, unruffled. "Emma, what do you think

Travis is feeling right now?"

"I don't know." But she does. "I guess he's...tired. And angry. And probably scared, like me. I just don't want the FBI to jerk him around like he's a puppet."

"Travis has been considering a career in law enforcement, though, hasn't he."

"Yes? But he's been kind of on the fence about it lately."

"And have you and Travis talked about the future? Do you feel like you've made a commitment to each other, with shared goals, or a shared trajectory?"

"We..." Emma gnaws the edge of a fingernail. "I guess we haven't talked about it much yet."

"Emma, listen," Audrey says gently. "Unless you and Travis have discussed a future together, and the compromises required for that, your decisions rest on each of you individually. Which means that Travis has to use his own powers of reason and discernment in this situation."

"I know that. But he's here in Massachusetts, where his dad died, and he's under so much pressure..." She liked it better when he was the real Travis Bell, back at the ranch, back at Quantico. But they're far from those places now, and this is the question that's pressing on her. "What if he makes decisions that are against his best interest? That are bad for him?"

"I recognize what you're feeling, Emma," Audrey says. "But here's some hard truth – are you ready for it? *You* can't be the one to judge what's in Travis's best interest. Only he can do that. And sometimes, the people we care about choose a direction that we don't agree with. We don't have to like it, and we don't have to go along with it, but we have to accept it, because it's not up to us. It's their life, and their choice."

That's the thing really scaring her, isn't it? That Travis might choose the FBI. The prospect of waiting for him to decide, waiting for the hammer to fall, is making her nauseous.

"Emma, I know trusting people is difficult," Audrey continues, "but you have to trust that Travis can work it out. And whatever that outcome is, you have to accept it, and decide whether to engage with it or whether to walk away."

The idea makes her throat constrict. It's like being strangled. "Okay."

"You still have an active role, though, and that is to be a friend to him."

"We slept together," Emma blurts, and her face goes hot enough to combust.

"That's no barrier to friendship," Audrey says, without missing a beat. "If anything, it should make you both more motivated to be considerate of one another. It's about respect. It's about being kind. That's what a friend is — someone who is kind, who gives strength and understanding and honesty, who offers encouragement and unconditional support."

It's all true, all correct. Above everything else, Travis has always been her friend. He gave her consideration and support, even when he didn't like where she was going with it. He gave her the most important gift: The space to make her own choices. And she has to return that gift to him now.

"Okay." Emma finds her eyes are wet. "Okay."

"I know this is hard. When emotions are involved, there's a lot of tension, and you're already under a great deal of strain."

"Yeah." Emma throws down her pen, swipes her nose on the sleeve of the robe. She clears her throat, but her voice still comes out muddy.

"I'm trying to keep it together here, Audrey."

"I understand. Calling me to talk, and clarify, and process things is a good strategy. You can call me anytime you need me."

"Thank you." A whisper is all she can manage.

"You're doing okay, Emma," Audrey says. "You'll get through this."

This, too, is correct, Emma knows. It's the phrase she's had on repeat for the last three years: that she has been in much tougher situations and survived. She's lived through circumstances that would've killed most people, and she's still standing.

But somehow, when it's not about you, when all you can do is watch someone you care for as they endure, keeping that awareness front-of-mind is so much harder.

CHAPTER SIXTEEN

Boston, 2 November 1982

Travis gets distracted looking at his forearm, where it rests on the beige laminated desktop. The hair on his arm is soft and dark, the skin beneath darker still. He got browner while he was in Mexico, he got a lot of sun. For a second, he lets himself think of the enormity of the sky above his uncle's ranch. Then he thinks of something from last night – the contrast between his brown forearm and the pale, delicate skin of Emma's stomach. Then he puts the memories away.

He's not the only man in the Boston field office bullpen with his sleeves rolled – he's not even the only non-white – but he's the only man in a Henley and jeans. Part of him wishes he had something more formal to wear in these meetings with FBI brass. He's got the FBI jacket, and he's doing all the things an assisting agent would do in this situation: He's followed up the videotape and evidence analysis with DC, sat in on incident-response briefings, collated statements, relayed Quantico information, and acted as a go-between for Carter. But Travis isn't wearing the suit, so as far as Boston FBI are concerned, he's not much more than an interested bystander.

The tile lighting in here is hurting his eyes. But every time he closes them, all the nightmare images come back: Sullivan's exposed heart, Mike

Martino's bloody hands, nose, feet, ears, dropped with careless abandon at points along the way to the rest of his remains in the second-floor bedroom. And the worst image: Jack Kirby's pale gray eyes staring forward endlessly, his upper body propped up in a dripping pool of his own organs in the wingback leather chair in the Gutmunsson family's living room. His tie was still in place and his limp hands lay flopped on the arm rests, but red had seeped up the white fabric of Kirby's dress shirt. His lower torso, still in his suit pants and buffed shoes, was seated in the other wingback beside him.

Travis blinks, pushes the images away. The brutal murders of three agents have galvanized a cross-state FBI response. The death of the local man, Sullivan, has given the Boston bullpen a particular harsh, outraged energy, which Travis finds a little infectious. There's a helluva lot to do, though.

Across the room, Shaun Fidler detaches from a knot of men at the section chief's office door and steps closer. "Carter's asking for you."

"Got it." Travis shakes off his exhaustion and stands, steadies himself against the borrowed desk. He's been running all day on Percocet washed down with cold coffee, so now it's like he can see through time.

Carter himself emerges, carrying a folder and his jacket and coat. "Let's go."

"Where are we going?"

"Dinner debrief at six, remember?" Carter sets his armful down on the desktop, starts rolling down his sleeves. "It's five-thirty. Probably take that long to get across town, with the traffic."

They take a bureau Ford. On the way in the car, Carter asks Travis how he's holding up and he says fine, despite being in a certain amount of pain. While he's busy, he can mostly ignore it, but it's like a piercing tinnitus, the background hum of telephone wires. If he were at the ranch, he'd have lain down about eight hours ago.

Emma meets them in the hotel restaurant, and he knows she can see it. Her face is soft and serious. She doesn't say anything, though, just does these small things, offering to fill his plate at the buffet, passing him hard-to-reach stuff. It's not the response he was expecting: He thought she'd still be pissed from their argument at the hospital. But now she presses her leg against his under the table, a warming brace. He remembers doing this kind of thing for her last June, and again in September – how did their roles get reversed?

But now, while Carter's getting second helpings, she's asking him what's been happening.

"It's been busy." Travis's tongue feels thick in his mouth. He tries to eat a few more bites. "It's been real busy. Carter called Becher's family again, then he's spent all afternoon in meetings with FBI Boston, the local medical examiner's office, state police, Boston SWAT. Quantico has been on the horn, coordinating forces. Plus there were the calls to Kirby and Martino's families."

"Heavy," Emma says.

"Yeah. I'm just trying to pick up the slack." Travis gives up pushing his food around and sets down his fork. "Gerry Westfall and Carlos Dixon have to go back to DC tonight, so they're sending in reports and I'm setting up their travel arrangements. I've been putting all the statements together – you need to give me a statement, by the way."

"I can do that."

"Boston thinks the Gutmunssons are still in Massachusetts. They've set up a joint taskforce with Virginia to begin a state-wide search."

"Everyone's riled up," Emma notes.

"With good reason. Obersby wants Simon Gutmunsson's head on a pike."

"He's not gonna get it by tossing every pile of leaves in Massachusetts." Emma sips from her water glass. "This is just my opinion, but I don't think they're still here. Simon's too smart to hang around after something like this."

"Wouldn't he want to watch and gloat? You know how he loves to see the FBI jump."

"He's seen the FBI jump before, he'd get bored with it pretty quick." She considers. "I think his priority is keeping Kristin safe. He knows what the repercussions of these murders will be – every FBI agent on the eastern seaboard will be gunning for him, not just Obersby. I think he and Kristin have already left Massachusetts."

Travis wipes his mouth with his napkin and tosses it on his plate. "It's all theories, though. We don't know, we're just guessing."

"What does your gut tell you?"

Travis blows out a breath. His gut is telling him to find a horizontal surface, and fast. It's telling him to recline or suffer the consequences. But he can't lay down now.

"My gut says Gutmunsson and Kristin are in the wind," he says finally. "But we have to follow up every scrap we've got, just so we can say we did all we could."

"Due diligence." It's Carter, back with his plate re-filled and seating himself at the table. "You're talking about due diligence. That's how we work in the bureau – it's about being methodical, covering the bases. But once we find Gutmunsson, we're going to stomp on him."

Emma pushes her plate away and leans on her forearms. "Have you heard any more news about Dr. Becher?"

Carter lays his napkin on his knee. "He's holding stable in the ICU, but his family has flown in. We're putting them up at the Wyndham on Blossom Street, closer to the hospital."

"I've still got his effects," Travis remembers. "His jacket and briefcase. All his case notes. I'm not sure what to do with all that stuff."

"Personal items go to the family once they've been cleared by Scientific Analysis." Carter starts on his shrimp salad. "We'll have to go through his case notes and see if there's anything there that might have operational use."

"I could read through the case notes," Emma offers. "I'm not doing anything."

"Really?"

She shrugs. "I'm supposed to be here to consult, you might as well put me to work."

Straight after dinner, that's what they do. Carter drives them back along Congress Street to the John F. Kennedy Federal Building, where the Boston field office occupies the entire ninth floor.

Wind whips through the dark plaza as they approach, tossing their coats; Travis pulls up his collar and grits his teeth. A bizarre mid-sixties sculpture stands outside, very simpatico with the building's pre-cast concrete panels and punched windows. Emma tucks her hands in her pockets, gives the sculpture a wide berth.

She looks around once they're through the giant revolving glass doors, out of the wind. "The FBI seems to have a real commitment to brutalist architecture, and I can't say I'm a fan."

"Hey, this place is twenty years old." Carter fishes for his ID. "The bureau used to be in the Sheraton Building on Atlantic Avenue."

"I can see why they moved. That would've been too nice."

Travis would snort if he wasn't so tired.

They all show their credentials and head for the white-glazed banks of elevators. The JFK building's internals look like something out of a science fiction movie, and in his depleted state, Travis half expects to see people in color-block spandex tunics in the lobby: He gets an inappropriate urge to laugh. But as the elevator car rises, the massed weight of all the additional tasks he needs to perform settles onto his shoulders like a yoke. When the doors open, there's the immediate and ever-present sound of ringing phones. Men are still taking calls and ferrying paperwork; it's nearly eight o'clock at night.

Carter excuses himself to go back to work, and Travis leads Emma around filing cabinets and cubicles until they reach the desk he was assigned. Becher's brown houndstooth jacket is in a plastic evidence bag on the wooden tabletop, but Emma's not interested in that. She picks up the briefcase that once looked like a toy in Becher's large hands, examines the clasps.

"Can we get these locks opened?"

"Yeah, sure." Travis tries not to let his weariness show. "Honestly, if you can go through the case notes, it'll really save us some time."

"Can I take the whole briefcase back to the hotel?"

"Um, good question, let me check."

"You should come back to the hotel with me," Emma suggests. "Aren't you worn out?"

He's not hiding his weariness all that well, it seems. "I can't, Emma – I've got a bunch more phone calls to make before I'm done."

Emma's gaze travels gently all over his face. "You should really rest. Not just take painkillers."

"I will, I swear." He rubs at his chest. "I'm gonna be right behind you. But today has been a five-alarm fire, and while I'm still capable, I need to help Carter see it out."

He gets the briefcase opened, and the permissions from Carter, and calls a cab for Emma so she can go back to the Harborside. Once she leaves, he returns to the borrowed desk and his final tasks, including a wrap-up debrief.

It's just after 10:30PM by the time he and Carter make it back to the hotel. Travis is swaying with exhaustion and there's a dragging feeling in his chest, beneath his scar. He has to pass by Emma's door before he reaches his own. He hesitates, knocks.

"Come in," she calls.

Then he's inside her room, closing the door. She's sitting on the bed, propped against the headboard with pillows, examining a hardcover logbook while jotting down notes on a yellow legal pad. Becher's briefcase lies open on padded dressing table stool nearer the wall. The light in here is a low, warm orange from the lamp she's working by: It feels homey, and he realizes dully that's because Emma is here, that she represents home to him now.

She waves Travis closer, moves a pile of papers and exercise books across for him. "Here, lay down. You must be ready to fall over. Did you read any of this stuff? Becher was meticulous."

Travis gets his shoes and belt off somehow, and his FBI jacket, and he tries not to simply topple onto the bed – or if he's going to topple, to at least do it gracefully. But when the cool pillow hits his cheek, he lets out an involuntary groan, can't help it.

Emma pats his shoulder. "You okay there?"

"I'm good, now. I'm great." The comedown from the Percocet is going to be brutal tomorrow, but at least today is finally over. He rolls carefully and stiffly onto his side toward Emma.

"Rest." She pulls the corner of the blanket up to cover him. "Stop thinking for tonight – I can do some thinking while you're out of it. Go to sleep."

His brain is barely working, but he remembers one thing. "You were mad."

"Yeah, but we're not talking about that now. Just get some rest."

Everything below his breastbone is numb. Emma kneads his shoulder with one hand as he curls against her, but she's still reading the book propped on her knees.

"What did you find out?" he murmurs. He doesn't really want an answer, but the sound of Emma's voice is soothing.

"Becher's got a bunch of theories about Kristin. I think he's onto something, but I'll tell you tomorrow."

"Tell me something now."

"Becher thinks Kristin is more important than we previously believed, that she's the key to Simon's psychology. He thinks she's repressing memories somehow, and I think he might be right. And I spoke to Audrey – she says Simon and Kristin's sexual relationship is about mutual co-dependence."

"Because they're fucked up." Travis's eyes are closed and he's fading fast.

"Their whole lives have been fucked up from the start. They've only ever had each other." Emma strokes his hair. "Go to sleep. I'm gonna stop talking now."

He falls into sleep like his brain has a blackout. About 3:00AM, he jerks out of a dream in which Jack Kirby – just the top half of him, propped in the sodden mess pooled in the seat of the wingback armchair, silver eyes gleaming and blood dribbling from the corner of his mouth

– talks in a rambling way about how the FBI will always be a home for Travis if he wants it to be…

The blankets are smothering and Travis pushes against them, his mind swimming around in dark spaces. Finally, he calms: He's in a Boston hotel room, in Emma's bed, still in his clothes. Emma is nestled beside him. He shifts closer to her, listens to her deep breathing. The warmth of their bodies together loosens his muscles, and Travis starts to breathe with her. If only this could go on a while, he thinks, just a few days so he could make a full recovery, but then the tide of sleep pulls him back under.

Soon enough, it's seven in the morning and his eyes are reluctantly opening. There's no alarm, but this seems to have become his default wakeup time.

Emma is curled toward him now, her eyes fixed on his. Dark feathers of her hair frame her face and her voice is quiet. "Hey. Are you okay?"

He's no longer as rattled as he was yesterday, although he still feels ache-y and tired. He tests the muscles of his diaphragm, which the doctors worked so valiantly to put back together. "I'm…sore, but I'm okay. Thanks for letting me sleep."

"You needed it."

"I probably need a shower just as much."

"I had one last night, it was so good. Go shower. I'll wait."

"Hold on a second." He owes her this much. He takes her hand. "You were mad."

"I was mad," she admits. "I was worried about you, and it came out wrong."

"Don't worry about –"

She puts her fingers to his lips. "I worry, okay? Can't help it. But

I'm dealing with it, and it'll be all right. Let me use the bathroom, then you should go shower."

The shower is good, and needed, and there's a fresh toothbrush, which is a bonus because he left the other one behind at the hotel in Sudbury. Travis leans into the spray and lets the hot water do its valuable work. There's a restless itchiness under his skin, from the Percocet hangover; he can barely stand the idea of getting back into his three-day-old Henley.

But when he comes out of the bathroom in his jeans, Emma tosses him a clean thermal shirt. "Here you go."

"You got me a shirt?"

"And a toothbrush – I left it on the bathroom sink." She wrinkles her nose. "I got stuff for me as well. I had to do something, our clothes were starting to smell."

It's such a mundane thing, this gesture, but it pulls some kind of trigger in his mind.

"You're taking care of me," he realizes.

"We do that for each other." The smooth curve of her neck is honeyed in the early light as she tucks away another sheaf of papers. "I wrote out the statement you asked for, by the way. Do you think we're going back to the federal building this morning? Because there's some calls I could make to –"

Travis pulls her by the wrist, not sudden but firm, until their bodies connect. He kisses her long and slow. He likes the way she seems to hum into his mouth, and how her palms flatten against his bare chest.

When she drags herself back, she's breathless. "It was only a shirt…"

"Kiss me again," he whispers, drunk on these sensations.

He knows this is a bad time, but it's always a bad time somehow, and Emma doesn't pull away. He draws on her tongue and strokes the arch of her spine – three deliberate strokes, and she makes a soft moan each time. He has a sudden urge to rub her feet, just to listen to her reaction.

Is this genuine desire or emotional escape? He has no incentive to figure that out right now. The need to take comfort and pleasure with each other, to find refuge and release, is very strong. He wants to tell Emma that he isn't walking away from her, wonders if she would believe it. And now her warm hands have fluttered down to the damp skin of his stomach, above the waistband of his jeans –

The phone rings on the dresser. Their lips separate with a smack.

"Shit." Emma's cheeks are pink as she glances between him and the phone. "Front desk or Carter?"

"Carter for sure," Travis sighs, but Emma is already detaching to answer.

"Yes?" She looks back at him with one short nod. "Good morning, Mr. Carter. No, I haven't seen him yet. Why do you…" Her posture and expression suddenly become more alert. "What happened?"

Travis feels his exposed skin goose-bump immediately.

"Okay. I understand. I'll find Travis, we'll be down in two minutes." Emma hangs up. "Quantico received a letter from Simon, mailed priority express."

"We have to go," Travis says.

"Right now. You need to grab anything from your room?"

"My dad's jacket."

"Do it." Her martial demeanor falters briefly as she blushes. "Maybe put your shirt on first."

She's close enough that he can step in and snatch a kiss, which she seems to like, before he pulls on his shirt and finds his shoes. He ties the FBI jacket around his waist by the sleeves, leaves the room to fetch his other jacket from his assigned room. When he meets Emma near the elevator, she's got her pea coat over her arm, the briefcase in her right hand, and a brown paper bag tucked in one armpit.

"Hold this?" She unloads the paper bag onto him as the elevator doors open.

"What is it?"

"Laundry. One sec." She sets the briefcase down, yanks her coat on, recovers the paper bag and kneels to open the briefcase and tuck the bag inside. "That'll do for now."

"Wait a minute." He looks down at himself. "I'm wearing two jackets."

Emma squints at him from her lower position. "I can put one in the briefcase?"

He tugs the more lightweight FBI jacket from around his waist, hands it to her. She stuffs it into the briefcase, snaps the clasps shut.

"Done." She stands again, hefting the case. "You should know – Carter wants me to fly back to DC."

It hits like a wasp sting. Travis straightens involuntarily. "Not me as well?"

"He didn't say." Emma's studying the elevator numbers as the car descends, which is one of her tells when she's being evasive. But then she looks at him directly. "Carter could probably use you here, if you want to stay."

This is her giving him options, Travis realizes. There's still some color in her cheeks, but her tone is even-handed, impartial, as the doors open and Carter greets them in the lobby.

The man's wearing his coat over the same brown suit, somehow weirdly unrumpled. He looks tired around the eyes, but Carter's nothing if not professional: His manner is crisp as he ushers them toward the hotel lobby doors.

"Good morning to you both. The letter was mailed from Wallingford, Connecticut, and we've got a team heading there now to take statements from the employees and collect any physical evidence."

"He must've mailed it right after committing the murders," Emma says as they walk.

Carter slips on his glasses and checks details from a small spiral notebook held in one hand as they steer around a lounge setting in the lobby. "Best estimate is that Gutmunsson would've had to mail it no later than 9:00AM yesterday in order for it to reach Quantico so fast. Wallingford is a USPS sorting center, that helped it move."

"Quantico staff recognized the letter as Gutmunsson's straight away?" Travis feels very awake after the conversation with Emma in the elevator.

Carter nods. "We're real lucky they were on the ball. Miss Lewis, you've dealt with Gutmunsson's written communications before – I want to send you down to see the letter in person. You can follow up on other evidence as well, like the videotape film, and I'm giving you chain-of-evidence papers to deliver Dr. Becher's jacket. There's a car outside for you, heading for Logan. When you get to the airport –"

"Sir, you're not going to DC?" Travis interrupts. He wants to get this clear.

Carter slows his roll and they all stop. "I can't – not yet. My responsibility is here with the joint taskforce for another twenty-four hours. I was hoping you could stay here and provide support."

Other guests eddy around the three of them as they stand in the middle of the lobby like a boulder in a fast-running stream. Travis is suddenly aware that he has to make the right decision, and he has to make it now.

Emma turns to him and proffers the briefcase. "Hey, I have to return our keys. One minute."

Travis takes the briefcase, and she walks toward the hotel reception desk. She's doing it again, he realizes – giving him space to talk to Carter, to make a call.

Carter can read the hesitation in his face. "Are you worried about your fitness? We can arrange things to make it easier."

"It's not that." Travis knows hasn't got much time, so he'd better use it. "Sir, maybe this is talking out of turn, but why do you have to stay in Boston? If the letter was sent from Connecticut, we know the Gutmunssons have left Massachusetts."

Carter narrows his eyes. "Due diligence. Section Chief Rasche wants me to bring some weight down here. Two Quantico people are dead – we need to give it one more day."

"Sure, but why not hand it off to the Boston field office?"

"Rasche isn't completely confident about their special unit." Carter looks around, looks back, lowers his voice. "There've been rumors about corruption problems within Boston FBI, and he doesn't want Obersby running the play."

Now they're getting to the heart of it. Travis squints. "So it's a political thing."

"With the FBI, always," Carter says dryly.

"Okay, that puts you in a tough spot."

"I'm aware," Carter grimaces.

"But the goal here is to catch Gutmunsson," Travis can see Emma making her way back. "And this whole thing started when Kirby used Emma to lure him home. Gutmunsson's focus has been on Emma, it's always been on Emma."

"Maybe originally," Carter says. "But now it seems like Gutmunsson is taking out his ire on the FBI."

"Both those things can be true. And Becher said Gutmunsson has a 'psychological attachment' to Emma. Leaving her alone would be a bad idea."

Saying it aloud, it's like a lock clicking into place, and Travis steadies. He's not completely sure, but he has a feeling. He's flying by the seat of his pants, but this is right; somehow, he knows it's right. The Sudbury murders were horrifying, but they need to be thinking about Gutmunsson's long game.

"She won't be alone," Carter points out. "She'll have a SWAT escort."

"Respectfully? After seeing the crime scene yesterday, I don't find that reassuring." Travis keeps his tone polite but firm. "If Gutmunsson's as fixed on Emma as I think he is, I need to be with her, not here in Boston."

Carter winces. "You can't give me twenty-four hours? Even a little less time than that – you could fly back to DC tonight. I could surely use you."

Travis exhales. *Last call.* "This new Quantico letter. Was it addressed to Emma?"

"Yes." Carter doesn't seem thrilled about the admission. "Yes, it was."

"Okay." That's it, the final domino falling. Travis's fingertips are cold, but it's the cool weight of clarity. "Then, sir, I appreciate your confidence in me, but I don't think I can stay."

"I've only booked Miss Lewis's ticket from Logan," Carter says doggedly, but then he relents. "All right, I can see your point. Give me a minute to make some calls and change the arrangements."

Emma arrives and reclaims the briefcase, just as Carter walks away toward the payphone area in the lobby. Her expression is so determinedly neutral it looks painful. "What's Carter doing?"

"He's booking my ticket to DC," Travis says, and he feels his posture loosen. "I'm coming with you. I go where you go."

But Emma's hand is on his forearm, her eyes searching. "I don't want to mess you up with the FBI."

"You're not messing up anything. It's my call. You let me worry about the FBI – let's just catch Gutmunsson first."

Carter returns, having managed to get them both booked on a plane. After asking Emma to sign a chain-of-evidence document and handing over Dr. Becher's jacket, still in its plastic bag, Carter prepares to take a cab back to the JFK building from the hotel.

Before departing, he shakes Emma's hand, then Travis's. "Good luck in DC."

"Good hunting here in Boston," Travis says. "We'll see you back at Quantico in a few days. And sir, I apologize –"

"It's all right, son." Carter shakes his head. "I'll be sorry to lose your help, but I understand. Call if you need me." He lifts his chin toward the car. "Okay, you two better motor."

True to his word, Carter has provided a Boston SWAT team member as an escort: Garron again. He seems happy to see them. He's also extremely efficient at the airport, expediting their passage through flight check-in and security. They still have to race to make the American Airlines flight. It helps that they're not travelling with any luggage, just the briefcase and the plastic-wrapped jacket and what they're wearing. The only downside to the flight change is that they're going to be arriving in Dulles.

The flight is half empty. Travis asks for water and coffee from the attendant, swallows a single pill, to take the edge off. Then he turns to Emma in the seat beside him. "Here, I want you to hold onto these for me."

She frowns at the white-capped plastic bottle in his hand. "But don't you need –"

"If I need a Percocet, I'll ask you for one. But I don't wanna be carrying them around anymore." It's making him sweat a little, giving her the bottle, but it's the smart thing to do.

"Okay." Emma tucks the pill bottle away in her coat pocket. She's eyeing him. "What's going on?"

"What do you mean?"

"Well, yesterday we were arguing about you working with the FBI, and today you're leaving Carter behind to come with me to DC, and giving me your pills…"

Travis isn't sure he can answer the question. How can he tell her it's everything? The orange lamplight in her room last night; the shirt she bought him; the way she gasped when they kissed this morning. It's all of that, and other stuff, too. Even the argument they had played a part. Is he sure about the theories he pitched to Carter? That Emma can't be left alone, even for twenty-four hours? Not completely. He's going on instinct, gut feeling…He doesn't think he's wrong, though.

It's a bit maddening that now the chips are coming down, he's relying solely on instinct – it makes him feel rudderless and shaky. But while his defenses are so low, while he's still tired and in pain, it's harder to make his brain work. Gut feeling is the only thing he has left. Travis hopes it's enough.

"I guess I'm just thinking about what I really want," he says at last. "And I have a feeling that if we're going to catch Simon Gutmunsson, then I'm exactly where I oughta be."

Emma still looks dubious. "And you sure you're okay?"

"I'm okay," he insists.

"All right. Then…should we talk about this letter?"

"Good idea." He needs a distraction.

"Right." Emma sugars her own coffee. "So, Carter said Simon's letter was mailed from Wallingford before 9:00AM yesterday, which meant it reached Quantico this morning. Dixon said the murders in the Gutmunsson's mansion were committed no later than 5:00AM yesterday."

"Let's pace out the timeline." This is territory Travis is familiar with. He takes his notebook out of his inside jacket pocket and puts it on the tray table, clicks his pen. "Okay – here's the murders. The twins finish at five, clean themselves up afterward, get to their vehicle and drive away by no later than, say, six. Then Gutmunsson wants to post his letter."

"Right. But the post office doesn't open until…" Emma gropes for the knowledge.

"Post office always opens at eight."

"Okay, eight. What are the chances that Wallingford is two hours' drive from Sudbury?"

"Extremely high," Travis realizes. "So you were right about the Massachusetts search being a waste of time – they were already in Connecticut by eight, yesterday morning. They're heading south."

"Yes. But *why*? Why didn't they just run for Canada after the murders? They could've cut through New York or Vermont and been over the border before lunch."

"Um, good question." He tries to think about it in a detached way. "Okay – Carter called in the alert as soon as we arrived at the Sudbury house. Boston FBI would've contacted border guards to be on the lookout. Maybe Gutmunsson was worried they'd get grabbed trying to cross into Canada."

Emma shakes her head. "Carter contacting Boston, Boston contacting agencies at the border, agencies disseminating the information about the Gutmunssons up and down the line…The timing for that would've been really tight. So there'd have been plenty of gaps for the twins to slip through."

"I don't know." Travis frowns, butting up against the limit of his understanding. "Gutmunsson wanted to post his letter, but he could've done that in Vermont – he could've done that anywhere north of Sudbury. Choosing to go south…It doesn't make a lot of sense."

Emma has that absent expression she gets when she's thinking hard. "We always assume that Simon's playing chess with us. That he's always a dozen steps ahead, making his movements hard to understand or predict. But…maybe this isn't his move."

Travis narrows his eyes. "You think it's Kristin?"

Emma shrugs. "Whenever the twins do something that doesn't make sense, I always think of Kristin."

The flight is less than two hours, and when they emerge from beneath Dulles airport's vaulted ceilings and soaring columns, the Washington DC air is heavy; it's an overcast morning, like they've brought the bad weather with them from Massachusetts. He and Emma keep talking, trying to work through a couple more scenarios on the way to the Scientific Analysis lab. Garron drives the rental car, a Ford Escort, and Becher's briefcase and plastic-wrapped jacket sit on the passenger seat beside him.

Just before they reach Pennsylvania Avenue, Emma looks out the window at the gray skies, looks back. "I'm glad you didn't stay in Boston."

"I probably should've stayed," Travis admits. "Carter wasn't happy."

"Why didn't you?" Emma asks. "It was only twenty-four hours."

"I'm not sure." He doesn't want to tell her that he thinks Gutmunsson is still gunning for her – he's sure she knows. He's also not completely certain his theories hold water. So that's all he's got, and it sounds a little crazy. "I just didn't want to. It didn't feel…right."

Emma looks like she wants to ask more, but they've reached the federal building. They sign in; Garron doesn't have clearance to go up to Scientific Analysis and stays with the Escort. Emma carries the briefcase in the elevator and Travis takes the plastic-bagged jacket. When they reach the labs, their ID doesn't work on the door release, so they have to knock.

Dr. Linda Brown opens the white door, waving them into the central storage-container room. "Welcome to the madhouse, folks. Come on in."

This is the first time Travis has seen Brown look anything but serene. She's in a nice burgundy-colored dress but her makeup is mostly worn off and her lab coat sleeves are rolled. Her hair is pulled back in an Alice band; escaped strands in front have gone a little silly from perspiration.

Travis looks around. "Is everyone here?"

"You bet." Brown's white coat hems flap as she leads them through the storage-container maze. "Gerry's here, but he was up half the night, then he had to do all the prints from the Quantico letter – he's taking a nap in his office. He said to thank you for arranging the flights back from Massachusetts, by the way. Carlos is still working, which is crazy, but he's on a mission. The letter was just bad timing."

"Why's that?" Travis hands over the jacket in its bag, relieved to be offloading it. "Something else to add to the collection – that's Dr. Becher's jacket."

"Wonderful," Brown sighs. "Make sure to sign it off, I'll give it to Glenn."

"Oh, I've got the chain-of-evidence paperwork for it." Emma rummages in her jacket, finds the handover papers and a pen. She signs the papers, passes them to Brown. "Why is the letter bad timing?"

"It arrived in the middle of the crunch with the Sudbury material, so everyone's under the gun." Plastic-bagged jacket and accompanying papers tucked beneath her arm, Brown stops at the door to the forensics lab. "And you should know. We got a call from Carter while you were still in the air – Stanley Becher died about an hour ago."

CHAPTER SEVENTEEN

Washington DC, 3 November 1982

"Dr. Becher passed?" Emma feels her breath hitch.

"Yes, I'm afraid so." Brown ducks into the lab to drop off the jacket, then ushers them onward. "Come into my office, let's look at the letter first."

Emma's not sure why she finds the news of Becher's death affecting. She didn't even like the man. But she's developed more respect for him, after reading through his comprehensive case notes on the Gutmunssons. And it's the sobering finality of it; Becher was the only person to survive the horrors of Sudbury, and now he's gone. No one made it out of the Gutmunsson's mansion alive.

Once they get through the door decorated with the framed, illuminated quote, Brown seems more herself – she's in her own space, her neat, orderly office glowing with light from the table lamp. She walks straight to the shelf beside the wooden filing cabinet in the far left corner, pours from an elegant glass carafe into a paper cup.

"Water?" Brown offers, and when Emma nods, she passes over the first cup, pours another for herself after Travis declines. "Please, have a seat."

Emma finds a chair beside Brown's big desk. There's a flat plastic evidence container on the pale leather blotter on the desktop, and Brown returns to sit at the cushioned chair in front of it. She sips from her paper cup, then sets it well away from her work area before taking a pair of nitrile gloves from an easily-accessible box.

"Travis, you don't need to hover – grab that chair there and drag it over. That's it. Now let's go through this." Brown pops the plastic clasps on the side of the evidence box. "All right, first of all, tell me what you see."

Travis squints, still adjusting his seat. "Uh, looks like watercolor paper again."

"That's right," Brown confirms. "Carlos said there was a sketch-book on a table in the greenhouse at the Sudbury location, and the paper was torn out of there. Glenn confirmed the match."

"That was Kristin's sketchbook," Emma notes, peering at the single sheet of paper in the evidence box. "What's he written the letter with? It looks like marker."

Brown nods. "Good guess – it's a green felt-tipped pen. Simon Gutmunsson has written with green pen a number of times, I'm going to go out on a limb here to say that I think it's his preferred color. Okay, I've done a thorough examination of this piece and taken phots of everything. The composition of the paper isn't relevant, so I'll spare you, but you can see it's soaked up some blood here in the bottom right corner."

Emma swallows down her revulsion. "Whose blood?"

"Jack Kirby's." Brown's eyes are dark, pained, before she looks back at the letter. "This isn't a spatter or a splash pattern, and it's not a smudge. It's a passive stain, probably from a pool. Which suggests this was written in the living room of the Sudbury house, where Kirby was killed, rather than a stain transferred from Simon's hand or clothing. He probably rested the paper on a surface near Kirby's body."

Travis's nostrils flare. "Okay. Anything else?"

Brown shakes her head. "In terms of trace, not much that wasn't native to the Sudbury location. Nothing that gives us any clues about where the twins might be now. You can see where the letter's been folded – this kind of paper holds creases extremely well – and how it's been fitted into the envelope. Gerry already fumed the envelope and took prints, and he'll fume this after I've shown it to you."

"But it's probably only Simon's prints," Emma says.

"Probably." Brown meets her gaze again. "Okay, time for the contents. Are you ready?"

Emma finds herself a little breathless once more, but almost as soon as she notices that, she notices something else; Travis has snuck his hand over and his fingers have laced with her own. She appreciates his presence more than anything. She doesn't know what made him choose to leave Carter in Boston, and come with her to Washington, but she's sure grateful now.

She nods firmly. "I'm ready."

"Okay, I'm going to read it aloud." Brown starts in her steady contralto. "*Dearest Emma…*"

Emma follows the words on the page as Brown reads –

I hope you've recovered from the shock you no doubt received upon viewing my ancestral home. My apologies for the mess. But you've seen such things before, haven't you? You're no blushing virgin in this regard - in many regards, I'm sure.

You will likely consider this missive vulgar in the aftermath. But as this may be my last opportunity to communicate with you, permit me a final indulgence, and allow me to say this:

Can you feel the wind stirring? Fall is a strange season, a time of flux. It brings one in mind of change, to see the leaves shift into ruddier hues. It's a suitable backdrop for drawing this stage curtain closed.

Principessa, I feel we may have reached the end of our dance. It's poignant, but often the best things in life are bittersweet. So let it be over and done. Let the old things fall away. The FBI set their hounds on me, and I have dealt with them in a way I deem appropriate - let that be an end to it.

This means an end to our connection as well, dear Emma. I will not call you an opponent - let us say instead that you have been a worthy dance partner. Do the FBI realize what they have in you? I doubt it. They should appreciate you more, but they never will. They don't understand you like I do.

And to the FBI analysts examining and picking over my final words: You have spent years trying to understand my 'behavior profile', my 'backstory', the 'psychology' of me. The whys and wherefores of my life. This is my chance to confess the truth at last...

There is no why. I did it because I enjoy it. Because it was easy.

You made it all so very fun, you see.

xxSimon

Brown sits back in her chair, her mouth working in distaste, as if reciting Simon's words has left behind a sourness in her soft palate. "That's it."

"Right." There's a swirl inside her mind; Emma blinks hard against it, refusing to succumb. She turns to Travis, addressing the obvious. "Okay, so he knows we're more than partners."

Travis's jaw is clenched. "What makes that clear?"

"*No blushing virgin, in many regards*?" Emma finds herself expelling a huff of air that sounds like wry amusement, although there's heat in her cheeks. "He knows."

"The stuff about you being a *worthy dance partner*…" Travis shakes his head. "Why are these guys always obsessed with 'worthiness'?"

"Just part of the messed-up serial killer psychology, I guess." Emma rubs her palms against her jeans. "Anyway, it sounds like he's planning to return overseas with Kristin."

"Yeah." Travis refocuses; he's making a mighty effort to sound objective. "But does he really think he can just say *Let that be an end to it*, and the FBI will let it go? He murdered four more men."

"The tone and phrases before the sign-off seem like a goad," Brown confirms. "This letter may have been addressed to Emma, but Simon's reference to 'FBI analysts' means he's addressing the bureau as well."

"*Apologies for the mess*, my ass." When Travis loses control of his expression, it becomes stormy. "What's the 'principessa' reference?"

"It's what he called me at the Kennedy Center," Emma admits. "It's a term from the opera."

"So he's just being a jerk, as usual." Travis sighs. "And he doesn't mention his sister at all."

Emma can feel the significance of that. "Do you remember the time I saw him at St Elizabeths, and wrote down what he said after the interview? You read the transcript and said he was fixated on Kristin. *Guys shut down sensitive talk*, that's what you said. You were right – and he's doing the same thing here. He's protecting her by not talking about her."

"*Fall is a strange season, a time of flux…*" Brown squints at the script on the page. "The whole thing is very poetic, although that's a regular feature of his style. If there's coded language here, I can't make it out yet. But I think I'm a little close to it and I'm also tired, so I'm going to pass this on to a friend at Langley for a second opinion."

"Okay." Despite his determined calm, Travis still has a stiff, angry energy. "So we've got Print and Trace evidence, and Langley will give us anything they can find on the language."

"Once I've compiled all the information, I'll fax the report and a copy of the letter to Howard Carter in Boston."

"Should we be sending the letter to someone to dig into the meaning a little more?"

Brown closes the lid of the evidence box and clicks it shut, peels off her gloves. "Dr. Becher would've been the person to contact, before yesterday. But there's someone – Lila Gretsky, she's a forensic psychologist at Georgetown U, and she sometimes guest lectures at Quantico. I can get in touch with her and get an opinion."

"I mean, we could try to psychoanalyze the contents of this letter all day," Emma says. "But I don't think it's that complicated – he wants to leave the country."

"Then why are they travelling south?" Travis asks.

"Because they're moving to Kristin's beat. And even *I* can't figure out what that will mean…" Emma cuts herself off as a new person arrives at the open door to Brown's office. "Hey, Mr. Dixon, how are you?"

Carlos Dixon is in fresh clothing, but his face is haggard, moustache sagging, his short beard a little furry and overgrown. Emma's never seen Dixon without fancy shoes, but today he's wearing scuffed Nike sneakers.

"Hola." He's holding a coffee mug stamped with a stylized red fingerprint and a logo that reads *Forensic scientist aren't petty, they just love minutiae.* "I'm keeping it together. Travis, thanks for getting us back to DC in one piece."

Travis nods. "Hey – no hay problema. You seem pretty wrecked, though?"

"Yeah, and now I have to go to the ME's office to go through the autopsy protocols from Boston." Dixon grimaces, takes a sip from his mug. "Linda, Gerry's up, he's got the jacket. And Glenn said to tell you that the videotape is ready."

"Really? Then I guess we should watch it." Brown stands, leaving her gloves on the top of the evidence box as a signal to others not to touch. "Glenn and I managed to make some headway with that videotape, although we had to call in reinforcements – videotape isn't really my area. It's taken this long to clean and prep it so it's viewable."

"And you want to watch the videotape?" Travis looks unnerved. "The tape that came out of…"

"Dr. Becher, yes." Brown grabs a notepad and a pen from a small pile on a nearby shelf. "We need to log the contents of the tape. Best case scenario, it's some kind of home movie, although I'm quite apprehensive about the kinds of home movies the Gutmunsson family may have produced."

"*I love new toys…*" Her words have come out in a whisper: Now Emma lifts her head. "That's it. Simon's videotapes."

"Come again?"

"I reminded Carter about it, but then it got away from me." Emma's annoyed with herself, that such an important memory took this long to surface. "When he was in Allegheny, Simon told me he'd made his own videotapes."

Brown has become more alert. "You think this could be a document of Gutmunsson's crimes?"

"It's a possibility. He said he'd made videotapes, but he could have lied, or this tape could be something else." Emma stands from her chair. "I guess we won't know until we watch it."

"Are you sure you want to watch this now?" Dixon looks concerned. "It might be really rough, Linda, maybe you should hold off." He checks his watch. "I've got to be at Whitman's office before noon, but if you wait a few hours –"

"Go, Carlos, it's fine." Brown pushes in her chair. "Glenn's here, and we can manage."

Dixon heads back to his office to collect paperwork for the medical examiner. Brown leads the way to the big examination lab, Travis following. Emma is just behind, and takes a moment to really look at him: He's holding some tension in his body, mainly in his neck and shoulders, but he doesn't seem to be as tightly-wound as he was yesterday. Emma hopes he's not in as much pain. The outline of his pill bottle rests in her coat pocket – he said he'd ask for them if he needed them. She hopes he doesn't need them.

The lab is bright with fluorescent light, and on the far side of the room, a weary-looking Glenn Neilsen is quietly arguing with a woman in a white shirt and blue canvas bib overalls who is connecting black cords between a rectangular metal box on the low lab table and a large television set on a stainless steel trolley. The woman seems to be in her late-twenties, although her soft face and Molly Ringwold-styled brown hair make her look younger, and her big glasses have a strange synchronicity with Neilsen's glasses.

"...but like I said, there's no coaxial port, so we'll just have to make do with the AV cables," the woman says, and when she spots Emma and Travis and Brown arriving, she pauses. "Sorry, slight delay, I had to go back downstairs to get a mono audio jack."

"That's fine." Brown's eyebrows lift. "You two are coping okay?"

Neilsen spins his wheelchair around when he realizes they have an audience. "Oh hey, Linda. Miss Brumbelow and I were just having a difference of opinion about which cable goes where."

"Except Mr. Neilsen doesn't know anything about AV cables, so his opinion is immaterial," the woman says sweetly.

"*Ella*." Neilsen's lips are pursed but he doesn't look genuinely angry. He runs a hand through his untidy brown hair. "Oh – sorry, introductions. Emma Lewis, Travis Bell, from Quantico training base, this is Ella Brumbelow, from technical archival support."

"Hi." Emma offers a wave in greeting.

"Pleased to meet you." Brumbelow smiles, and the spray of cables in her hand wobbles like a collection of black licorice strands. "We've nearly got the machine hooked up – it's the one from my lab, for delicate materials, only I usually hook it to the other television set downstairs? So we've had to mess around a little. This would be a lot easier with a coaxial, but here we are."

"And what's the state of the videotape? Can we view it?" Brown asks.

"We can view it," Neilsen reassures, glancing at Brumbelow. "Although Ella, you said you had some concerns about making sure the tape was dry enough to wind?"

"Oh no, that worked out okay." Brumbelow ducks behind the big Sony set and plugs something in, bobs up again. "I'm actually surprised at how simple it was to process, considering that wet contaminants on magnetic tape are usually time sensitive, and blood has a *lot* of salt in it – like, this is definitely one of the weirder damage-mitigation-and-recovery jobs I've worked on? But I washed the tape with distilled water and air-dried everything, then just sent it through the pinch rollers. Although, I'm really sorry, I had to splice some stuff."

Neilsen clarifies. "Apparently some of the tape was mangled when the doctors removed it, and there was damage as well from pre-surgical X-rays."

Brumbelow winces. "I *hate* X-ray, it just fogs the crap out of magnetic tape – we actually lost a bunch of footage. Just under a thousand feet, or about a third of the tape, was irreversibly destroyed. Like I said, I'm really sorry! I've saved the cut sections if you want them, although they're not viewable."

"She did her best, and we managed to save more than we lost," Neilsen offers in Brumbelow's defense, and Emma finds the energy between the two analysts amusing.

"That's unfortunate," Brown says, "but if there's nothing we can do to recover the footage, we'll just have to live with it. So now we can view the tape?"

"Oh, yeah," Brumbelow says. "One sec."

She ducks behind the TV set once more, fiddles with something, then pops back up, leans to press the button on the front of the set. White snow appears on the TV screen.

Travis looks around the lab. "Let's grab some chairs."

"Over in the corner, or out in the storage room," Neilsen suggests. He turns his own chair back to the table-top to collect a cloudy plastic videotape case. "Should I do the honors?"

Brumbelow is checking the back of the VCR machine. "Sure, go ahead."

Neilsen cues up the videotape cassette in its slot at the top of the machine while Emma and Travis and Brown find seats. Brown rests her notepad on her knee. Emma watches the snow on the screen, feels a hush settle. They're about to view Simon Gutmunsson's videotape, potentially a documentation of earlier murders he committed – the footage could be ugly.

Travis's mind-reading ability kicks in. "This might be bad, right?"

"Yeah," Emma confirms. "It might be bad."

"Pardon?" Brumbelow looks up, in the middle of squeezing around the VCR table and the TV set to come out and watch.

"Oh, of course." Brown winces, maybe that she didn't consider this herself first, and raises a hand. "Ella, one moment – do you really want to view this?"

"Uh, yeah?" Brumbelow looks slightly bewildered. "I mean, I've been working on it for over thirteen hours, so I kind of want to see if the recovery process was successful –"

"Ah, okay," Neilsen says, realizing the issue needs more explanation. "Ella, this tape is material from a homicide case, so it's potentially disturbing viewing. It'll be…a little like watching a snuff film."

"That's not a real thing," Brumbelow scoffs.

"In this case, it is," Emma says quietly. "It's a home movie made by Simon Gutmunsson."

"Ohhh." Brumbelow looks like she gets it now. "Oh wow. Okay." She chews her lip. "Look, I need to watch at least the first part, so I can check and resolve any playback problems."

"Just so long as you're aware," Neilsen says gently. "And hey, if everything's playing fine, then you're welcome to duck into my office while we view the rest."

"Thanks. I may take you up on that." Brumbelow appears to steel herself. "All right, it's go time. D'you wanna hit Play?"

The lights dim in the room; Travis has stepped over to the switches. Now he comes back and finds his seat beside Emma again. She controls the nervous urge to take his hand again, focuses on the Sony's giant screen and braces herself mentally.

The picture blips, resolves – it's a sunny, summer day. The image is steady, the camera clearly on a tripod. The focus pulls, until green and white fuzz in the foreground transmutes into a moving picture of Kristin Gutmunsson sitting in the long grass surrounded by white field daisies. There's a soft graininess to the image, suggesting wholesome authenticity: The Gutmunssons at home.

Kristin looks about fourteen. She's in a white shirt and long ecru skirt to match her shoulder-length white hair, and she's mugging for the camera with a bouquet of daisies that she holds to her cheek, blowing kisses and batting her eyelashes, like the star of an old silent film.

Here she is, in a simpler time: before Simon's court case, before her confinement at Chesterfield. Before she developed that unhinged mote deep in her eye.

Emma finds everything about the images poignant. "My god, Kristin's so young."

Travis leans forward in the dark of the lab. "Where's her brother?"

His question is answered: There's a jump-cut, the scene still outside in the grass, but with an altered sun position. Simon and Kristin are lying opposite each other; between them, a chess board. Simon is in a long-sleeved white shirt and fawn trousers, his hair a sharp reef of ice. Matched like this with his twin, he looks relaxed and shockingly juvenile, his pouting lips tender. Only a year after this footage, he will commit his first murder.

Simon makes a move with his bishop, and Kristin swoops in to make a move with one of her pieces – she shouts in victory, sitting up and waving her hands ecstatically. Everything is mimed: The film has no sound.

"This doesn't look so bad." Brumbelow, standing to the side, frowns and hooks her thumbs in the sides of her overalls. "But where's the damn audio?"

"Could it be the sound circuit on the player?" Neilsen asks.

"Nope. There could be damage to the outer edge of this section of the tape, but let me check here…" She walks behind the set to check the cables.

On screen, another jump-cut. On the stone patio of the Sudbury house, Simon and Kristin are older. Their hair is longer, their gestures more studied and sophisticated. They're with friends, everyone lounging outside on giant cushions and rattan garden furniture in the early evening. There are candles in glass holders on the coffee table; the quality of the light is poor. Despite the party's youth, everyone is drinking wine. Simon and another boy are smoking.

"That's Marlowe Drury," Emma says softly.

"Gutmunsson's first victim." The angles of Travis's face are rendered harsh with shadow in the TV glow.

This isn't a professional film, and maybe there was some damage from the cleaning treatment; there's a reddish grain to the footage, and a certain delay that gives peoples' movements an echo effect. When Kristin leans back and Drury takes her hand and pulls her off balance, kisses the side of her neck as she squeals, it's like Simon is in slow motion. He turns and looks straight into the camera, his expression utterly blank as he raises his wineglass to his lips.

"I could try another cable for the audio?" Brumbelow calls from the back of the set.

"Don't worry about it for now," Brown says, her eyebrows knitted and her attention distracted by the screen.

Jump-cut. The picture is black, but there's subtle movement within and at the sides of the frame that indicate this is a deep close-up. Then the camera draws back, and what has been unseen is revealed: Marlowe Drury's face, his drugged eyes blinking silvery tears, his tongue glistening as the lens withdraws from the cavern of his mouth, held open cruelly with hooks and fishing line.

"*Oh.*" Emma claps a hand to her own mouth.

The camera pulls back farther, and the dim afternoon light is still enough to show what's been done to his lips, his cheeks. The skin of his neck is separated in a clean cut down the center line of his throat, peeled outward to show the wet, red muscles and cartilage of his larynx.

Brumbelow reappears at the side of the TV. "I'm sorry, I don't know what's wrong with the –"

"*Ella, stay there.*" Neilsen's hand is raised, his cheeks blanched. "Don't...don't come out just yet."

Jump-cut. Morning in the garden of the Sudbury house. Kristin, about sixteen, lies in the grass. She is shirtless, her soft breasts strewn with green oak leaves and chamomile flowers. The camera zooms in on her, admiring her white hair streaming out around her. Kristin smiles at the camera, coquettish, and blows the lens a kiss.

"Oh my," Brown says.

Jump-cut. Low light, and the footage is gritty. Three figures recline in a jumble together on a leather sofa by a massive stone fireplace – not Sudbury, another house. A girl with long brown hair sits between the twins, who stroke and caress her from each side. Everyone is clothed, but it doesn't look as if that condition will last much longer.

"That's Philippa Robotham," Travis says. "Pippi, everyone called her. She was in the twins' friendship group. Another nineteen seventy-nine victim."

Ella Brumbelow peers around the side of the TV. "Can I, um, see what's going on yet?"

"Hold on one sec," Neilsen cautions. He glances back at the screen, uncomfortable. "Watching this feels gross."

On-screen, Simon reaches up and turns Pippi Robotham's head towards him, kisses her deeply on the mouth. On the girl's other side, Kristin takes a drag from a cigarette, her expression perturbed. Her gaze strays toward the camera, and she frowns, gets up from the couch and stalks forward, until the lens is obscured by her skirts.

Jump-cut. An afternoon party in a woodland clearing, everyone sitting around a table set incongruously with high-backed chairs, rustic floral arrangements, crockery and silver and crystal glasses.

"Oh no," Emma whispers. She recognizes the tableau from crime scene photos.

One guest seems to be asleep, face down in a bowl. Another guest

237

is positioned awkwardly upright, their chin flopped forward and their hands secured to the table with carving forks.

"*Jesus.*" Travis glances away.

Neilsen clears his throat. "Ella, give us a minute."

In a chair at right, Pippi Robotham still seems to be awake, although her shirt is open and her intestines are piled on the plate in front of her: She stares at the purple mess, blinking slow. Another boy reclines, head angled back, his face peeled away into a crimson mask. The tablecloth is, astonishingly, still mostly white.

Simon, in a cream linen shirt, sits at the head of the table and raises his glass in a toast. He says something inaudible, sets down his glass and reaches for a piece of fruit from a platter, tears the fig in half. His hands are blood-stained. He winks at the camera before squeezing the fig's innards into his mouth.

The camera moves, circles the table: The infamous tea party, a primary feature of the Gutmunsson mythos. The Artist in action.

Travis straightens abruptly. "This isn't on a tripod. Who's holding the camera?"

"Don't you already know?" Emma whispers.

The picture wobbles for a moment as the camera is thumped down on the far end of the table. Now the boy with his face in the bowl of soup is in focus, and Simon's figure is blurred in the background. Kristin Gutmunsson strolls into frame, walking behind the right-hand row of chairs, patting the eviscerated Pippi Robotham on the head in passing. She reaches her brother and climbs into his lap, kissing him, the two of them curling their arms around each other...

"Turn it off," Linda Brown says thickly. Her voice sounds loud in the lab. "I'll review the rest later, but I think we've seen enough."

Neilsen hits the VCR button, turning the screen black. His lips are twisted in a grimace. "That was…revolting. I need a shower. Ella, you can come out now."

Brumbelow scooches carefully around the TV, adjusting her glasses over big eyes. "Okay, judging from your faces, I'm glad I didn't watch."

"Kristin participated in Simon's murders." Emma says the most obvious thing straight away. "The prosecution team were right from the start."

"I still can't believe it." Travis seems genuinely shocked, but he's always had a lot of sympathy for Kristin.

"I can," Emma says softly. "And I wasn't the only one. Before he died, Becher was following up on something exactly like this."

Travis shakes his head. "In her testimony, Kristin was always so adamant that Simon was the perpetrator. That she knew nothing about it."

"It's pretty clear from that video how things really were." The lab lights flicker on; Neilsen rolls back from the wall switches. "Honestly, I always had some suspicions. Kristin Gutmunsson had no alibi for a bunch of the homicides, and a lot of her legal defense rested on her stabbing her brother when he was captured."

"Was there ever any physical evidence connecting her to the murders?"

"Nope. Not so much as a hair. But some of the crime scenes were in places you'd expect some cross-contamination."

"And maybe she wasn't there for all of them," Emma suggests. "Just a few. It didn't look as if she was present for Marlowe Drury's murder, for instance."

Travis is obviously thinking about other logistics as he lifts his chin toward the VCR. "That tape must've been stored somewhere in the Sudbury house. They didn't drag it around with them in Morocco. Boston FBI need to search the house again to see if there are more tapes."

"All right, so this information needs to reach Howard Carter as soon as possible." Brown has been rubbing her eyes; now her hands drop as she stands. "Glenn, are you and Ella okay to pack this up? And I want to send a copy of that tape to Lila at Georgetown University, along with Simon Gutmunsson's letter."

Neilsen nods. "We can pack it up."

"I'll make the copy." Brumbelow is already removing the video cassette from the VCR, packing it back into its plastic case.

Emma is returning her chair to the side of the lab when Gerry Westfall, clad in his usual Carhartt pants and suspenders, with a black cotton drill button-up, appears in the doorway to the lab.

He fishes a pack of Camels out of his pants pocket, warily eyeing off the television set. "You guys been watching soaps?"

"Hey, Gerry. It's the Boston tape," Brown replies.

"Great." He sticks a cigarette in his mouth and lights up. "Please don't tell me the details, I'll read the report. Linda, go wrap up your chores and take a break, you look beat. But before you do that – I just got through with that jacket you gave me. Did you know there was a note from Kristin Gutmunsson in the pocket?"

CHAPTER EIGHTEEN

Virginia, 3 November 1982

They're in the Ford Escort again, with Garron driving, by now only about fifteen minutes away from Quantico on the I-95. The trees on either side of the expressway are a rich russet-and-gold, and they've just passed an overhead sign for *Truck Rest Stop – ¼ Mile.*

Travis has been looking out the back passenger seat window, trying to lighten his mental load – the videotape shocked the hell out of him, and he can still feel the reverberations. The incest stuff wasn't a surprise to him, but the murders…

Emma has the briefcase full of Becher's papers across her knees, a photocopy of Kristin's note smoothed out on top of the dark brown leather. Westfall gave them a photocopy of the note before they left Scientific Analysis, but they're no closer to understanding it now than they were back in the lab.

It's one of Kristin's weird lists, much like the list she once shared with them about Simon's preferences for red wine. Except this time, the note – in Kristin's looping cursive – was tucked into the pocket of Becher's sport coat rather than tumbled in the bottom of her drawstring satin purse, full of pencil stubs and acorns and rose petals.

The team at the labs explained in detail that the note is on 300gsm watercolor paper, exactly the same paper as Simon's letter and probably from the same source: Kristin's sketchbook in the Sudbury house. It's written with a Faber-Castell watercolor pencil, #20 in Reddish-Brown. The note is about the size of Travis's palm, a torn-out piece, barely a scrap, and it's composed of only six words: *Diary, Mother's keys, Ring, Sheba, Tagore.*

They don't know what it means, but everyone has a theory: It's items Kristin wanted to gather from the Sudbury house before she and her twin departed; it's a list of things that Kristin likes, or is fixated on, or wants to remember for some reason; it's a code, and all the letters of each item can be rearranged to form a legible message…Somebody at Langley is actually working through the six words on the note, with the code idea in mind, right now.

Travis isn't convinced by any of these theories. The note seems like a reminder list, like what you'd write before you went grocery shopping. Something ephemeral, throwaway.

"But it wasn't thrown away," Emma muses. "Kristin put it in Dr. Becher's jacket."

"Kristin also helped her brother murder a whole bunch of people," Travis says dryly, "which probably makes her clinically insane, and you know she's always been a magpie. She could've slipped the note in there for any reason. Or for no reason at all."

Emma looks over – soft cheeks, gentle eyes beneath her pixie hair. "You sound like you're angry with her."

"Maybe I am." Travis rubs at his temple, searching the outside landscape of high cloud and sun and birch trees for relief. "Does that sound stupid? I feel like a fool for believing she was innocent."

Emma flattens the photocopy with her palm. "This is going to sound nuts, but I don't think Kristin knows what she's done. I don't think she even knows she's a killer."

"How the hell is that possible?"

"Repressed memories," Emma says. "It's a kind of self-hypnosis, or maybe actual hypnosis, with Simon involved."

"You're saying Simon *hypnotized* her?"

Emma shakes her head. "I'm saying that selective amnesia is an adaptive response in a situation like Kristin's – growing up with a twin brother who's a manipulative sociopath, who she depends on for emotional support, even romantic fulfilment, who's twisted her all out of shape."

Travis thinks of something Kristin once said about herself: *I'm like marshmallow. Soft and amorphous. There's nothing to hold onto...* Maybe Kristin contorted herself one too many times, and this is the result.

Emma smooths the pads of her fingers over the gold latches on the briefcase, like the metal is grounding her. "There's all these articles in Becher's papers about selective memory and the impact of trauma on memory. Becher believed that Kristin's pushing all this stuff down, shoving it into her subconscious, keeping it locked away. That's how she's able to present so convincingly. You, me, law enforcement, the legal team – she isn't trying to fool us. She really *believes* she's innocent. But it's affected her behavior in subtle ways."

"And not-so-subtle ways," Travis points out. "She's never come off as normal."

"No, and I guess that's part of her presentation. People understand flakiness, they understand eccentricity. Kristin has always seemed peculiar, but it was just put down to her personality. And law enforcement never had anything concrete to link her to the murders."

"But now we do." He can't prevent the bleak tone in his voice. "Now we know."

"Folks, we're on Russell Road," Garron says from the front.

A few minutes later, they reach the first MP checkpoint. There are a few delays as Garron's identification is confirmed, then they're on base, and Travis is providing directions to Jefferson. It's weird how the sight of the austere brick building brings a feeling of relief – even Emma's posture seems to relax a little. For Travis, it's the knowledge that the long miles of the last three days are over. Not for Garron, unfortunately: Now he's delivered them safely to Quantico, he's driving straight back to DC, returning the Escort's keys to the Hertz desk, and getting on the next flight back to Boston.

Crisp wind pushes Travis up the concrete steps, and he's weary. "Okay, it's nearly two-thirty. Let's check in, change clothes, go downstairs and call Carter."

Emma lugs the briefcase into the lobby. "I need to make photocopies of these papers, so I can stop carrying this damn case everywhere."

"Upstairs first? If I wear these jeans much longer, they're gonna start walking around on their own."

"Upstairs," she agrees.

They show their ID and make for the elevator. In the car going up, Emma puts the briefcase down and leans against him; Travis puts his arm around her. On their floor, they get out and separate in the hallway.

His room is exactly as he left it, all the items still in place: The dressy clothes from the Kennedy Center operation lie in a pile on a chair; his duffel, with his worn familiar sweatshirt peeking out, sits on the floor, neglected; the bed is still messy with tangled sheets. In the bathroom, he tosses his toiletries into the old leather washbag he's had since he was thirteen. His face in the mirror looks tired and he badly needs a shave.

Is there anything else you need? That insistent little murmur at the back of his mind.

244

No. He's had one pill on the plane, and he's not in pain right this minute. Emma has his pills. The physical distance is a safeguard and it's good, knowing he has to take a moment to think about it before automatically reaching for the plastic bottle – even if that momentary personal assessment is one more goddamn task, amongst the multitude of energy-draining tasks he's been asked to perform lately...

But it's fine. It's okay. He'll get through it. This isn't going to last forever.

And that thought makes Travis pause. Take stock again. Because it's the first time he's really acknowledged to himself that he's ready for this case, this return to law enforcement duty, this time at Quantico, to be over. And maybe he isn't planning on coming back here.

Is that what you really want? Emma's voice in his head, and all the memories of what happened that night.

What the hell *does* he want? He's being pulled hard from both sides. He's got an ID card and an official jacket and the promise of advancement: The FBI has offered him a law enforcement career. Emma...Emma has offered him a home.

He doesn't think he can have both. Emma's fought with him and bled with him, but he's pretty sure she's had enough of bleeding.

They just keep taking until they use you up. He knows her feelings about the FBI, and she's so sick of this war. Maybe, the way he feels after the last three days, he's sick of it, too. Oh, he gave it his all in Boston, to support Carter, but that felt like obligation, and he was dragging himself to the finish line that night.

He looks at his face in the mirror. He's nineteen, and he's been badly injured, burned hard, and he's barely at the start of his career...

He used to think that a job like this could be handled, that it didn't have to destroy you, that the role was more significant than just serving as cannon fodder. It would be different if he could convince himself of that. But after seeing Jack Kirby propped in his own guts, seeing Mike Martino chopped up and discarded – or why not go farther back, to Ed Cooper's death? To Barton Bell's? – Travis isn't sure he believes that anymore.

But if he's not good for law enforcement, what is he?

Under the bathroom lights, his reflected eyes look haunted. Travis splashes water on his face and dries off. *Quit it with this.* Let this day, before it's even fully over, be enough. No decisions, not yet. He just needs to concentrate on the task at hand.

He zips the washbag, goes back to the bedroom. Pulls off his warm jacket, lays it on the bed next to his duffel so he can find a fresh pair of jeans. Once he's changed, and has checked that the thermal shirt he's wearing still smells okay, he folds up his spare clothes, packs them neatly.

Go down, call Carter, talk to him about the videotape evidence, about Kristin's note…

Something about the note keeps repeating on him, he's not sure what it is. Something's swirling there in his brain pan. That stiff paper scrap, the six words – it's ringing off to the side, an incessant, tinkling bell.

He tries not to think about it. Pulls his boots back on, moves to fold the dress pants and shirt on the chair, hang the jacket off the chair back. If he gives them to Betty, she can return them to their owner.

Kristin, and her selective memory, and her grocery list: *Diary, Mother's keys, Ring, Sheba, Tagore.* A girl twisted out of shape, contorted by her dominant twin's psychopathic desires. The girl he first met in a sanatorium, under green trees, like an echo of the woodland grotto where she and her brother set up a tea party to slaughter their friends. *They thought twins were two halves of one soul…* Kristin pouring coffee from a silver service, laughing at the antics of the puppies at her feet –

It slams into him hard enough to knock him off balance.

"*Holy shit.*" Travis steadies. "Holy shit, it's –"

He lurches for the door, flings it open, then he's out in the hallway. Nobody else is in the hall right now and Emma's door is there, he pounds on it. When she opens it, he's still so shocked that he struggles to sound coherent.

"It's the *dog*," he says. "*The fucking dog.*"

Emma has changed her shirt, her hair rough and damp from a shower. "Travis, what are you –"

"*Sheba.*" The briefcase is on the floor, near her door, and the photo-copied note is resting on top. He steps in and grabs it up. "*Diary, Mother's keys, Ring, Sheba, Tagore.* Sheba is the name of the labrador at Chester-field. Don't you remember? The first day we met Kristin, the coffee and the dogs..."

"Chesterfield." Emma's eyes blow wide as it comes to her. "Kristin's private asylum. *Diary, Mother's keys*...It's a list of things she wants to get from *Chesterfield.*"

"*That's* why they're going south," Travis says. "Because Kristin wants to pick up her stuff and say goodbye to the damn *dog.*"

In the beat, he can hear Emma's shallow breathing and his own ears ringing.

Emma recovers first. "What time is it?"

He shakes the tinnitus away, checks his watch. "Two-forty."

"We should call Carter."

"Carter's in Boston. Who's lead investigator on the case down here?"

"You don't know?" Emma squints. "I-I honestly have no idea. Have they even worked that out yet, now Kirby's gone?"

"We need to go to Chesterfield," he insists. "The twins have probably already been and gone in Richmond, but they can't have got far. We can find more evidence –"

"Wait." Emma presses the edge of her thumbnail against her front teeth for a moment, deciding. Then she drops her hand. "Okay, can you arrange transport?"

"I'll organize a vehicle." That's his cue, the sign that Emma is on board with his train of thought. He starts walking backward. "You talk to Betty, get her to pass a message to Carter."

"Meet at motor pool?"

"Yep."

Travis is really glad he didn't have to convince Emma this was worth following up. He's already reached the open door of his room; jogging inside, he goes to the bed and grabs his ID lanyard and a couple other things he needs from his luggage – he shoves everything into a small canvas rucksack he's brought along specifically for this purpose. Then he scoops up his jacket, walks out, heads for the elevator.

Motor pool is one level below Behavioral Science, and it's chilly in the garage. Wind from the open bay doors creates little eddies of dust near the exit ramp. It takes longer than he'd like and some serious finagling, but Travis gets permission to take a beat-up brown Chrysler Valiant with enough gas in the tank to get them to Richmond. After that, they're on their own.

As he's signing for the keys, he sees Emma arrive from the direction of the elevators. She's got the strap of a black haversack over one shoulder and she's using both hands to carry two precariously-balanced polystyrene cups with lids. He meets her halfway, already smelling the coffee.

"You're a goddamn hero." He takes a cup from her stack, leading forward to the Valiant. "Car's this way. What's the story with Betty?"

"She's calling Carter now. I've got sandwiches in my bag, too. Let's go."

Travis unlocks and they load all their crap into the backseat. The car smells faintly of body odor and there's a depression in the vinyl front seat from a heavier driver.

Before they get in, Travis meets Emma's eyes over the roof of the Valiant, compelled to say it. "Look, I'm just going on instinct here, from a remembered conversation five months ago. We can't be sure this is a real lead."

"Feels like a real lead to me." Emma shrugs, slides into the front passenger seat.

"Okay." Travis exhales hard, takes his position behind the wheel.

Emma's making a face because there's no cup holder, grimaces again when she sees the car's transmission. "Can you drive a column shift? Give me your cup back."

"Three on the tree is fine." He's longing for that coffee, though. Travis starts the engine. "Emma, did you hear what I said? This could be a mistake. We could be driving to Chesterfield for nothing. Or it could be a false clue, a deliberate distraction."

"I know." She nods. "But we do the due diligence, like Carter said. And I trust your gut."

"My gut just got sewn back together a month and a half ago," he blurts out.

Emma grins. "You're fine. Just drive."

He guns the Valiant out of the bay. For the first time in a while, Travis recalls the afternoon when Ed Cooper drove them to Scientific Analysis through gridlocked Washington DC streets; Cooper was always great at managing traffic. Travis wishes he had his own set of flashers.

He gets them off base as quickly as possible, and back onto the I-95. "Listen, are we sure this isn't just an old note that Kristin found in her own pocket and stuffed in Becher's jacket?"

"Pretty sure," Emma says. "It could even be Kristin trying to communicate with us."

"What do you mean?"

"Think about it." Emma curls one foot up under herself, passes him a to-go cup now they're on the expressway. "Kristin's got a headful of memories that she's spent years squashing down. She's got no choice but to be pulled along by her brother. You said, after the Kennedy Center, that she might want to get out. So…maybe she stuffs the note in the jacket of a man who she and her brother murdered, leaving it behind for authorities to find. Maybe she hoped we'd read it. Maybe she's on the fence about Simon. About all of it."

"That's a lot of maybes." Travis frowns. "You think she's cracking?"

Emma sips from her cup. "I think she's a mentally unwell person who's talking to us the only way she knows how."

It's over an hour to Richmond. The pines and birches unspooling out the window are a lesson in fall contrast: deep rich green and shimmering yellow, like gold confetti. Above, clouds scud high in rippling waves. It's so sunny and nice today, and here they are, stuck in this government car, on their way to god knows what kind of situation…Travis shakes his head, takes the Doswell Road overpass.

Emma digs two saran-wrapped sandwiches out of her backpack and divides them up. "Dr. Brown and the others will have contacted Carter about the letter and the videotape evidence. Betty's already called to let him know we're checking out the Chesterfield lead…What do you think Carter will do with this new information?"

Travis wolfs down Wonderbread and bologna, tries to think about it like a bureaucratic puzzle. "He'll get moving pretty quick, I think. Contact Justice about relitigating Kristin's charges. Start getting some bulletins out to teams with additional warnings – I mean, he has to let folks know that Kristin is as much of a physical threat as her brother."

"And Boston?"

"Rasche tagged Carter to take the lead on that for political reasons, but now they know the Gutmunssons are on the move, that gives Carter some impetus to unhitch from Boston's state search. He'll probably be back here tomorrow, putting together a bigger team. He'll have to fill some investigative roles, but Carter's no slouch, he's got enough clout to select good people."

Emma nods, considering, as she chews. "What do you think he'll say about this stuff with the note?"

"Are you wondering if he'll be okay about us going to Chesterfield?" Travis takes a swig of coffee. He thinks about the timing. "Wallingford, where Gutmunsson posted the letter, is about seven hours from Richmond. The twins have been on the road for nearly sixteen hours, so they've had plenty of time to get from Connecticut to Virginia, visit Chesterfield, and cut loose. That's just my opinion. I'm hoping we'll find something at Kristin's old bungalow that will give us a clue about where they've gone now."

"If the note is Kristin leaving us breadcrumbs, I'd like to follow them."

"Agreed. And if we can nail down the twins' trajectory, that would be huge."

"Last question." Emma glances at him. "Are you feeling okay? Do you need meds?"

He wipes his fingers on his jeans, thinks about it. For what they're about to do, he needs focus, and he doesn't want to be distracted by pain. "Gimme one more."

Emma grabs her coat from the back seat, scrounges for the pill bottle in the pocket, puts one pill in his open palm. He washes it down with the coffee.

"Those pills are pretty strong," Emma reminds. "I can always spell you with the driving."

"I'm okay."

There's the road sign to Richmond. They stick to the '95 all the way through the city center, emerging on the south side of the James River. Another twenty miles to go. The river follows the road until Bellwood and they turn right toward Afton, before finally reaching the soft rolling green of Chesterfield Clinic.

Travis parks in the gravel lot near the discreetly-worded sign, and they both just sit there for a moment. The car is full of the susurrus of fall wind outside.

"You said this could be a false lead." Emma is looking out the window at the manicured lawns of the facility, the white blocks of residential bungalows. "Also that the twins have had plenty of time to visit and then go."

"I did, and yeah."

She runs an anxious hand through her hair, short wisps between her fingers like dark grass. "What do we do if they're still here?

Travis leans back to retrieve his rucksack from the rear seat. He unzips it and shows her the Colt Python that belonged to his father. It's still in its holster at the bottom of the bag, along with a box of shells.

"Oh." Emma bites her lip, glances at him. "Every eventuality, huh?"

"You got it."

They open their doors, slide out, lock up.

They don't look very FBI – both of them in jeans – but at the reception office, they lean on their FBI identification to get access to Kristin's room. The words *This is in connection to a current homicide investigation* help, too; Travis has always been good at talking the talk. An older nurse agrees to escort them across the grass to the bungalow.

"I hope this doesn't in any way reflect on Chesterfield's reputation –" the nurse starts.

"Not at all, ma'am," Travis reassures. He's sweating a little in his jacket, despite the cool breeze. "There's just a couple things we need to check."

The bungalow's lock doesn't appear to have been tampered with, but Kristin would have her own key, of course. Inside, the space is dusty, light-filled. A draft lifts the bottom edge of the long muslin curtains, making them sway.

The nurse stands sentry dutifully as they check the rooms, the shelves.

"Tagore is an Indian poet." Emma calls from the bookshelf in the open living room. "I can't tell if any of the poetry books are missing, though. It's not like a single damn thing on this shelf is alphabetized."

Travis walks back from the bedroom, having found more significant traces. "Jewelry box has been cleared out."

"So they *did* visit."

"Yep."

"What about Kristin's diary?"

"Hard to tell," Travis admits. "I checked her nightstand, her wardrobe shelves…There wasn't anything. She could have taken it, or it could be somewhere else."

"Keys might be another tough one to figure out. Let's check the 'Sheba' reference and come back to do a more thorough search." Emma turns to the nurse. "Excuse me, ma'am? You have dogs on the property, yes? Labradors?"

The woman seems flustered to be answering FBI questions. "Oh, uh, yes – yes we do. The residents often respond to the dogs."

"Of course." Emma's smile is tight, her impatience reined. "Could you tell us where they're kept?"

"The old barn, near the woodland side of property."

"On the state park side?" Travis clarifies.

"Yes, sir."

They abandon the bungalow, leaving the nurse to lock up, and walk across the soft, spongy lawn, past a stand of oaks. With the breeze making the red and orange leaves rustle, it's like walking past a cold forest fire.

"I just want *one* clue," Travis says. "One piece of evidence to say she was here – not the *absence* of something."

"I hear you," Emma says, shoving her hands in the pockets of her pea coat.

The barn is straight ahead: tin-roofed, unpainted, an old post-and-beam stables with goldenrod growing around the stone footings at its base. They stand there for a moment, looking at it.

"Very picturesque," Emma says quietly.

"Yeah." He feels it, too: Something about the isolation of the place, there on the edge of the trees, is making Travis's hackles rise. He unzips the rucksack and takes a knee. Loads the Python inside the bag, pulls it out, ditches the bag and the rest of its contents on the grass.

Emma's eyes go big.

"You said you trust my gut, right?" Travis whispers.

"Uh-huh." She gets in close behind him.

He grips the gun across his body in a left-side, low-ready position with two hands, and they move forward, losing the sun as they enter the open, shadowed doorway of the barn.

It's not big inside – a shotgun shack with six simple wooden stalls, three on each side. This front entry area is designed for storage, and there's junk piled up by the left wall: antique chairs, old dressers, patio furniture, glass jars full of old dirt, a metal bucket piled with cobwebbed kindling, a collection of gardening equipment – shears, spade, hayfork. On the right, a stack of hay bales. Green-tinted light streams in through the open doorway on the far side of the building, which shows a view of forest undergrowth.

On the right-hand side, the gate of the center horse stall is ajar. Travis can hear playful growls, and a girl's cooing giggle. All his skin comes alive with goose-bumps. Emma clutches his shoulder.

A barn swallow swoops out past them, and they walk forward.

Kristin Gutmunsson is sitting on the floor of the center right-hand stall, which is scattered with hay. She's cuddling two dogs, one an old golden Lab bitch and the other a more frisky juvenile. Travis knows dogs, he shouldn't be surprised that this is one of the month-old pups that he and Emma saw in their June visit, all grown up. Has so much time passed?

Kristin's white hair frames her face, flows down her back. She's wearing black ballet flats, black culottes – dusty at the seat and on the knees – and a white broderie blouse. Her face is open, relaxed, and she laughs as the juvenile dog licks at her neck.

She looks up at Travis and Emma as they step into view. Her blue eyes, so like her brother's, are like twin sapphires.

Her smile seems almost relieved. "You found me."

Travis finds his throat has gone very dry but his grip on the pistol is sweaty. They've found her – this eccentric girl, murderous and sweet.

"Hello, Kristin," Emma replies evenly.

"I wondered if you'd figure it out." Only a close examination reveals how Kristin's eyes are slightly vacant, how they track a beat too slow. "The note was very vague, of course, but you are both reasonably bright, and I just had to trust that you would remember…"

"I remembered," Travis says at last. He doesn't lower his grip. "How's Sheba?"

"Oh, she's doing *very* well." Kristin's smile cracks at the edges. She shakes off the tremble in her lips, smooths a hand across the back of the young dog, who twists to gnaw at her fingers. "And this is Lucky. He's going to get to stay here in Chesterfield for ever and ever, so you can see he's well-named."

"Where's your brother, Kristin?" Travis says softly.

"Oh he's…" She gestures vaguely toward the open door at the rear of the barn. "On the other side of the wood, in the car. I asked for a little private time. You know that's quite hard to find, with Simon. He's very attentive."

"Smothering," Emma suggests. They are standing about five feet away, giving Kristin space.

"Goodness, no, nothing like that." Kristin's laugh is a little too high-pitched and cuts off too abruptly. "He cares about me, you see. He just wants to keep me safe."

"He loves you too well," Travis offers. "Is that it, Kristin?"

The girl blinks up at him. "We were together in the womb. We've always been together. We've always loved each other…"

Emma is slowly, carefully moving to the right. "You were together at the tea party."

"Yes," Kristin says, her expression distracted. The young dog, Lucky, growls and tugs at her fingers. "Until I was called away…"

"You went to get the video camera."

"Yes." Kristin stops, corrects herself. "No. I had…I had an appointment with Mother."

"That's what you told the police, and your mother backed you up."

Travis takes another step toward the left, keeping his attention on Kristin, surrounded by golden dogs. "And what about that afternoon with Marlowe Drury?"

Kristin shakes her head as if something is buzzing around inside her skull. Sheba licks her neck. "I wasn't there for that. I wasn't there for any of them."

"But you were, Kristin," Emma says gently. "We saw it on the videotape."

"I don't believe…I don't think…" Kristin looks up at them, eyes crystalline with unshed tears. "Why would you lie to me so cruelly? That's an *awful*…Just an awful thing to say."

"I'm sorry, Kristin," Emma says, "but we're not lying to you. The videotape – the one you left inside Dr. Becher. We watched it. We saw it all."

"That can't be true." Kristin blinks, frowning, as the dogs bump against her. "I don't believe that's true."

"You were there for the tea party, and you were there for Pippi, and you were maybe there for Marlowe…"

"*That's not true.*" Kristin glares up at them. Then her chin dips and her gaze loses focus again. "That's not…That *can't* be true…I don't…"

Travis glances at Emma, both of them stuck in place as Kristin

Gutmunsson's consciousness surfaces, sinks again, bobs away. Travis is torn by the plaintive sight of this girl he's always felt something for, whether it be sympathy or suspicion. He's always found Kristin incredibly unnerving, from the moment they first met, and here she is, on the dirty floor of this barn, trying to reconcile her own memories with a reality that seems to make no sense. Pity rises up in him, tempers his caution.

Travis lowers his weapon in his left hand, releases his right hand so he can hold it out, palm-up, as he sinks down slowly on one knee. "Kristin, I know it's hard to understand. I know there's a lot you don't recall."

Their eyes are level now. Kristin looks at him, tear tracks shining white on her cheeks and her voice a whisper. "It can't be true, Travis. It can't be real. I don't remember anything like that at all, and I'd *remember*."

Emma moves nearby, and Travis can't look at her right now, but he senses her hunkering down. "Do you have dreams sometimes, Kristin?"

"No." One of the dogs – Lucky – licks at Kristin's cheek and she curls her arm around him, bringing him close. "I don't have dreams. I never have dreams."

Wrong approach. Travis isn't sure how he knows this, but he glances over at Emma, willing her to let him try. Emma's said before that he has a good read on Kristin; he has to take advantage of that now.

"Kristin, look at me," he says softly. "You left us that note for a reason, didn't you? You wanted us to find you. To help you remember. Do you remember Sudbury?"

"The house…" Kristin's gaze is floating as she nuzzles at the dog.

"That's right. The house with the lions at the gate." His chest is starting to ache from holding his body at tension. "You were there with Simon, and it was dark."

He never says Gutmunsson's name – not ever. It's a kind of rule with him, not to give Gutmunsson the privilege of a Christian name. But Travis has to bend that rule now to connect with this girl.

Kristin's attention hovers somewhere above the dogs she's petting and her voice is almost sing-song. "It was very dark. Simon said we had to wait in the maze. We waited and waited. It was so cold, and there was a storm…"

"That's right," Travis encourages quietly. "There was a big storm."

"I've never been so cold…" She shivers, and Travis can see she's in it, back there in the hours before she and her brother committed the Sudbury atrocities. "Simon went ahead to the house. He told me to bring the other things, the duct tape and the saw…"

Travis swallows, feels that same cold as he remembers the appalling state of the men's bodies inside that dark Tudor mansion.

"The *saw*…" Something clicks into place, Kristin's vision clearing, recognition coalescing in her brain. As the dogs whine around her, she looks at Travis with genuine understanding for the first time, her expression filling up with horror. "*Oh my god*. Oh my *god*, I didn't…I can't…"

"Stay with me, Kristin," Travis insists, leaning forward.

"I *can't*…" Kristin gasps, lists away. She begins to stand, clinging to the side of the stall to get herself upright, casting around, sightless. "All the noise – my god, there was so much *noise*, you can't imagine. I put duct tape over their mouths, I couldn't bear it…"

Emma winces, rises from her crouch. "Kristin –"

"It was too much, too much…" The girl's gaze is deep inside now, reliving the tangled jumble of images, memories she's never let herself acknowledge. She shakes her head, as if to relieve pressure. "There was so much *noise*, so much *blood*, and I…"

"Take my hand, Kristin," Travis says, standing to match her.

She suddenly looks at him, eyes piercing. "A man can stay alive a long time with his heart outside his chest. Did you know that?" Then her expression sags. "Oh. Excuse me –"

Kristin holds one hand on the stall and angles sideways, vomits quietly onto the straw. The dogs mill excitedly. Travis doesn't know what to do – this girl is going through an abrupt, harrowing process of instant recall which she may not be built to endure. If they're not careful, they could lose her to a full psychotic break.

He steps back, uncertain, even as Emma steps carefully forward. "Kristin?"

"Are you bothering my sister?" a cold voice says, and Travis looks left, immediately feels the barometer drop.

Simon Gutmunsson is standing inside the rear door of the barn, blocking sunlight. His tall, wide-shouldered figure is dark, almost in silhouette with the bright green and yellow foliage beyond the door. He's wearing dress trousers and a white shirt, a black wool coat.

Travis jerks up his gun, although it's in his off-hand and there's no time to aim.

Gutmunsson is on him faster than should be possible, covering the distance in one long stride. He smacks Travis's southpaw hand away to the left. The gun goes off – a deafening BOOM inside the tiny space – and spins through the air, landing inside the horse stall close by. Dogs start barking.

Gutmunsson uses the same striking hand to punch Travis full in the solar plexus.

"*No!*" Emma cries.

It hardly registers, except that he's falling backward. But that only lasts a moment, then there's no oxygen, nothing but an explosive agony in his diaphragm as he tumbles, lungs full of cement. He feels a secondary pain and a *gong* as his head strikes the edge of the metal bucket.

He can't breathe. He's drowning on dry land. Tears leaking from the corners of his eyes, he rolls, retches, vaguely hears Simon Gutmunsson say, "Hello, principessa," before his chest seems to seize up.

A soft hand touches his shoulder and Emma's voice quavers urgently in his ear. "*Travis*. Travis, *breathe*. Roll onto your front –"

Travis clutches at his chest, neck straining, pushed onto his side and finally finding the thinnest sip of air. Every gasp he makes is like knives. Somewhere in the background, barking, growling, and the sound of the Gutmunsson twins reuniting.

"Kristin, dearest, what have they been doing to you…"

"*Simon*." A heartfelt sob. "Oh, Simon, I'm so sorry, I should never have brought us here, to this place…"

Travis opens his watering eyes, breath coming in like he's sucking through a tube, wire in his lungs, alive to pain. The Gutmunssons are hugging each other in the center aisle, between the two sets of stalls, Kristin with her back to them, her white blouse outlined against her twin's black coat.

Her brother is stroking her hair. "Oh, love, you've done nothing wrong…"

"I *have*, Simon, I *have!*" Kristin turns and looks back at Travis and Emma, her gaze distressed and scattered. "All their blood is on my hands!"

And even as his chest burns and his lungs hitch, Travis remembers: The day in the garden, the feel of acorns crunching under his boots, Kristin standing beneath a green oak. *That's the difference between Simon and me – I know what he's done is wrong.* Unlike her brother, Kristin has a conscience, for all that it's been suppressed and abused all these years.

But Gutmunsson is pulling her back to face him. "That's not *true*, love. They're *lying* to you –"

"The big man I helped you get onto the kitchen table." Kristin's voice is toneless once more, as if she's walking through a dream. "I cut his belly open…"

"*Keep breathing.*" A whisper in Travis's ear, and before he can make eye contact, Emma leaves his side. He makes a futile stretch for her, but the action causes his chest to seize once more and she's already gone, crawling away for the gun to their left while the twins are wrapped up in their private drama.

"Dearest," Gutmunsson croons. "Kristin…"

"You wanted me to take everything out, like we did with Pippi." Kristin Gutmunsson sounds wretched, as if talking to her brother is hurting her. "But I put something in, instead…"

But Simon Gutmunsson has caught Emma's movement as she creeps on all fours for the stall – he steps away from his twin, steps forward and grabs her. Emma squeals as his hand fists in her short hair, yanking her up to her knees.

His angular face is contorted, his voice curt and angry. "Emma, *what did you do to my sister?*"

Travis makes a hollow wheeze, pushes himself up on one hand, collapses back down. More pain, a paroxysm of pain, a *starburst*. Dogs mill and whine, then dash out the barn door behind him, barking an alarm.

With their departure, Kristin wakes enough to plead. "Oh, Simon, please don't!"

"What did *I* do?" Emma's hands are up, scratching at Gutmunsson's fingers, her expression acid, gutsy even on her knees. "What did *I* do? When you've been mind-fucking and *actually* fucking Kristin for years, you selfish prick –"

Gutmunsson snarls, pulling Emma's head higher, and she shrieks.

Emma. Travis has to help her, has to…He rolls onto his left side. The dusty air tastes thick, sawing in and out of his lungs. He reaches blindly, finds something solid: metal tines, a wooden haft–

The hayfork.

Gutmunsson yanks Emma up to standing. *"You dare to –"*

"I DARE," she spits, twisting in his grip, yelling in his face, every bit of animosity inside her resonating in her voice despite her disadvantage. "I dare! And you can't *handle* it, that someone stands up to you! Kristin, the sister you say you love – she wanted to stay in Morocco, but you had to come back, had to give in to your *ego.* Everything is about *you!"*

With a tortured grunt, Travis pulls himself up with the hayfork's haft.

"STOP TALKING!" Gutmunsson screams, and it's the first time – ever – that Travis has heard him lose control.

But Emma will not stop, her voice babbling, enraged. "You think you're different from the Hoyts, the Huxtons, every killer I've ever met, but you're *no different,* Simon. Under the veneer, you're just a petty, cruel, vindictive *loser,* like all the others –"

Simon Gutmunsson roars, pulls hard at Emma's hair, wrenching her neck back. Emma screams, and Gutmunsson bares his teeth like a rampant wolf ready to bite, and Travis knows he's going to kill her. Black flares shoot across his vision as he lifts the hayfork's double tines.

"Simon, no!" Kristin shrieks, and grabs for Emma's arm, hauls Emma aside.

Travis has a clear shot. He winds up and spears the hayfork forward with all the strength he can muster–

Kristin Gutmunsson steps in front of her brother.

The tines stab flesh, pass through, disappear into the long fall of Kristin's white hair from behind.

"*NO*," Travis gasps, his voice all wheeze, feeling his eyes expand in shock.

There's a choking sound, a horrible weight on the end of the hayfork. It's quivering in his grip and his hands are wet, Kristin Gutmunsson's warm lifeblood oozing down the handle.

Emma turns around and sees, makes a strangled cry, her hands flying to cover her mouth.

Simon Gutmunsson's expression is confused. "Kristin?"

"No," Travis whispers, his chest on fire as he releases the hayfork and staggers to the side of the stall. "No no no…"

Kristin spins slowly, the wooden handle of the hayfork jutting obscenely from her back. Tines extrude out four inches in front of her at chest, at throat – the one in her throat has miraculously missed her windpipe and pierced through the muscle at the side of her neck. Blood pulses from the wound with the rhythm of her heart.

"*Simon*," she croaks, eyes unfocused.

Her twin catches her, cradles her shoulders with one arm, his other hand fluttering in bewilderment above the metal projecting out of her. "Dearest? Kristin?"

"Oh my god," Emma sobs.

Travis sags against the stall, vicious lightning under his ribs competing with this new horror.

"Simon." Kristin makes a wet swallow. Her white blouse is turning soggy red, her head sinking back. "Simon…"

"I'm here, Kristin, I'm here, don't…" Her twin tries vainly to keep her upright, tracks the blood spattering from her lips with an expression of perplexity. "Love, don't talk."

"I'm sorry." Travis's knees give way. "Oh god, I'm so sorry…"

"*Travis.*" Emma steps in and grabs for him, lets him collapse against her.

Together they sink to the floor of the barn, and it's as if Simon Gutmunsson has only just recognized they're still here.

His eyes narrow, the intense blue of a spring storm. "You did this."

"I don't…" Travis can hardly feel Emma's arms around him, can hardly breathe, words whistling out. "I didn't mean…Oh god –"

"*Simon.*" Kristin's white hand floats to her twin's cheek. She's paler by the second, her voice faint, liquid. "Brother…"

"Kristin," he whispers. "Please."

Kristin smiles, blood on her teeth. "Simon…D-do you love me?"

"Dearest…" Simon Gutmunsson gulps, his eyes glinting wet, voice thready and catching as he's rendered suddenly, shockingly human in this moment. "Can you…Can you not feel how much?"

Kristin's expression softens, her eyes glazing as she turns into a beautiful, blood-soaked mannequin, skin like wax. Her fingers fall away from Simon's cheek. Her red-streaked hair hangs down.

Simon, his face still tender, blinks and tries to lift his sister's hand, press her fingers to his mouth. Her hand flops away.

"Kristin. Kristin."

He touches her cheek, her lips. Sees her wide-blown, empty eyes. Only then does he seem to realize what has happened, the way his life has irrevocably changed.

His head lifts. He looks around blindly, makes a thin, quavering wail.

Travis wants to be sick. No air in his lungs. It's like the moment of impact when Gutmunsson punched him: the beat of silence, the mind-altering purity of pain. Emma is weeping above him, her arms hugging around him.

Simon Gutmunsson looks over, sees them. He bends, lets his sister's body slide to the floor. Stands again, all his limbs loose. Hands and shirt covered in Kristin's blood, he regards them with an expression of blinking focus. The sharp angles of his face turn to stone and he takes one step, toward the gun on the floor of the stall.

Sirens sound, away in the middle distance.

Simon pauses, like an animal sensing a predator. Pale-cheeked, eyes glittering, lips as white as his hair, he looks at his twin's body. Looks back at Travis and Emma. Then he turns and walks through the rear door of the barn, into the forest.

Travis totters on the edge of unconsciousness. A few minutes later, the state police arrive, and he can let go.

CHAPTER NINETEEN

Richmond, 4 November 1982

There's a small smoker's garden in the hospital courtyard, and at 6:30AM, in the half dark, nobody else is there. Emma sits on a cold wooden bench under a silver birch, pulls her coat closer and waits for the sun. Cardinals are waking up and making their morning calls. The sky is starting to pale and lighten. Behind shrubs on the other side of the courtyard, a heating unit comes on.

Emma lets herself cry for a little while. She thinks of the smell of lavender on the patio of Travis's uncle's house in Guanajuato.

A nurse in a blue Chippenham Hospital uniform covered by a thick khaki field jacket steps out for a cigarette, looks over. "You okay, honey?"

Emma dabs her numb cheeks with the sleeve of her coat. "I'm okay."

The nurse lights her smoke, puffs a couple times, face up to the trees. "Listen to those birds."

They listen for a while. The sun rises, blue and gold.

"Gonna be warmer today," the nurse remarks.

Emma tucks her hands in her armpits. "You think so?"

"For sure." The nurse takes one more drag before butting out. "Cafeteria's open, if you want coffee."

"Thank you," Emma says.

She doesn't go to the cafeteria. Instead, she pushes through the heavy glass door and turns right, walks along the corridor lined with blue bump rails to the elevator, where she rides up to the fourth floor. At this early hour, the hallway is coming alive with staff on morning rounds. Gray linoleum leads Emma forward to Room 441, where a SWAT officer in black fatigues sits on a padded chair beside the closed door, reading a copy of the *Richmond News Leader*.

"Cafeteria's open," Emma says.

"Thank you, ma'am." The SWAT officer folds his broadsheet. "I'll go down and get a brew when the shift changes at eight."

Emma lets herself in.

The room is dark with the blinds closed and the fluorescents off; Emma stands for a moment, allowing her eyes to adjust as the door hisses shut behind her. A bluish nightlight at floor level is helpful. Last night, she slept – if that's the term – on the large, upholstered recliner in the corner on the right, and her blankets are still mussed on the seat.

She's about to return there when she hears Travis whimpering in his sleep.

She goes to the hospital bed on the left, where he's a bulky shape under the starched sheets and pilled wool covers. He's in a hospital gown, and there's a nasal cannula delivering oxygen, the thin clear tubes hooked over his ears and meeting at his throat, as well as a chunky piece of plastic attached to his forefinger and trailing black cable; the nurse said this is a new thing, a pulse oximeter. His lips are swollen and dry. He's a couple days past needing to shave, and his dark hair curls on the pillow.

Emma watches Travis's eyeballs roll under his closed lids, the way his chest moves, his breathing low and jagged. She's not sure if she should call someone to attend, but it looks more like a reaction to things in his head. He's fighting devils in his sleep.

She brushes back his hair, then puts a hand on his forearm. "Travis."

"Muh…" His head turns, his eyelids flickering, brows scrunching. Then the dam breaks and he gasps awake. "*Uh –*"

"Hey." Emma makes sure her face is in his field of vision. "Hey, it's okay. It's me. You had a dream."

"Fuck." His eyes focus and he exhales, raising a hand to his mouth. It's the hand with the bothersome plastic attachment, so he flops it back down again. "Goddammit…"

"It's okay." Emma strokes his hair back some more. "It's all right. Give yourself a minute to wake up."

He uses his other hand to rub at his mouth. "Jesus."

"Bad dreams, huh?"

"Yeah." He closes his eyes like they're sore; his eyelids and fingernail beds are mauve, but the doctor said that the signs of cyanosis aren't that severe and should fade soon. His voice is rasping. "Have we got water?"

Emma gets him the water with the straw. She's spent way too much time in hospitals over the past five months – and she already had plenty of experience with them – so she knows where everything is and how to arrange items on the nightstand and tray trolley for easy accessibility. She raises the head of the bed a little, so he can drink comfortably.

When the straw pulls out of his mouth, he says, "I guess Kristin's still dead, then."

"Yeah." She takes the cup, squeezes his free hand. He's not trying to be glib or belligerent, he's just finding it tough to talk about. "Yeah, she's still dead. Are you okay?"

"Not yet." He lets his head sink back, eyes closing. "Maybe not for a while."

"That's all right." Emma's trying to be matter-of-fact about it. It's going to take them both a while. It doesn't seem quite real.

"Did you feel like this, after Kirke?" he asks softly.

"Yeah. It's pretty much the worst feeling in the world."

"You got through it, though." He needs some reassurance.

"With some help." What helped a lot was talking to Travis on the phone, and she hopes he remembers. But it's not as if the feeling's completely gone away, either. "Some of it lingers…I don't know how long that lasts. But it gets easier."

"Okay."

She wants to remind him of the circumstances. Wants to remind him that Kristin was the one who stepped in to take the blow intended for her twin. That it was – above everything – an accident. She knows that saying all this won't help. She squeezes his hand instead.

"Listen," she says, "Agent Carter arrived from Boston last night. He's coordinating the search for Simon with Virginia state police and the US Marshal Service. He said he'd come talk with you this morning."

"Great." Travis's rough voice is colorless.

"The doctors want to check you over first."

"Okay."

"They said maybe one more X-ray to be sure everything's where it should be," Emma says, and as she's saying that the door opens, and a middle-aged woman leans her upper half into the room.

"Hey, that's me! I'm the 'one more X-ray' lady." She steps closer, lets the door hiss. She's wearing navy blue Chippenham scrubs and she's sturdy, Black, wearing orange pumpkin-themed earrings, and smiling enthusiastically at Travis. "Glad to see you're up, sir – are you ready for your starring role in the spotlight?"

"I guess," he says.

"You guess? You guess right." The woman's nametag reads *Washington* and she takes a quick look at the clipboard chart on the end of Travis's bed, then glances over at Emma. "Are you coming along for the ride?"

Emma defers to Travis. "You want me there?"

"I should be okay," he says.

Nurse Washington is pleased. "Excellent, now let me get you set up here…"

She begins the process of taking Travis's blood pressure, then ripping off the Velcro band and checking his oxygen readings, unhooking him from machines in order to wheel the bed away. After a few minutes, once he's been cleared by SWAT, another orderly comes in to help.

It takes a few minutes, and Emma returns to her recliner so she's out of their hair. "If you need me, I'll just be here. I have to write out a statement."

Travis meets her eyes as he's wheeled away. "See you soon."

After he's gone, and the bed with him, the room seems peculiarly half-empty and hollow, and Emma herself feels half-empty and hollow. The modern heating unit under the window hums deep and low, like a gothic choir. Emma wants to sleep more, but she suspects she's still too tense, so she settles back amid the blankets and uses the hardback Gideon Bible from Travis's nightstand to rest her paper on as she writes out a full description of what happened yesterday afternoon in that old barn on the wooded boundary of Chesterfield Clinic.

At 8:00AM, the SWAT protection shift changes over. Travis is back from X-ray and poking at the items on his breakfast tray when Howard

Carter arrives. He hangs up his coat and jacket, sits on the end of Travis's bed, and asks if he's ready to make his statement.

"Yeah," Travis sighs. "Let's get it over with."

As Carter gets out a small micro-cassette recorder, like the one she used to listen to the recording of Agent McKnight's death at the Kennedy Center, Emma asks Travis if he wants her to stay.

"Not for this," he says quietly.

"Give us a minute," Carter says.

Emma nods and leaves the room. She goes downstairs in the elevator and visits the cafeteria, takes her time buying four coffees. She piles cream and sugar sachets on the tray to bring them back upstairs. The officer at the door appreciates the gesture.

When she comes back into the room, Travis looks exhausted from talking, but he cheers fractionally at the smell of coffee. Carter accepts his cup, adds sugar, and rather than dashing back to work, he stays a while, spending some time that Emma is sure he doesn't have, sharing information and asking how they're tracking and looking at them both with a great deal of compassion.

"Oh, here – I've finished my written statement," Emma says, and hands him the pages she labored over earlier. "So what do we have now?"

"Okay, this is where we're at." Carter sips, sets down his cup and pushes up the cuffs of his sleeves. "State police and the Marshals have widened the search for Simon Gutmunsson, and they're coordinating with the Massachusetts unit. We've got the tracks from his car and we're chasing the registration – we think the twins ditched their Sudbury vehicle and acquired a new one in Connecticut. We're checking all Gutmunsson's old haunts, and properties listed under the family name. Another APB went out broad last night at 8:00PM, and Gutmunsson is currently in our top five Most Wanted. I've also put together a new team at Quantico to keep us current on all this, because we've been operating without crew for the last forty-eight hours. Now, we won't be spread so thin."

By 'we', he means him – Emma can see the signs of intense weariness in Carter's face. He's at least had a chance to change his clothes since Boston, but he looks like he could use some sleep.

"One other thing I wanted to tell you both in-person," Carter continues. "Your families are safe. Miss Lewis, we've moved your parents and sister to a more secure location – here's the number." He passes her a card. "Mr. Bell, I've been in touch with your mother, she's decided to go with your sisters to Guanajuato, they flew out late last night."

Some cloud Emma hadn't even realized was there seems to melt off Travis's face and he rests easier. "Okay, that's good."

"She's made the right call," Carter agrees. "It's better for them, and it means you don't have to worry. And that's all I've got for now, so I guess I'd better get back to it."

"Thanks for coming in," Emma says.

"Honestly, it's a relief." Carter stands and pulls on his jacket. "I've been talking to grizzled cops for days. Here, I get to talk to you young people and sit down in a quiet room."

"Will you keep us in the loop?" Travis asks.

"Absolutely. But you should concentrate on healing up." Carter collects his coat. "I feel like we're close. We've hit Simon Gutmunsson where it hurts, and he's going to make a mistake soon."

"Or he'll do something crazy," Emma suggests. She's been thinking about this a lot. "Kristin wasn't just his sister – she was his heart, and what was left of his conscience. Now he's conscience-free and angry. We've seen Simon when he's scheming, we've seen him be cold and malicious…But we've never seen him when he's truly angry."

She's afraid of it, she knows, but she wants to impress on Carter that she's not speaking purely out of fear. She's hoping he'll take it as a warning.

"At least this time, we're better prepared for him," Carter says, then he wishes them both a quick recovery and departs.

Emma takes Carter's still half-full cup and puts it on the tray, checks the time: It's nearly ten. Nearly time. Travis is lying back, his eyelids drooping.

"You sleepy?" she asks.

"Yeah," he admits. "Which is nuts, because I just woke up a few hours ago."

"Sure, but they woke you every two hours in the night to take your blood pressure, and you've got a bunch of drugs in your system, *and* you just gave your statement to Carter – that's all exhausting." She pulls the covers up for him. "Go back to sleep. I'm gonna go call home."

"Okay."

"You need anything?"

"Nope."

Emma leans a hand on the bed near his pillow, bends close. She nuzzles her nose against the side of Travis's throat, where his scent is strong, and rubs her soft cheek against his rough one, before pressing her lips to his.

"I haven't had a shower, and I haven't brushed my teeth," he protests softly.

"I don't care," she says. She's noticed how his eyes glance away from her now, like he's ashamed of existing, and she aims to fight that. And for herself, she needs it, needs this promise of sweetness to get her through the next few hours. "I'm gonna go now. Get some rest."

Grabbing her pea coat and letting herself out, she checks that the card is still in the back pocket of her jeans, then makes her way once again to the elevator and its downward momentum. In the car, she's alone, and she gives herself a moment to find her center. On the ground floor, she goes to the phone banks, calls the number on the card. Talks reassuringly to her parents. Talks to Robbie.

"How's Julia?" she asks her older sister, and she can almost hear Robbie's double-take through the phone.

"Um, she's fine, I guess," Robbie says, with phony cheer. "She's good. Where's this coming from?"

They haven't really discussed this yet, and Emma's pretty sure her sister doesn't know that Emma saw them kissing in the barn.

"Does she make you happy?" Emma asks. "Just tell me she makes you happy."

Robbie goes quiet for a whole minute, until Emma's ready to ask if she's still on the line, before she finally replies. "Yeah, she makes me happy. She's wonderful. She's...everything."

"Good." Emma smiles, her eyes getting wet. "That's all I wanted to know. That's the only important thing. I love you, Rob."

"I love you, too, Em."

They leave it there, and Emma hangs up. She wipes her eyes with back of her hand.

Then she returns to the elevator and presses the button for the basement level: Just like at Quantico, this stuff is always at basement level. In the car, she pulls on her coat. She gets out in a long, cold corridor with two branching corridors and many offset doors, and has to check the directions she wrote down on a slip of paper to make sure she's heading true. But she finds the right path and is directed to the right area.

She pushes through the wood veneer door and finds herself in a dim, gray, echoey room, not much wider than a hallway, with a couple white plastic chairs against one wall and a large viewing window on the other. To the right of the window, an older intercom unit attached to the wall, and another door with a mounted plastic box sign above it that reads *Controlled Area* – the sign is currently unlit. A green curtain covers the window on the opposite side of the glass.

Emma buttons her coat and spends a moment bracing herself for what's to come.

As she's finishing her mental preparations, the door she entered through opens and a squat, familiar figure walks in. Carlos Dixon looks better than when she last saw him, more put-together in brown plaid wool trousers and a mint-green bowling shirt and a sport jacket. He has an overcoat caught inside the crook of his elbow.

"Miss Lewis, hey," he says, smiling. "They told me you were here already."

"Hey, Mr. Dixon," she says.

Dixon lays his overcoat across the arms of one of the white plastic chairs. "You holding up okay?"

"Mostly.

"How's Travis?"

"Physically, he's all right," Emma says. "The doctors want to keep him at least until tomorrow. They were worried about reinjury so soon after surgery – something about a traumatic diaphragm rupture and surgical adhesions – but he hasn't got a fever, and his tests and X-rays have come back clear. They don't think he's a lung collapse risk anymore."

"I'm real glad to hear that, we've been worried about –"

Dixon is interrupted by a rap on the glass of the viewing window. The green curtain is pulled aside along the top rail.

Behind the glass, a stark white room with a large, high surgical light, and a metal benchtop against the far wall holding equipment. A tall, rangy older man in navy blue scrubs stands near the glass, a scrub cap covering his cropped gray hair.

The man steps to the side, touches something Emma can't see, and a rough, smoker's voice issues from the intercom. "Hey, folks, are we all good? Carlos, good to see you – did you drive all the way down from DC to say hi?"

Dixon smiles and hits the intercom button on their side. "Hey, Clay, no, I got in last night. They brought us in by chopper – Gerry had his usual conniptions."

The man behind the glass rolls his eyes and grins, nodding.

Dixon hits the button again. "Clay, this is Emma Lewis from Quantico. Miss Lewis, this is Dr. Clay Simmons, out of Central."

Dixon holds the button so Emma can step closer and reply. "Nice to meet you, Dr. Simmons. Thanks for attending."

Simmons opens out the hand he's not using on the intercom. "Thank *you* for doing the identification, it's saving me a major headache. Now, are we ready?"

"We'll need comprehensive photos, Clay," Dixon says.

"I'll get you photos," Simmons replies. "All right, time to go to work."

Simmons releases the intercom and turns his back so he can go to the metal bench and don a paper gown, latex gloves, a paper mask. He begins setting up a set of metal scales, a small dry-erase board with markers, a measuring tape, a set of stainless steel instruments.

A nurse – an older white woman with bobbed hair, wearing examining gloves – enters from an opaque plastic swing door at left, and sets a camera on the benchtop, walks over to the place near the intercom and touches something: The *Controlled Area* sign comes on. She exits again, and the doors sway, then she returns, walking backward carefully and towing a metal gurney. On the gurney, a long shape covered with a white cloth.

Simmons waits until the gurney is in position, its entirety centered length-wise in the viewing window, before turning on the big, glaring surgical light and returning to the intercom. "We'll get the identification out of the way, then Miss Lewis can leave."

"I'll stay," Emma says, not bothering with the intercom.

Dixon frowns. "Are you sure?"

"I want to stay. I owe her that much."

"Okay." Dixon seems unsure of Emma's decision, but he hits the intercom anyway. "Miss Lewis is staying for the whole procedure, Clay."

"Really?" Simmons" eyebrows raise, lower. "Okay, it's up to you. Tap out anytime, and there's chairs behind you if you feel dizzy. Shall we get started?"

Emma swallows, nods.

Now she's delivered her burden, the nurse retreats. Simmons goes back to the gurney and, without ceremony, removes the drape.

Lying on the silver steel under that harsh, glaring light, Kristin Gutmunsson is naked, her body white as marble. Emma can see the faint blue tracery of veins at her wrists, her closed eyes, her breast. Her belly is concave, and her pubic hair is dark. Long legs and arms, a graceful neck...She looks like a sculpture of a nymph, a statue of a girl, something you might find in a gallery somewhere. The bruise-like marks where the hayfork tines pierced her are the only blemish on her skin.

She looks as if she could wake at any moment, but at the same time, it's patently clear that she will never wake again.

The back of Kristin's skull rests on a plastic cadaver head block. Her blood-stained white hair, freed now from the drape, flows down and swings gently off the edge of the autopsy table.

Simmons approaches the intercom. "Miss Lewis, do you attest that this, the deceased, is the body of Kristin Margret Gutmunsson, lately of Chesterfield Clinic, Virginia?"

Emma finds her breath coming in short. There's a sense of unreality, of time collapsing. Kristin, here, like this, on an autopsy table...Kristin on the night of the Paradise sting, applying eyeshadow with soft brush strokes...Kristin on a plane, giving her a manicure...Kristin giggling, saying, "Oh, goodness!", and swirling her long skirts...

Simmons and Dixon stand expectant, these two men waiting on a response. Emma recognizes this poignant fact: She and Kristin have, many times, been the only women in the room. Now, here they are again. She thinks she made the right decision, to stay. She doesn't want Kristin to be alone for this.

She presses the intercom.

"Y-yes." She clears her throat. "I mean, yes, I do attest."

"Thank you, Miss Lewis," Simmons says. "All right, let's begin."

The bonesaw is switched on, and Emma breathes deep.

CHAPTER TWENTY

Virginia, 5 November 1982

About 3:00AM, Travis wakes from another nightmare, one he can't fully remember. He's woken Emma, too; she's standing by his bedside in the humming dark of the hospital room, her hand warm through his cotton gown, squeezing the muscle of his shoulder.

"Hey, hey…" She rubs his arm. "It's a dream. It's a dream, Travis, it's okay."

The pressure in his chest is back, and he tries to breathe slowly. He's never wanted a Percocet more, something to make him numb, something that would render him unfeeling, something to block sensation out for good. The nightmare is over, but flashes remain: a sense of crawling dread, Kristin Gutmunsson in her long emerald gown, her brother snarling, the dogs Sheba and Lucky bounding from the stables…Travis's hands on the hayfork as they spear through solid flesh, that feeling of weight and liquid warmth…Kristin in her red-soaked broderie blouse, blood on her teeth as she turns to him and smiles – *You found me…*

"Hey," Emma says. "Okay, fuck this, I'm getting in with you now. Make a hole."

She unwraps the blanket around her shoulders, lays it over the other blankets on his bed, then climbs in beside him, burrowing under the covers. Her body heat and the smooth skin of her bare legs against his own is a jolt, enough to be confusing. The bed is wider than a twin, but it's not made for two; she pulls up the rails so they're not in danger of toppling out, then pulls the blankets so they're both tucked in.

Now she's turned on her side in the quiet night, facing him when he can barely face himself.

"Talk to me," she says. "Tell me."

"I can't," Travis whispers hoarsely. How can she even stand to be near him?

"Travis, look at me," Emma says. "I've killed someone. I killed Kirke. I shot him in the face."

"It's not…" His throat is closed and tight. "Kristin was innocent."

"Uh, she really wasn't. She murdered –"

"*She didn't remember.*" Travis smears his hand across his wet eyes and rough cheeks. "You saw her in the stables. And you said it yourself in the car on the way to Chesterfield – she'd suppressed all those memories of what she did."

Emma shakes her head against the pillow. "Whether she was innocent or not, it doesn't matter. She stepped right in front of you. It was an accident."

His voice comes out thick. "Saying 'I didn't mean it' doesn't make me feel better."

"I know. I know, and I'm sorry." Emma subsides, her dark hair tufted, her pale face blue-tinged, sharp eyebrows and cheekbones shadowed. "I killed Kirke because he threatened me, and he was hurting you."

"Kristin wasn't a threat."

"Maybe not at that moment. We can't know. But at the end of the day, you didn't mean to hurt her."

"No, I didn't," Travis finally allows. "But I don't think her brother is going to give much weight to my intentions."

He doesn't give them much weight himself. What had he *meant* to do? Had he even been thinking clearly?

"Look at me," Emma says again. She leans in close. "You're not a bad person."

She is frighteningly good at sensing his mood and his thoughts. There are thoughts in his head that he sometimes wants to keep screened, keep private, maybe because he knows they're unhealthy, but she digs them out, unerring, like she's doing now.

"Travis, I've been where you are," she says. "Let's talk about innocent people dying, okay? For a long time, I felt like a monster for escaping Huxton and leaving those other two girls to be killed. Oh, I tried to tell myself, after the fact, that I'd always planned to reach help and save Vicki and Tammy – but in my heart, I knew there was no plan. There was no *thought*. I just fought him, and I got clear, and I ran. Like a coward."

"No," he says softly.

"It's true." Her exhale comes out unsteady. "I abandoned them, and they died before the police even got to Huxton's house."

He wants to spare her this, wants to tell her to stop yanking out all this painful personal stuff to make him feel better, but she's determined to keep going.

"So it took me a long time to accept that it was understandable, even okay, for me to just want to save myself," Emma says. "To feel like I deserved to be saved, deserved to live, as much as the other girls. That anyone in my position would want to escape. That being completely debilitated, being injured and abused, meant it was hard enough for me to get *myself* out, let alone to expect that I was capable of saving anyone else." She blinks, swipes her face against the sleeve of her T-shirt. "I had to let that responsibility go. It was never mine to hold. I escaped, and I tried my best for the other girls, but there was nothing I could do."

He's transfixed by the play of light and shadow across her features, and by the absolute courage of her. Her presence, her existence, her continued survival is a testament and a reminder: *I've survived this, so can you.* He once called her a force of nature, and now he understands exactly what it means, how fitting that description really is.

She takes his face in her hands and stares deep into his eyes, speaking plain. "You didn't mean to kill her, Travis. She stepped in front of you, and there was nothing you could do. You'd been injured – you could barely stand up. And if Kristin's death hadn't distracted Simon long enough for the state police to arrive, he would've killed both of us for sure. You can count on that."

Emma's words are a balm, but the acid burn of guilt smarts inside him, making his voice rough and hitching. "It feels so bad."

"I know, baby," she says. "I know."

"Let me hold you," he whispers.

"That's why I'm here," she says, and draws him close.

They can sleep after that. In the morning, the new nurse on shift is a little scandalized to find Emma in Travis's bed with him, but that's okay.

There aren't that many more hospital tests to complete – the doctors check his lung sounds, and are keeping an eye on his oxygen levels, but everything else is done. Travis finds his chest pressure has eased, and his cannula is no longer necessary, so he's sitting up drinking awful hospital orange juice when Carter arrives. He can't stay long, but he's brought some of the cool outside air in with him, as well as coffee and crullers from downstairs. Travis switches up the OJ for coffee while listening to updates on search progress.

"We may have a positive sighting in North Carolina," Carter says, nudging the cafeteria tray to squeeze a manila folder onto Travis's overbed trolley, taking off his coat. He's looking more refreshed, like he's managed to get some sleep, and possibly a meal that wasn't from a gas station. "A trooper claims to have spotted Gutmunsson in a car outside Mooresville – we got the plate number."

"I hope you've told people not to go near him." Emma, dressed again in her T-shirt and her jeans and running shoes, is folding blankets and stacking them on the recliner that she didn't use last night. "Simon isn't sane, has never been sane. But he's completely off the leash right now. If he's pulled up for a traffic stop or something, there's no predicting what he might do."

Carter nods, demolishing a cruller as he slips his glasses on with his other hand and examines the notes in the folder. "We've issued thorough warnings – don't interact, don't approach – in all the APB and BOLO dispatches for both law enforcement and members of the public. The last thing we need is more casualties because somebody was trying to be a hero. But listen, this term from Kristin's note, 'Mother's keys'. We've been digging into it, and Agent Reyes –"

"Agent Reyes from Pittsburgh?" Emma stands straighter, finished with the blankets and now folding her arms in front. "Who worked with us for the Paradise operation?"

"Same guy," Carter acknowledges, finishing his pastry and taking a slug of coffee. "I got in touch, he was floating between units in Pittsburgh. I asked him if he'd like to come aboard, he said yes. He's a great addition. He's been trying to work out if the *Mother's keys* reference is alluding to an object, like keys for a vehicle or a post office box, or whether it might mean keys to a location."

"Or whether it means anything at all," Travis says. "Kristin wasn't what you'd call stable. It's not hard to imagine that she was just scribbling random stuff down."

"But she was rational enough to mention Sheba, so we'd know where to find her," Emma says. "I think the note was for us, but it was also a real list. She took the jewelry, and probably the poetry book, and nobody's found her diary."

"I agree," Carter says. "I believe the keys are real, and that they correspond with something. Something we don't know about yet."

"Mother's keys…" Travis blows on his coffee. "What do we know about the mother? Is she still alive?"

"She's still alive," Carter confirms. "Last we heard of the Gutmunssons Senior, they were in Madrid."

"Can we talk with her?" Emma helps herself to a cruller from the bag on the tray trolley. "She might know what the keys reference means."

"If she's happy to cooperate with us." Carter brushes pastry sugar off his shirt and closes his folder. "She and Ivar Gutmunsson left the States to avoid legal and financial repercussions here, after Simon's court case. She might just ignore our requests. We'll try other angles, just in case. Look, I've got to go, but there's one other thing I need to talk with you about."

Carter's standing, facing Travis and looking serious. Travis braces himself for it, wishing he weren't in a hospital gown.

"Mr. Bell, you've been declared not legally culpable for the death of Kristin Gutmunsson." Carter removes his glasses. "No charges will be brought by the Richmond PD or by any other agency. Chesterfield Clinic has negotiated to sign a release. Kristin's COD has been registered as accidental death by Clay Simmons, the medical examiner."

Travis isn't sure what to say to that, is unprepared for the swoop in his stomach at the idea that he'd maybe been on the hook for murder and hadn't even realized. "Okay."

"It's a just outcome," Carter says.

Travis swallows the peach pit in his throat. Last night with Emma was a salve to a lot of the wounds, but like she said, the painful sting lingers. "Still feels kinda shitty."

"I understand. But don't take it on, son. That's not your load to carry." Carter takes one more slug of coffee, reaches for his coat again. "Oh, and the Richmond PD still have your sidearm. They've requested to keep it for a few days while they complete ballistics tests, but after that, you can get it back."

"It's my dad's gun," Travis says.

"We'll get it returned to you, I guarantee." Carter wipes his mouth and hands with a paper napkin, picks up his folder. "I'm heading to Quantico, now I'm packed up here in Richmond. Being back in the office is holding a lot of appeal. What time do you check out?"

"Soon," Travis says.

"About five this afternoon," Emma says, glancing at him. "Depending on what the doctor says."

Travis makes a face. After two weeks of hospital in September, his patience for this stuff has run dry. "The quicker I can get out of here, the better."

Carter nods, already holding the door. "Okay, then I'll see you folks back at the ranch this afternoon. Catch you soon."

The door hisses shut behind him, and Travis is surprised to realize that he feels a certain detachment from Carter and the bureau now – he's invested in catching Gutmunsson because it's personal, but his connection to the FBI feels blurred as a tombstone rubbing. He wants it to be the same, but it's not. Something has changed, and he's not sure how to fix it, or if he's supposed to fix it. Will he get back to Quantico and feel out of place there? And wasn't he having these doubts and concerns before?

"You good?" Emma asks.

"Yeah." Sand seems to be shifting under his feet, and it rattles him. Being in this hermetically-sealed room with the humming heating unit isn't doing much to help. He pushes the covers off. "I think I'm gonna take a shower."

The shower clears his head, makes him feel more human, more grounded. Back in his shirt and jeans, he starts agitating for release, but there's still some fucking around before they'll let him leave. Emma's not convinced he should go early, but in the end, the wheels of the hospital process move so slowly that it's 3.00PM before he gets permission to go, and ultimately, as he points out, what real difference is two hours going to make? He's out of bed, he's upright. A little devastated, but basically okay.

They get a SWAT escort back to Quantico and reach Jefferson by four-thirty. There's nothing in his hands – Emma has her black haversack, but his rucksack, with the shells for the Python, will probably only come back with the gun. Luckily, he finds his FBI lanyard in his jacket pocket, so there's no hold-ups checking in.

"Upstairs?" Emma asks.

If they go upstairs, she'll try to make him rest, and he's had plenty of rest. He's moving slowly, but he can still move. "Honestly, I'm fine. I wanna go see what the folks in the basement are up to."

When they reach Behavioral Science, Betty is at her post, wearing a blue wool skirt suit with an ivory blouse tied in a bow, a cameo at her throat, like she's just walked out of a 1970 Sears catalogue.

"Miss Lewis, Mr. Bell, nice to see you. Special Agent Carter has invited you to attend the meeting in his offices." She proffers a small business card. "Also, this is for you, Mr. Bell. It's the phone contact for the main switchboard of the Office of Personnel Management, regarding your mother's survivor's benefit."

"The what?" Travis squints at the card. "Why is this coming to me?"

Betty explains. "As the spouse of a fallen federal officer, your mother is the recipient of an OPM survivor's benefit, in the form of a monthly annuity. OPM has been trying to contact her, but as she's out of the country, and you're listed as next of kin, and also as a temporary federal employee…"

"So, they tried to phone Mom, but they couldn't reach her, so they want to talk to me. Great." He's still confused. "What is this in regards to?"

"I'm afraid I don't have that information," Betty says serenely.

"Okay, I guess I'll call them." Travis snorts, tucks the card in his jacket pocket. "I'm not doing anything else right now."

Emma leans forward. "Betty, which office is Mr. Carter in?"

"They're all in BSU10," Betty informs.

Through the beige-and-gray warren of cubicles, BSU10 is revealed to be a large managerial office with the partitions removed. Carter and his new team have colonized it into a working space by adding the hard old couch from the Cool Room, and hanging blackboards on the cinder-block walls. Four paperwork-loaded desks are squeezed in, plus a corkboard with all the photos and notes from the Gutmunsson file, tacked up in a more sensible order.

Carter is holding court, one foot up on a metal file box, pointing the end of a pen at the blackboard, his shirtsleeves rolled. Four other heads swivel as Travis and Emma arrive at the door.

"You're back already?" Carter straightens. "Excellent – let me introduce you to the team. Jonah Reyes, who you know from Pittsburgh. Sam Mitchell is on temporary loan from US Marshal Service. Dr. Lila Gretsky is our psychology consultant. And Reggie Bowen…" Carter makes a dry grin. "We don't know why we Reggie's still hanging around. Folks, this is Travis Bell and Emma Lewis."

"Hey, nice to meetcha." Closest to the door, Bowen is a white guy in his early thirties, also in shirtsleeves, with a red tie. A toothpick hangs in the corner of his grin; Travis suspects he's the new Martino. His handshake is of the hearty 'one and done' variety common to football players Travis knew in high school. "Oh man, you folks nabbed Hoyt *and* Kirke, and now you've taken Kristin Gutmunsson off the board…"

"Yeah, well." This is where he'd usually say something politic and friendly, but Travis isn't in the mood. It's disorienting to realize that Kristin's death, which he's been agonizing over, is considered a win here.

"You came straight from the hospital? That's some commitment." Mitchell is a clean-shaven Black man in a black polo and hard-wearing chinos. His USM badge is on his belt. "Come on in, we've got coffee somewhere."

"Coffee's terrible, but it's free." Dr. Gretsky is white, closer to forty, also in chinos, with short, curly hair and a cheerful face. "Pleased to meet you both, I'm looking forward to sharing notes."

"All right, let's share some notes up here." Carter, drawing everyone's attention back as he stands beside Reyes, a lean Latino man in his late forties with big, brown-tinted glasses, bow legs, and sleek dark hair, already thinning. "Mr. Bell, Miss Lewis, we've found a lead but we're on a time limit. Jonah, do you want to give us the brief?"

Reyes – who Travis remembers fitting him with a wire for the Paradise sting – consults his notes. "Right, okay. So we examined and re-searched all the Gutmunsson properties, but then we got the *Mother's keys* thing. Digging hard into Alice Gutmunsson's history – which included some phone calls to Europe – turned up some real juicy info. We now think *Mother's keys* is a reference to a property that Alice had in her maiden name, du Hammel, that she never sold and never divulged on tax records."

"There's a house nobody knew about?" Emma finds herself a seat.

Reyes nods, holding up a curling paper. "This just came through on the fax. The whole thing's been very cleverly managed – property taxes and maintenance costs handled by an estate manager, all the bills sent to du Hammel's brother in Luxembourg. Low key, under the radar."

"I guess the Gutmunssons Senior wanted a landing pad if they ever decided to come home from Europe," Travis suggests.

"You got it." Reyes pokes at a spot on a wall map. "And here's the property, outside Wells in New York. It's right on the edge of the Silver Lake Wilderness area." That sounds significant, and now Reyes explains why. "It's isolated, plenty of forest to get lost in, but there's easy access to Syracuse and Albany, and most importantly, it's close to the Canadian border. The twins could've been hanging out there since their return from Morocco, for all we know."

"Sounds exactly like what Simon Gutmunsson needs right now."

"Exactly." Mitchell nods, leaning his chair back, one foot on his desk. "We're flying out with a Rapid Response team to check it out."

"Uh, not me," Gretsky says, raising a hand.

"No," Carter acknowledges. "I want you and Mr. Reyes holding the fort back here."

"Good, because I'm really hoping to pick Miss Lewis's brain about Dr. Becher's notes regarding the Gutmunssons' psychological makeup."

Emma looks surprised. "Um, sure, whatever you need."

Travis waves a hand. "So you're going to Wells – what's the play on the ground?"

"We're coordinating with USM, New York staties, and Syracuse SWAT." Mitchell gets up to point at spots on the wall map. "All groups meet up in Johnstown, here, so's not to spook our guy if he's in residence. Advance to here, near Hope Falls, then do a swoop raid."

Travis tilts his head. "And we don't know if Gutmunsson's there? No pre-raid surveillance?"

"We don't want to put any of the local staties in danger." Bowen's tucked his toothpick behind his ear and is running a finger down a checklist on a clipboard. "I'm talking to Deputy Chief Evan Taylor from NYSP, and Sergeant Bill Hickok – yes, that's his actual name – from the Syracuse unit, and we're updating all the APBs to tell everyone how we really don't want folks going near our guy."

Carter is nodding. "We saw what Gutmunsson can do to the unprepared, after Royce Sullivan in Boston. If he realizes he's being surveilled, he won't just bolt, he'll retaliate. I'd rather simply go in hard – if he's there, we've got enough force to grab him, if he's not, we look someplace else. But this seems like a pretty solid lead."

"When do you leave?" Travis asks.

"In about an hour."

So fast. Travis gets a sense of people and events moving around him at a pace he's currently not equipped to keep up with. "Okay. So what do you need us for?"

"Right now, I need you both to stay on base, stay safe, and if you want to discuss the videotape and Gutmunsson's letter with Dr. Gretsky, that may be helpful."

Travis knows what this is – busywork, and the tying up of loose ends. "Sure, we can do that."

"Excellent. Now, let me remind everyone real quick about VHF communications…" Carter says, and the rest of the discussion is about the raid operation logistics, coordination, and the likelihood of Simon Gutmunsson being at the location. It's all pretty rapid-fire, and wrapped up quickly. Then Carter, Mitchell, and Bowen don their jackets and pull on thick coats as they prepare to head for the roof. In fifteen minutes, a chopper will be ready to transport them to the location.

The three men accept departure jokes and commendations for the hunt, then the office is cleared out. Reyes jumps on the phone. Dr. Gretsky has snared Emma into a conversation, presumably about Simon Gutmunsson's psychopathology.

This all feels…a little like having whiplash. Travis walks over to the corkboard with all the photos. The ones in which Kristin is smiling are particularly painful. He tries to focus just on the ones with her brother: Gutmunsson looks smug in almost every shot. Travis should feel vindicated about wiping the smirk off Gutmunsson's face. Gutmunsson killed Barton Bell – now, Travis has killed Kristin. Natural justice has been served. He should feel righteous about it.

Instead, the memory of Kristin's body on the hayfork recurs, and he just registers a sense of disgust about it all.

He's glad Carter is dealing with it, and the new team – younger, energized, hungry for the hunt – seem like they'll work well together. But for Travis himself, the thrill of the chase and the adrenaline of live action is curiously absent. The fluorescent tile lights in Behavioral Science make everything stark, and he feels…non-operational. Distant.

"Travis?" Emma's come up on his left and he hadn't even noticed. "What's happening?"

"Not much." He nods at the photos. "Just…remembering old times."

"Listen, Dr. Gretsky wants to talk, and I'm going to get Becher's briefcase from upstairs, okay?"

"Absolutely."

"Travis." Emma steps in to squeeze his hand. "You look a little lost."

"I feel like dead weight," he admits.

"Do you need to rest?"

"I been resting…" He shakes his head, sucks his teeth, reminded of how Emma had been testy during the Crafton raid in Pittsburgh: *I can't just sit here.* "I need something to do."

Emma's suggestion isn't one he was expecting. "Have you called your mom?"

It's such a good idea that he does it straight away.

Rather than going upstairs to his dorm room, he simply walks over to the empty cubicle outside BSU10, near the water fountain, and pulls up a chair in front of the desk. The plate glass window shows the view into Carter's team office, where Reyes is taking down information on the phone, where Dr. Gretsky makes notes as she waits for Emma to return.

Travis pulls the phone closer, presses a button for an outside line, starts to dial – stops. He's forgotten the card Betty gave him. May's well do that chore first; he finds the card in his jacket pocket, dials again.

"You've reached the United States Office of Personnel Management," a prim voice says. "How may I help you?"

Travis hunts for a pen on the desk he's borrowed. "Uh, I'd like to speak to someone about survivor's benefits, please."

"Certainly, sir – forwarding you to the Retirement Information

Office now, please hold." Ten seconds of incredibly twee music, then a new voice: "Hello, Retirement Information Office."

"Uh, hi. My name is Travis Bell, I'm returning a phone contact from the Office of Personnel Management regarding my mother's survivor's benefit? She's not available to call back right now, so I'm acting on her behalf."

The older female voice on the line sounds put-out. "Well, thank you for getting in touch, Mr. Bell, but we don't discuss benefits over the phone. If your mother received a contact from us regarding her benefit, it would've been by mail."

Travis frowns. "So you don't have a record of the call? Because I was given this number –"

"I'm very sorry, sir, but like I said, I'm not at liberty to discuss benefits over the phone."

"But *you* called *her* –"

"Well, I'm afraid there must be some mistake. As I mentioned, this office conducts all business relating to benefits exclusively via certified mail. If you have any further concerns, please do contact your state branch. Is there anything else, sir?"

"Uh…no." Now he's really confused.

"Thank you for your time, sir, have a good day." The lady hangs up.

Travis taps his pen against his bottom lip, before getting up and walking through the cubicle corridors. At the foyer reception desk, Betty is packing personal items into her handbag as she prepares to call it a day.

"Excuse me, ma'am?" Travis holds up the card she gave him. "Can I ask how this message from OPM came to me?"

Betty nods. "Of course. I received a call from Special Agent deVere, who is in charge of your family's protection detail. He explained that

OPM had called your mother at her home. Another agent at the house informed them that she was temporarily out of the country, so OPM asked for a local contact, which was you. Agent deVere subsequently passed on the message about it to us here, so we could get in touch with you. He didn't want a communication delay to create a problem with your mother's benefit payments."

"That was nice of him," Travis says, "but OPM don't seem to have a record of their initial call."

"I can try them, if you like?" Betty offers.

"Thanks, but…I'm sure it's fine." Maybe he just needs to try calling the local branch.

"Is there anything else you need, Mr. Bell?"

"Um, no. Oh – wait. Can I call international from the office phones?"

"Yes, just dial for an outside line, like normal, then dial the country extension before the number."

"Thanks, Betty."

"You're welcome, Mr. Bell. Have a nice weekend."

Is it Friday night? He hadn't even noticed. Travis walks back toward the borrowed desk. As he's taking a drink at the water fountain, Emma returns to the team office with Becher's briefcase. Through the window, he sees her place it on a desk and pop the clasps, sees Gretsky peering at the paperwork.

Travis sits down at the phone once more and calls his uncle Luiz's ranch.

The phone rings seven times before being picked up. It's Sofia on the line, then Luiz, then Sofia again, and Travis switches to Spanish so he can make his responses understood, fielding high-speed questions from his aunt and uncle, reassuring everybody that he's okay, really, he's fine, yes, Emma is fine, too, they're all right.

Finally, they bring his mother to the phone. "Travis? Are you okay?"

"I'm okay, Ma – are you okay?" He's still speaking Spanish. "How're Lena and Connie?"

"They're complaining about being away from San Angelo, Lena especially, but they're fine," his mother says. "You don't sound so good."

You can fool mostly everyone, he reflects, *but you can never fool your mother*. "I'm okay, but I'm tired. I'm still a bit doped up, and kinda sore."

"Uh-huh," his mother says, her suspicions confirmed.

There's a pause, and he remembers that as the widow of a US Marshal, she knows it all, has heard it all. She's familiar with what Travis is experiencing, in ways he's never really considered before. Rosa Bell has been direct and pragmatic and insightful her whole life, and sometimes it fucking stings, but maybe that insight and honesty is what he needs right now.

"I killed someone, Ma." He takes a breath after saying it, testing how the words taste. Bitter, so bitter. He swallows hard. "I killed someone, and it wasn't for no reason, but I still did it."

"Were you protecting yourself? Protecting Emma?" his mother asks.

"I guess I thought so."

"Then you did the right thing."

"It doesn't feel like it." His mother's voice has unstoppered some kind of cork inside his heart. "Did Dad…Did he ever regret the things he had to do as a Marshal?" And maybe this is the better question: "Do you think he'd approve of what I'm doing here?"

"Everyone carries regrets," Rosa Bell says. "No one is immune from that – not even your father. But he's proud of you, Travis. You never need to worry about that."

Now his eyes are damp, for all the reasons he's starting to get a better understanding about. "What if I don't stay in law enforcement? Would he be proud of me then?"

"You're not a parent yet, Travis," his mother says softly, "so you'll just have to believe me when I tell you that what every parent wants is for their child to be happy. To find satisfaction in life and to be happy – that's what we wish for our kids, always." Her voice gets more light-hearted. "You could be a peanut farmer, and so long as you're happy and satisfied, your father would be proud."

It's a family joke. Travis sniffs and tries to smile. "I don't think I want to be a peanut farmer, Ma."

"I mean, somebody has to be, or there'll be no more peanuts." His mother snorts, sobers. "How long will all this keep going, Javi?"

It hits him hard, then. She's down in Mexico, temporarily uprooting her life so that she and the girls can stay safe from one of the monsters that Travis is tracking: Only the monster's death or capture will give her release. He feels guilty, and he knows she understands, but dammit, she shouldn't have to.

"I don't know, Mama," Travis says. "They'll get it done as quick as they can."

They. The recognition of what he said jolts him. It used to be *we*, but it's not that anymore. Wow.

He rubs his eyes. "Are the girls there? Does Lena want to yell at me some, for dragging her away from her boyfriend?"

"They're in the next room," his mother says. "I'll go get them. Lena's pretty angry."

"Oh, great," he jokes.

"One moment."

The phone is put down with a clunk. Travis stops capping and uncapping the pen in his fingers, sets it back down on the desk.

The phone is picked up, and he braces for a tongue-lashing. "Lena?"

"No, it is me." A growling, familiar female voice; Mariana smokes a couple cigarettes a day. "Are you healthy? When are you coming back?"

Travis grins at the blunt questions. "I don't know, abuelita. Are Lena and Connie driving you crazy?"

"They're less trouble than boys. They help with the dishes. I'm not worried about them, I'm worried about the dogs."

Travis picks up a paperclip. "What's wrong with the dogs?"

"Chico died."

"What?" He drops the paperclip, sits straighter.

"He died this morning, we don't know why. He was dead in the stables. Now Paco and Oscar and Kuku are sick. Mateo is worried it is the distemper."

"So Chico died, and now three more are sick?"

"Yes, that is just what I said, did you not hear?" Mariana coughs, clears her throat, goes on. "Mateo is wrong, it does not look like the distemper. There is no fever, and no pus in the eyes. It looks more like the time Sofia's brother's dog ate the poison for the rats. But Mateo and I have an agreement that he uses no poison, because of the dogs. So where would the dogs eat it?"

Travis looks at the paperclip, there on the desk. He holds the plastic phone receiver to his ear. But he's not connected to the physical world right now: Instead, he hears a series of ratcheting cogs clicking, pieces aligning in his head. Experiencing it is something of a revelation;

many times, he's wondered what kind of internal system gives Emma the ability to recognize evil when it crosses her path. Now, as cogs shift, as he ticks off all the red flags waving, he realizes it's not a psychic power – it's just joining the dots.

Simon Gutmunsson has dropped off the map…OPM called Travis's mother's house; it was not their usual process, and the OPM representative was informed that his mom is out of the country…In Mexico, on his uncle's ranch, four dogs are dead or dying for no clear reason…In 1973, terrible things happened to the dogs at the Gutmunsson residence, when Simon was a child…

Two days ago, as he cradled his twin's body, Simon Gutmunsson stared into Travis's face and said, *You did this.*

Travis stands abruptly from his chair. Through the window of the BSU10 office, Emma notices his movement, meets his eyes.

"Abuelita," Travis says evenly, "is uncle Luiz there? Can you pass the phone to him?"

"Your mother is coming with your sister –" Mariana starts.

"Give the phone to uncle Luiz for one minute, abuelita."

"Travis?" Emma has left Gretsky's side and stepped into the office doorway. "What is it?"

Travis covers the phone with his hand. "I'm not sure. One second." He checks the time on the wall: It's 5:32PM.

His uncle gets on the line. "Hola?"

"Uncle Luiz, I need to talk to you for one minute, okay?" Travis wets his lips. "Were the dogs in the stables last night and this morning?"

Luiz is a little confused, but he says that they were.

"And they got sick this morning?"

"Yes."

"You don't know what's wrong with them?" Travis listens to his uncle's reply, but he's thinking of timing, of driving and flight departures. How would Simon Gutmunsson know about the address of the ranch in Guanajuato? It seems impossible. But his alarms continue to peal like deranged church bells. "Okay, uncle, this is going to sound a little weird, yeah? But I want you to get everyone together and leave the house. Can you do that for me? You need to do it straight away. Yeah, I'm sorry. No, I don't know where you should go – someplace busy. Maybe to Luisa's in San Miguel…"

When he glances up, Emma has come closer. She's biting her lip.

Travis has to concentrate, and his hands are sweating. "Look, I don't want to panic my mom or the girls. Tell them I'm gonna come to you, okay? Soon. Like, as soon as possible. I'll fly into León. Yeah, okay. But uncle, the important thing is to get everyone out right now. Understand? Don't stay at the ranch. I don't know if it's safe…"

The rest of the phone call is just reiterations and assurances. Then Travis hangs up.

Emma has moved to stand right beside him, her face a mask of throttled concern. "I didn't get all the Spanish – tell me what's going on."

"Someone who said they were from a government office called my mom in San Angelo and was told she was out of the country. And now someone's poisoned the dogs at the ranch…" When he explains it like that, it seems thin. Emma knows about the Gutmunssons' dogs, though. Travis grips the nape of his neck. "I don't know. Am I being paranoid?"

"How would Simon know about the ranch?"

"I'm just trying to figure that out." Travis's heart is racing, uncontrolled. "I got no idea. Maybe I'm going nuts."

"What's your gut telling you?"

"That something is wrong. That I need to be in Guanajuato."

"Okay," Emma says simply. "Let's go."

CHAPTER TWENTY-ONE

Virginia, 5 November 1982

The first part of the trip is like a quick-step barn dance: fast movement, rapid manoeuvring. Emma goes upstairs to grab their bags while Travis explains everything to Reyes. When she gets back down to Behavioral Science, Reyes is pulling on his coat.

"You've got no cover between Quantico and Mexico." Reyes digs for his keys, pulls open a drawer to collect other things. He's a neat, fox-faced man with a taciturn manner and quick dark eyes, and Emma thinks he might be reasonably smart. "Just to cover the bases, I'll drive you to the airport."

"Are you sure?" Dr. Gretsky stands by the desk with Becher's briefcase, looking as if she wants to wring her hands. "This is all happening very suddenly."

"That's the way things usually happen here." Emma tries not to sound dry as she tugs on her own coat. "What's the likelihood that Simon Gutmunsson could be threatening Travis's family in Guanajuato?"

Gretsky's mouth twists. "Psychologically speaking, it makes sense that Gutmunsson would consider Mr. Bell's family a viable target for retribution."

Reyes spreads a hand. "Look, I don't know, it seems thin. But I run the odds, Miss Lewis. It's no more unlikely than the idea of Gutmunsson being in a random house in upstate New York, and we sent a strike team for that."

"No strike team for this," Travis notes, zipping up his jacket.

"We have no jurisdiction in Mexico," Reyes agrees. "But I can talk to Carter about contacting local authorities for cooperation."

"That may take time to set up that we don't have."

Reyes nods. "I think you're going off-book for this one, at least for the time being. Are you folks ready to leave?"

Reyes's car is in the lot outside Jefferson – a dark blue, two-door Ford Mustang Ghia with a racing hood vent. The car is two years old and in absolutely mint condition, and now Emma is doing a thorough reappraisal of Special Agent Jonah Reyes.

She tosses their luggage in the rear seat and raises her eyebrows at the leather upholstery. "Do you spend a lot of time under this car at weekends, Mr. Reyes?"

"At least as much time as I spend driving it fast." Reyes has the shadow of a grin. "Hurry up and jump in the back."

Reyes gets them to Washington International in under an hour – Emma's impressed. The whole way there, he's talking, calm and unhurried, strategizing with Travis about travel arrangements, emphasizing that they should keep receipts for reimbursement, getting Emma to write down phone numbers, encouraging them to stay in contact. Close to Alexandria, he starts discussing equipment.

"You can't take a weapon on the plane," he notes, "and definitely not over the border."

"My sidearm is still with the Richmond PD anyway," Travis says.

"So you're gonna have to find something once you arrive." Reyes gives Travis a glance. "You got people down there you can talk to?"

"I got people," Travis confirms.

"Good. One other thing." Reyes fishes something out of his inside jacket pocket. "Take this."

Emma receives the small, thin piece of plastic with the Chase Manhattan logo, along with the sticky note it's wrapped in. "An FBI credit card?"

"Not a credit card – it's for one of those automatic teller machines. You'll find them outside the banks at the airport. The number on the sticky note gives you access, even on a weekend or after hours. You get a limited amount of cash, three withdrawals only, and I mean it when I say I want receipts."

Travis frowns at the card. "Are you sure that thing will work?"

"It's new, but it works."

Then they're pulling up at Domestic departures, Reyes is wishing them good hunting, and they're hustling hard to make the next plane to Texas.

Three and a half hours later, Houston Intercontinental is a mess of harried-looking travellers, crying toddlers, and weird, square-panelled ceiling lights. They hit their first snag – there are no flights to León, Guanajuato, until 3:00AM. With a lot of sotto voce cursing, Travis buys their tickets.

"Call your family again," Emma suggests. "Hopefully they won't be there, but at least you can check in."

Public payphones are ranked in a row beside the entrance to the business class lounge. Emma stands nearby with Travis's duffel and her own backpack as he makes the call.

Travis presses the plastic receiver to his ear and squeezes the metal phone housing as the dial tone rings and rings endlessly. He finally hangs up. "No answer."

"Great. That's what you were hoping for, right? If nobody's home, that means they got out."

"It's good news," Travis agrees, nodding, but he still looks super stressed.

"Where will they go, d'you think?"

"Luisa's in San Miguel is most likely. Her house is pretty small, though. And I don't know her number."

They dropped off some celebration food for Luisa, Travis's aunt Sofia's sister, on the day Kirby arrived, Emma remembers. It was the day this whole mess started.

Emma checks the time on the huge digital display over the service desk: 11:41PM. "Let's call Carter."

"He may not be back from New York."

She's running out of road. "Then let's get coffee."

Before coffee, they find the bank branches with the automatic kiosks and use the plastic card Reyes gave them. It works like magic. Travis suggests they do all three withdrawals in succession, pointing out that they may not have either kiosks or bank access in Mexico. Emma puts the money in her black haversack along with the kiosk card, in case it's something they're supposed to return.

After changing some dollars into pesos for the trip, they buy coffee and sit in a corner of the departure lounge. Travis confesses that he needs to lay flat for a minute, so he stretches out on the blue carpet, with Emma's haversack under his head: At this hour, nobody seems to care. On the other side of the lounge, across a bank of blue-cushioned chairs, an older man in a white coverall works a Hoover commercial vacuum cleaner up and down the hall.

"If we'd driven, we'd be an hour away from Border Colonia by now," Travis frets, staring up at the ceiling.

"And then we'd have another eleven hours of driving to get to San Miguel," Emma reminds him. These lost hours feel galling, but there's nothing they can do. "We'll be there soon. Do you need painkillers?" She tries to be mindful of how she's framing this. "If you take painkillers now, I can't give you any more for another four hours."

Travis does the math, shakes his head. "We'll be arriving at the ranch right as the pills are wearing off. I'll wait."

They call Quantico again just before boarding their flight. Carter sounds exhausted and a little pissed at them on the phone: It's 3.15AM, east-coast time, his two adolescent consultants who he told to stay on base have flown the coop, and for all the unit's efforts in New York, they found nothing to show for it.

"Simon Gutmunsson was not in Wells." Carter clears his throat. "There were no signs at the Wells property at all, which means we're twisting here."

"I'm sorry to hear that, sir," Travis says. Emma is holding the receiver this time, but they're both huddled in the booth, standing close to hear Carter's voice.

"Now I hate to add fuel to your fire, but Reyes has done some more digging. He believes he's figured out how Gutmunsson might know about your Mexico address."

"How?" Emma meets Travis's eyes.

"Jack Kirby had copies of both your personnel files as part of an operational folder he took with him in an attaché case to Boston," Carter says. "Neither the attaché case nor any of those papers were recovered in the aftermath of his death."

"No papers were recovered?" Emma feels her skin flood with cold. "So you mean, Simon took them."

"Fucking great," Travis whispers, his chin lifting.

"We can't confirm –" Carter starts.

"Mr. Carter," Emma says, and she's giving herself kudos for maintaining calm, "those personnel files have *everything*. Social Security. Psychological assessments. Family contacts…"

"I'm aware." Carter sounds frustrated with himself. "We were so focused on the murders, we forgot about the paperwork."

"I guess Gutmunsson has it now," Travis says bluntly. "Sir, we're about to board. Is there anything else we need to know?"

"That's it. Now listen, I know you're on your way, and I'd probably do the same in your position, but please don't panic. There's no evidence that he's hopped the border, and we have that lead in North Carolina, plus another potential sighting. You'll likely get to Guanajuato and find that everything's just fine, Mr. Bell."

"Maybe, but I doubt it," Travis replies. He seems to be trusting himself more and more. "Good luck, sir."

"Same to you," Carter says. "To both of you."

It's not until they hang up that Emma realizes Carter's words had a strange finality. She's not superstitious, and she tries to push the awareness down, refusing to spook herself.

Fifteen minutes later, they board a DC-9 aircraft – silver, with a broad orange stripe running the length of its body – by walking straight across the tarmac. Emma encourages Travis to take the window seat as she finds a place for her haversack in the overhead bin. The flight is full, even at this dark time of the morning, and the cabin resonates with the sound of Spanish.

Emma's been on a few planes, now: This one seems small. She curls up next to Travis, who squeezes her hand and leans against the bulkhead, both of them staring out the glass at the Aeroméxico logo stretched across the plane's silver wing as the flight taxis, launches, speeds into the night. In the enfolding bass drone of the aircraft's passage, with the lights low and the air conditioning making everything soft, they're both finally able to crash for a few hours.

At five-thirty in the morning, they land in León.

CHAPTER TWENTY-TWO

Guanajuato, 6 November 1982

Outside, it's still dark. Travis shakes off his coat – he's dragging his duffel behind him, and Emma has her backpack on her shoulder by one strap – and discovers it's already way warmer, although he's been in air conditioning for the past two days and it's hard to tell what's normal anymore.

They're under the plain rectangle of the airport portico with *Aeropuerto San Carlos de León* written in white letters that reflect the sulphur of the streetlights. This is a rural airport, and there's a bustle of pre-dawn movement: green or yellow taxis jostling, dusty industrial trucks and farm pickups farther away, a dog sniffing in the gutter. People flag their rides, and cab drivers spruik for fares from the folks just disgorged from the flight. Two guys in brown uniforms are sitting on the curb under a big oleander bush across the street, smoking cigarettes and talking before work. An elderly woman walks past carrying a huge roll of striped fabric on her back. A police cruiser rolls by.

"Now where to?" Emma says.

As she speaks the words, a red two-door Datsun covered in a metric ton of dust screeches into the parking bay, and the driver's door opens. A guy stands half out of the car, while the engine's still running. He's about thirty, shaggy dark hair, a solid guy in a grubby white T-shirt and jeans.

"You're Travis? Javi?" He's speaking in Spanish. When Travis nods, his face relaxes. "Thank god, this is the second time I've driven a round trip to León in the last five hours. Jump in – I'm Emilio and Gabriela's son, Joaquín Delgado. My dad and Luiz are at the ranch, I'm gonna take you there."

For a second, Travis can't feel the concrete under his boots, only the sense of freefall as his stomach plunges. "Joaquín? What's going on with my family?"

"What's happening?" Emma can't understand the Spanish, but she's good at body language. "What's going on?"

"We're going to the ranch." Travis is already moving, getting the car door open, slinging in his duffle, directing Emma to a seat at the rear. "*Joaquín –*"

"They're all okay," Joaquín says. "Calm down, they're all okay. Are you guys in?"

He doesn't wait for a reply, already slamming his door. Travis shuts his own door in the front passenger seat, feeling like the interior of the car is tight and close. Emma makes a squeak as the car starts reversing, bracing her hands on the upholstery. The Datsun does a full J-turn and starts forward on the road through Silao.

"Tell me," Travis grinds. His fist is already clutching the panic bar.

"Okay," Joaquín says in English. "The rancho is burning...was burning. But the people, the families..." He grimaces, trying to speak too fast in a language not his own, and flips back to Spanish. "Shit, I can't do this in English, let me just talk in Spanish, okay?"

Travis wants to pull his hair out by the roots, replies in Spanish. "Just fucking tell me."

"Luiz got the family out okay." Joaquín is driving at least ten miles over any kind of speed limit along the Silao road in the half dark, past concrete road barriers and electricity poles with sagging wires. "The women are all at Luisa's house in San Miguel –"

"My mom and my sisters?" Travis's grip on the bar is white-knuckled. If the car keeps moving like this, he's gonna throw up.

"They're safe. Nobody got hurt. But the –"

Joaquín slams on the brakes and the car skids about six feet. There are goats in the road, a young boy leading them with a long stick. Travis hears Emma yell, but he's too busy unclenching his jaw to reply. Joaquín starts swearing a mile a minute, some of the filthiest language that Travis has ever heard in Spanish, before veering the car carefully around the goats and driving on.

"Jesus Christ." Joaquín clears his throat. "Sorry about that."

"More haste, less speed," Emma says hoarsely from the back, in English.

Joaquín doesn't hear her or doesn't understand. He talks directly to Travis again after the brief interruption. "Okay, the main thing you need to know is that everyone's safe, your family's safe."

"But the fire?" Travis asks.

"Luiz and Emilio and Mateo took everyone into San Miguel, then went back to check on the ranch, and there was a fire in the night. They managed to control it in time, so the ranch house wasn't completely destroyed. But they're still there, and I'm gonna take you to them." Joaquín is handling the car smoothly now, still driving fast, but they're about to leave Silao and the road is more open. "Luiz said he wasn't sure when you would arrive at Léon. Emilio sent me to the airport for the midnight flight arrival, just in case you came in earlier. I'm really glad you finally made it."

"Me, too," Travis says, although the idea of the fire, of what might have happened if he hadn't given Luiz a warning, is ricocheting between his ears. "Thanks for all the driving, and for meeting us."

"It's fine." Joaquín has strong, white teeth when he smiles. "Everyone else is busy, or tired, and my mom is with the girls in San Miguel."

Emma leans between the front seats, one hand on the center console, looking at Travis's face. "What's happening? Are you okay? You went completely white for a second."

"I'm all right. Give me a minute." Travis finds he's rubbing his breastbone. But his heartbeat has settled down to some extent. "Okay, there was a fire at the ranch, but everybody's safe. My mom and my sisters are in San Miguel. We're going to the ranch right now."

"All the family safe," Joaquín says to her in English. "We come to rancho soon." He snorts, looking back at the road and reverting back to Spanish. "Sooner, if I can avoid any more goats."

"Okay, thank you." Emma sits back, still a little wild-eyed.

"Welcome back to Mexico." Joaquín grins, eyes in the rear view. "How you doing?"

Emma wets her lips, thinks about the Spanish before she speaks it. "Last night is very long."

"You're telling me," Joaquín guffaws in his own language. Foot steady on the accelerator, he glances at Travis. "Hey, it's a terrible way to meet, but nice to meet you. My mom says you're a good guy. Don't worry about the fire, it's gonna be okay."

Travis is pretty sure he won't believe that until he sees it for himself, and he's glad now that Joaquín is driving fast. Out the window, the country he knows: Tree cholla and the smell of dust have replaced US east-coast autumn foliage and steel urban landscapes. The air is starting to lighten as dawn approaches.

Travis feels like he's in a state of suspended animation. There's a drying marigold in the ashtray. The sky is bleeding orange, opening up, and he wishes the sunrise calmed him, but that's impossible right now.

Joaquín, who seems to be a considerate guy, keeps talking and providing distraction – mainly he talks about himself, sharing information. Travis now knows that Joaquín is the middle son of Gabriela's kids, of which there are five all together. His other siblings are scattered around Durango, Guanajuato, South Mexico. He works as a leather cutter sometimes, but he's been doing more work for Emilio lately in the family business as a courier, and arranging sales of horses.

"You've been up in the States, doing law enforcement work?" Joaquín seems intrigued. "What's that like?"

"Not so great, I'm discovering," Travis says dryly.

But they've passed a *Entronique Peligroso* sign and a brick-walled yard with a hand-painted hoarding reading 'Materiales Para Construccion' and now they're nearly at the turn-off road past the Laja River. In the middle-distance, a thin, rising column of dark-gray smoke.

"Is that it?" Travis swallows. "Holy shit."

Emma leans forward again. "Are you okay? Listen, it's been hours."

"What?"

"You're sweating." She frowns, digs in her pocket, shakes out two pills from the orange container and puts them into his palm. "Take these, and let's try to stay on top of your pain levels."

"It's not pain so much," he tries to explain, but actually it *is* pain – the very thought of arriving at the ranch and seeing the damage is making his chest hurt. He swallows the pills with orange soda from a bottle of Topo Sabores that Joaquín nods toward in the front passenger footwell.

They've cut along a bunch of dirt roads, and now it's nearly seven in the morning, and the landscape is hazed with pale orange as they come up on the entry to the long driveway.

Travis doesn't hear the soft groan he makes, his eyes on the smoke. Emma reaches through and squeezes his arm.

"It's okay, it's not as bad as you think," Joaquín says, as they bump up the sandy ribbon of driveway.

But it looks bad. It looks real bad, and even Emma whispers, "Oh no," as the full tableau comes into view. The right side of the house is shrouded in a pall of smoke that wreathes amongst blackened timbers – those bedrooms that he and Emma occupied are now non-existent. There's damage to the roof and the front patio on the right, although the stone and adobe is still standing. One of the mesquite trees near the house appears to have gone up; Mateo, in work clothes, is throwing buckets of sand at its base.

Luiz is standing by the century plant in trousers and a filthy blue shirt unbuttoned over an equally filthy T-shirt. He's talking to another man, some local guy Travis doesn't recognize, who's wearing coveralls and wielding a hose connected to a small white truck with a big cartage tank of water on the back – the truck's yellow emergency lights blink off/on, off/on. Water sprays from the hose, and where it lands, ash puffs and rises.

Joaquín has stopped the car near the open gate, and Travis struggles out. The smell of char is overwhelming. "Jesus Christ."

Emilio, in a dark shirt and trousers, leather boots and gloves, walks over holding a rake. "You found them, Joaquín? Good, good."

"I can't believe this," Travis groans.

"It happened last night," Emilio says in Spanish. "But if you hadn't warned Luiz, the whole family would have died in their beds." He waves Luiz closer. "Let your uncle explain."

Luiz flaps his hat to cool his face as he comes close. He has ash in his hair and a fat blister on the side of his temple, and he grips Travis's arm. "It looks bad, but we were lucky."

"Uncle…" Travis's eyes are watering with the smoke and he hardly knows what to say.

"Here, I'll tell you," Luiz says, and lifts his chin toward Emma. "You'll have to do the translation."

As his uncle talks, Travis gives Emma the summary.

"So, Luiz took Mariana and Sofia and Mom and the girls to San Miguel…" There's a lot of translating, but Travis is glad to have something to focus on. "They went to my aunt Luisa's house. All the women, plus Elias, Mateo's grandson, are still there with Tómas, Luisa's husband."

Emma is staring at the destruction wrought on this part of the ranch. "How did they catch the fire before it burned the place completely out?"

"Luiz and Mateo…" Travis listens to his uncle's explanation. "They'd contacted Emilio…The three of them came back here late… about midnight? The house was burning."

Emma has a hand shielding her nose from the smoke, and looks like she's going to be sick. "So Simon set the house on fire?"

Travis nods, continues. "Luiz says that Mateo…He saw someone running away from the fire, a tall man with white hair –"

Emma wipes her eyes, distraught. "*Goddammit.*"

But Luiz, even with the burn on his face that must be smarting, looks resolute when he speaks to Emma in English. "This, this is not your fault. You did not do this."

Travis understands guilt, though. "Maybe we didn't light the flame, uncle. But we brought this to your house –"

"No." Luiz frowns, wiping his sweaty face in the relatively clean fabric in the crook of his elbow, replying in Spanish. "The bastard who killed your father is trying to kill you, and your family – it's a vendetta. Well, now he's made me very angry."

"We need to catch this boy," Emilio agrees.

Luiz waves at the section of the house that's now a ruined mess. "The fire settled down about three o'clock this morning. We've been working to keep the embers from damaging other areas of the house, but I also called some friends – Nestor, Gael Pérez, Juancarlo – to help me find this white-haired asshole –"

"He's insane, uncle," Travis warns. "People need to be careful."

"Yeah," Joaquín says, "but he's not in his own country now. Everybody knows everybody here, so it's harder for him to stay under the radar, and he's not being quiet. We already know he hired a car in Léon to get here, bought gasolina in San Martin de Terreros…He's not local, so he stands out. People remember his hair."

The smoke is too much and makes a burr in Travis's throat, and now he's filled with another kind of horror. "So where did he go from here? God – not to San Miguel?"

"No." Luiz shakes his head, lifts a hand toward the fire's remains. "We thought he'd probably make a run for it after he did this, and he did."

Emilio looks pleased with himself. "We contacted people to keep lookout. One of them said they saw him in the car, driving too fast near Mompani."

"Joaquín has friends at the airport in Querétaro," Luiz adds. "So we found out where he went."

"Get this." Joaquín snorts. "The airport in Querétaro isn't commercial, right? It's just a civilian aerodrome, so there's a bunch of little planes and loose pilots. Your asshole guy, he splashed money at the airport to get a private flight to Villahermosa."

This seems like something worth explaining to Emma, who's been very patient, waiting for news in English.

"Gutmunsson's gone south-east, to Villahermosa." Travis tells her, before turning back to the other three men. "I don't get it – what's in Villahermosa?"

"Well, he can fly from there to Cuba," Joaquín points out.

"*Fuck.*"

Emma caught the last part, and a hot thread of tension enters her voice. "If Simon gets to Cuba, he can't be extradited. He can also come back anytime he wants and try to attack your family again."

"It's all right," Luiz replies in Spanish, in this strange multi-lingual exchange. "We can catch him."

How? Travis wants to scream. He rubs his mouth. "We'll have to go back to León and get a flight –"

"No need," Emilio says, loosening the handkerchief at his throat, shaking it out to wipe his brow. "I told you – Joaquín has friends at the airport. That's because he has his civilian pilot's license."

Joaquín grins. "I can fly you to Villahermosa to catch this asshole. But we need to go now."

CHAPTER TWENTY-THREE

Querétaro, 6 November 1982

I t's just over an hour and a half to Querétaro in the Datsun with Joaquín Delgado, and then they swap the tiny car for a tiny plane.

"The planes on this trip keep shrinking," Emma says, while they're watching Joaquín use a tow bar to pull the Cessna 152 out of the aerodrome warehouse onto the concrete tarmac.

"You flew in that Piper Navajo from DC to Pittsburgh," Travis reminds her.

"This is way worse."

He frowns. "Are you sure you don't want to stay in San Miguel with my mom and the others?"

Emma looks straight at him and says, "There is no way on god's green earth that you're going to chase Simon Gutmunsson without me. Package deal, remember?"

But they had to leave their bags with Luiz, back at the ranch, because this plane won't carry more than the pilot, one passenger, and fifty-four kilos worth of luggage. In this situation, she's the luggage. Once they get in, she's sitting on a small square of carpet in what's usually a baggage compartment behind the two front seats.

Emma puts her headset on, and to her relief, the world goes quiet. This is the moment she needs, the space to breathe and hear her breath return, and if it had to happen inside this miniscule aircraft which she's terrified will break apart on take-off, then so be it.

Travis and Joaquín climb into the Cessna's front seats and close doors, strap in. There's a concertina-ed silver cover on the windshield to protect the cabin from sun damage – just like you'd have in a car – and Joaquín removes that, folds it and passes it back to her. She's also holding a small satchel which contains her and Travis's passports, money – pesos and dollars – and Emilio's Smith & Wesson Model 19, with a box of .357 Magnum shells. Travis checked the action on the gun back at the ranch, and promised Emilio that the gun would be returned to him.

Joaquín taps the instrumentation, glances her way and speaks in English. "Are you all right?"

"I'm good," Emma reassures.

He grins. "Then let's get this little boat up in the air."

The steering yoke is just like the steering control of a bumper car that Emma drove one time at the funfair in Canton, when she was about thirteen – it seems too flimsy to be real. The rest of the instrumentation panel is a mystery, and she knows there are foot pedals too, which she can't see.

It really is like a bumper car, but now this flying bumper car is buzzing around them, like they're inside a hornet's belly, and the little plane seems to strain toward movement.

Travis looks back and waves a finger, shows her how he flicks a switch on his headset so it's just them talking to each other. "Are you okay?"

His voice is warm and deep in the cavern-quiet of the headset earphones. It feels like he's talking directly into her mind and Emma gets a shiver. "I'm okay. This is crazy."

"I know," he says. "Hold on."

Joaquín is talking now, although his voice sounds more tinny, and he's exchanging instructions with the airport control tower in Spanish that she has to strain to follow.

He adjusts his mic. "Querétaro, este es Cessna 2600, listo para ir."

"Escuchándote, Cessna 2600." A nasal voice from the control tower in Emma's headset.

"Gracias." Joaquín flips a series of switches, gives a long series of phrases in technical Spanish.

"Cessna 2600, estás autorizado a pasar a la pista tres."

The bumper car is shuddering as they move slowly forward, and Emma watches the instruments so she won't feel so nervous. As the knots-per-hour hit fifty, Joaquín lifts the aircraft's nose, then they're at seventy-five knots and the plane is up, is being held by the hands of the sky.

Travis's voice again, soft and real. "Holy shit, this is wild."

The noise from the engine and propellor creates a bone-deep vibration that Emma's sure will have her ears ringing for hours after they land. But even at just under ten thousand feet, the landscape looks vast: Flying under cloud cover, she can look down at swatches of beige and brown, the dust of marginal land, square cubes of buildings, the majestic phthalo green of distant rising mountains.

Joaquín speaks in English for her benefit. "How are you, Emma?"

She remembers to toggle the switch, so she can be heard by everyone. "I'm fine, so long as I don't look straight down."

Joaquín laughs. "You are very good! You are no problem!"

"Nope, no problem," she replies; even with a slight wobble in her voice, she sounds okay.

She's happy to sit and watch Travis as he switches to Spanish and asks questions about every piece of instrumentation, and about when and how Joaquín learned to fly. It's impossible to understand everything in Joaquín's reply, but she gets the gist – he was fifteen, and bored, and one of his dad's friends took him up in a light plane one time, and then he was hooked.

He's an extremely competent pilot, at least in a plane this size. Travis seems to want to hear more about the details of flying, so Emma settles back on her carpet square, a cold vinyl cushion at her back which protects her from the bulkhead, and looks out the windshield at the brown land, the crimps and buckled folds of it, the clouds spreading out like a rippled blanket above. For a few minutes, at least, she can forget that they're chasing Simon Gutmunsson.

A little while after, Travis looks over and flicks the switch on his headset. "Hey, we've got about an hour to go. Are you comfortable back there?"

"My back is a little sore," Emma confesses. "Other than that, it's kind of weird to say it, but so long as I don't think about how high we're flying, or what we're doing once we reach Villahermosa, I'm having fun. How about you, how're you feeling?"

"I'm okay," he says. "I'm good."

It's ten thirty in the morning, and he had pain relief about three and a half hours ago. She doesn't want to push, but she needs to mention it. "We've been travelling non-stop for seventeen hours."

He looks over his shoulder. "I know. But my family's okay, so everything feels more manageable."

"Don't go all tough guy on me," she says.

"I'm too tired to play tough, Emma," he says, and seems to surprise himself with a laugh. Then he turns his head to look through the windshield again and goes on. "Honestly? I'm tired of all of it. I want to end this. My dad is dead. Kristin is dead. I don't want to be stuck in Gutmunsson's loop anymore – act, react, spill blood, move onto the next thing…I want to get off this merry-go-round and just have a life."

It's like he needs to be facing the blue sky, facing eternity, as he says it, yet his deep voice direct in her ears creates a surprising intimacy, like he's whispering to her. Emma finds it strangely moving.

"I get that," she says, and she hopes her own tone is coming through the headset, loud and clear.

She sees his throat bob as he swallows. "Um…How would you feel about having a life with me, once this is all over? No FBI, no crazy serial killers. Just a regular, boring guy who doesn't know what he's doing next?"

Emma feels her eyes getting damp. Out the windshield, the fuzzy blue-green of Mount Tlaloc reminds her that all things pass away, and that the best moment is the one she's in here, right now.

"I could handle a little boring," she says, her voice coming out thick and soft.

They can't really touch, and he doesn't say anything more, but from her angle, the slow smile spilling over his face is like seeing the sun come up on the mountains.

Joaquín adjusts some instruments. "Hey, friends, hope you are okay, we are getting some rain coming maybe?"

He indicates to their left, and Emma notices how the clouds have changed, the darkness low down, like they're dragging the wet black hems of a dress across the sky.

"Yeah, that doesn't look great," Travis murmurs, then, "Emma, I'm gonna ask Joaquín what we're doing once we arrive in Villahermosa, okay?"

Emma gives a thumbs-up, and he opens the channel. She doesn't understand all that conversation either, but she gets the rough version she can confirm the details of later: Simon is unlikely to still be in the airport at Villahermosa, because the embargo on US citizens flying to Cuba means he'll be questioned if he flies commercial with an American passport. Travis asks if they'll have to search the...boats? The ports. Joaquín says no, that Simon will most likely seek out the mulas – people from Cuba who take contraband items and passengers to and from the island.

"Drug mules," Emma suggests.

"No," Travis clarifies in English, "although it's the same term. But the contrabandistas aren't just transporting drugs. People need things like medicine, electrics, clothing, car parts, other stuff they haven't been able to get since nineteen sixty-one. Contraband flights come in and out pretty regularly, folks know about them – hold on..."

He asks Joaquín if they'll have to find someone who can connect them with a contrabandista flight, but apparently Emilio is already making phone calls about it and they'll be met at the airport.

"Your dad is doing a lot for my family," Travis says to their pilot. "I don't know how to thank him."

Joaquín laughs again and says something about how his dad is a hard-ass, but that he and Luiz go back a long way.

Then he asks a question neither of them were expecting, and he asks it in English. "Why does this boy hate you? He burns your uncle's house, he is dangerous to your family, he has this...la venganza de sangre, yes?"

Travis presses his lips and glances out the window before replying. The twists of the Rio Grijalva are gray down below, and the land looks much greener than it was when they crossed Hidalgo. "I killed his sister while I was protecting Emma. It was an accident, but it happened."

"Ah." Joaquín nods. "This I can understand."

"He killed my father, so we're…matched somehow with this." But Travis looks back at Emma, his eyes lingering before looking away, and she knows he's going to say more. "And I have something he wants. In Simon Gutmunsson's whole life, no one has ever refused him. It's made him crazy. He thinks he's a king, and the world should bow at his feet. The people who won't bow, he punishes. I just never learned how to bow, I guess."

Joaquín seems to approve of this reply, but he gives a warning. "Then be careful. The man who thinks he is king will not accept to lose. He will cheat."

"We'll be careful," Travis reassures.

Ten minutes later, the rain starts, a fitful drizzle that blurs the windows of the plane. Soon after that, the Cessna lands in Villahermosa, Tabasco.

CHAPTER TWENTY-FOUR

Villahermosa, 6 November 1982

Joaquín shakes their hands and wishes them good luck before taxiing the plane over to the refuelling station. Travis jogs across the tarmac with Emma, both of them sheltering under his jacket from the drizzle. When they get through to the Arrivals area, he shakes off the damp and looks around for a sign of whatever arrangements Emilio Delgado has put in place for them in this city.

The Arrivals area is small and looks kind of new. A half dozen people are drifting between the main doors, the bathrooms, and the row of phone kiosks. A middle-aged man in a ball cap is eating from a bag of duros and reading a sign. A very senior lady, wearing a men's Hawaiian shirt over a white embroidered dress, sits on one of the plastic chairs near the door. Travis doesn't know who he's looking for, which makes it trickier.

"Maybe we should wait outside?" Emma suggests.

The glass door opens, and a very short woman in an embroidered hipil blouse and black pants, with a fanny pack around her waist, waddles inside. Her age is indeterminate, closer to Mariana than his mom, but her braid is still black, and she's wearing blindingly white hi-top sneakers and aviator sunglasses.

She looks around the people in the small Arrivals foyer, then – maybe seeing their air of confusion – heads straight for them.

"Taxi?" She peers over the top of her sunglasses. "You want a taxi? I can take you wherever you want to go – hotels, Palenque, wherever."

Her English is great. If only they were here to sight-see.

"Gracias, señora," Travis says, "but we're waiting for someone –"

"Javi? You're Javi, right?" Now she takes off the sunglasses completely. "I don't usually work today, but I got a call from a friend who said I should come find you."

Travis has to do a split-second reassessment, but he manages not to fumble too hard. "Hi. I mean, yeah, I'm Javi – Travis. And this is Emma."

The woman takes his extended hand and shakes vigorously. "Great, great, pleased to meet you both. I'm Fernanda. Come on, I got my car parked in an illegal zone outside."

"You got a call from Emilio?" Emma asks.

"About two hours ago," Fernanda says. "He called José next door, and José gave me a message. But hey, Emilio is an old friend. He said I should help you get to El Cobá, who's on the south side of town, so we need to move fast."

She leads them through the door, down the steep ziggurat-style steps and across a tiled pathway to a parking zone surrounded by grass and palmetto. The airport façade looks off toward green pasture dotted with thatch palm. Travis is sweating in the sun, but the temperature drops whenever a cloud comes across the sky. At least it's stopped raining.

"Who's El Cobá?" he asks.

Fernanda is continuing her sailor's walk across the parking zone. "Just a guy who arranges things for people. Okay, this is us here."

She makes for the driver's-side door of a white Datsun A10 that looks as if it's seen better days, and is covered in decals of pink and purple hibiscus flowers.

Emma seems uncertain. "Where are we going?"

"South side of town, like I said." Fernanda takes her seat, arranges her fanny pack. "Not right in Villahermosa. There's a suburb, Playas del Rosario, and that's where we go."

"To see El Cobá," Travis repeats.

"You got it." Fernanda pulls her door closed, grinning.

Emma looks right at him, but what else are they supposed to do? He shrugs. They get in the back seat.

Fernanda is revving the engine, which yowls twice before they pull away from the curb. "All right, here we go!"

The inside of the car is a riot. Decals and little curtains decorate the interior. Hanging off the rear-view mirror, a St. Christopher medal, a thin plastic skeleton, rosary beads, and a piñata-shaped air freshener all sway in unison with every bump in the road. There's a garland of marigolds across the dashboard.

Emma is pulling her satchel strap off her shoulder. "So this guy, El Cobá, he's the one who arranges flights to Cuba?"

"I don't know much about that." Fernanda puts her sunglasses back on and lights a cigarette, winds the window down halfway. "El Cobá's business is his business, you know what I mean? Hey, you're from America, right?"

"Yeah, from Ohio," Emma says. Outside, tall fancy streetlights give way to thatch palm. "Travis is from Texas, but he has family in Guanajuato."

"That's cool," Fernanda enthuses. "I love America – I love the movies from there. That's how I learned English, watching American movies. *Taxi Driver*, right? What a movie, I love it. Okay, this is the one-eight-six road, we go onto the one-ninety-five and then we'll be in Playas del Rosario before you know it. There might be some traffic, because there's a parade today."

Trees flash by, lots of tulipan chino. Travis peers at the threatening clouds. "Nice weather for a parade."

Fernanda waves her cigarette. "I know, right? But if you wait for a day without rain, you'd never have a parade. So you have cash? Can't see El Cabó without cash, the man's a true capitalist."

"We have enough," Travis says. "What happens when we get there? We pay El Cabó…"

"You pay El Cabó, he makes a call, you take a ride to the location and wait for the plane." Fernanda glances at them in the rear view mirror. "The plane comes, some things are loaded, other things are unloaded, the plane flies away – that's all I know. I don't like to know too much, you understand? El Cabó's business…"

"…is El Cabó's business," Emma finishes for her. "We understand. Have you always lived in Villahermosa?"

"My whole life!" Fernanda's head bobs. They've come to a turn-off, and she takes them over a road bridge past a whole stand of jacarandas decorated with papel picado. "I mean, I lived in Ciudad del Carmen awhile, when I was a kid, but not for long. Villahermosa is really my place."

"You have family here?" Travis asks politely.

"Of course!" She slaps the driving wheel as they speed down a four-lane roadway on the outskirts of Villahermosa, with more lush greenery, and blue-and-orange painted buildings on their right. "I support my family driving this taxi. I love driving a taxi, you know? It's a window to the world. You meet everybody – Mexican, American, Guatemalan, Cuban. I even met some Russians, and an Australian once. People are coming to Villahermosa from all over the world…"

She keeps talking about the joys of Villahermosa, and of taxi-driving, and the buildings become very mixed: an auto shop with plastic chairs under an overhang, an antojitos place called 'El Guadalupena'. They go past a lagoon, and over the Grijalva River, and then they're out of town, driving through a sparse residential area called Parrilla, which has the same concrete road barriers as Silao. Here, decorations for Día de Muertos still wave as they go by, then the gray backs of buildings peter out and the jacarandas resume.

"You said we take a ride to the location for the plane," Emma asks. "Is that far away?"

"A couple hours?" Fernanda replies. "Not so far. But you can't land a plane here, even a little one – people would notice, right? So you find a place out of the city, past Palenque, maybe someplace closer to the jungle, so it's harder to see from the road. That's how it's done."

"Uh-huh." Travis thinks Fernanda knows an awful lot about 'how it's done', for someone who doesn't like to pry into contrabandista business. And he's not sure how listening to her gets them any closer to Simon Gutmunsson. "And you know the place?"

"Everybody knows the place! People don't know, but they *know*, you understand? Like El Cabó – he's not the only man who arranges things. Other people do it, I could give you ten names. They mostly use the same little planes. One plane here and there is plenty, you know? Otherwise you'd have little planes flying all over the place."

More spitting drizzle on the windshield. The landscape is so green here, Travis can't get over it. Emma touches his arm, lifts her chin to the window as a man riding a mule goes by.

The first sign they're approaching Playas del Rosario is a car junkyard by the side of the road. People are in the street, yellow streamers and banana leaf flags are flipping back and forth, and there's the echo of music.

They turn off onto a right-hand street, nice and wide. Ironwork gates of some fancier houses are covered in marigolds. More traffic, and more people everywhere, many in costume: swirling Spanish skirts, flower garlands, skull face paint. There's a convenience store, a refrigeration mechanic place called 'El Arca'. Then a left turn down Bulevar Olmeca, and suddenly they're in the middle of what looks like a market – street stalls are dotted up and down the sidewalk, and there's an explosion of people dressed in yellow.

"Is this the parade you were talking about?" Emma asks.

"Oh yeah." Fernanda leans forward and squints at the people criss-crossing the road in front of them. "Are you in a hurry?"

Travis wants to gently grind his teeth. "We're in a little bit of a hurry, yeah."

Fernanda shakes her head. "Terrible policy to be in a hurry in Mexico. To be in a hurry anywhere, but especially in Mexico. What do you two kids want with El Cabó anyway?"

"We're looking for someone – a guy who wants a ride to Cuba."

"He wants to go to Cuba?" Fernanda snorts. "What for? Nothing in Cuba that you can't get better here."

"He's a bad guy looking for a way out." Travis grimaces.

People are pressing against the side of the car, and the sounds of Huichol music compete with drums, and also recorded pop tunes from somebody's boombox. Traffic is moving at walking pace. People shuffle by in costume – as giant skulls, as La Catarina, as dancers, everyone wearing celebratory clothes, dodging traffic cones. Kids wave palm leaves.

Travis thinks it could take them a while to get through this. "Is there another way we can go?"

Fernanda twists to glance through the rear window, turns back. "Uh…Look, I'm sorry, what can I say, it's Día de Muertos. The rest of the country celebrates one day, maybe two, but not around here – we celebrate for a week. It's fine, except when it holds up traffic." She presses on the horn, leans out the window. "Hey, come on!"

Parade-goers startle at the horn, but most of them laugh. Emma is peering out the window at the people in the street – at drummers in skeleton costumes, at gold-clad pedestrians lining the sidewalk and pressed up against lime-washed buildings. Travis forces himself to stop clenching his jaw. If they're hitting obstacles, then it's guaranteed that Simon Gutmunsson is also hitting obstacles…

"Travis," Emma says.

"Ai-ai-ai," Fernanda says, adjusting her sunglasses. "We're only going about another two blocks." She lays on the horn again.

"*Travis.*" Emma clutches his forearm, eyes wide. "That's *Simon.*"

Every hair on his body springs up. "What?"

"That's *Simon*, fuck –" Emma grabs for the door handle. "He's right there on the side of the street!"

"Who's on the street?" Fernanda says, edging the car forward.

"Where is he?" Travis's radar is pinging hard as he leans to see out the window.

"No! No!" Emma is tracking movement past her door, contorting herself to see out the rear window. "He's walking back the way we came in! *Goddamnit* – Travis, come on!"

Before he can say, *No, wait*, she's popped the door handle and jumped out of the car. Travis gasps, grabs for the satchel she's left on the rear seat, pops his own door handle and –

"*Shit.*" Too many people, crushing against his side of the car. "*Fuck*, let me –"

"Hey!" Fernanda shouts. "You gotta pay me!"

"One minute!" Travis says, then he gives up, scrambles across the rear seat and out Emma's door.

In the street, the music is even more deafening; people in yellow, screaming with laughter, shaking noise-makers, throwing streamers and marigold petals into the air. Travis cranes to see Emma, finds her dark head and pale white neck above her T-shirt as she weaves to some spot on the sidewalk about twenty feet back.

Fernanda has opened her driver's side door and is standing one foot out. "Hey! Hey! What the heck are you doing?"

Travis ignores her, pushing to where Emma is swimming in a tide of people before she…disappears.

"*No,*" he gasps, then he's shoving people out of the way to get to where she last stood on the sidewalk.

His heartrate decelerates when he realizes it's the entry to an alley. Cobblestoned underfoot and not much more than ten feet wide, with a skinny Dodge Dart and some other car parked a little way down, the whole lane is quiet, and in blessed shadow.

Emma stands near the iron grille of somebody's laneway window, slamming the side of her fist into the bricks. "*Fuck!*"

"Emma, for god's sake –" he starts.

She spins to look at him. "He was *here*, Travis! He was *right here* –"

"I still am," Simon Gutmunsson says, as he steps out of the black doorway and grabs Emma by the wrist.

Travis's skin freezes.

Emma's reactions are better: She screams, punches out, tries to twist away. "*Get off me!*"

Gutmunsson slaps her hard across the face.

By the time Travis has pulled the Model 19 out of the satchel he's holding, Gutmunsson has Emma wrapped up from behind like a python. As Travis lifts his arm to aim, there's the snick of a spring-load, and the point of a six-inch, black-handled stiletto digging into Emma's right temple.

Travis can hear his own harsh breathing, Emma's sobbing gasps; in the background, the sound of drums.

"Well, here we are again." Gutmunsson snugs his arm around Emma's collarbones and presses the sharp tip in, his eyes the color of ice submerged, hollowed deep in brown-bruised circles. His expression is utterly flat. "Shoot, and I will shove this blade into her brain."

"Don't you do it," Travis hisses, but his aiming arm is shaking.

"Travis, just *shoot* him," Emma rasps, bucking in Gutmunsson's hold.

"I don't recommend you test me." Gutmunsson's arm across her is taut as iron. His white linen shirt and cream trousers are immaculate, but his sunglasses are pushed up into his hair, and his face looks gaunt.

"Emma –" Travis starts.

"Lower the gun," Gutmunsson says.

"*Shoot him,*" Emma begs.

Gutmunsson claps his left hand over Emma's mouth and shoves the point of the blade deep into the joint of her shoulder. Emma squeals behind his hand, her eyes going wide and white with shock before squeezing shut.

"*Stop!*" Travis yells, stepping forward without thinking.

Gutmunsson hasn't even changed facial expression. He's still holding Travis with that eerie, intense stare as he tilts his head. "Did it feel like that when you stabbed my sister? Lower the gun."

Emma's body trembles, a dark rose blooming on her T-shirt near her collarbone. The knife in her shoulder quivers. Gutmunsson keeps his eyes on Travis as he slowly draws the knife out of her – she makes a muffled, high-pitched keen as the blade comes free.

Travis's nerve-endings are electric with the need for violence. "For *fuck's sake* –"

"Did you think I wouldn't hurt dear Emma?" Once more holding the knife against her temple, Gutmunsson leans forward; she's forced to bend with him, groaning. "Oh, I'm sorry – didn't you know the rules had changed? Lower. The. Gun."

Travis does as he's told. Emma whines behind her gag, in pain but angry, too, her eyes blinking back tears as she looks at him.

"This is cute," Gutmunsson says, his tone so sardonic it almost dries the air. Far away, guitars strum, crowds cheer. "Are you both chasing me? Here, without your FBI pals? How dedicated of you."

Nervous sweat makes his eyes sting, but Travis can't help himself. "*You're* the one who tried to burn my family alive."

"*And I'd do it again in a heartbeat,*" Gutmunsson spits. Then his snarl calms. "I'll get them eventually, don't worry. I'll just wait until you've dropped your guard. You'll have to live with fear forever – just like I have to live with grief." His expression cracks for a moment, recovers into a sneer. "You make me sick. Slap yourself."

"What?"

"Go on. Slap yourself in the face."

Emma makes a desperate, furious noise behind Gutmunsson's hand.

"You're insane," Travis says.

Gutmunsson digs the blade tip into Emma's temple again, and her angry buzz turns into a pained whimper. She squirms in his grip, as dark blood runs in a line down her cheek.

"She's a wriggler, isn't she?" Gutmunsson grins. "Now – slap yourself."

Travis cracks a hand across his own cheek, moving on automatic. The sting feels justified.

"*Again*," Gutmunsson commands.

The second time, Travis slaps harder. It doesn't combat this feeling of helplessness.

"Well, it's a start." Gutmunsson seems to find all amusement bitter. "Drop the gun and kick it away."

Travis does that, too. Emma sobs, frantic.

"Now, I know it's hard to process concepts with your *gorilla brain*," Gutmunsson hisses, "but listen very carefully. This is what is happening. *I* am flying to Cuba. *You* are going to do nothing. Because if you pursue me, if I suspect even for a moment that you're trying to stop me…Then my sweet little insurance policy here will suffer." Gutmunsson's visage turns frighteningly brutal. "I will make her hurt. The way you made Kristin hurt."

There is nothing left to try but the truth.

"I never meant to kill Kristin." Travis's voice is shaking. "You have to believe me."

"I don't think I believe anything anymore." Gutmunsson's eyes go entirely blank and exhausted, before hardening again. "Now back up."

"*Emma…*" Travis whispers.

Gutmunsson flicks the point of the knife against her forehead, creating another line of red. Emma jerks and writhes. "Should I cut something off?"

Travis backs to the entry of the alley.

Knife notched in the hollow behind Emma's ear, Gutmunsson pushes her toward the Dart. He removes his clamping hand from her mouth, grips her by the throat from behind. "Open the driver's side door, and the one behind it. Then get in the driver's seat."

Her breath sobs out. "*Simon* –"

"Shut up," he says.

Then they're both in the car – Gutmunsson in the rear, sitting behind Emma, who's at the wheel – and Travis can't hear any more of what they're saying as the engine starts. The Dart pulls out slowly, putters to the other end of the alley, and the blood rises in Travis's face so fast he thinks he's going to black out.

He leans over his knees. *No time. No time for that shit.*

As soon as the car turns left at the corner, he runs forward, grabs the Model 19 out of the gutter and stuffs it into the satchel as he spins, sprints for the mouth of the alley.

Out on the sunny street, it's like nothing has changed. People are smiling, yellow and orange spilling off their clothes. Dogs are barking. Great paper skulls weave on processional bamboo crosses as mariachi music plays.

Travis runs, dodging people, bumping into some, until he reaches Fernanda's white, hibiscus-covered Datsun; she's made it almost to the intersection. Travis steps in front of the slow-crawling car and slaps both hands on the hood. He has no idea what his facial expression is in this moment.

Fernanda stomps the brake. "Hey! What are you –"

He slings himself around to the front passenger seat and gets in the car.

"*Hey!*" Now her sunglasses are off. "What the heck do you think you're –"

"I know you're El Cabó," Travis wheezes. He can't control his panting.

"Listen…" Fernanda says, but she looks rattled.

"I *know*," Travis says. "So please don't lie, because I don't have time to fuck around. Do you know where the contrabandista plane is supposed to land?"

Fernanda sucks her teeth, gives in. "Near El Sacrificio."

He nods. "Take me there."

"But what about your girl?" Fernanda looks back through the rear window, as if Emma will magically materialize there. If only.

"That bad guy we're chasing…" Travis masters himself. "He has her. And I need to get to that plane location before he hurts her. Can you take me?"

Fernanda winces, uncertain. "Look…"

"I'll give you two hundred American dollars," Travis says. "And another two hundred when we get there."

The woman makes a considering face, shrugs. "Okay."

"Good," Travis says, settling back, "Put the car in gear and let's drive."

CHAPTER TWENTY-FIVE

Chiapas, 6 November 1982

The first part of the trip, as she drove Simon's car out of Playas del Rosario, Emma thought about what she could do to thwart him. It was hard to concentrate because the pain in her shoulder was very loud. Simon, by contrast, was quiet, giving low-voiced directions and instructions: *Turn right,* or *Turn left,* or *Slow down.* His voice, sibilant in her ear, was the only reminder sometimes that this was real, that this was happening – apart from the blade tip at the nape of her neck that provided a stinging, jabbing reminder each time her head moved.

She thought seriously about crashing the car. Because that was the vulnerability of letting your hostage drive, wasn't it? A smart kidnappee figures out quick that a car crash might kill them, but that the knife at their neck will *definitely* kill them, so they might as well take a shot...

But about two miles out of the little township, Simon told her to pull over, then his cold, long-fingered hand was around her throat. Emma tried to swallow, couldn't, tried to breathe, couldn't. She's been choked unconscious before, and it sent her back: In her panic, she scratched at Simon's fingers, drummed her heels in the driver's side footwell, but he just kept pressing – almost delicately – against her carotid until she thought she might die, until her alarm-blaring brain could think only of

Travis, of his quiet voice saying *How would you feel about having a life with me?* as her whole world went black...

Now, when Emma wakes up – rising to the surface of consciousness, head breaking the oily waters, gasping at that first breath, dry lips gummed and desperate – she's in the front passenger seat.

Her head feels like it might split open, just burst like a ripe pomegranate, skin splitting as her mind tumbles out. The pain in her shoulder is a low, deep gong resonating through her whole body. Her wrists are tied together, then tied to the window crank with some white rope, and when she looks over, Simon is relaxed behind the wheel, smoking a cigarette, the metal edge of his sunglasses glinting. She can see herself mirrored in the dark lenses when he glances at her.

"Welcome back," he drawls.

His white hair ruffles in the breeze from the open window. His linen shirt is unbuttoned, the front panels flopped apart to show off his lean chest and stomach, and Emma realizes he's tied her up with torn strips of his undershirt.

She tries to think past the iron hammers ringing in her head like the inside of a blacksmith's forge. "Where are we?"

"Just past Palenque."

Her tongue is thick. "Water?"

"I'll give you some in a minute." He glances over, reproachful. "Emma, what am I going to do with you? I gave you a chance to transcend, you know. Now I'm not even sure if you're worth it."

She absolutely cannot be fucked with this. Oh god, her head. "So let me go."

"This whole experience with you has been so...disappointing." Simon ashes his cigarette out the window.

I don't know what to tell you, she thinks, *I never wanted this experience in the first place.* The engine hums beneath her. Outside, the sky is cloudy and troubled.

"You were so adorable when you first came to see me at St Elizabeths," Simon continues. "Do you remember? You didn't want to say boo to the ghost." He grins, then gets contemplative. "Brave in other ways, though. I miss that."

"Please give me some water," Emma says, words like gravel.

Simon is oblivious. "And so angry! My god. It was this flame of fury that just sprang out of you. All-consuming…" He looks at her, his cheeks hollow with disdain. "You've mellowed since, and I don't believe the change is an improvement."

"What do you want me to say?" Emma swallows, but her voice still comes out hoarse. "I'd be angry now, but I don't want to waste my energy."

Simon pouts. "It's very boring of you."

"I'm not here for your entertainment." She tries to straighten, can't, tugs on the rope, hisses with pain. "I don't *know* why I'm here. Jesus Christ, Simon – I don't think *you* know why I'm here. You're just acting on old instincts, on and on, repeating the same old tired pattern –"

"Is that what you believe?" He glances over, dark glasses and swollen, sullen lips in a too-thin face. "That this is all repetition?"

She leans her head against the window. Her energy is flagging. "I don't know, Simon."

"But things have changed, haven't they, this go round? Kristin…" His features work, then he exerts control. He pushes up his sunglasses; his sharp blue eyes are baleful and exposed. "You're wrong, you know. I'm not like all the others – I've never been so ordinary. Kristin knew that. She

340

knew me, on every level. She recognized me. Gave me purpose, gave me a tether to the world, gave me...existence." Cold wind through the car pulls at the icy tangle of Simon's hair. His gaze flicks Emma's way. "And you – you recognize me. You've known who and what I am, from that first moment at St Elizabeths. You see me, and you don't flinch."

Emma hardly knows what to say. She could tell him that recognition is not the same as acceptance. She could say that if he hasn't seen her flinch, it's because she's been good at hiding it – because she was trained for that. But her voice has withered on her tongue, and he doesn't want a reply anyway.

Simon looks through the windshield and sniffs. "You've fallen short of expectations, though, Emma. I offered you a gift. I offered you transcendence, the chance to evolve, to rise. And you threw it back in my face."

Emma swallows again, breath catching in her parched throat. "You never offered me anything I wanted, Simon."

His mouth twists. "Well, you never understood it, so you never really appreciated it. And you think this is repetition? You *still* don't understand. This is what I mean by transcendence, Emma. The old way is gone. My old mold has been broken. Nothing but this new road ahead." Simon eyes her, speculative. "And here you are, inside the cage bars with me. Maybe I should bring you along to Cuba. You could be my consort... or my house pet."

Emma looks away. "Just kill me and be done with it."

"Or perhaps I could teach you." Simon bites his lip, glances over, and his voice becomes slithering, seductive. "You're still young, still malleable. I could change your mind about me. It would take time, but you'd learn to understand. Learn to respond. I can be very persuasive..."

Emma had thought she had no energy left, but when Simon extends a hand to touch her, she explodes, whipping her head around to bite, teeth snapping on air as his hand pulls back.

He laughs. "You've still got some fire in you, I see."

"Put your hands on me and find out," she rasps viciously.

He grins. "Maybe you're worth it after all."

And Emma wants to rail then, wants to cry. She needs Travis's arms around her so badly, just the sense of being warm, of being loved, and she is so *sick* of this shit, so tired of this homicidal boy who always gets what he wants. *No one has ever refused him,* Travis said, *and it's made him crazy.* Simon raves about evolution and existence – but what about the promise of *her* existence? Because she wants more than the role Simon's pressing her into: As a mirror in which he can see himself reflected, or worse, as a bulwark for him to crash against.

What she wants is a rebuke to Simon's fantasies, and Emma clings onto that, a glowing coal of rebellion in her mind: She just wants to be herself. To live. To claim the right – the power – to be ordinary. To simply *be*, just another part of the world, and at the end of it all, to resolve back into the dirt from which she came.

It's what Simon's forgotten, or doesn't understand: That there is no transcendence, no evolution, that brings escape. At the end of everything is nothing, the same for everyone, and there's poetry in that, and meaning.

But Simon's entire worldview revolves around himself, and she's not arguing philosophy with a madman. All she can do is wait for her chance and do her best to fight.

Emma rests her head against the window. The sky through the windshield is darkening, storm-heavy. They've been driving for hours, it seems, and outside in the fast-flowing landscape, trees have now started to whip. The wind coming in through the car is agitated, and Simon extinguishes his cigarette and rolls up his window, consults his map.

Emma cushions her injured shoulder as much as she can, tries to ignore the pain, to quiet her head. When the car turns left past a huddle of small village houses and onto a bumpy dirt road that extends ahead into the jungle, she takes some bracing breaths.

Because they must be nearly at the runway for the plane.

Because whatever Simon has in store for her, Emma knows her chance to fight is coming soon.

CHAPTER TWENTY-SIX

Chiapas, 6 November 1982

To get the box of Magnum shells out of the satchel, Travis has to dig past Emma's coat – and the smell of her fills him up for a second. He lets himself breathe deep once before releasing, pulling out the box, focussing his attention on the task at hand.

Fernanda casts quick, furtive glances at him as he loads the gun. "You know, I really don't know who your bad guy arranged his flight with. It could have been one of a half dozen brokers in Villahermosa –"

"I don't care about that." Travis adds another bullet to the chamber.

The Datsun bounces along, approaching a collection of small houses. Overhead, the clouds are a deep, glowering blue, pregnant with imminent rain. The land under these dark clouds is spread out in pasture, with some cattle here and there, but they're moving into a more lush area and the grass on the roadside is almost as high as the car. The road edges are a mosaic of African tulip trees, cassias, smothering vines, everything lashing in the slowly building wind.

Fernanda lifts a hand off the wheel to gesture. They've been speaking in Spanish for a while now. "This is why I became El Cabó – to keep things ordered. To avoid getting caught up in drama like this."

Travis slots another bullet, refuses to engage. "Can I ask you a question? What does *cabó* mean, anyway? I don't recognize that word."

"One moment." Fernanda slows the car, and they turn left onto a dirt road, bumpy and soft at the shoulder. Keep driving as the crow flies, and they'll end up in Guatemala. "Okay, let me tell you. It's a Yucatán word, from Maayat'aan. A cabó is a kind of little chicken."

He side-eyes her. "A little chicken, huh?"

She snorts, drives on.

It's getting more crowded at the road edge with trees, with creepers. A huge jacaranda looms farther ahead, branches shifting, and thatch palms rise up. The road is disappearing into the jungle.

Early drizzle starts, and the last vestiges of civilization fall away from the landscape. Travis puts spare shells in his jeans pocket, holds onto his own uncivil urges, the desire for violence coming upon him in waves: The clawing need to sprint to the runway location, and make Simon Gutmunsson eat his own teeth.

Fernanda pulls the car onto a hard-packed, shadowed track. Progress is slower now, and more winding. Water drips off the leaves above and spatters the Datsun's roof: The car itself feels like an intruder here, where roots of strangler figs encroach on the leaf-littered road. Travis spots small animals – red, with striped, upright tails – flitting amongst the trees.

Fernanda pulls the car into a seemingly-random spot before a big ficus, cuts the engine. "We're here."

Travis frowns at the location. "His car's not here."

"There are two other roads he could have come in on. We try not to turn this into a parking lot, you know?" She lifts her chin. "Okay – you see that path there, behind the strangler fig? Go along there about fifty feet, you'll find a break in the trees. The runway is just dirt."

Travis cracks his door, looks out dubiously. "They really land a plane in the middle of a jungle like this?"

"They could land it on the highway, but that might be a little noticeable," Fernanda quips dryly. "Listen, there's no shelter near the runway. I don't know how you will manage once this rain really gets going."

"I guess I'll just get wet." He can hear a gentle roar, far away. "What is that noise? Is it the rain?"

"It's the river," Fernanda says, waving toward the path. "The border is very close here, and the river is the marker. There's a little waterfall past the runway, that goes toward Cascada Busilja. So do you have a plan for this rescue or what?"

"A plan?" Travis considers a moment. "No – there's no plan. I go in, I get her out. That's it, that's all I've got."

"Mother of god," Fernanda says, and crosses herself. "I'll pray for you."

"I mean, prayers couldn't hurt." Travis digs once more in the satchel, then reconsiders and just hands her the whole bag. "Your money's in here."

"What about the bag?"

His grin is a little sad. "If I don't come back sometime in the next hour or so, it's all yours. And hey, if I don't come back, can you please call Emilio and let him know? That's…" He shrugs. "I didn't make that arrangement with you before, but I probably should have."

"Of course." Fernanda looks torn, now, as if she's finally figured out the stakes. "But…I have to stay here with the car."

"Absolutely," Travis agrees. "I don't expect you to come. What time is the plane due?"

She frowns. "Within the hour. But the exact time varies greatly, depending on the pilot."

"Okay. And hey, Fernanda – thank you." Travis puts his gun in his left, reaches across the center console to shake her hand. "I appreciate everything you've done."

She seems surprised by the gesture, makes a small smile. "This little chicken wishes you good luck."

That's all there is. Travis gets out of the car, shuts the door, takes the path.

Rain still drips through the jungle's canopy, and he can hear the soft tapping on the leaves around him. He's not worried about the rain; his T-shirt is already wet with sweat, from the drive and the heat and the panic.

His Percocet bottle was in Emma's coat, in the satchel, and he took two on the drive here to combat this feeling of compression in his chest. Now his vision feels sharp but skewed, like each rain-drizzled tree and leaf has a subtle glistening aura.

The gun is in his right hand, a slick, heavy weight; he's missing the rubber grips on the Python. Debris crunches under his boots, but he doesn't much care about the noise, all his FBI training backburnered now as he strides forward, his heart beating a steady rhythm of *Emma, Emma, Emma.*

The muddy path spills out onto the clearing: a long strip of bare orange dirt and sedge grass that stretches out to his left for what he estimates is at least half a mile. It's weird, seeing this strip of destruction in the jungle.

What's almost as weird is seeing Simon Gutmunsson standing forty feet away in his white shirt and cream pants, a leather satchel slung over his shoulder. He's pushing up his sunglasses as he stares down the length of the runway, waiting for his ride like he's waiting for the bus.

Beside him, Emma – wan and limp and shivering, her hands tied in front. The collar and shoulder of her T-shirt is a red-stained wash, and she's hunched, protecting her injury.

Travis's heart clenches so hard and so fast he's worried it might spasm. He suddenly remembers there's no plan. He has no plan, just a gun and his own body. But if he can use both those things to give Emma a distraction, to give her some small chance to get free, then maybe the sum total of his life will have meant something.

Wind picks up, and the rain is starting to come down in earnest. Travis exits the tree line, leaving himself exposed. "Hey!"

His gun arm lifts and he shoots, still walking forward.

The sound ricochets through the trees, and birds nearby scream and take flight. It's an impossible shot at this distance, but Gutmunsson ducks, his expression shocked, and Travis takes a certain dark pleasure in that.

"*Travis!*" Emma cries.

"Emma, *GO*," he yells.

He lets his next shot be his follow up. And his next and his next, as he closes the distance, still too far away to be accurate but it's enough – enough to keep Gutmunsson hunkered down and seeking cover, enough to satisfy the rage in his heart.

Enough to give Emma the chance to do exactly what she does now, as she turns and runs into the jungle.

CHAPTER TWENTY-SEVEN

El Sacrificio, 6 November 1982

No thought but flight, just *Emma, GO,* and nothing else. Not thinking about Travis and his rain-curled hair and desperate face, not thinking about the pain in her shoulder. Not thinking about Simon close behind her as she runs, dodges trees, runs, slides in mud, runs, and finally – *finally* – gets this fucking cotton rope off her hands to run some more.

She's crashing through branches, blasting through spider webs, bumping, exhausted, from one tree trunk to the next. Trying to get out, to *GO,* that same blind *GO* that impelled her three years ago, that made her a coward, that made her a hero, that saved her life.

Palmetto whips her in the face, vines catch in her hair. Simon is behind her, roaring; something else is roaring in front of her. Then she hurdles a log, bolts through a gap, and suddenly she's on rocks.

Emma teeters at the edge of a drop.

Nothing but air in front, pure empty air. Below her, rocks and water tumble to a river. Her feet slip, catch, she waves her arms, her shoulder exploding with pain as the breath gasps out of her. Gray-green river water rushes below, and water rushes from above, the rain is now a downpour and she's soaked in it.

But she's pulled herself back.

"I mean, you could always jump," Simon's acerbic voice says behind her.

Emma gasps. Spins, half-stumbling, around.

The devolution of Simon Gutmunsson: He's not a suave charmer anymore. The chase has ripped his dapper clothes, made dark stains and green smears. He's in the process of raking back his wet white hair. His breath is coming hard and he's advancing fast, light catching on the thin silver blade of the stiletto in his hand.

"Simon, please," Emma wheezes, glancing between him and the drop. "You can't make me into the thing you want – "

"Shut up and *LOOK AT ME*," Simon snarls, his blue eyes rabid, arm slashing down.

Emma cries out as she dodges, twists, avoids the knife.

"You think you know…" Simon's voice is panting, his face contorting, hand stabbing wildly, "…what I want? You have *no idea* what exists in my – Jesus Christ, *stand fucking still!*"

Emma swivels, screams, slips on rock, stumbles to one knee. There is nowhere for her to go but back into the ravine. She's trapped. This is the end, and now she finally understands: This boy wants to kill her – because she is a girl, because she refused a king, but mainly because the act of killing is his nature. He is Death, trapped in this loop, and the best way to defeat him is to close the circle, let the snake eat its tail.

Emma sobs a breath, forcing down fear. She's been fighting a long time, but sometimes the only way to fight is to yield. She launches herself up, grabs Simon's wrist –

Impales herself on the blade.

It slides in just left of her navel, and it hurts like a soft punch. Emma gasps. Simon's eyes bulge. Rain pours over them. They've never been this close before – her body pressed against his, his breath on her face, his cold hand between them, gripping the knife. She feels cold as well, except for the radiant warmth starting to spread at her belly.

"Okay," Emma whispers hoarsely. "I'm still."

Simon swallows, rain dripping off his eyelashes. "I wasn't...You shouldn't have..."

His blue eyes are huge, they go back and back endlessly, and Emma almost feels sorry for him. But the warmth at her stomach is distracting. Being stabbed is not like she expected; she thought there'd be more pain. She turns them both with one neat spin, and it's Simon who seems more hurt, more confused.

His grip on the knife releases. If this is him letting her go, then she'll go.

Emma steps back. Looks down and sees the black handle of the stiletto projecting from her belly, how strange. Simon – who has seen and caused more wounds than anyone has a right to – seems appalled.

She's not feeling it yet. It's just a numb spot on her body. She feels it more when Travis bursts out of the trees behind her and collides with her back.

"*Yes,*" he pants, and he has a clear shot – Simon's standing on the rocks above the river, outlined by gray sky.

Travis's arm lifts, breath wavering, and he shoots.

Simon jerks, blood blooming on his white shirt at the top of his right arm. He wobbles on the rocks, but it's not over yet.

He corrects and straightens, smiling. "You missed."

"I won't miss twice," Travis rasps.

But his body's tense – too tense. Emma can feel it through her spine. She puts both her hands over Travis's on the gun.

"*Emma*," Simon warns, eyes widening. His palm lifts toward her, his expression suddenly scared – she's never seen him scared before.

"Emma..." Travis says in her ear.

"Just breathe," Emma whispers, and she and Travis shoot together. Their last bullet sings out.

A whipcrack: Simon's head snaps left, like he's looking over his shoulder. He turns back slowly, laughing.

"'*Oh marvel,*'" he giggles. "'*Oh dream.*'"

But his left eye is bloodshot. His left temple, a red ruin. Emma recognizes the line from the *Turandot* libretto. Rain hurls itself from the sky.

Even as the side of Simon's mouth sags, he's still trying to smile.

"Did you really think you could..." He stumbles, falls to his knees. Blood runs down his face. His blue eyes meet Emma's, hazed but unerring. "Principessa..."

Simon tips sideways, hits a rock, rolls back, and tumbles off the cliff.

Emma watches, feeling absent, remembering a line of her own.

"'*Only nothingness exists, in which you are annihilated,*'" she says softly, and then she, too, is falling.

Luckily, Travis is there to catch her.

EPILOGUE

Mexico, 1984

The lumber arrives about 3:00PM, and it's all hands on deck to unload it off the truck and get it laid out and covered. But they're done by five-thirty, and can retreat to the patio, away from the sun. Mariana brings out four glasses and a jug of fresh hibiscus tea with ice, carrying everything on a tray with a dish towel for spills, just as Travis is taking off his rawhide gloves.

"No orange juice?" Emilio looks disappointed. He's lighting a cigarette he bummed off Mateo, having claimed the best position on the wicker couch cushions.

"There *is* no more." Mariana flicks him with the dish towel. "You drank it all. Sofia says, you want more orange juice, you need to help us pick more oranges."

"But we carried all the wood!" He pouts, wounded.

"You are pretending like this is a hard job, it is not harder than orange picking. I'll carry wood, you pick fruit."

"Mariana, you are a tough woman," Emilio intones. "Every day, I give thanks that I'm married to Gabriela and not to you."

"I would not have you, old man," Mariana scoffs, wiping the coffee table and stalking off, but Travis can see that she likes being called tough.

He pours himself a tea and slakes it off, still standing as the other men sit. "Uncle, will that be enough timber?"

"It will be enough," Luiz nods, slapping the dust off his own pair of gloves. "This shed is only twelve by twelve, thank god. The price has gone up so much, it's crazy. The lumber we used for the house repair? If we bought that now, it would kill me."

"It's terrible," Emilio agrees. "It's putting me off extending the fences."

The house behind them now looks much the same as it did when Travis first arrived here to recuperate in '82 – although the damage from the fire took some work. Four lavender bushes had to be replanted, and sometimes on warm nights, Travis catches a whiff of smoke. But once the rooms were rebuilt and the adobe painted over, the repair was hardly noticeable.

"The price of nails has gone up, too," Mateo complains, and there resumes a conversation about local expenses, until Mariana comes out again to collect the jug.

While the men continue talking, Travis waves to catch Mariana's eye. "Did she go for a run?"

"No, she's in the stables," Mariana says. "Tell her a letter has come."

"Okay, I'll tell her," he says, before walking back along the patio in his jeans and heavy boots.

Down the steps, he goes around the stone mounting block and the century plant, reaches the fence. A small gate there leads to the path through the garden, then to the door of the stables. Inside, the stables are cool and dark. Travis can smell fresh hay and manure, hear horses blowing.

He finds her currying Sofia's bay mare, the horse still in the stall and Emma working the brush along its neck. For a moment, he just stands there admiring Emma in her jeans. That is also his shirt she's wearing, he notices. She's still got the pixie cut, which she says is cooler for summer, and she looks toned and lean and tan from being outside.

She finishes the bay's neck and gets started on its mane. The horse snorts with enjoyment, which Travis understands completely. He comes closer.

"If I ask nicely," he says, "will you brush my hair like that?"

Emma looks over, laughs as he approaches. "Your hair definitely needs brushing."

"Does it now?"

"It does." She squeals as Travis slides his hands around her waist from behind, pulling her against him. "Ohmigod, you're all over with sweat!"

"But you liked that last night..." Travis laughs, nuzzling his lips at the place where her neck meets her shoulder, running his hand up under her – his – shirt and touching the little scar on her stomach near her navel.

When she turns around, he kisses her, and this is the part he will never get over, how intense their contact feels. Every kiss is like a slow, drawn-out lightning strike.

Her arms curl up around his neck. "You taste like...agua de Jamaica," she whispers.

"Because Mariana gave us hard-working guys agua de Jamaica," he says, nipping gently at the soft spot under her ear. "She said to tell you there's a letter."

Emma sighs, softens. "It's the letter from Howard Carter. I'm avoiding opening it. He wants me to write everything out for the archives."

"Then write him back and say thank you, but no, like I did. I'll help you, if you like."

"No, you're right, I can do it." She pulls back and tugs on his hand. "Come on, it's sunset."

She puts the curry comb away, gives the bay horse a pat on the nose, then walks with Travis out of the stables. As soon as they reach the garden, Bebe and Panchito – the latest additions to Mariana's pack – come wagging over, so they walk out the small gate and farther down toward the driveway with these puppies trailing around their legs and trying to trip them over.

Once they're at the main gate, Emma puts an arm around his waist and leans on him as they watch the sinking sun, part of their ritual. "Are you going down for a flying lesson tomorrow?"

"Joaquín had to take a raincheck. He said Saturday." Travis plays with the soft hair at her nape. "I'm gonna miss you while you're in Ohio."

"I'll miss you, too, so much. But it's been too long. Robbie and Julia are giving me shit about it. Mom and Dad are wondering if I'm ever coming home."

"Are you?" He keeps his voice quiet. "Ever going home, I mean?"

"Don't you know, Travis?" She touches a hand to his cheek, brings his face around. She's smiling. "I'm already home."

They kiss gently, until she draws away to take in the dusk. The salmon-colored light makes her tanned face glow.

"Oh, wow," Emma says wonderingly. "Look at that sky."

"I'm looking," Travis says, but it's her he's looking at.

After a while, they walk back to the house.

Guatemala, 1984

When Juan Ortiz first cut his finger on the fencing wire, it seemed like nothing. Just a clean cut, like slicing it on the edge of a maguey leaf, and he wiped it on his trousers and carried on planting. That night, it was still stinging, so he ran some water over it and wrapped a piece of higuillo leaf around it, and the next few days he kept working.

By the fourth day, the cut is oozing and nasty, and his wife says she won't let him touch her with that hand unless he sees the médico in Piedras Negras, so he takes the mule and goes.

The médico del pueblo has a small house with a kitchen and two rooms, and another room which is for seeing patients. It is not fancy, and the médico's assistant assures him that it will not be expensive, if he wants to pay with a few pineapples, that will be okay. Juan sits in the plastic chair near the médico's desk, unwraps his finger and lets the man poke at it.

"You should have come to see me the same day you cut it," the médico says.

"My wife also said this."

"Your wife is a wise woman, you should listen to her more often," the médico says, and they both have a laugh about that. "Okay, it's pointless to stitch it now, but I'm going to wash it out, put some medicine on it. Then I will give you some medicine to take home, okay?"

"Okay."

"One moment." The médico stands up and calls out through the open door. "Haw! Can you bring me a bottle of amoxicillin? Just the Roche two-fifty bottle."

While they wait for the medicine, Dr. Flores cleans out the cut and puts some sour-smelling salve on it. Juan thinks Dr. Flores is a little fussy with the cleaning, but it's of no matter. The médico's assistant comes in with the bottle, and once the wound is bound up, he gives Juan instructions about the pink liquid medicine.

"Drink it all, until it's completely gone," the assistant says. "If you don't take it all, it won't work."

Juan agrees that he will take all the medicine, and says he will come back in a day or two to pay with pineapples.

"Bring back the medicine bottle, when you come," the assistant says. "We can wash it and reuse it, there's never enough medicine bottles."

Juan agrees to this, then he compliments the assistant on his Maayat'aan. The assistant thanks him for the compliment, and humbly explains that he is still learning, before collecting all the rubbish and bloody materials from the wound cleaning and taking them away.

As Juan unties the mule to go home, the médico and his assistant are out on the little tin-roofed porch of the house, drinking from small glasses of cusha corn spirit and smoking cigarettes at the end of the day.

"Goodbye, and thank you," Juan calls.

Haw, the assistant, looks up from the medical textbook he is reading. "Remember to bring back the bottle!"

"I will," Juan says, and later that night, he tells his wife that she is wise, and that the médico del pueblo is very affordable, and that he has a foreign assistant with blue eyes, who speaks Maayat'aan and brushes his brown hair over the terrible scar on his head..

Ellie Marney, Yandoit, 7 November 2024

ACKNOWLEDGEMENTS

This book only exists because of you.

I'm talking about *you*, dear reader – because it's readers who've pushed for the conclusion of this series from the very start. You made the first book, *None Shall Sleep*, a bestseller, and your support gave a greenlight for the release of the second book, *Some Shall Break*. Then my publisher abandoned this final book…but I had three-quarters of a manuscript, and a heckuva lot of people checking in to say, "Please, you *have* to tell us how the story ends!!" so I decided that, dammit, *I* wanted to know how the story ended, too…

First thanks, then, must go to the die-hard, bloodthirsty crew from my newsletters, both The Black Hand and Nailbiters. This book is dedicated to you. Without your unwavering commitment and encouragement (and in the case of Nailbiters folks, financial support), *All Shall Mourn* would never have been finished. You've seen the behind-the-scenes dramas at every stage of this book's journey, and I've had a ton of fun sharing peeks and updates and early chapters with you all! Every author should have such an amazing cheer squad at their back, my god. I'm humbled to be the author *you* support, and I'm enormously grateful – seriously, you're all the best ♥

Second thanks go to the inimitable CS Pacat – pep talker, plot wrangler, and one of the smartest people I know. I don't want to get all mushy or anything, but I couldn't have done this without you, my friend.

To my House of Progress buds – thank you all so much. Especially for brainstorming sessions, and your encouragement on the days when I wanted to throw both myself and my laptop into the ocean.

My agent, Josh Adams, tried *so hard* with this book – Josh, we went a very roundabout way, but here you go! We got there in the end. Special thanks to Nailbiters readers Ella Brumbelow and Julia Rezuto, who were both kind enough to allow me to immortalize their names in print – I didn't even kill your characters off! But hey, there's always next time…

Ben Marney knocked it out of the park with this book cover, I honestly think it's the best cover of the series – and I'm not just saying that because I'm biased ♥

The long-suffering Alison Croggon did an amazing job smashing this book into a shape and format that other people could actually read, and I'm hugely appreciative.

Finally, my partner Geoff, and all my sons – Ben, Alex, Will, and Ned – were integral to the creation of this book at every stage (especially the "help author mother come up with ideas" stage, and the "ensure author partner does not starve to death/work herself to exhaustion" stage), as they are with every book I write. Guys, I know living with a writer can be A Lot sometimes, but I hope I have other good qualities that make up for it! Love you all so much ♥

xxEllie

If you enjoyed this book, please leave a review at any platform of your choice!
Reviews and recommendations help books succeed and support authors.

ELLIE MARNEY

is a multi-award-winning, internationally bestselling author of thrillers for teenagers and adults. Her titles include the *New York Times* bestseller *None Shall Sleep*, the Kirkus-starred sequel *Some Shall Break* and trilogy finale *All Shall Mourn*, as well as *The Killing Code*, *White Night*, the *Every* series, and many more. Her books have been published in multiple countries and optioned for the screen. Ellie has spent a lifetime researching in mortuaries, interviewing law enforcement and autopsy specialists, and asking former spies how to make explosives from household items – now she lives quite sedately with her family in south-eastern Australia while she writes her next book.

Discover more about Ellie at www.elliemarney.com or catch up with her on social media @elliemarney and @elliemarneyauthor

For all news and book updates, read Ellie's newsletter, The Black Hand

Find all Ellie's books at www.linktr.ee/elliemarneybooks